SEARCH

for

AQUASAURUS

OTHER WORKS BY ERNIE LEE

NOVELS

AQUASAURUS, Aim-Hi Publishing, Canyon Lake, Texas
ISBN; 978-0-9971284-0-6, Trade paperback, 2016
ISBN; 978-0-9971284-2-0, Mass-market paperback, 2016
ISBN; 978-0-9971284-1-3, E-PUB, 2016
ISBN; 978-0-9971284-9-9, Hardcover

HIM, Aim-Hi Publishing, Canyon Lake, Texas
ISBN; 978-0-9971284-4-4, Trade paperback, 2017
ISBN; 978-0-9971284-5-1, Mass-market paperback, 2017
ISBN; 978-0-9971284-7-5, E-PUB, 2017
ISBN; 978-0-9971284-9-9, Hardcover, 2017

POETRY

Where the Wild Rice Grows, Aim-Hi Publishing Canyon Lake, Texas
2017
ISBN: 978-0-9971284-3-7, Mass-market paperback 2017

Available: WWW.Aim-HiBooks.com

SEARCH
for
AQUASAURUS

by

ERNIE LEE

AIM-HI PUBLISHING

AIM-Hi Publishing
1542 Lakeside Dr. West
Canyon Lake, Texas 78133

Publisher's Catalog-in-Publication Data
Names: Lee, Ernest (Ernie), 1946 - ; *cover illustration: Raphael Frankavilla, Saint Genes Lerpt, France © Aim-Hi Books 2019*
Title: Search for Aquasaurus / by Ernie Lee
Description: Aim-Hi Publishing LLC, 2016. | Summary: A group of college students set off to find a previously thought extinct species of crocodile.
Identifiers:
Library of Congress Control Number: 2019902427

ISBN 978-1-7321131-2-1 (Trade paperback) (c) 2019

Subjects: Fear – Fiction. | Crocodiles – Fiction. | Romance – Fiction. | Fracking – Fiction. | Mythology – Fiction.

To my sisters:

BETTY HENSON MOSIER
GLENDA LEE DEAL
POLLY LEE LIVELY

Acknowledgments:

There is much more to writing a book than telling a good story and putting sentences and paragraphs down on paper. This book is the product of a diverse team of people who helped put it together in a readable form. You are holding in your hands the product of many people who spent countless hours reading, editing, and suggesting solutions to the many challenges I created for myself. I would especially like to thank the following:

Susan Eisenbrey, who suffered through extremely rough concept ideas and drafts **twice!**

Sandra Gayle Young, whose editing skills and sharp eyes were ever on the hunt

Liberty Dove Fredericks, who proofed and gave valuable feedback on continuity

Finally, especially to those loyal friends who also read each chapter along the way, made useful comments and suggestions, and provided inspiration and support:

Billy James Wall who has been a friend since high school, and whose encouragement, love and support are irreplaceable

Maria Elena Alvarado who has stuck with me through three novels and a book of poetry

Shawn Wolfe who took time from his military duties to help make this book a better read

Jorge Gracia for his help in proofreading the manuscript, and for his guidance on Mexican culture and language

Janice Murphy who asked all the right questions at the right time

Robert Carpenter and the inmates of the James Crabtree Correctional MSU, who read the first rushes

Without all of your help, support, and assistance, I could not have completed this book. My heartfelt thanks to each of you.

WRITING IS GIVING

The author's goal is to give away **2,016** copies of *the novel AQUASAURUS* to **Cancer Fighters**. If you or someone you know is currently fighting cancer or has survived a cancer fight, please go to www.Aim-HiBooks.com and sign up on the website. Then send a personal message to Ernie Lee (contact button at the top of webpage) with the name, details, type of device (e-Pub, Kindle, .pdf, or other) and contact information of your nominee. A copy of the award-winning novel AQUASAURUS will be provided to the nominee in your name, free of charge. For details on the number of books distributed to date, please check the **Writing+is+Giving** page on the website. Your purchase of a book on Amazon, Barnes & Noble, or your favorite outlet helps pay for this campaign.

CHAPTER 1

"No shrimp here," Binh Gnu told his crew as an assortment of trash fish and useless litter spilled from the dripping net.

Binh looked out across the calm waters of Laguna Madre just north of Brownsville, Texas. In years past, Binh had been successful on this stretch of the deserted lagoon. The fishing in these waters was usually excellent in the interval between the mandatory evacuation of thousands of spring breakers and the invasion of winter Texans. Not this year. This year they would have to go deeper for the shrimp. He ordered his three-man crew to pull the nets and secure the outriggers.

Bihn studied the maps to find fishing spots where he might try next. His fishing permit gave him rights to a specific area in south Texas, but this time he might have to bend the rules a little. The State wouldn't know so long as none of his competitors complained. He studied an area just off the Brownsville coast that was permitted to his cousin Quang. The water was deeper and colder there. He marked a circle on his map in pencil so he could erase it later if necessary. Quang's boat was up on blocks in his backyard, so nothing but eighty miles of Texas Gulf water prevented Binh from fishing in his cousin's quadrant.

A disturbance on the deck caught his attention as he slid aside the window to peer down at the crew pulling the nets.

"It is hung on something!"

"Careful!" Binh shouted. "Don't tear the net. What is it hung on?" he asked.

"We can't tell!" his nephew Phue yelled back. "Too deep!"

"Well, go in and free it!"

"Uncle, I'm not going into the water. I can't swim."

"You don't need to swim. Just pull yourself down the net to the bottom and free it. We'll pull you in with the net once you free the net."

Phue made a crude gesture at Binh and mumbled some profanity beneath his breath.

"That boy is just like his father," Binh mused as he shook his head. He knew from experience no amount of argument was going to get his nephew into the water. He should have left the boy at home to paint Quang's boat. The other two boys were no better. They got paid to fish, they said, not to swim.

"What kind of sailor doesn't know how to swim?" Binh grumbled as he peeled off his pants and shirt. "What the hell is this younger generation coming to?" Binh recited a steady stream of complaints about the state of Asian millennials as he stomped down the steel ladder and across the wet steel deck in his underwear. Pushing past his young nephew, Binh flung himself into the briny waters of lower Laguna Madre.

Surfacing, he shook water from his head and swam toward where the fishing net disappeared beneath the surface. He gingerly tugged the lines, but it was stuck fast to something on the bottom. Binh knew that the lagoon was only ten or fifteen feet deep at the most; so he took a deep breath, grabbed the netting, and pulled himself beneath the surface. There was no telling what it was snagged on in this aquatic garbage dump.

On the bottom, Binh found they had netted a nice antique Sears washing machine that some previous boater probably shoved overboard. Freeing his fishing net from the rusted appliance, Binh swam for the surface. Bobbing in the small swells, he was tempted to scold his young crew for being too soft; but he simply ordered, "All right! Pull it in!"

Not wanting to be netted himself, Binh swam a few yards to starboard and floated on the surface until the crew hauled the net past him.

He floated on his back and watched the clear blue sky as he enjoyed the cool salty water lapping across his chest.

"Drop a ladder!" he yelled to Phue.

Suddenly, the net stopped moving toward the boat. *Now what?*, Binh thought to himself.

"Come on! Get that net aboard! We don't have all day, and drop me a ladder!"

He looked up at his crew standing along the edge of the bulkhead. The net lay slumped across the gunwale as the boys stood with eyes and mouths held wide open.

Binh had reached the end of his patience and was ready to explode. It was bad enough these slackers would not go into the water to free a hung net, but now they were not even going to pull it on board. He was about to unleash a string of profanities when his nephew raised a shaking hand and pointed to an area just behind Binh.

"What?!!!" Binh shouted as he used his arms to turn himself around in the warm water and came eye-to-eye with the largest crocodile he had ever seen.

"It's him," thought Binh. *"It's that escaped crocodile – the one they call Aquasaurus. The one that has been attacking people on the coast for the last three months. It has to be him; no other crocodile is even half that large. Good Lord, look at the size of his head. What's he doing here? Crocodiles were not even supposed to be in these waters."*

Binh hollered over his shoulder, "Phue, get the rifle and shoot it! Hurry! And don't shoot me!"

Binh decided to stay as still as possible. *"He's trying to figure out if I'm food. Maybe he thinks I'm a dolphin or something to eat. Don't panic,"* he told himself. The crocodile floated motionlessly only a few yards away. All Binh could see of it was an enormous bulbous snout and two unblinking yellow eyes above the water. Binh calculated how fast he could swim to the boat and decided he would not make it if the crocodile wanted him. Binh slowly reached for the knife at his waist before realizing he was swimming in his underwear. *"Why didn't they shoot it yet?"* he wondered.

Bihn was mesmerized by a small, red, light that flashed on and off inside the crocodile's snout. Binh could not understand what the light was. *"Maybe it is part of the last guy he ate."*

The croc slowly blinked. A lens like a cataract slid downward over its eyes. Binh could see little frothy bubbles in the corners of the croc's eyes.

"Well, what do you know?" Binh thought. *"They really do cry."*

The television was on in the waiting room as Katie settled into a soft leather chair.

"… Texas Attorney General is suing the EPA over the rejection of the Texas clean air program. The lawsuit is the state's second battle against the EPA in two months. We will be following this story for you as it develops out of Austin. Stay tuned to News 12 for more details."

The camera switched to the news anchor. "Thank you, Hannah. We are following another continuing story this day. That large crocodile, dubbed Aquasaurus, surfaced again off South Padre Island this morning. A local fisherman was snatched from the water by the huge beast. The body of thirty-nine-year-old Binh Gnu of Port Isabel has not been recovered as of air time."

The camera pulled back to reveal both newscasters sitting at a desk. A photo of a massive crocodile and the word 'Aquasaurus' showed behind them. "Is it just me, Larry, or is that thing moving south?"

"Indeed it is, Hannah. The last reports of it were in the northern tip of South Padre Island; now, it's at the southern tip of the island in Laguna Madre. Coast Guard officials have been trying to track the creature for the past three months without much success. Its location is marked each time there is a sighting, and it does appear to be moving south. You remember, Hannah, this monster crocodile first appeared during the earthquake and flood that hit San Antonio. How a gigantic crocodile worked its way into the Gulf of Mexico without being detected is remarkable."

"Yes, Larry. Those poor spring-break kids on South Padre last April – what a tragedy that was …"

Katie turned her attention away from the television and looked around the waiting room. The outer office of Bruner, Bartholomew, and Zackery was professional, comfortable, and designed for intimidation. The lighting was subdued, lit only by shaded lamps in a Texas ranch motif. The entire waiting room looked like the spacious living room of a large ranch house – exactly what you would expect an oil magnate's attorney to own.

Katie Marshall sat on the luxurious leather couch and hoped the back of her legs would not stick to it when she got up to greet Mr. Bruner. Katie reminded herself for the hundredth time that Mr. Bruner was on her side; there was no need to worry. Since her father, Clint, was dead, Katie guessed Mr. Bruner was her attorney now. Thank goodness for Hootie Johnson, without his advice and guidance she would have been entirely lost. Hootie had been her father's right-hand man. She had not even known who her father's attorney was, much less all of the assets Clint owned. She wished for the umpteenth time that Hootie had come with her to this meeting.

"Don't like lawyers" was all he would say. Then he pulled down his cowboy hat and jutted out his jaw in such a way that made his dimples even more pronounced. The man had no clue how handsome he was. Katie wished again that Hootie was fifteen years younger.

Katie did not like lawyers either. They had far too much power. They knew things – things no one else was supposed to know. Their knowing made them powerful. Mr. Bruner had filed paperwork with the court to declare Clint Marshall officially dead, as was required by law. Clint's body was not in the charred, twisted wreckage of Dilley Chalk #1, but there was no doubt he was deceased. They found his truck still running, and gasoline was still in the tank when they pulled the vehicle away from the fire. It was still drivable even though the paint had bubbled and cracked in the heat. Not much remained inside that burned-out pickup. The bare metal springs protruded through the charred seat covers. Clint had disappeared within the enormous fireball that soared high above the fiery wreckage of the oilrig. Trying in his awkward way to give her comfort, Hootie said Clint had probably vaporized in the inferno. It wasn't much comfort.

The past three months had flown by, and Katie had struggled to understand it all. Most of her father's business dealings were beyond her knowledge; and without Hootie, she could never have figured it out. She felt overwhelmed by the wealth her father had accrued. Katie had no idea how to handle her father's assets. She had no clue where it all was, but Hootie had been immensely valuable tracking it all down. Thanks to her father's personal assistant Darla Dunn and Mr. Bruner, it made quite a list. There was the condo in Houston, a villa in La Pesca in Mexico somewhere below Brownsville, a boat named Miss Katie, two airplanes, a couple of motorcycles, a Mercedes, and one burned-out truck. The lawyers could not transfer anything to Katie until the law declared Clint officially dead. Without a corpse, complications stalled the transfer of ownership. She had no idea what she would do with everything, except she planned to put the condominium on the market. She had no intention of living in Houston. The rest she would decide later.

A well-dressed woman entered the waiting room and greeted Katie warmly. She introduced herself as Lisa and escorted Katie into Mr. Bruner's office. Mr. Bruner rose immediately and came around his large wooden desk. He took Katie's hand and placed one arm around her shoulder. The model of a typical Texas attorney, Charles had perfectly styled silver hair, which gleamed in the light. He could have stepped right out of central casting. Katie wished her hair would shine that way.

"My dear Miss Marshall," he cooed. "It is so nice to see you. Your late father always bragged of your beauty, but I'm afraid he missed the mark. He said you were beautiful, but he never said you were a living angel!"

Katie blushed. "Thank you, Mr. Bruner. He never told me his attorney was a matinee idol!"

"My dear! You age me!" Mr. Bruner waved her off, but she could tell he was flattered. "I much prefer rock star," he laughed.

"Call me Charles, dear," he continued. "Your father said you were quick-minded. I'm afraid he did not do you justice in that quality either, Miss Marshall."

"You can call me Katie, sir. I am honored to meet you. My father spoke so highly of you and your firm."

Mr. Bruner patted her on the shoulder and gave her another hug.

"Our entire firm extends its solemn condolences, Katie. Please have a seat. May I offer you anything: coffee, tea, or ice water?"

"That depends on what you are about to tell me, Mr. Charles. I take it as a good sign you did not offer me bourbon."

Laughter bubbled out of Charles' face as his large belly jiggled up and down behind his expensive suit jacket.

"Bourbon!" he repeated several times until he could get his breath. "Just exactly what your father would say! Oh, my! How we are going to miss his sense of humor. I'm sure you do, too, my dear."

Using the southern custom of putting a "mister" in front of an elder's first name, Katie smiled at Mr. Bruner. "Very much, Mr. Charles – I just can't believe he is gone."

Charles extended his palm, indicating that Katie was to use one of the plush leather chairs that sat beside a richly carved coffee table. Everything in this office was designed to impress.

"Tea," Katie requested as she nestled into the lavish leather chair, "iced, please."

"Lisa, please bring us a couple of iced teas." Then, he turned back to Katie. "We can always spike it if the need arises," he laughed again.

Once he settled into the matching armchair, Charles got down to business.

"Well, Katie. I have some good news and some even better news for you."

Katie breathed a sigh of relief.

"That is good to hear, Mr. Charles. Am I right to assume that since you were my father's attorney, you represent me as well?"

"Indeed, my dear. You inherited everything, including me – as long as you want us, that is."

"I wouldn't dream of making a change."

"Thank you, hon; your father was a brilliant man. A few years ago, we advised him to place everything in a trust to protect his assets from personal liability, and I am happy to say that he followed our advice. Since you are his only beneficiary, you stand to benefit greatly from that decision. As trustee, we manage your father's entire holdings, The Marshall Family Trust; and since he is deceased, that means – you. Young lady, you are a very wealthy woman."

"Thank you, Mr. Charles. But, I don't know how to manage that kind of wealth."

"You don't have to worry about that, dear. *That* is what we do. We are specialists in asset management. Your father put us in charge of everything – however, you are free to make changes if you wish. If not, things will continue under the same terms we gave your father years ago. If you care to make any changes, all you need do is call me. Here is my private number." He handed her a card. "Meanwhile, I can tell you that you will draw a monthly stipend; and if you need more, you call that number. Would $10,000 monthly be sufficient to start?"

Katie's head swam as she realized that money would no longer be a problem in her life. The big challenge now would be how to hang on to it.

"Yes, sir," she mumbled. "What about the will?"

"The will," Charles leaned back in his chair and laced his fingers together. "As I told you earlier, you inherit everything. With no siblings and with your dear mother deceased as well, there should not be any reason to expect anyone to contest. Probate will go through without a hitch. Besides, the trust is not subject to probate. There are a few cash accounts, a retirement IRA, personal property and real estate, and some assets from a couple of oil companies – let's see …"

Charles reached over, pulled a file from his desk, and opened it. "I see a preliminary application for transfer of 25% of Rio Frio Oil Company, who your father worked for along with HNH Oil. We will execute a change notice listing you as the owner now that your father is deceased. I will keep checking on that and keep you informed. In all likelihood, the transfer will go through without a hitch."

He flipped through some additional pages, "Here is what I wanted to discuss with you about Rio Frio Oil Company. The transfer was recent, but it will be included in Clint's trust. Rio Frio is not making any money, and it looks inactive. It does have substantial losses for the year. The fire that killed your father also destroyed one of your well sites. And, you have an employee in that company, but I am sure that will pose no problem if you want to divest your ownership in Rio Frio."

"An employee?"

"Yes, as I said, you only own a quarter of Rio Frio shares. The other three-quarters belongs to Mr. T.J. Howlett of HNH. Your father employed Mr. Hootie Johnson to manage a project for Rio Frio. He was an HNH employee, but the company recently transferred Mr. Johnson to your dad's company. I don't know all the details, but the division of assets is final. Mr. Johnson *is* your employee, but we will handle payroll and human resources for you, including termination if you choose. Do you know Mr. Johnson?"

"I do know him? He is waiting downstairs, and I certainly do not choose to terminate him. Should I call him in to meet with us?" Katie asked, amazed.

"I'd love to meet Mr. Johnson, but it may not be appropriate at this meeting concerning your father's assets. Why don't we bring him in on our next meeting when we discuss what you want to do with Rio Frio? You have several options, not the least of which is to sell it outright."

Katie did not even have to think. "I don't want to sell it," she announced.

CHAPTER 2

When Katie came down the elevator from Bruner, Bartholomew, and Zackery, she found Hootie where she had left him in the first-floor lobby. He leaned with one hand against the windowsill, looking out on the heavy traffic moving up and down the Gulf Freeway. His starched tight blue jeans had a crease down each leg, and he kept his starched shirt tucked neatly inside. His hat lay on its crown in the seat next to the window. Katie liked the look.

"Hi, cowboy," she kidded, as she walked to the window.

"How'd it go?" he asked.

"It went ok. You could have come up," Katie assured him.

"Well," he drawled, "I thought it was best – Y'all were discussing private stuff."

"Not exactly," Katie teased, "since you work for me now!" She laughed aloud.

"Oh, yeah – Rio Frio, I forgot about that," Hootie smiled. "I guess we are kind of tied together – sort of."

"Sort of? What does that mean?"

Hootie shrugged and ducked his head. "Look, Rio Frio ain't much. It sure isn't makin' any money. You might not even want to keep me on. Most of the assets burned up in the fire. I guess we still hold the leases and the hole, but that won't do us much good – we don't have any way to drill anymore. I guess you could sell the leases to HNH Oil – if they will take 'em."

"I can't do anything until after Probate Court, and then we can decide," Katie raised an eyebrow, "Hey! Do you want a condominium in Houston? I've got one I don't want."

Hootie laughed, "Well, I've got my trailer down in Dilley. I guess it's enough until you decide what you're gonna do."

"What does *that* mean?"

"I don't know – maybe you might sell Rio Frio, and I'd have to find me another job."

Katie felt a little disappointment, "You've got a job! You still work for me. Let's get out of this place and find something to eat. I'm not too fond of lawyers either, but I have confidence in Mr. Bruner. Come on; let's go get some bar-b-que and we'll talk."

It was already broiling in the parking lot for late June. They switched the air conditioner on the max setting as they pulled out on the freeway that led to I-10 and San Antonio. Somewhere before the town of Katy, they pulled off the interstate into a restaurant parking lot.

They sat in the refrigerated dimness and shared a rack of ribs and a couple of beers. Hootie was very quiet, and Katie could tell something was on his mind. Whatever it was, he was not ready to talk about yet. Katie was afraid he might be planning to leave and go somewhere else for work. She decided to distract him from thinking along those lines. She did not want him to leave.

"Hootie, do you know how to fly an airplane?"

"Sure," he nodded, "spent four years in the Air Force."

"Do you know how to sail dad's boat?"

"You bet. Your daddy had me bring it down from New Jersey last year. He even sent me to captain's school so I could move it for him whenever he wanted."

"So you did more things for Dad than work on oil wells?"

"Oh, yeah," Hootie nodded, "whenever he needed something, I'd get it done. He trusted me."

"Hootie, I don't know how to do any of those things. Couldn't you do all that stuff for me? I need someone who knows about all those things, and where all Dad's stuff is, and how to find it…"

"Whoa, girl. Slow down. I thought you were going to sell all of that stuff."

"Why should I? I want to travel, Hootie. I've decided, I'm not going back to school for a while. With an airplane, a boat, and plenty of money, I can go anywhere I want, but I need someone to drive. Will you do that? I'll pay you whatever Dad was paying you. Besides, I'm sort of stuck with you."

"How can I refuse an offer like that?" Hootie grinned.

Rita Martin paused on the Barton Creek Trail and looked back at Jesse Perrine stumbling along behind her. He was making good progress since his injury in the cave. She would never forget him leaping into the water to save her from that monster crocodile. He had no regard for himself. He claimed he could not remember his encounter with the giant beast, but sometimes at night, he would thrash around in his sleep. She recalled how she thought he was dead after the crocodile's huge tail had knocked him into the rocks of the dark cave. It had taken four of them to carry Jesse out of the cave.

Jesse was still using a cane, but Rita figured that in another month he would abandon it just as he had ditched the crutches. He was tough, no doubt, and Rita was proud of his progress. Right now, he was lagging, but by the end of summer, she knew Jesse would be out front, putting pressure on her to catch up. Jesse was already itching to get back in the saddle – especially the seat of his mountain bike. Katie made sure to keep an eye on Jesse to make sure he didn't give it a try. She had a padlock on the bike just in case.

"Come on, slowpoke! Get a move on; we want to get out of this gorge before it gets too hot!" Rita goaded him. She knew that would get his goat.

"Shut up!" Jesse grumbled.

"Another half mile and I'll buy you a smoothie and take you for a swim in Barton Springs!"

"Late June might as well be summer," she thought as she trudged up the gravelly slope. Down in the bed of the rocky creek no air circulated, and the sweat rolled down between her shoulder blades. *"Another month and we won't be able to stand it on this trail."*

A sudden shout from Jesse interrupted her thoughts.

"Jake! Hey, Jake!"

Jake Haw stood at the trailhead watching them climb out of Barton Creek. In a few quick steps, Rita was on top of the bank and reached down to help Jesse climb the sharp incline.

"You're doing pretty good for an old man," Jake teased Jesse.

"Yeah? Well, you'd be walking like an old man, too, if this girl was pushing you up the canyon!" Jesse pointed at Rita.

"If I weren't pushing him, he'd still be lying in bed," Rita laughed. "Don't let him fool you; he's itching to get rid of that cane. The doctor says he's about six weeks ahead of schedule," Rita bragged.

"Gotta get back on the bike, fool!" Jesse laughed.

"How's Katie?" Rita asked. "I haven't talked to her in about two weeks – guess I need to give her a call."

"Don't feel like the lone stranger," Jake agreed. "She doesn't seem to have much time anymore, wrapping up her father's affairs and stuff. I talked to her last week, and she seems to be doing fine. I've been kind'a busy myself."

"I heard," Rita slapped him on the shoulder. "You climbed Widow Maker in less than four hours! Way to go, hotshot – wish we could have been there. That is one heck of a climb. I'll bet that was something!"

"Right out of a Marvel comic," Jake bragged.

"With you as The Joker," Jessie quipped.

"That's a DC comic, you hoser! Keep your books straight!"

"Pardon me, Mr. Superhero – Mr. College Senior – still reading funny books!" Jesse dug at his friend good-naturedly.

"At least I can read, Skater!"

"We're going over to Barton Pool, Jake. Come on; go with us," Rita offered.

"Sounds like a deal," Jake nodded. "I'll wait for you there. It's goin' to take you a while to lug this guy up to your car! Laters!" Jake laughed as he peddled off down the trail. "Nice shot, Gimpy," he shouted back at Jesse as he ducked a rock that whistled past his ear.

Representative Sara Hughes answered her private line when fellow representative Pokey Marin's name showed in the display.

"Sara, something is going on in your district you should know about. Remember those two hoot owls that came up here from Houston the day Cody got hurt? How is the boy anyway, Sara?"

"Cody's doing great, Pokey. Graduated on time, and he takes his bar exam tomorrow," Sara answered as she flipped through her calendar.

"That's wonderful, Sara, just wonderful. I know you are so proud of him."

"I am! Yes, here they are," she tapped her calendar, "Gunderson and Strickland – what about them?"

"Well, after you left, I sent them over to the resources commission, and apparently, they got enough attention that Judge Isaac issued a stop order on Dilley Chalk #2."

"I remember," Sara said. "I've got a file on it here somewhere."

"Well, before the Judge could have his hearing, Dilley Chalk #1 blew up and killed that guy – Clint Marshall – down there at Cotulla."

"Boy, do I remember that – the worst fracking incident in Texas history. San Antonio is still reeling from the effects of that one."

"Yeah, and now the Railroad Commission is swarming like bees. They've subpoenaed Gunderson and Strickland, along with the owners of HNH Oil Company down in Houston. If they can prove that Marshall dropped something down that well, there might be some restitution coming along – *if* they have any money left after the fire."

"That's a big *if*, Pokey. No one has that much money."

"Probably not, but just wanted to give you a heads up. The Commission called me to sit on the panel – you can come if you want. Say! What was that big news you wanted to tell me yesterday? I'm sorry I didn't get back to you."

"It's okay; I know you have your hands full. I just wanted to tell you something."

"What's that, hon?"

"I'm getting married!"

"Mr. Bruner, you have a call on line three. It's Mr. Nobles from HNH," Lisa announced on the intercom.

Charles picked up the phone, "Phil, how the heck are you?"

"Doin' fine, Charles. Thanks for askin'. You doin' okay? Family doin' fine?"

"We're just great, Phil. What's up, buddy?"

"I just got off the phone with our in-house attorney over here."

"How is old Anson? What's he up to these days?"

"Well, Anson had some bad news for us, Chuck. It seems like the Railroad Commission has subpoenaed T.J. and me, along with Gunderson and Strickland. That judge up there in Austin, Solomon Isaac, the one that shut down Dilley Chalk #2, has them looking into improprieties at Dilley Chalk #1 now. You know they're going to swear us in, and we're going to have to disclose our relationship with Clint and Rio Frio."

"Of course you will. There's nothing to hide there. What do you think they're looking for, Phil?"

"After they shut down #2, Clint moved his operation back to #1."

"Yes, that was a true tragedy. Too bad Clint was up on the rack when it kicked back."

"Well, I don't know how to tell you this, Chuck; but, the state boys don't think it kicked back."

"They don't? Why the hell not?"

"Chuck, they think Clint put something down the well."

"What?"

"You better come over here, Chuck, and read this case file. You are going to be in this up to your ears."

Hootie was silent on the drive from Houston back to San Antonio. Katie tried to start a conversation several times, but they soon lapsed into silence. Katie had never been with a man who was not trying to impress her. He was surely a man of few words, but he seemed worried about something. Katie decided to let him work it out alone. He would tell her when it was time. Still, she could not help but wonder what was on his mind. *"Downside of a cowboy,"* she thought.

When he dropped her off at her apartment, he still had not opened up. He only mumbled, "Call me when you need something, boss."

"Where are you staying, Hootie?"

"You know, I've got a trailer down south – between Cotulla and Dilley," he reminded her.

"That is quite a drive, isn't it?"

"It's not too bad, I guess. I can move the trailer later if I need to. I don't have a lease or anything – nothing to tie me down. It's just an old RV, and I hook it up and move wherever I need to go. I may park it closer up here; it just depends on how often you're going to need me, and what all I'm going to be doin' for you."

Katie handed him a folder she received from Mr. Bruner that contained all of the insurance information on the vehicles and airplanes. "You probably need to keep this," she offered.

Hootie leafed through the documents. "I'll go out and service the airplanes tomorrow – make sure they are up on their inspections – if you won't need me for something else."

"Where are the planes?"

"One is in Cotulla; the other one is at Hobby Airport in Houston. I'll check out the one in Cotulla tonight, then fly over to Houston, and do the other one tomorrow. If you don't mind, I'll check out the boat while I'm down there, too – if that's okay?"

"Hootie, you don't have to ask – you go do what you need to do. You are in charge of that department. If I need something, I'll call."

"Sounds good," he nodded.

Katie got out of the truck and closed the door. Hootie put the window down.

"Katie?"

"Yes, Hootie?"

He looked at her with sad eyes, and those dimples popped out again. "Ah, never mind. It'll keep. See you around, Boss." He smiled and tipped his hat and then he was gone.

Katie watched his truck turn out of the parking lot and wondered what was bothering him.

Hootie was a handsome man, only fifteen years older than she was. She was attracted to him but not "that" way. Besides, she had Jake. Jake! *"OMG! I forgot Jake!"* She made a mental note to call Jake as soon as she got inside.

Charles Bruner looked up from the file into Phillip Nobles' worried eyes.

"What are you thinkin', Phil?"

"I don't know, Charles. I need to talk to T.J. and see what he knows."

"It looks like they think Clint put something down the well at Dilley Chalk #1. I thought the investigation was focused on well #2 where they closed you down. Did Clint do that?"

"Not that I know of. At the last board meeting before Clint died, he *was* talking about an experimental method called Pawson's Bitter Pill. Of course, we turned him down."

"What is Pawson's Bitter Pill? Some kind of explosive?"

"No, not an explosive – exactly; it's thermite, mostly, mixed with some aluminum nitrate and white phosphorous as I understand it."

"What's it do?"

"It gets real hot – hell hot! It gets so hot the stuff will melt rock, which is why Pawson invented it. No one has ever used it in a live well – it's experimental – strictly theoretical stuff."

"I'm not going to ask," Charles teased.

Nobles laughed, "Don't worry – Clint didn't use it so far as we know. The Board voted it down. Gunderson, the geologist down at the site, thinks he saw a delivery slip with some thermite on it. He and Strickland – you know Paul, our Safety Officer? They went up to Austin on their own and ended up with the Railroad Commission – and then Judge Isaac got involved. He ordered Railroad to pull our permit and to shut down Dilley Chalk #2 because of it. I reamed Strickland and Gunderson out for it, but it was too late – the cat was out of the bag. The last contact we had with Clint was that he was moving back over to DC#1 to try to break through to a huge oil field he had been trying to get at for a year."

"Is there any reason he would use thermite at a well site?"

"Naw – not really. Some drillers sometimes use thermite to dry up settlement ponds. When that stuff comes into contact with water, it has a violent reaction – vaporizes water in an instant."

"Is that legal?"

"Well… It ain't *illegal*," Nobles smiled, "as long as he didn't put it down the well, that is."

"Of course my client didn't put it down a well."

"Of course not – that's our story, and we're s-s-stuck with it!" Nobles repeated the old joke.

"What is Strickland saying?"

"Strickland didn't see an invoice. All he knows is what Gunderson told him. Gunderson is still claiming he saw a delivery ticket. The Texas Rangers and the regulators inspected that site and did not find any thermite, aluminum nitrate, or white phosphorus at DC#2. Who knows about DC#1? If there was anything there, it burned up along with everything else within a thousand yards."

"Well, I think this will blow over," Charles declared. "It's not illegal, even if it's a little unusual to have thermite on the well site; but without that invoice, no one can prove it was even there. We can throw enough reasonable doubt on that unless they find the shipper. Supposing Gunderson was right, so what?"

"It would have been nothing, except that DC#1 blew up," Nobles admitted.

"Well, maybe it kicked back because of the earthquake out west of there. That earthquake sure screwed up a lot of stuff. Who can say if the kickback caused the earthquake or vice versa? Maybe that well and Clint were victims, and the thermite was just a coincidence."

"Chicken or the egg, huh?"

"I can sell that in court if I have to," Charles decided.

"Well, neither you nor Anson will get a chance to talk. This thing is a hearing, not a trial. You might get a chance to give your two bits, but probably not. Anyway, I know you know how to get a message through to those boys when it's needed."

"You boys go do what you got to do – be sure to get the board minutes of that rejection of the Pawson idea on the record. That's going to be key; I'll start lining up character references to say Clint would never go off the reservation. It probably won't go any further than this hearing – unless there is something else you need to tell me."

"You already know we don't own Dilley Chalk #1 or #2, don't you? We only manage it."

"Yeah," Charles nodded, "Rio Frio Oil Company – owned by your partner T.J. Howlett."

"And your client, Katie Marshall," Nobles reminded him.

Hootie sat in his truck and gazed for a long time at the burned-out hulk of Dilley Chalk #1. The sun was setting, coloring the western sky with rich, red velvet clouds. Those clouds reminded him of the terrible inferno that had caused the death of his mentor and best friend.

Hootie was not at the site when the fire began. Maybe if he had been there he could have done something – anything – to help Clint. The last thing Clint told him was not to "push the red button." He wished Clint had followed his own advice; he might still be alive.

"What am I going to do?" he wondered. *"You are going to do exactly what Clint told you to do and keep your mouth shut, boy."*

He thought about the telephone call that he had received while he was waiting for Katie to talk to her attorney. It was T.J. warning Hootie of some bad news. There was going to be a state hearing about the Dilley Chalk #1 incident. Someone was trying to tie Clint's accident to the earthquake. The quake cost billions of dollars and took dozens of lives. Regulators were going to want to know what Hootie knew about the fire. Without saying it aloud, Hootie knew that T.J. had intended to keep Hootie in the dark. If the attorneys could pin the fault of that fire or the disaster on Clint, then Katie might lose everything. No one would gain, and everyone Hootie knew would hurt. Hootie sighed, *"I can't win; I can't break even; and, I can't even get out of the game."*

Hootie knew that when he testified, Katie would hear it all. There was no way he was going to let her find out that way. She deserved to know why her father was dead. Hootie had to figure out what to tell her and what he must conceal. He was sure that the hearing would cover, in part, that shipping invoice Gunderson saw. Knowing Clint, Hootie knew no one was ever going to find the source of that shipment. No one on the planet, other than himself, knew where that invoice was. Hootie planned to keep it that way. As soon as he could, he planned to make sure that invoice never saw the light of day. If he had his way, neither would the second device that Clint had him hide on the night of the fire.

If the attorneys could not prove that Clint had thermite and white phosphorus, then all they had to go on was Gunderson's word. Even so, no one would ever know whether Clint dropped anything into the well. Hootie intended to deny everything, just as Clint wanted. No one would ever find that briefcase with the second device.

He wished he could talk to Mr. Bruner. However, he knew he could not take that chance. Attorney/client privilege only went so far. As he sat in his truck, looking at the greatest failure in his life, Hootie formulated his story. No shipment described by Mr. Gunderson ever happened. Mr. Gunderson must have read it wrong. Clint died while checking DC#1 *after* the massive earthquake shook the countryside. The *quake* set off the oil well explosion and fire that killed Clint, not the other way around. That was all there was to it. If push came to shove, he would tell Katie about the allegations against Clint. He would assure Katie that the rumors were all lies. Hootie hoped he was a good enough liar.

CHAPTER 4

T.J. Howlett looked at Phillip Nobles as if he were the dog that messed on the Turkish rug. He had little respect for his father's old partner, and he had less regard for him now that Nobles controlled a majority of HNH Oil. After his father died, T.J. knew it was only a matter of time before Nobles either bought or forced T.J. out of the company. HNH was not the company his father built anymore.

"If you are asking me if Clint put something down that well, then you should be ashamed of yourself, Phillip!" T.J. glared at the older man.

"T.J., we're being subpoenaed. We are going to have to tell the commission everything we know – straight down the line. I've got to know what you are going to say under oath. Painful or not, if Clint used Pawson's we damn sure better know about it before we go into that hearing."

"Not that he ever told me about," T.J. fumed between clenched teeth.

Phillip Nobles looked at his partner with narrow eyes. Those were weasel words; they did not fully answer the question. He knew better than to push the younger man too far. He was like his old man; if pushed he would shut down completely. Phil needed T.J. on the team. Phillip wished once more that his former partner Wilson were still alive. Wilson would know what to do – Wilson would know how to handle his son.

"Look, T.J., I liked Clint just as much as you did. He was a good man – he made us a lot of money. I'm not sitting here throwing rocks, damn it – you've got to know that! The future of this whole company rides on what comes out of this investigation. If we screw up this hearing, it'll end up in a trial court next. It was Clint himself who brought up Pawson's Bitter Pill, not me. I'm just trying to find out if he went through with it."

"How would I know that, Phillip?" T.J. was exasperated. "I'm here in Houston, and he's down in Cotulla somewhere drilling for oil. What makes you think I know anything?"

"Because he respected you. Besides, you made him a partner of Rio Frio."

"How do you know about that?" T.J. asked, surprised.

"I know everything," Philip assured him. "Clint wouldn't take a dump without clearing it with you."

"That's bull! Clint had a mind of his own. You might as well ask Darla Dunn as ask me; here she comes right now!" T.J. pointed through the glass window at a tall brunette walking rapidly toward their door, her heels clattering on the hall floor. "Go on! Ask her."

"I already asked her," Nobles frowned. "Come in, Darla. What did you find out?"

"Phillip, T.J.," she nodded at the two men and delivered her message. "They are moving the hearing up to next week. It will be in Austin on Monday in front of the Railroad Commission. Judge Isaac has ordered HNH and Rio Frio to preserve all files and records we have. The Attorney General will be there, too. And that's not all."

Phillip put his head in his hands. *Can this day get any worse?*

"Now what?" he said wearily.

"They've subpoenaed me, too!"

Hootie sat in the round booth at Jim's Restaurant waiting for Katie to arrive. Katie said she had something important to share with him. As Hootie waited, he went over the story he was going to tell about the fire that killed her father. Hootie hoped she wouldn't ask too many questions. He wondered how she was going to take the news that the state suspected her father of causing the horrific earthquake and fire that ended his life.

He watched through the window as Katie pulled into the parking lot. She parked her car and walked toward the door, her blonde hair bouncing in waves as she walked. *"She's got a boyfriend,"* he reminded himself. *"Besides, she's your boss."* Anyway, she was way too young for

Hootie. Still, she was an attractive young woman. Katie reminded him too much of Alice. *"Maybe someday I'll find a girl like that again,"* he wished, almost kicking himself for thinking it.

Katie was in a happy mood. He could tell by the way she walked that she was feeling good. Hootie was delighted for her. He knew too well it was not easy getting over the death of a parent, and Katie had lost both of hers. They had that much in common.

Hootie hated to spoil her mood, but she needed to know how serious this hearing was. If the courts decided that Rio Frio had some liability, she might lose everything. Hopefully, Mr. Bruner had sheltered her assets. Katie whirled past the waitress, ordered coffee, and slipped into the booth. She smelled like coconut oil sunscreen.

"Guess what?" she asked him.

"What?" Hootie asked, barely listening; he was still planning on how and what to tell her.

"The will passed probate! Let's celebrate! I want the surf and turf! What about you?"

"The same, I guess." He did not feel hungry. He was too nervous.

Katie kept a constant stream of talk going through the entire meal, occasionally pausing to take a bite of food or a sip of coffee. He had never seen her in such a good mood. Hootie was not listening. His mind was fifty miles away in Cotulla.

"Katie ..." he drawled slowly, "Katie, have you talked to Mr. Bruner since we left Houston?"

"Of course, silly, how do you think I know about the probate?"

"Did he mention anything about a hearing on the oil well fire?"

"Oh, that! Yes, he did. There is going to be an investigation and a hearing Monday in Austin. He told me I didn't have to come unless I wanted to be there. They didn't subpoena me. What about it?"

Hootie rubbed a finger across his lips as she sipped her coffee.

"It may be a little more complicated than that," he hinted.

"What do you mean?"

"They subpoenaed me. I've got to go testify. I'll have to tell everything I know about your dad, the fire, and the operations of that well…"

"Hootie! I've got it all figured out!" Katie interrupted, so excited she could not sit still. Hootie's heart skipped a beat at her words. What had she figured out? He stared at her with the deer-in-the-headlights look. "You did?"

"I did! You asked what I wanted to do after things settled down – remember? Now that the judge approved the probate, I know exactly what I want to do. Will you help me, please?"

Hootie breathed a sigh of relief – she had not figured out the worst part – what caused the fire. "Of course, I will – what?" Hootie shook his head, confused.

"I want to go after it!" She was bouncing up and down, almost popping out of her seat.

"Go after what?"

"It – that thing!" she exclaimed, the excitement shining in her eyes. "I want to go find it and get rid of it! I want to stop it from killing people!"

"What?" He shook his head, still not yet realizing what she meant.

"Aquasaurus – I want to go after it, and you are going to help me!"

CHAPTER 5

Hootie sat in the crowded hearing room and looked at the clock hanging behind the head table. It was a government clock with the State of Texas seal on its face. The red second hand jumped every second as the time inched toward 9:15. As soon as the second hand reached the twelve, the gavel rang throughout the room as spectators rose. They watched as the Commissioners filed into the room and took their seats.

The Chairman banged the gavel and read off a long script required for formal hearings, which included all of the legal announcements. After the Chair completed the formalities, he put down the text and spoke directly to the audience.

"This hearing of the Dilley Chalk Incident is called to order. Ladies and gentlemen, let me begin by introducing the members of this panel."

He introduced himself and went down the line for all fifteen members of the commission. The men and women who sat on the dais were all members of the Railroad Commission and had direct authority over oil drilling in the State of Texas. Whatever these regulators decided would affect HNH's drilling permits. Every oil company in the state lived or died by their rulings. A hearing was serious business.

"Also," the Chair added, "we have added Senator Compton from Del Rio and Representative Pablo Marín to this panel. Welcome, everyone. Also in the interest of public disclosure, the Attorney General has sent a representative from his office to serve as an observer: Mr. Doug Griffin." Mr. Griffin waived his hand at the room. "Mr. Griffin will not be a deliberating member of the panel; he is here to observe for the State."

Everyone knew why Mr. Griffin was there. If anyone broke the law, then someone's head was going to roll.

The Chairman called the roll from a long list that included Phillip Nobles, T.J. Howlett, Paul Strickland, Jim Gunderson, and Hootie. Hootie responded when they called his name, but he did not recognize several of the names on the list.

Hootie was surprised to hear Darla Dunn's name. *Was she here?* Hootie looked around the room for Darla but did not see her. He looked forward to seeing Darla again. He dated Darla a few times. They got along well, and Hootie liked her a lot. The only problem was Clint. Hootie could not avoid thinking that Darla was a little too close to Clint, and Hootie did not want to get between whatever might be going on between them. Hootie was glad they had not called Katie.

After the Chair admonished the audience to keep order, he called Paul Strickland to the small table facing the panel. After taking the oath, Paul eased his large frame into the narrow wooden armchair that must have been a hundred years old; you could hear it squeak from across the room. Hootie stifled a laugh. *If Sam Houston sat in that chair, it wouldn't be worth much when Strickland got through with it.*

"Sir, please state your name for the record and tell us your role with HNH Oil Company."

"Paul Strickland, the corporate safety officer for HNH Oil Company. I have worked in this capacity for fourteen years, and I oversee all field safety operations for the company."

"Are you familiar with the Dilley Chalk #1 and #2 operations?"

Paul assured the panel he was, that he was responsible for the safety of the men employed by HNH, and that he oversaw all the operations at dozens of drilling sites, including both Dilley Chalk wells.

"When did you first become aware that there might be a problem with something on the Dilley Chalk sites?"

"Well, Dilley Chalk #1 near Cotulla shut down because something blocked the borehole. A huge granite dome was down there that covered the whole area. Mr. Marshall believed that a huge oilfield lay beneath the blockage and, if he could get around it, he could get to the oil. He thought if he went a little ways north to Dilley, he might be able to get under or around the blockage."

"Was he able to succeed in that plan?"

"No, sir. When he got down far enough, he ran into the same formation – just from a different angle. Mr. Marshall believed that the granite dome wrapped over the entire oil bed. It was going to be very costly and take a very long time to get through that half a mile of rock."

"We understand that at some point #2 was ordered to shut down. Do you know why?"

"Yes, sir, I do. I got a call from the geologist on the site, Jim Gunderson. He said he thought Mr. Marshall was going to try to break through the rock with some illegal method. Jim was so adamant about it that he convinced me to come to Austin with him to report his suspicions; we ended up with the Railroad Commission. They pulled the permit and shut the well down."

"Why did they do that, Mr. Strickland?"

"Jim Gunderson saw a delivery slip that had some suspicious chemicals on it. He believed Mr. Marshall was trying to build Pawson's Bitter Pill."

Strickland spent the next few minutes explaining Pawson's Bitter Pill to the panel.

They asked, "Did you see that invoice?"

"No, sir."

The panel excused Strickland and called Jim Gunderson next.

"Mr. Gunderson, please tell us what you saw on that delivery slip that caused you such concern."

"I saw an order for thermite and some white phosphorus."

"Is that unusual?"

"No, not the thermite – that's pretty rare on a well site, but not unheard of. However, the Willie Pete – now that's really odd – that's another story. That stuff is dangerous."

"Willie Pete?"

"That is what they call white phosphorous. Together, those two ingredients form the main components of Pawson's Bitter Pill."

"Is it your opinion Mr. Marshall was going to introduce those chemicals into the well?"

"Yes, it is. I don't know any other reason why you'd want Willie Pete on a drill site."

"Do you know the source of that delivery?"

"I gave it back to Mr. Marshall," Gunderson admitted.

"So," the Chairman summed it up, "you have no actual evidence of delivery to the well site?"

"No, but … but I saw the invoice. I'll testify to it."

"Thank you, Mr. Gunderson; you just did. We'll call you back if we need anything more."

The Chair called Mr. Philip Nobles to the stand next. After he introduced himself, the panel got down to business.

"Mr. Nobles, do you know anything about Mr. Marshall's plans to use a device known as Pawson's Bitter Pill on Dilley Chalk #2?"

"Yes, sir, Mr. Marshall came to the HNH Board of Directors meeting with a proposal to do that. Pawson's is highly experimental. No one has ever used it on a live well. The board turned him down because we didn't feel it was warranted."

"Do you think Mr. Marshall may have gone ahead with his plans despite being overruled by the Board of Directors?"

"No, sir! Mr. Marshall was a devoted and dedicated employee of our firm. He was tough, but he would not take that kind of risk on his own. He would not do anything the board did not approve. There is no way he would have put Pawson's down Dilley Chalk #2."

"What about well #1?"

Phillip paused before he answered and considered his words carefully.

"He never suggested using Pawson's on Dilley Chalk #1, and we never discussed that either. At the time the state closed Dilley Chalk #2, #1 was inactive and capped for eight months. When the state shut down #2, I believe Clint felt he had no choice but to start up operations on #1 again. We gave him the authority to do that. He was not a man to give up easily, which is why he was so valuable to us. However, with the board so adamant against Pawson's, I don't believe Clint would have taken that step on his own. There was more riding on this than just his finding oil."

"Like what, Mr. Nobles?"

"A lot of investment had gone into this project. The owner was going to go broke if this well didn't come in." Hootie looked across the room as T.J. clinched his jaw and stared back at Philip. There was no way to avoid answering the next question. Besides, they already knew the answer.

"HNH did not own the project?"

"No, sir, we only managed it for the owner – Rio Frio Oil Company. HNH collaborated with Rio Frio and underwrote the project."

"Who owns Rio Frio, Mr. Nobles?"

Phillip Nobles turned and pointed at T.J. sitting along the back wall. "Mr. T.J. Howlett."

"Mamá! Mommy!" Isabela screamed with laughter! "Look at me!"

Hermosa Flores looked up from her book at her daughter. "Be careful, M'ija! Hold on tight!"

Her daughter was riding the Shetland pony so close to the ocean waves the hooves kicked up watery globs of sandy mud with each leap. Isabela liked to ride fast. Nothing could stop that girl.

"Come away from the water!" Hermi shouted although she knew it was a waste of time. Exasperated, she lay her book aside and got up from the beach blanket. She looked out from under the umbrella shading her spot and moved her sunglasses down from her head to her eyes.

The pair enjoyed their stay at the Laguna Madre y Delta del Rio Bravo State Park, in northeast Mexico. The park had everything: great cabins, an excellent restaurant, and plenty of activities to attract all ages. Hermi wished they didn't offer horse rentals though; but other than that, everything was going well. Isabela loved the horses, and it was hard to drag her away from her favorite rental pony that she named Bravo.

Except for a couple of falls on the soft beach, Isabela had improved her horse skills this summer. Hermi planned to give her some riding lessons this fall when they returned to Mexico City. Hermi decided to talk to her husband, Hector, about buying a pony when he arrived over the weekend. Meanwhile, she would try to keep Isabela from breaking her neck.

She walked toward the shoreline enjoying the warm sandy beach. The water was so blue and pristine; Hermi could not believe how beautiful it was. It was hard to tell where the sea stopped and the sky began. She was glad they came here; it was so much less crowded than Cabo or Acapulco. She waded in the warm surf, waiting for Isabela to ride back down the beach. She waved as her daughter trotted in her direction. Hermi moved deeper into the refreshing water and ducked beneath the waves, forgetting to take off her sunglasses.

Wiping the water from her face, she shook water from her sunglasses and looked out on the expansive lagoon that bordered the park. No sharks here, she thought – nothing but dolphins and porpoises. She was glad that big crocodile, *Acuasaurio*, she had heard about on the news was up near the Texas border. "*We don't want a thing like that down here,*" she shuddered and winced at the thought of those massive jaws closing around her only daughter.

Hermi came ashore as Isabela trotted up. She grabbed Bravo's reigns to bring him to a full stop before Isabela could take off again. The warm water lapped her ankles playfully.

"M'ija, vamos a buscar un cono de nieve," she pointed. "There is a raspa stand up there. We can get a snow cone!"

"Si, Mamá, but what about Bravo?"

"Leave him here. You can tie him to that huge driftwood log there. We'll be back soon. It's just a few feet."

"Ok, Mamá. You go ahead, and I'll catch up."

Hermi was halfway to the raspa stand when she heard Isabela's shrieks, and Bravo's loud panicked screams. She had not known a horse could scream. Horrified, she turned to see her daughter swinging a big stick at something in the water. Hermi broke into a run towards her child. Something was dragging Bravo into the surf with such force that Hermi heard the reins pop as they snapped in two. Isabela was following the horse into the water, still striking at something. Suddenly, a massive scaly tail swept out of the water and swept across Isabela's tiny body. Hermi watched as an enormous wave washed her helpless child ashore.

Isabela was not badly hurt; she was on her feet by the time her mother got to her. Hermi grabbed her child before Isabela could go back into the water. She covered her daughter's eyes to keep her from seeing, but she could do nothing to prevent her from hearing the screams and the crunching of the horse's bones. The crocodile rolled over repeatedly, turning the water into a frothy red foam. Mercifully, the horrible sounds stopped as the crocodile quickly took the horse into deeper water and disappeared.

Hermosa kept Isabela's eyes covered until they were back in the condominium. Hermie prayed and rocked her crying child to sleep until Hector arrived.

Katie sat at an outdoor taco stand with her friend Rita Martin as the two friends caught up on their summer activities. Katie wanted to know how Jesse was recovering from his injury in the cave. As expected, the talk finally turned toward the giant crocodile, Aquasaurus.

"That's one thing I wanted to talk about, Rita. That crocodile is killing people. It almost killed us. I want to go find it and try to kill it or capture it – and I want you to go with me!"

"Are you crazy? That thing almost killed us. It was a miracle that we got out of that cave alive! It broke your arm and almost disabled Jesse – he still uses a cane to get around! He'll probably have a limp for the rest of his life. I'm not going anywhere near that thing!"

"I've got help – a man that worked for my dad. His name is Hootie. He can fly my dad's airplane and drive his boat. We can find it. You all won't have to do anything except be there with me – sort of as a chaperone. You don't want me going off alone with some strange man do you?"

"No, but – school. Classes start at the end of August. Will we be back by then?"

"I promise if we don't find it by the end of August, we'll come back. That gives us two months. I'm going with Hootie, Rita. You want me to go out there all by myself?"

"Of course not, but what do you know about this Hootie?"

"Only that he is gorgeous! You should see him, Rita!" Katie could not hide her admiration of the older man.

"I better go – you'll come back in trouble if I don't keep you two apart," Rita laughed. But, what about Jesse? I can't leave him alone yet."

"Jesse and Jake can both come. Look, Rita, it will be fun. Probably all that is going to happen is we will sail around the Gulf for a couple of months on a long holiday. The sea will be good for you and good for Jesse."

"What about Jake?" Rita asked.

Katie slapped her hand to her forehead. "OMG! I forgot about Jake!"

CHAPTER 6

T.J. Howlett eased into the squeaky chair.

"Yes, sir. I am the majority owner of Rio Frio Oil Company. I am also a minority owner of HNH Oil Company. Until my late father's death, I was the majority owner. Let me explain it this way: Rio Frio owns the leases to the Dilley Chalk project, which includes both #1 and #2 well-drilling sites; HNH manages the project under contract."

"Isn't that a conflict of interest, Mr. Howlett?" the Chair asked.

"No, sir. I don't think so. Everything Rio Frio does goes through the HNH trustees. Rio Frio pays HNH under contract for their involvement. Rio Frio leases HNH employees, but they own their equipment outright. You will find all the books and records in order. There is no conflict."

"So, what if HNH and Rio Frio disagree on a course of action?"

"HNH holds the purse strings; Rio Frio would have to find funding for operations if they went out on their own. There are contracts in place to protect HNH interests and to allow Rio Frio to continue to produce. Rio Frio understands the contract and has agreed to follow it to the letter."

"Absolutely?"

"Absolutely," T.J. emphasized.

"Once HNH rejected the Pawson method, what was Rio Frio's position?"

"Are you asking me as an owner of HNH or an owner of Rio Frio?"

"Both. Is there any difference?"

"No. Both HNH and Rio Frio abandoned all thought of using Pawson's."

"What about Mr. Marshall?"

"Mr. Marshall was a great employee and a partner in Rio Frio. He would not take that kind of risk. If HNH pulled its support, it would ruin Rio Frio financially – it would ruin both of us, frankly."

"Thank you, Mr. Howlett. You are excused for now, but please stay here in case we have some follow-up questions. The panel calls Sergeant Neal Howard."

T.J. went back to his seat, thankful the panel had not pressed any further. He wondered who Sergeant Howard was. He had never heard of the man.

"My name is Sergeant Neal Howard of the U.S. Border Patrol."

"Sgt. Howard, did you detain a delivery driver named Francisco Herrera at the border checkpoint near Encinal, Texas last April?"

"Yes, sir, I distinctly remember him."

"Why, Sgt. Howard?"

"He was a funny guy – calls himself Paco. We thought he might be running drugs, but we didn't find anything. He was carrying a few boxes, but he had the correct hazardous cargo placard posted. Funny thing though, he was making his delivery in a classic 1955 GMC pickup – a real gem of a truck. He was real picky about it – didn't want us to scratch it, I guess."

"Do you have your log book with you Sgt. Howard?"

"Yes, sir, right here."

"Will you turn to the date you stopped Mr. Herrera and read your notes?"

"Sure." Sgt. Howard flipped through the pages. "Here it is. It is just like I told you. Herrera came through the checkpoint, no drugs found, and he was carrying cargo with the proper placards attached. Another thing about that placard," Sgt. Howard laughed, "he stapled it to a wooden slat stuck in a stake hole – he would not let anyone tape it to the truck. As he left, the placard blew off, and he had to stop and go back to pick it up. He stuck it back into the stake hole and went on his way. He had a manifest and delivery ticket for some oil company in Dilley. I did not make a note of the source of the shipment, but I believe it was in Del Rio or Laredo."

"Did you note the name of the company it was marked for?"

"No, sir, I did not. We don't normally do that once we make sure the shipment is legal."

"Would it have been for Rio Frio in Dilley, Texas?"

"It could have been – that seems familiar."

"Sgt. Howard, did you make a notation of the type of materials Mr. Herrera was hauling?"

Sgt. Howard looked back at his notes, "Yes, sir, he was carrying thermite and white phosphorus."

Katie mentally calculated the number in her group. With herself, Hootie, Rita, Jesse, and Jake there would be five. Hootie told her there would be plenty of room in the plane so long as they did not bring too much baggage with them. The 65-footer had four cabins below and one cabin behind the wheelhouse for the captain, so there would be plenty of space. Hootie already had someone stocking the boat for a two-month cruise. Katie called a meeting with her friends to discuss the trip.

They met that evening in Austin at a quiet place off Lamar so Hootie could attend. Hootie was still involved with the hearings. He seemed distant and troubled, but Katie believed it was because of the legal problems with the oil wells. She thought that if it were something she needed to know, then Hootie would tell her. After she introduced Hootie to the group, she laid out her plans. First, she would need to know how long the hearing would take.

"I'm not sure," Hootie shook his head. "It might be over tomorrow, or it might go a week or more."

"Do you have to be there all the time?"

"Yes. I'm on the call list; it's a formal subpoena. I'll be called to testify first thing in the morning. I might be able to leave after that, but I figure I should stay until the end. I might be needed again."

Hootie hoped she would not ask any more questions about the hearing. Things were not looking good for Clint, and he did not want to tell her that with all of her friends around.

"OK, so we can't leave right away; but we can get ready," Katie announced. "Here is the plan. As soon as we can leave, we'll take the plane to Galveston to pick up the boat. Write down your identification numbers on this form so Hootie can fax them to the port in Galveston. That will take care of the paperwork. Everyone carry your passport. There are enough cabins for all of us. Take your summer clothes, but we'll probably live in swimsuits and shorts for two months. Bring your cameras, but watch your baggage weight. The airplane will be heavy enough without a lot of luggage. Whatever you need, we'll buy on the way."

"How long will we be gone," Jake asked. "School starts in August."

"We'll be back by the end of August," Katie promised. "While we wait, go ahead and get registered or get your paperwork ready. We may get back just in time for classes to start. Are all of you pre-registered?"

Receiving nods from everyone but Hootie, Katie continued. "We are going to just motor around the coast for a couple of months hoping to spot that crocodile – Aquasaurus. We know the croc is in Mexican waters now. It ate a little girl's pony at a park called Laguna Madre Rio Bravo. That park is on the way to our villa at La Pesca. We can make that our home base while we search. That way we won't be on the boat all the time."

Jake scowled at Hootie. "You can't talk her out of this?"

"I work for her, Hoss. She's the boss." Hootie admitted.

"Well, I think it's crazy!" Jake raged. "That monster almost killed us in that cave! It's already killed more than twenty people. What chance do we have – even if we can find it? Hell, the Navy can't even find that thing. And, even if we do find it, what are you going to do *Hoss* – rope it?"

Hootie's only response was to smile, wink at Jake, raise his beer, and take a sip. Jake was fuming.

Katie searched for a way to make peace, "If we find it, we'll call the Mexican Navy. They will know how to deal with it. All we need to do is find it."

"Mexico has a Navy?" Jake asked.

"They must have; every country has a Navy," Jesse stated. "Don't they?"

No one in the group knew for sure.

Darla Dunn was working late as usual. She closed out Clint's files and emptied his office. She had already boxed up his personal effects and would ship them off to his daughter. There was only one thing remaining to do for him – she had to check his apartment. She decided she might as well do it now. She was leaving the next morning to testify at the hearing. She used her key to let herself in and picked up his mail beneath the mail slot. It was quite a lot of mail – most of it junk.

The apartment still smelled of Clint. She inhaled deeply. Lord, she missed him so much. She looked at his portrait on the table by the couch.

"Damn your blue eyes! Why did you have to go and die?" She sadly turned the photo on its face and sat at the table to go through the mail.

His daughter could come later and pack his clothes; Darla did not think she could do it without crying. It had been almost three months, but her heart was still broken. Darla's only role at this point was to make sure all of HNH's property and paperwork was collected and brought back to the office, as well as to pay any bills that had come to the apartment instead of the office. *"Just get it over with and get out of here,"* she told herself.

She pulled a large trashcan over to the table and began sorting through the cards and letters. There were no personal letters, cards, or anything like that. It was all business – just like Clint – all business. She dumped most of it without even opening it. He did not need any credit cards, insurance, magazines, or vacation offers. She found a bill for gasoline and placed it in the "To Be Paid" stack. There was not much else. She was tempted to sweep the entire pile into the wastebasket when a new credit card bill caught her eye. *Better keep that.*

It was a month late she noticed as she opened the envelope. She located the late notice in the stack and looked at the statement. Her eyes scanned down the list of charges until she got to the final one on the list. It was the last thing Clint charged before the accident. He had stopped at the Dairy Queen in Cotulla. She scrutinized it closer as she scrunched up her eyes. Something triggered a thought in her mind, but she could not figure out what it was.

She scrutinized the entry, searching her memory for a clue as to why it bothered her. When it came to her, a loud gasp escaped her mouth. She searched through the stack of bills and opened Clint's cell phone bill. She ran her finger down the list of calls to the final entries. With a loud whoop, she stuffed the statements into her purse, slipped on her heels, and ran from the apartment, locking the door behind her. She fired up her car and immediately drove toward Austin in the middle of the dark Texas night.

CHAPTER 7

"The Chair re-calls Mr. T.J. Howlett."

As T.J. returned to the squeaky chair, the Chairman reminded him that he was still under oath and instructed him on the line of questioning that would follow.

"Mr. Howlett, we would like to question you this time in your capacity at Rio Frio Oil Company. Please respond in that regard. The Commission believes your thought process may differ from one organization to another as both firms have their own unique objectives. We are most interested in your testimony about your role in Rio Frio."

T.J. indicated he agreed and understood, but he wondered about the line of questioning. Did they know more than he thought they did?

"Yes, sir, I understand. However, both firms are subject to the same regulations and laws."

"Understood, sir, but your decisions may change because in one role you are a contract administrator; and in the other, you are an owner. Wouldn't you say that might affect your response?"

T.J. nodded his head, "It might, but not much. It is what it is."

"Indeed it is, Mr. Howlett. How many people own shares of Rio Frio?"

"Only two, Mr. Marshall and me – I guess now, his daughter inherited his share. That would be Ms. Katherine Marshall and me."

"Is she here today?"

"No, sir; I don't think so. I believe her attorney is present."

"Is there someone here that represents Miss Marshall?"

A silver-haired man in a gray suit stood and addressed the panel.

"I do, Mr. Chairman. My name is Charles Bruner. Miss Marshall became an owner upon the recent death of her father; she does not know of the incidents we are discussing. I represented her father, and I am far more knowledgeable about his business dealings than Miss Marshall would be. She was not subpoenaed; but I am here and will speak for Miss Marshall if needed – and for Clint Marshall as well, as far as that goes."

"Thank you, Mr. Bruner. We will call upon you if needed." Mr. Bruner nodded and sat back in his chair.

"Mr. Howlett, you have heard testimony here that Rio Frio received a shipment of thermite and white phosphorus at Dilley Chalk #2. Were you aware of that order or shipment?"

"In all due respect, sir, I believe the testimony did not claim Rio Frio ever received such a shipment. I certainly did not authorize such an order."

"So, Mr. Marshall ordered these supplies on his own?"

"I was unaware of any such order; nor did an invoice for an order like that ever come to the accounts payable department of either oil company – HNH or Rio Frio. There is nothing to establish that any such order ever existed."

"Who pays the invoices for Rio Frio?"

"Miss Darla Dunn, Mr. Marshall's personal assistant, handles all of Rio Frio's payables."

"Did you and Mr. Marshall have any discussions concerning Pawson's method?"

"Well of course we did! After he brought the suggestion to the HNH Board of Directors meeting, we had a heart-to-heart discussion about it. He should have cleared that idea through me first, and he did not. I nailed him to the wall over it. If he had checked with me, he would never have brought the idea before the board in the first place."

"So you were not in favor of using Pawson's method?"

"Mr. Chairman, I am quite sure the use of that experimental method falls outside our permit authorizations. In order to use it, we would need to file an amendment with the commission and get approval before taking that action. We have done neither, so Mr. Marshall's suggestion was premature and out of line. I told him so in no uncertain terms."

"Yet the components for such a device were delivered to the site, were they not?"

"I do not know, sir. Mr. Gunderson testified he saw such a delivery ticket, but I do not know anything about it. It could be that Mr. Gunderson was mistaken! Maybe it was for some other operation nearby, and we simply received it on their behalf. I don't know. But I *can* tell you that neither Rio Frio nor HNH used those items on either Dilley Chalk site."

"Received for another operation?" the Chairman asked.

"Mr. Chairman, have you ever worked on an oil well site?"

"Well, of course I have, Mr. Howlett. I even worked with your father for many years on the same sites. You know that. What is the purpose of your question?"

"Then you know how those sites work, sir. Crews are in and out checking on other sites and running to get supplies all the time. Sometimes we lock the gates and leave for three or four days on some sites. We all help each other out. If a shipment comes for one site, it's not unusual for a neighbor company to take it until they come back. I don't know if that is what happened, but surely you can see where that could happen – *if* it even happened at all."

There was a disturbance in the back of the room as Mr. Gunderson rose to dispute Howlett's statement. The Chair gaveled for order and asked Mr. Gunderson to take his seat. Once he had order restored, the Chair continued.

"Mr. Gunderson's testimony seems to be corroborated by Sgt. Howard, who has official documents showing the chemicals passed his checkpoint."

"Yes, sir. However, Sgt. Howard also said he did not know if the destination was our site or not. He was not there, and investigators did not find evidence of those chemicals at either site. It may be the delivery ticket Sgt. Howard saw was in error, or the materials were intended for some other location. I don't know, and apparently, neither does Sgt. Howard."

Heads nodded up and down the line of panelists. It was going to be difficult to prove beyond a reasonable doubt that Rio Frio ever received the shipment since Sgt. Howard had not annotated the destination on his forms. One of the members of the panel tried another tact.

"Mr. Howlett, do you have any reason to believe Mr. Marshall may have wanted thermite and white phosphorus at his site? After all, didn't he request board approval to use them?"

"No to both questions. I do not know why or even *if* he had those items at the site; and no, he did not request permission to use them. He merely brought the idea up for discussion at a board meeting. He did not request using Pawson's at any time. It is not against the law to talk about doing something."

The commissioner muted his microphone and sat back in his seat, yielding questioning back to the Chair.

"However," T.J. continued during the delay, "let me be clear on this matter. *If* Mr. Marshall did order those items, it is not illegal for them to be on a well site. We use a great number of materials in our operations for some purposes. If they were on-site, it would prove nothing. It would only be illegal *if* he put it in the well! I already testified that both HNH and Rio Frio's position was that Pawson's would not be used at Dilley Chalk #2, and Mr. Marshall was fully aware of that. I am not going to sit here and disparage the character and reputation of a man who died trying to do his job."

"Mr. Howlett, the board offers its sincere condolences on the death of Mr. Marshall. Also, we want to add our sympathies on the recent death of your father, Mr. Wilson Howlett. Wilson had many friends in this industry and on this panel, and we had great respect for him. We understand that your father was gravely ill during the time of this incident."

"Yes, sir, he died on the same day as that terrible earthquake and the resulting fire that killed our friend Clint Marshall."

The Chairman noted the sequence of order T.J. used. Howlett was trying to get into the record that the oil well fire was a result of the earthquake. If the panel believed that the quake caused the fire, then the issue of the chemicals would be mute.

"How important was it to you that this well at Dilley Chalk #2 strike oil?"

"Very important – we had invested a great deal of money on this project. You're an oil man – no oil driller wants to come up with a dry hole."

"Isn't it true that if your father died, Mr. Nobles would end up with the controlling shares of HNH?"

T.J. turned and stared at Phillip Nobles. There was only one way they could know that information. *What was Phillip trying to pull here?* He forced a smile and a nod at Phillip and turned back to the panel.

"Mr. Chairman, my father and Mr. Nobles created HNH from the ground up over fifty years ago. They fought hand-in-hand to build the company through lean times and years of struggling. They were partners almost all their lives. They wildcatted wells from east Texas to Odessa back in the days when you had to use your own money. Back in those days, no bank would touch a wildcat well – it was too risky. Mr. Nobles and my dad risked everything they owned. It was natural and right that my father would leave half of his shares to Mr. Nobles. It was part of his personal code of ethics. I'm not so sure anyone else in this room would have been as principled as my father was."

"How did you feel about that?"

"I inherited the other half of dad's shares and ended up with more than I had before. I was satisfied." T.J. crossed his arms and stared at the panel, offended by the line of questioning.

"Thank you, Mr. Howlett. I am sure these questions are painful for you, but we must get to the truth."

"You want the truth?" T.J. could hold it in no longer.

"Yes, we do."

"The truth is the world lost a lot of good people that day. I think the death toll from the earthquake is somewhere near a hundred, and we were lucky it wasn't more. The epicenter of the earthquake was nearly a hundred miles west of our well site. To suggest that Mr. Marshall caused an earthquake from that distance away is egregious and grossly unfair. There were some innocent people killed that day, but none more so than my partner and friend Mr. Clint Marshall."

"Thank you, Mr. Howlett. The Chair calls Mr. Hootie Johnson."

"Who the crap does he think he is, anyway?" Jake complained. "This guy – this cowboy – what do we need him for? Why doesn't he go back to the oilfields where he belongs?"

Jesse looked at his friend. *Boy is he worked up.* "We don't need him, Jake; but I guess Katie thinks she does. She inherited a lot of property and oil fields and stuff. I guess she needs him to help her sort all of that out."

"Yeah, but why do we need him hanging around all the time? Now, he's going on a trip with us. We don't need that."

"Jake, do you know how to fly an airplane?" Jesse laughed, trying to humor his friend.

"No, but…"

"Do you know how to captain a boat?" Jesse added.

"No, of course, I don't! But, but why him? We can hire someone to do those things. We don't need him for that. This – this Hootie! What the hell is that anyway, a Hootie? What are *we*? Blowfish?"

Jesse laughed, "Blowfish!" He punched his friend in the arm. "Good one. Come on Jake, let it go; he's going whether we like it or not."

"Then help me get on this bike. I'm not going to be crippled all my life!" Jake carped.

"Jake, if Rita finds out about this, she'll kill us both! You're just going to balance on it, right? You're not going to ride; right?"

"If she kills us, we won't have to worry about Hootie going on the trip."

Jake helped Jesse swing his leg over the bike. "I'm not sure about this," Jake waffled.

"See, I can hold it up with my good leg!"

With a sudden unexpected whoop, using his uninjured leg, Jesse pushed his bike over the edge of the rim.

"See ya' at the bottom sucker! He yelled as he bounced headlong down the rocky trail to the bottom of the canyon.

"No!" Jake shouted as he scrambled for his own bike.

CHAPTER 8

Now that Hootie was in the squeaky chair, he did not find it nearly so funny. He was nervous, so he clasped his hands together to steady himself. He could stand on an oil rig while it bucked and roared beneath him, but sitting in this room with everyone looking at him was something different. He did not trust these people. He wished he was anywhere but here trying to keep that chair from squeaking.

"Mr. Johnson," the Chair began, "Hootie is such a different name. Is that your birth name?"

"No, it isn't, but it's the only name I've ever used, except for my time in the Air Force."

"Thank you for your service. What name were you born with?"

Hootie dropped his head and mumbled, "Harry – I've legally changed it to Hootie now."

"Was that short for Howard Johnson?" the Chair asked unaware of the snickers slowly spreading around the room.

"No – it was Harry." Several people in the room laughed aloud as Hootie's face turned crimson. The Chair sternly looked out at the room until they settled down. "My legal name is Hootie – I've been called that all my life anyway."

"Hootie, what is your position with HNH Oil Company?"

"I started out as a roughneck and rose through the ranks to day shift leader for the crew on the Dilley Chalk projects."

"Was Mr. Marshall your direct supervisor?"

"No, sir, my supervisor was Mr. Hugh Shipman until he left HNH in April."

"What about after that?"

"Soon after that, I was transferred from HNH to Rio Frio by Mr. Marshall. I was offered the foreman slot on Dilley Chalk #1, but the accident ended those plans."

"So your employer is Rio Frio?"

"It is now; but since the accident, we have been shut down. Everything we had was wrapped up in the Dilley Chalk projects."

"From the time you were transferred until the accident, you were supervised by Mr. Marshall. How long was that?"

"I don't recall exactly, but it was probably two days or maybe less."

"Who ordered supplies and materials for your operations in the field?"

"Mr. Marshall would, or he would tell me what he wanted. Sometimes Miss Dunn back in the office would make the orders," Hootie said.

"During your entire time on the Dilley Chalk projects, both #1 and #2, did you order a shipment of thermite and white phosphorus?"

"No, sir," Hootie said truthfully. He knew what they were getting at, but he would let them ask the right question before he answered.

"Do you recall receiving a shipment from a man named Paco who drove a 1955 GMC pickup?"

"Oh, yes! I definitely remember that! At the time, I thought he was looking for work; but it turned out he had two boxes to deliver. We were told to expect a delivery intended for a neighboring operation."

"What was in those boxes, Mr. Johnson?"

"I'm not sure. I didn't read the packing slip or open the boxes. I just signed the driver's delivery ticket and placed the items in the pump shed like I was told to do."

"You weren't curious?"

"No, I had plenty to do. We were in the middle of shutting down Dilley Chalk #2 because the Judge shut us down. There were valves that had to be set in certain positions and pumps that we had to shut down and lock out. We had already laid off half the crew. I didn't think any more about it. I figured the owner would drop by and pick them up in a day or two. It wasn't unusual because we got shipments delivered to our site all the time."

"Who was it marked for?" the Chairman pressed.

Hootie considered his words carefully. "I wish I could tell you, but like I told you, I didn't open the packing slip. I just signed the manifest."

"How did you know it wasn't for HNH?"

"Because Mr. Marshall had told us to expect the delivery. He asked me to put it in the pump house, so I did. I didn't have time to be curious; I had stuff to do."

"But, don't you work for Rio Frio?"

"I do now, but at the time I was still working for HNH. I did not know Rio Frio was involved in our operations. I worked for HNH then. It wasn't until after I was transferred – *after* we moved operations back to Cotulla, that I learned who Rio Frio was. Up until then, I didn't know anything about them."

"But you signed a shipment for them?"

"If it was for them. An oil field is a different kind of business. A lot of times, there is no one at all on the sites. We take deliveries and hold them for each other all the time – all the delivery companies know this. If you can't find anyone at the delivery site find someone nearby to take the delivery – we all work together. At the time, I thought Rio Frio was some other operation out there."

"What happened to the shipment you placed in the pump house?"

"Mr. Marshall told us to move it over to Cotulla to Dilley Chalk #1 after we shut down #2 – along with a lot of other materials, equipment, and tools."

"What were your instructions concerning that Cotulla site?"

"My instructions were to prepare the well according to the work order issued on the schedule. It seemed to me like we were going to resume drilling – or we were going to pull pipe back out of the well – either one."

"Why would Mr. Marshall ask you to do that after Dilley Chalk #1 was already shut down and written off as a failed well?"

"I believed Mr. Marshall had decided to reopen Dilley Chalk #1 because it was clear that we would not be able to continue to drill at #2. Please understand, he did not discuss any of this with me at my level; but we all understood that we were moving back to #1 to resume drilling. Besides, once the State locked us out of the Cotulla site, the site in Dilley, #1, was the only option we had left."

"What became of that shipment you took to Dilley Chalk #1?"

Hootie paused. *Here was the point of no return.*

"I put it in the pump house like I was told to do. I suppose it got burned up in the fire along with everything else." *It was a safe answer.*

"Do you think those items in that shipment increased the intensity of the fire?"

"I suppose so; they probably did. That was pretty powerful stuff."

"Do you have any reason to believe Mr. Marshall used those products in the well?"

"No." Hootie laced his hands together on top of the table. "I never saw or heard him mention anything like that, sir."

The Chairman looked up from his notes at Hootie. That was not the question. He had not asked Hootie what he had seen. "But do you believe he did it?"

"No, sir," Hootie shook his head. "I don't believe he did."

"Why do you think that, Mr. Johnson?"

"Because Mr. Marshall was not crazy! He would not have endangered his crew without warning us ahead of time."

"We understand the crew was not on site at the time, Mr. Johnson – everyone was on standby. Mr. Marshall was the only person on site when it exploded. Is that correct?"

"We have to offer crew rest – it's the law. We were going to insert the drilling bit the next morning. It was on the work schedule – you can see that for yourself. We filed the schedule with HNH a few days earlier, and I'm sure you have a copy. The crew was on-call and scheduled to report at eight a.m. to begin their shift."

The Chairman picked up the work order sheet and showed it to Hootie.

"Can you explain why it would be necessary to place an insertion port on the well?"

"For the mud," Hootie looked at them with an amused look. *Didn't these people know anything about drilling oil wells?* "We were going to start drilling again."

Jesse slid to a half-turn stop at the bottom of the trail. Gravel and dirt flew across the rocky path as Jake arrived in the cloud of dust Jesse had kicked up. Jesse's shouts of joy echoed off the canyon walls as he laid his bike down and rolled onto his back. He raised his fist into the air in jubilation.

"Man! That was so great! That felt *so* good!"

"You crazy butt! You're lucky you didn't break your damned neck," Jake yelled at him. "You weren't supposed to do that! We were just going to see if you could hold the bike up. Then you take off like a bat out of hell! You are lucky you aren't dead!"

"We aren't dead – we're alive! I'm alive!" Jesse shouted to the deep blue Texas sky.

Jake leaned his bike against a rock and gave Jesse a hand to help him to his feet. "Come on, let's get you back in the truck before you do something else squirrely! Hopefully, Rita won't find out about this – you fool!"

"You'd have done the same," Jesse retorted.

Jesse used his bike as a rolling crutch as they moved off down the trail to where Jake had parked the truck. Jesse got into the passenger seat as Jake loaded the bikes into the bed before they roared off down the dirt road toward the highway.

"You got all your stuff ready to go? " Jesse asked.

"Yeah, I wonder how long it's going to take. Time is running out – we need to be back here in about four weeks."

"As soon as Hootie's ready, I guess."

"I still don't see why we need to wait for that cowboy jerk!"

Jesse sighed deeply, "Oh, no! Not that again. Give it a rest won't you? Katie wants him there, and that is all there is to it."

"Yeah, that's what I'm worried about," Jake blurted, despite himself.

"OH...M...GEE!" Jesse shouted. "You are jealous! You are afraid he is going to steal Katie!" Jesse was laughing and bouncing up and down on his seat. "This is so rich!"

"No, I'm not!"

"Oh, yes you are! Damn. You have nothing to worry about, man – he's old! He's probably as old as Professor Morrison!"

Happy to be out of the hot seat, Hootie returned to his place in the hearing room. During the short recess, Mr. Howlett came over, shook his hand, and told him he did a good job. Hootie didn't feel that way. He had played with the truth, toed the edge of integrity, and almost crossed the line. Maybe next time he would not be so lucky.

When the session came back to order, the Chair called Miss Darla Dunn. She entered through the door on tapping heels as she walked to the center of the room. Darla was not only strikingly beautiful; she was cool, calm, and completely aware that she had the rapt attention of every man in the room – and most of the women, too. Her dark hair curled around her dimpled face, and long shiny earrings hung nearly to her shoulders. She wore about 15 bracelets that jingled and rang out every time she moved her hand. She had hot red lips and green eyes that stared out from beneath curly bangs as she flashed a smile. Every man in the room hoped she was smiling at him. Even if a celebrity were standing next to her, Hootie knew every eye would be on Darla Dunn.

When she sat in the chair, it did not even squeak.

CHAPTER 9

Sara had set her wedding for the end of August, and an overwhelming number of things loomed large in Representative Sara Hughes mind. Should she use her current name, or would she become Representative Sara Bryan, wife of Dr. Colton Bryan? In addition to all of the wedding arrangements to make, she had to change all of her identity documents including her social security card, driver's license, IRS forms, and even her passport.

On top of that, she had to keep up with her job at the capitol. Luckily, the Texas legislature was not in session. Hundreds of friends and supporters would expect an invitation. She would need a huge place – thankfully her close friend, Ida Walsh, owned a wedding planning service. She knew Ida would handle everything correctly; but still, there were a thousand decisions that only Sara could make. Colors and coordinating, invitations, food selection, bridesmaids, and the list continued to grow. She would have to pick out a dress and decide on a hairstyle. She was going to need every minute of the next two months. *Men had it so lucky* she thought -- *all they had to do was show up.*

Cody, Sara's son, agreed to serve as best man. Colton was also happy for Cody to be the best man in the ceremony. He and Colton had developed a great relationship since Cody's recovery, and the close bond was evident. Sara had not realized how Cody must have missed having a father in his life after Frank died. Cody believed Dr. Bryan saved his life after the cave accident. Sara was so grateful his friends Jesse and Jake brought him into the hospital as soon as they did. It was a miracle there was no brain damage. Cody had been in the coma for three weeks. Cody's head still showed a small indention, if you knew where to look; but all the injuries had healed. His mental capabilities had not suffered, and he graduated on time with his class, despite being absent for nearly a month.

Cody not only graduated, but he also graduated at the head of his class with a Bachelor's Degree in Criminal Justice. Sara was not surprised when Cody announced he was going to take the bar exam right away as he had practically grown up in a law office. Additionally, he had spent almost all of his summer vacations clerking for his father's old partner who had offices in Wyoming and Texas. Wyoming did not require a law degree to become an attorney. Cody intended to pass the Wyoming bar and get that out of the way first before getting the law degree. It never seemed to bother him that Wyoming had one of the toughest bar exams in the nation. Barely half passed the exam even after law school. That did not deter Cody. He was just like his father – always in a big hurry.

A week ago, Cody flew to Cheyenne and took the Wyoming bar exam. Now they were waiting for the results, but Cody had no worries. When asked how he thought he did, he just snapped his fingers, "Aced it, Mom!" And, that was that. Sara could only marvel at her son. Right after the bar exam, he went down to Colorado to climb some mountain out there.

When Sara took the bar, she had fretted for three months until she got word she passed her bar – after the third try! She laughed as she proudly thought of her son – he will probably be governor one day.

Cody did have an excellent memory. He could read something and recall it years later. He could recite every name on his class roster from the first grade on. Once he saw something, he rarely forgot it. You quickly learned to watch your words with Cody, because they could come back to haunt you. He could already argue like a lawyer. He got in trouble with most of his teachers who could not recall what they said the first time around – Cody did, and he did not mind reminding them. His memory was not perfect, and some things he could not recall at all, but he could remember better than most people could. He passed almost every test he ever took. The injury in the cave did not seem to lessen his abilities.

What was unusual was that he could not remember anything leading up to the accident or anything that happened for the three weeks he was in the hospital. He never remembered going into the cave or falling and hitting his head. It was as if that part of his memory disappeared.

Therefore, when Cody reported, "Aced it, Mom," Sara was confident he had passed the bar exam. She anguished over this because it probably meant he would have to move to Wyoming to work and go to graduate school. He was already making plans to move to Laramie in the fall.

"Hi folks, this is KRTX talk-radio in Kerrville, Texas! I'm your host Bobby Deal, and this is Talkin' Texan! Welcome to the show. Our guest today is Professor Tom Morrison, of Southwest Texas State Univer… oops – I guess that is Texas State University now, isn't it, Tom?"

"Yes, sir, Texas State University. The name changed in 2003, Bob."

"You know, I knew that. I graduated Southwest in 1989, and when they changed the name, would you believe they sent me a completely new diploma with Texas State on it. So I have two masters' degrees!"

"I don't think it works that way, Bob."

"Ahhhh! What do *you* know, Tom?" Bob laughed. "Go dig up another dinosaur!" Bob bantered.

"Anyway, folks, Tom Morrison is that professor who identified the super crocodile that crawled out of the earthquake last April down by San Antonio – the one they call Aquasaurus. Is that right, Tom?"

"That's right, Bob."

"I see from your notes that it's a Carolinensis somethin' or 'another. What's a Carolina crocodile doing living in the aquifer?"

"We know that crocodiles somehow escaped the extinction event that killed off most of the other dinosaurs, Bob. We believe they did that mainly by hiding in subterranean formations – caves. As you probably know, Texas was once part of a vast inland sea. It was a tropical, shallow sea that served as habitat for a wide variety of animals. It is a good environment; one that crocodiles favor. When the Rockies formed, the uplift pushed all that water into the Gulf of Mexico. Then the mud turned into limestone. It was that karst limestone layer that formed all of the caves around this part of Texas – it's why we have so many of them – and why we have so many dinosaur tracks spread around the state."

"So, you are saying this prehistoric beast crawled into one of the caves and stayed there for thousands of years?"

"Pretty much, Bob. Of course, the croc changed over the years and adapted to its environment. It ate what it could find, and learned to live in the dark, wet, closed-in environment that describes large portions of the aquifer."

"Why didn't we know about it before now, Tom?"

"No one knows for sure what all is down in the aquifer, Bob. It is a vast underground lake, with high spots and low spots. It is a reservoir so large that if it were on the surface, it would have tides like the Great Lakes. I don't know why no one ever discovered Aquasaurus before. Perhaps it was trapped down there in a remote, unexplored section. It came out during the earthquake, as you said, in an isolated portion of the aquifer west of San Antonio. This particular section yielded briny water, so historically no one pumped water there very much."

"I understand you were trapped in the cave with the monster, Tom."

"Oh, yes! I got acquainted with it up close and personal. Some students of mine from the university and I were exploring the cave during spring break. Earlier they found a piece of skin and brought it to me to identify. When I figured out what it was, we went back into the cave to try to find it."

"What was that like being in the cave with that thing, Tom?"

"It was horrifying, Bob. Imagine being in a dark, wet cave knowing that something like that might be lurking around the next corner. The earthquake trapped us inside the cavern. We couldn't get out because a cave-in blocked the passageway. Suddenly, this thing just lunged out of a deep pool of water and attacked a couple of students. After we fought the thing off, we managed to work our way out. However, some other students were not quite so lucky. We found eight young spelunkers dead inside that cave – killed by the crocodile. We were fortunate to get out alive, Bob."

That is just horrible, Tom. Our sympathies go out to the families of those young explorers."

"It is a tragedy, Bob. The lives of those cavers are sometimes forgotten in the greater disaster that claimed the lives of hundreds in San Antonio. We mourn for all of them."

"So now, a prehistoric crocodile, Aquasaurus, is loose somewhere in the Gulf of Mexico. It is killing people down there. We got a news report just this morning that it ate a horse, and almost snatched a young girl from the beach. Did you ever figure out what kind of crocodile it was, Tom?"

"I did, Bob. It was *Carnufex carolinensis.*"

"Hey! That's Greek to me, Tom. What is that?"

It was time for the money shot. Tom lowered his voice as he always did and leaned into the microphone.

"Carnufex – **The Butcher!**"

After swearing Darla in, the Chairman began his line of questioning.

"Miss Dunn, please tell us your position with HNH Oil Company."

"I am an executive assistant, primarily in support of Mr. Clint Marshall. Mr. Marshall was a corporate executive and project manager for HNH until his death in April."

"Did Mr. Marshall discuss operations with you?"

"No sir, not normally – except as it applied to administrative things – things like getting permits, ordering supplies, filing legal papers, and making arrangements for a great variety of other activities."

"If Mr. Marshall ordered something for the company, then you would know about it, is that right?"

"I would," she admitted. "Someone had to pay the bill."

"And that would be you?" the Chair inquired.

"That would be me."

"Miss Dunn, did you get a requisition to order thermite or white phosphorus, or an invoice to pay for such an order?"

"No, I did not, sir."

"Is it possible that Mr. Marshall would have purchased those items on his own?"

"Yes, sir, that is possible. However, he usually sent in a receipt so we could log it in for reimbursement and tax records. He did not file any receipt for any purchase of anything like that."

"Do you also handle travel arrangements for Mr. Marshall?"

"When he needed that, I did. He was a licensed pilot and owned an airplane; so usually, he just flew himself wherever he needed to go – except out of the country. He would take commercial flights anytime he needed to leave the U.S."

"When was the last travel arrangement you handled for Mr. Marshall?"

"Late last year – to South America – Venezuela, I think."

"I see. Miss Dunn, did you have any discussions with Mr. Marshall on the progress of the Dilley Chalk projects?"

"Of course – almost every day. He would send in data from the well, and I would enter it into the system and compile reports. There wasn't a lot of that since much of the data collection was automated, but there was some. Plus, I would send data and information back to him as feedback."

"But, what about his strategies or plans or his intentions on the operations of the well – did he ever share any of *that* with you?"

"No, not unless it was something he wanted to be put in the records or presented to the Board. I worked with Clint long enough to know he was driven to succeed, and he hated it when he had to shut down a well. He really cared for all of those people he had to lay off. However, he never talked about those kinds of things to me – I handled the administrative and financial aspects of the project. Which is why I know Mr. Marshall did not cause the earthquake and fire that destroyed Dilley Chalk #1."

"What did you say, Miss Dunn?"

The room immediately became silent as they listened for what Darla would say next. Did Darla Dunn know something that no one else in the room knew?

"I said that I know for certain Mr. Marshall did not do anything to cause the earthquake or the fire."

"How could you possibly know that, Miss Dunn?"

Darla smiled and pulled a sheet of paper from her purse.

"Mr. Chairman, is it true that the earthquake that damaged San Antonio and much of south Texas occurred at about 3:20 p.m.?"

The Chairman leafed through his notes and responded, "Yes, Miss Dunn. The geological service puts the time of the earthquake at precisely 3:17 p.m."

"Then, Mr. Marshall could not possibly have caused that earthquake, and it is even more likely the earthquake caused the blowback that killed Mr. Marshall."

"Why do you think that, Miss Dunn?"

"I don't *think* it; I *know* it."

"*Why?*" The Chairman was losing his patience with her.

63

Everyone in the room was on the edge of their seats as Darla waved the paper at the panel.

"Because, Chase Bank says that at 3:05 that afternoon, Mr. Clint Marshall had a hamburger and fries at the Dairy Queen in Cotulla, Texas!"

CHAPTER 10

Chaos erupted in the hearing room. Darla Dunn passed the credit card statement forward to the Chair who read it and shared it down the row of officials on the panel. He called a short recess while he and the board went into a conference room to deliberate. Clint's supporters mobbed Darla with embraces and pecks on the cheek. T.J. was all smiles now.

After a few minutes, the Chairman returned and called the room back to order.

"Thank you, Miss Dunn. We will check the charges on the credit card statement. It is possible that the credit card company's clock was off and may not reflect the correct time. It is possible the meal may have been ordered earlier."

Darla pulled another sheet of paper from her purse and handed it up to the Chairman.

"If the clock at Chase Bank was off, then so was AT&T's! He also made a cell phone call while he was waiting for that burger." Darla smiled sweetly at the Chairman. Laughter and chaos erupted again as the Chair called another recess. The board adjourned back into the conference room with Clint's cell phone bill.

They returned shortly as the Chairman adjourned the hearing for verification of Clint's credit card and cell phone bills. He announced they would dismiss the investigation if the time on the documents were correct; if not, he would reconvene the hearing. Almost everyone believed the case was over. Sure, credit card machines were off sometimes, but Chase would have a record of the exact time Clint swiped his card. For both invoices to have the same time discrepancy would be an impossible coincidence.

As the crowd filed out of the room, Hootie found T.J. waiting in the hallway. He stuck out his hand for Hootie to shake.

"You did great, Hootie. I wanted to thank you for the way you handled that."

Hootie put his Stetson back on his head and shrugged as he tugged it down in front.

"I told the truth."

"I appreciate your loyalty to Clint and HNH – and to Rio Frio too. We haven't had much time to talk, Hootie, but I want you to know that your job with HNH Oil is still there for you – if you want it. Rio Frio is probably dead in the water for now. Anyway, what I wanted to say is since Rio Frio won't be drilling for a long time – if ever – we'll take you back at HNH. Hugh Shipman said he'd hire you up in Oklahoma right away if you want to go up there."

Hootie knew this would have been an entirely different conversation if things had come out different. He had no hard feelings about it, business was business, and he knew T.J. had been under a lot of pressure. He appreciated the offer.

"Thanks, T.J., I'll keep that in mind. I'm working for Clint's daughter right now, but I don't know how long that will last."

"Doin' what?"

"Just stuff, she's kind of overwhelmed with all of it right now. Clint had a lot of stuff; airplanes, boats, houses – things like that. Katie asked me to help her sort it all out until she figures out what she wants to do with it."

T.J. reached out, gripped Hootie's arm warmly, and smiled, "You'll always have a job with me somewhere, Hootie. You just call if you change your mind."

Hootie promised he would and walked out into the warm Texas sunshine.

"Professor Tom Morrison is calling," Tom said into his office telephone impatiently. He walked around his office as far as the phone cord would reach. He parted the blinds and looked out on the San Marcos

River that snaked through the Texas State University campus. After fourteen media interviews in the past couple of months, Tom had become a minor celebrity. Everyone wanted to talk to the man who had discovered Aquasaurus – a living example of a prehistoric crocodile. Talk was easy; what Tom wanted was coverage. He wanted *this* coverage – Discovery Magazine.

All of the other major magazines decided to wait for the DNA results to come in before they went national on the story, even though it would take another month at least to get the DNA results. The broadcast media, including all the major networks, did not have the same concerns, but print left a lasting impression. None of the majors wanted to be wrong.

Tom heard a click in his ear as Ryan Cash, the features editor for Discovery Magazine, came on the line.

"Tom! I intended to call you. We just got out of an editorial meeting with staff; they love your story! We're planning an all-aquatic issue in October – giant crocodile will fit right in – it'll be great!"

"Great, Ryan. I'm happy to hear it," Tom sighed with relief. *Take that, National Geographic!*

"We're anxious to get those pictures you mentioned, Tom. Can you send them on up to us?"

"Pictures," Tom repeated.

"Yes, pictures. You have them don't you?"

"Yes, Ryan. I have pictures, but as I mentioned to one of your editors, they are very poor quality. It is dark in a cave, you know – and the thing was never in full sight. All I've got is grainy portions of its body."

"Oh," there was a long pause. "We thought you had pictures."

"Well, I do, but they won't work well for publication – just red dots for the eyes reflected in the water, mostly. Can't we do artist renderings?"

"Tom, we're a visual medium – our readers want pictures. "We'll have to go back to the drawing board on this, then. Without pictures of the croc – that takes a lot away from the story..." There was a long foreboding pause.

"What if I can get pictures?" Tom interjected. "The croc is still out there, Ryan. Someone probably has pictures of it. It's been coming ashore down in Mexico – we can buy the photo rights."

There was another long pause on the other end of the line as Tom realized Ryan had covered the speaker with his hand as he talked with someone.

"Okay, Tom, you get us some photos, and you're on the schedule. Your deadline is two months. If you can't come up with pictures by the first of September, we'll have to run another story. I'll hold your slot until then. I want three shots – clear and close-up. Make them really scary."

"You'll have them, Ryan."

Tom hung up the phone and wondered where in the world he was going to come up with pictures of a monster crocodile. If he had to, he would track that damn thing down and take them himself.

Hootie paused on the top of the steps outside as he called Katie to tell her the hearing was over.

"Great! We can leave on our trip right away!" she exclaimed.

Hootie had halfway hoped she had changed her mind about tracking down the crocodile – but she seemed more eager than ever. She did not ask too many questions about the hearing because she had not fully realized how a different result would threaten her father's reputation. Now that the danger had passed, there was no reason to worry her about it. Hootie envied the bliss of her not knowing.

"You still want to do that, huh?"

"Yes! I'm calling everyone together tonight. Can we leave in the morning? Meet us at the Ice House at Judson Road in San Antonio tonight at eight. I'll have everyone there. You'll need to tell everyone what to do."

Hootie agreed to meet them. They would fly to Galveston the next day to meet the boat. Katie was excited.

He turned off his cell phone and snapped it back in his holster.

"Hey, cowboy," a voice came from behind.

He turned to face Darla Dunn. She gave him a warm hug.

"What are you up to?" she asked.

"Nothin'. I'm just glad this thing is over. Man! You turned this whole hearing around. You were great in there!"

"You didn't do so bad yourself," Darla smiled.

"Yeah, but you set 'em back on their hindquarters – a hamburger," he laughed. "Who'd have thought it?"

"Speaking of hamburgers – why don't you take me out for something more substantial?" Darla's eyes twinkled.

"How substantial do you want?" Hootie joked.

"More than a hamburger," Darla teased, giving Hootie that look and linking her arm to his.

"I can do lunch, but I have to be somewhere tonight. I have to go to work. There is a meeting tonight at eight in San Antonio, and I promised I'd be there."

"Rats! Just my luck," Darla whined.

"Darla, would you do me a favor?"

"Sure, what do you need, Hootie?"

"Can you have a rental van and driver at the HNH hanger at Hobby in the morning about nine? They'll need to take us to the dock at Galveston Marina."

"Going on a cruise?"

"Yeah, I'll be gone a month or so. It would help if you could do that for me."

"No problem, it's just a couple of phone calls. T.J. told me to take care of anything you wanted. You're coming to work for us, I hear. Say! You aren't taking some woman on a cruise are you?" Darla's eyes flashed again.

"Yes, as a matter of fact, I am."

Darla jerked her arm back. Her eyes flashed instead of twinkled. "In that case, cowboy, make your own phone calls!"

"It's Katie," Hootie explained, "Clint's daughter and three of her friends."

Darla placed her arm back in his, "Oh, in that case, no problem. Where are you taking me to lunch?"

"Anywhere you want to go," Hootie promised.

"Ah! I see, okay. Well, do we have time for a hamburger?"

"Or, something more substantial," Hootie laughed.

Across town, Katie wasted no time. She rounded up her friends, and they met that evening at the Ice House in northeast San Antonio. The group sat sipping a beer at a wooden table beneath the tin canopy and went over the details of the trip.

"We meet at Stinson Airport tomorrow morning at eight," she announced, "and don't be late," she eyed Jake and Jesse. "Do not screw this up! We'll leave without you if we have to," she threatened.

"Chill! We'll be there. Where are we supposed to be?" Jake asked laughing.

"Stinson Airport," Katie reminded Jake, handing out maps to the others. "You can park here, where Hootie marked on the map. Walk toward hangar C; you'll see the airplane there on the side, next to the building. Have everything you want to take with you – we won't be back for a few weeks."

Hootie took over the instructions. "The number on the tail is N980. Write it down on your maps. It's red and white, and, as Katie said, will probably be the only one next to hangar C. Remember, we're going on a "fishing charter" – if anyone asks. All the fishing gear we need will be on the boat. Be careful of the weight – the less you bring, the better."

Hootie paused for questions, but not hearing any continued with the instructions.

"We'll be flying into Galveston to board Miss Katie. Flight time will be about ninety minutes. If we leave on time om the morning, we can sail by noon."

"Board Miss Katie?" Jake asked with a big smile.

"My daddy loved me," Katie mugged making duck lips at him.

"We'll take a little sail down the Texas coast into Mexico. Make sure you have your passports with you. We have completed all the paperwork to sail in Mexican waters. As far as anyone knows, we are a fishing charter, with our own villa and dock at La Pesca. Our first destination will be below Laguna Madre at Rio del Bravo State Park."

"Mexico has a Laguna Madre?" Jesse asked.

"Mexico has state parks?" Jake laughed. "Why are we going there?"

"That is the location of the last sighting of Aquasaurus – just a few days ago. Chances are it's still around there somewhere. We'll search the estuary and low lying areas of the lagoon to see if we can spot it."

"The boat will go into shallow water?" Jake asked.

"No, we need about seven feet, but we have a motorized skiff on board, and a couple of jet skis to get close in."

Hootie saw Jake nudge Jesse and decided to add to the instructions in as nice a tone as possible.

"Listen, guys. These jet skis will be used for close surveillance and searching the shoreline. If you guys have ideas about racing around the bay kicking up rooster tails, forget it. We are trying to *find* the crocodile, not scare it down to Guatemala!"

Jake twisted open another longneck and gave Jesse a knowing eye. Hootie knew too well what that look meant – these two were going to need close supervision.

"What we are trying to do here," Hootie continued, "is to locate the crocodile. It is going to require close cooperation and staying with the plan. This is a dangerous animal. If you haven't been following the news, the croc has already upended two or three shrimpers and killed the entire crew. Those shrimp boats are about the size of our boat. That means every one of us needs to keep our eyes open and pay attention – no goofing off!" Hootie reasoned.

For some reason, Jake took offense and challenged Hootie right away. "Why the hell are you looking at me? I know what we need to do. Besides, who died and left you in charge?"

"My dad did, Jake!" Katie whispered sadly. "That's who died."

"Katie." Jake was immediately sorry he had mouthed off. His eyes softened as he apologized. "I'm sorry." Jake pleaded, "I didn't mean for it to come out like that."

"Let's get this straight right now," Katie stood and faced the group. "This trip is *my* idea. Hootie had nothing to do with it – I'm pretty sure he would advise against it – this is my deal. Understand?"

Everyone nodded as she continued. "This croc almost killed us. It tried to drown Rita and broke Jesse's leg."

"… and broke your arm," Rita added.

"Yes! Since then it has killed no fewer than eight people. I want to track it down and try to stop it. If we can't kill it, we can at least try to stop it. Since neither of you has a license to fly a plane or drive a boat, then Hootie is in charge. Every boat needs a captain – that's Hootie. I'm glad you are all coming with us on this trip. We are going to make this as fun as possible, but you have to be willing to do your part. You are my friends, and I love you, but if you can't get serious about this, then you need to stay home – no hard feelings. Understand?"

"Well, I'm going," decided Rita, looking at Jesse.

"Me, too," Jesse added immediately.

Jake looked at the group as he considered his options. He realized he'd have to get along or Katie would sail through Mexico with Hootie.

"All right, I'm in. I was just kiddin' around. You guys take everything so literal."

"Okay. Thank you," Katie replied as she sat back down and looked at Hootie.

Hootie looked at the group and continued. "Fine, we all agree. Probably all that's going to happen is we're going to float around Mexico for a few weeks doing a lot of fishing and swimming. We'll report the location of the crocodile if we find it and let the government take care of it."

Jake raised his hand. Hootie acknowledged him with a skeptical nod.

"You don't have to raise your hand, Jake – what do you want?"

"So, what happens if the giant crocodile – this Aquasaurus attacks us? What are we going to do then?"

Hootie thought for a long moment before he answered.

"I know how to kill it."

CHAPTER 11

When the meeting ended, Rita and Jesse left to make final preparations for their trip. Jake reached over for Katie's hand. His forefinger traced over the friendship ring of entwined hearts he had given her a year earlier.

"I've got to go to my place in Austin and pick up a few things for tomorrow. Do ya' want to go with me? I'll bring you back in the morning," Jake suggested. He glanced at Hootie, sure that the implication was clear: she would be spending the night with Jake.

With her free hand, Katie drained her bottle and placed it on the table, making sure to center it in the middle of the wet circle where it sat before.

"Jake, I've got some things to do myself – and I can't just leave my car here in the parking lot. You go on, and we'll see you in the morning."

Jake did not miss 'we'll' in her reply. He did not like the sound of that at all. He pulled his hand away from hers and gripped the edge of the table as he pushed back.

"We could take your car to your apartment before we go," Jake reasoned.

"No. Not tonight – I've got too much to do. Really. Go do what you've got to do, and I'll see you at eight o'clock – okay?"

Jake reluctantly agreed. Katie walked him to his car, and after saying goodbye, Jake roared off toward Austin. She realized that Jake made sure Hootie saw the kiss. After he was gone, she returned to the table. Hootie confided in Katie.

"I'm not sure taking Jake is a good idea – he's got some kind of beef with me – it probably has somethin' to do with you. I'm tryin' to be even-handed, but he's a loose cannon as far as I'm concerned."

"There's no way I can tell him he can't go," Katie chewed her lip.

"Are you two – you know – a *thing?*"

"We've dated, and we've been friends for a very long time. Jake is a good guy – he really is. We've been seeing each other for three years. I haven't seen anyone else, and I don't think he has either. Still, he feels more possessive than I do. I guess he thinks we are – *a thing*," Katie laughed repeating Hootie's word.

"I'm tryin' to walk on eggshells here, Katie. The last thing we need is Jake goin' nuts on us."

"He won't" Katie assured him. "Jake has his own mind, but he knows how to buckle down when he has to. He'll be okay."

Hootie nodded as he picked up his hat and pulled his truck keys out of his back pocket.

"Well," he commented as if it were a statement. "I've got some stuff to do *too* before we leave tomorrow. I'll see you at the plane in the morning," he said as he stood up.

"Where are you going?" Katie asked.

"I've got to go down south to run an errand. I have to do it tonight; it can't wait."

"To Cotulla?" Katie guessed.

"Yep."

"I want to go," Katie decided.

"You said you had some stuff to do – we wouldn't be back 'till after midnight," Hootie explained.

"I want to go if that's okay. You promised you'd show me where Dad died. I want to see it."

"It'll be dark. There's not much light out there. Besides, you said you had stuff to do."

"I've been packed for a week," Katie admitted. "Come on, let's go!" Katie urged. "Unless you have something personal to do," Katie winked at him.

"No, it's nothing like that," Hootie stalled. This could be a bad idea. "You can come," Hootie decided. "But don't say I didn't warn you."

After dropping her car off at her apartment, Katie climbed into his truck. Hootie looked for Jake's car parked nearby in the dark. He decided Jake was not spying on her. When Katie got in, Hootie turned his truck south, and after leaving the lights of San Antonio, Katie realized just how quickly it was growing dark. As they sped down the black tar pavement toward Cotulla, the cicadas sang so loudly they almost drowned out the engine noise. No one was following.

Katie looked out at the passing scrub brush. She knew most of them by name: stunted junipers, thorny bushes, agave, agarita, and fiddlewood. In this part of the country, almost every plant had thorns. The taller plants were black silhouettes against a vast yellow sky as the sun dipped slowly out of sight. It was her favorite time of day – between sunset and night – when strange shadows moved on the bare landscape, making strange fleeting shapes. It was far too beautiful for the word 'dusk' to do it justice. As the truck sped down the highway, Katie looked out on the area of Texas her father called "The Big Nothing."

By the time they got to Cotulla, it was full dark, and the crescent moon hung low in the sky like a thin scimitar. Hootie slowed the truck and maneuvered it around so the lights could shine on the twisted hulk of the burned-out oil well.

"Is this it?" Katie asked.

"Yeah," Hootie nodded. "Do you want to get out? I still have a key to the gate."

Katie nodded. Her stomach felt nervous. She felt like she was visiting her father's gravesite. In a way, it was. They never found Clint's body, so there was nothing to bury. Hootie unlocked the gate and pulled it open. They drove into the site and parked near a tower of twisted, melted metal that used to be the pump house. It was a blackened mess. Katie got out of the truck and placed her hand on the wreckage of the rig. It seemed warm to the touch instead of cold like she imagined. She looked up at the remains of the derrick. It slumped over like a play-dough figure left in the sun all day. The extreme heat of the fire had twisted and charred everything within 100 feet of the wreck.

"Where did they find his truck?"

Hootie pointed, "Over there. It was in pretty bad shape. And, no – in case you are wondering – he didn't die in his truck. I think he was up there on the rig," Hootie pointed.

Katie had seen enough. With one last look, she walked back to the truck and climbed in. It did not make Katie feel any closer to Clint as she hoped it might. She did not feel sadder either. She realized she did not feel anything – just emptiness where her father used to be. Katie did not know if there were spirits or things like that, but if there were, the sense of her father was not in this place.

Hootie backed his truck out and locked the gate behind them. They rode in silence back to the crossroads in Cotulla where Katie pointed out the Dairy Queen.

"Let's stop and get a hamburger," she suggested on impulse.

Hootie did not have the heart to tell her it was the same place her father had eaten his last meal.

Tom Morrison sat in the stiff wooden chairs in the conference room during the monthly meeting of the Natural Sciences Department as Professor Sheela Catalino went carefully through the agenda. Item by item, the meeting marched toward the point where Tom would rise to make his appeal to the staff.

He was still trying to fine-tune his pitch. How would he present the case? They had heard all of the stories – all of the excuses professors used to wring money out of the research fund. Sure, most of the requests

77

were legitimate – the professors were diligent about collecting data and reporting their findings. But, mostly, they were just a big fat excuse to fund a boondoggle. Most of the professors at the table were guilty of that from time to time, including himself. He had to convince them that this was legitimate –an actual prehistoric crocodile was running loose out there. Aquasaurus was his find. Tom deserved the chance to go collect data on it, and he did not want any company.

Tom still did not have a hook: those magic words that would capture the imagination of these guardians of the funds. Do that, and money would rain down on him in buckets. There had to be something, but he had no clue what it might be. He nervously tapped his fingers on the table so loudly that Wanda Higgins poked him in the ribs.

"Stop fidgeting," she whispered, as the agenda reached new business and new funding requests.

Finally, Sheela asked if anyone had any new business.

"I do," Tom raised his hand.

"Not so fast," Wanda objected. "I already filed. Wait your turn," she admonished. Tom lowered his hand and listened to Wanda's lame excuse for funding for a study of some blind salamander somewhere.

When she finished and got her money, the Chairwoman nodded at Tom. Before he could begin speaking, the Chairwoman addressed the table, "All of you know Professor Tom Morrison. Congratulations, Tom, on your recent discovery. What was it? A huge crocodile, was it not?"

"Indeed, it was, Professor Catalino. Thank you for asking." Tom breathed easier, grateful for additional time to search for a path to the pot of gold at the end of the financial rainbow.

"Please bring us up to speed. Have there been any results from the DNA testing yet?"

"Unfortunately not, I'm afraid. It will probably be another month before we hear back from the laboratory."

Tom launched into his radio interview script, telling of the students who found the mysterious hide in the cave. He divulged how he convinced them to take him back into the cavern and how they became trapped in the cold and dark cavity during the earthquake. He recited the story of the horrific encounter with the massive crocodile. He described in finite detail how the crocodile attacked and killed eight cavers and injured two of his exploration party. He told how the crocodile escaped in the raging flood after the Medina Dam collapsed. He spoke in such practiced, descriptive words that several board members shivered as they imagined the gigantic crocodile in a dark hole with them.

All the while, his mind kept trying to seize upon some angle he could use to fund his expedition to Mexico. He was nearing the end of his story, but he was still at a loss as to how to seal the deal. He was encouraged by their interest in the story. Maybe this would not be so hard after all.

Finally, he wrapped up by telling them the crocodile was still at large and was attacking unsuspecting people along the beaches of Mexico. *Yes, that was a good line.* He related the recent attack of a little girl on the beach. He described how the monster ate her pony right in front of her, and how her terrified mother could only watch at a distance, lucky to have saved her child. *Yes, they were feeling it.* He added how the beast dragged three students into the surf on South Padre Island during spring break.

"Are we sure there are no others?" Dr. Cantalino asked.

The spark went off in Tom's mind. Here was the irresistible hook he needed to get the money.

"We think so, Dr. Cantalino. Even if it *is* the sole specimen, you can imagine what might occur if it reaches a breeding population in South America."

Dr. Cantalino shivered. "It would be devastating," she admitted. "What exactly *was* the crocodile, Professor Morrison?"

"I'm afraid we won't know for sure until we get the DNA results back." He admitted truthfully, as he paused for dramatic effect before he fired his final shot.

"What do you think it was, Tom?" asked Wanda Higgins before he could pull the trigger. Tom could have kissed her!

"I think it was *Carnufex*," he responded casually, knowing they would ask.

"*Carnufex*?" Wanda repeated, playing right into his hand.

Tom leaned in closer, making eye contact with each of the professors sitting around the table, and lowered his voice as he responded with the line that worked so well in radio interviews.

"*Carnufex*," he paused for effect. "*Carnufex* – the Butcher!"

Tom could smell pay dirt. As he elaborated on his description of Aquasaurus as *Carnufax*, the committee's excitement grew. Tom decided to give them the full treatment.

"This crocodile is a descendent of *Carnufex Carolinensus*," he spoke as though the results were already in, ignoring the fact that he could not prove anything he was saying. He turned on the entire scientific litany.

"It was from the late Triassic period of North America. Paleontologists found the first remains in 2015; it was a young specimen, but it stretched over nine feet long. If it was related to *Sarcosuchus*, and most authorities believe it was, it could have reached thirty feet easily. The one I saw in the cave, I estimate to be about thirty feet long and over three tons."

Several people around the table shook their heads in disbelief.

"I was close enough to touch it – I did touch it! I can assure you this crocodile is the most fearsome thing I have ever seen. I wrestled alligators in Florida for years, but none of them were anywhere near the size of this monster. You have all seen the news reports of Aquasaurus attacking fishing boats and sunbathers on the beach recently. It is migrating south and has entered Mexican waters. Somehow, we must stop the introduction of this crocodile into southern waters."

"Why do you call it Aquasaurus, Professor Morrison?" asked one of the professors.

"I didn't. Because we do not have the true scientific name yet, some newspaper reporter gave it that name, and it stuck. Hardly a day goes by without some report of a new attack on some unsuspecting victim."

"What do you propose to do, Tom?" asked Chairwoman Catalino.

Tom looked at the others as though it was the most obvious thing in the world.

"Well, we must capture it, Professor Catalino. We must stop it and study it so that we can understand it better."

He spread his hands outward to take in the entire gathering at the conference table.

"We must not miss this opportunity to study an actual dinosaur – a living, breathing dinosaur. We may never get another chance."

"What do you propose to do?" Professor Higgins asked.

"We have to find it, of course. Find it, contain it, and study it. We have to do this soon before some gun-happy cowboy, or the Mexican Navy blows it away! Do you realize what will happen if this crocodile were to mate with the current species of crocodile found in Mexican waters? Aquasaurus is an apex predator! The environmental impact will be tremendous. Not to mention, the current population of already aggressive crocodiles, endowed with that DNA, would create the most violent and deadly crocodile that ever existed," Tom thundered, "Carnufex, the Butcher!"

The clouds opened, and the green rain of money fell in buckets.

Hootie turned his truck north toward San Antonio. They rode silently for miles until Hootie turned off to the east in Dilley, Texas.

"Where are we going?" she asked.

"I told you, I have an errand to run – remember? It won't take long – you won't even have to get out of the truck. It's not far from here; and then, we'll be on our way. Why don't you take a nap?" he suggested.

Katie laid her head against the glass in the truck door. The road was so rough her head bounced off the glass with each bump. Hootie reached behind the seat and pulled out his blue jean jacket for her to use as a pillow. That was better.

After a few minutes, Hootie pulled off the highway at a gated fence. He pointed through the windshield to a well in the distance.

"This here is Dilley Chalk #2. I can't take you in there; the State has it locked because of the investigation. I wanted you to see it because you own part of it. You have valuable equipment and supplies locked up in there. It's worth a lot of money. You can sell it once the state's locks come off the gate. That should be pretty soon."

"Does it have oil in it?" Katie asked.

Hootie laughed, "I wish! No, unfortunately, you don't have any producing wells right now, Miss Marshall. I'm afraid all you have is Rio Frio and two dry holes," he smiled. "Not to mention one old out-of-luck roughneck named Hootie," he joked, as he pulled back onto the road.

"I'll take that," she grinned as she watched the lights of the derrick disappear behind them.

"Where are we going now? To your place?"

"Nope. We're going to the Pump House Tavern – or at least what's left of it," Hootie disclosed, as he pulled into a gravel parking lot.

The building looked as though a tornado had hit it. The sign on the pole out front still read 'Pump House,' but it was leaning so far to the left Katie thought a strong wind might bring it down. There were no lights on, but Katie could see the building was abandoned and unusable for any purpose. The windows were all blown out, and the roof sagged along the back corner. The door stood wide open, and when Hootie's headlights swung past, Katie could see overturned tables and rubbish strewn about the room.

"What happened to this place?" Katie wondered.

"Earthquake," was all Hootie said, as he wheeled his truck around to the back of the destroyed building. Finally, he told her, "This is where my truck tried to kill me."

Hootie aimed his truck toward a gaping hole that was the back door. He left the motor running as he got out and rummaged around in his toolbox. Katie could see a slanted wooden platform sitting on four posts that led to an old screened-in back porch. The entire left side had collapsed along with the roof, but everything else was intact. She got out of the truck and walked back to where Hootie was still digging through the toolbox.

"How can a truck try to kill you," Katie asked.

"See that porch in front of the truck?" Hootie asked.

"Yeah."

"When the earthquake hit, I was parked about ten feet behind us facing the other way. I got out of the truck intending to go through that door," he pointed, "when it happened. It knocked me to the ground. I swear this truck started hopping off the ground about four feet high, as the ground rippled and moved beneath me. The parking lot was shaking so hard I couldn't get to my feet, and the truck started bouncing toward me. If the rear bumper hadn't landed on the edge of that porch there," he pointed at the platform, "my truck would have crushed me dead."

Katie's eyes were wide. She did not know if he was kidding her or not, but he seemed sincere.

"Weren't you afraid?" she asked.

"Yeah, I thought I was a goner! You can stay in the truck if you want to," he offered. "You'll be safe there; you can lock the doors if you are afraid – I won't be long."

"Afraid? What would I be afraid of?"

"I don't know, maybe that rattlesnake over there by the porch," Hootie laughed as he pointed to a dark coil by the front post. Katie quickly decided to wait in the truck.

"Look, I'm sorry, I laughed at you. I'll be back soon. You'll be safe in the truck, I promise. This place is full of snakes, and cactus, and who knows what else. Just wait for me here; you can keep the truck running and the lights on."

"Okay," she agreed, as she watched the snake slither beneath the ruined building. She rolled down the window and asked, "Why are we here?" Hootie was still rattling through the tools.

"I need to pick up something I left here for safekeeping," Hootie replied as he pulled out a shovel from beneath a lot of other tools and came around to open the driver's side door.

"Why do you need a shovel?" she asked while he reached under the seat.

"Snakes," he remarked, as he ran his hand beneath the seat. He pulled out a .45 pistol and stuck it in his belt.

"Why do you need that?" she asked wide-eyed.

"Bigger snakes," he quipped. "Wait here."

She rolled up the window, watching as he switched on a flashlight and walked beneath a large mesquite tree. He disappeared through a prickly pear cactus bed. She could see his light flash occasionally in the upper branches of the tree, but she could not see Hootie at all for the brush. She looked again at the back porch, bathed in the headlights of the pickup; but she did not see any other snakes. Regardless, she decided to stay in the truck.

It was not long before she could hear footsteps on the gravel; and looking in the rear view mirror, she could see Hootie coming out from under the tree. He had a dirty feed sack in one hand and the shovel in the other. He threw the shovel into the bed of the truck and rapped his knuckles against the glass so Katie would unlock the doors. Hootie opened the sack and pulled out a metal briefcase. It still looked new. He threw the bag aside and placed the case behind his seat. He took the gun from his belt and shoved it back under the seat, stomped dirt from his boots, and climbed back into the truck.

"You buried your briefcase?" Katie asked incredulously.

"Yep," was all he said.

"Why? I mean, honestly, why in the world would someone bury a briefcase?"

"Safekeeping."

She knew it useless to ask. Hootie was not going to tell her anything else. Katie tried to figure it out in her head, but it made no sense. She kept turning it over in her mind as she bunched his jacket up beneath her head and drifted off to sleep against the rattling glass.

CHAPTER 13

Hootie stretched and yawned as the sunlight flickered on the metal bulkhead inside the cabin of the airplane. He pulled on his boots and jumped to the ground to start his preflight inspection. He slept in the plane fully clothed after dropping Katie off at her apartment. The aisle between the seats was just large enough to fit his body. He wanted to get an early start to the day.

He watched the sun make its way behind the nearby hangar and wished he had told the group to meet at seven o'clock instead of eight. There was a red sky. Hootie wanted to get started to avoid any weather delays. He was anxious to get down to Galveston to board the boat, so he quickly completed his checklist; and by seven o'clock, he was ready to take off.

Surprisingly, Jake was the first to arrive, followed closely by Jesse and Rita. Hootie had already stowed his equipment and baggage in the cargo compartment of the plane. He greeted them as they unloaded their vehicles and carried their luggage to the aircraft. Hootie took each one and loaded it into the compartment on top of his gear. He mainly wanted to check the weight. They had followed instructions well, and their weight seemed reasonable. They would carry smaller personal items with them in the cabin. Katie drove up at a little before eight and, after loading her bags, they were ready for takeoff.

After each driver had parked their cars in the parking area, Hootie gathered the little group under the wing of the aircraft for a short safety briefing. There was not much to it, except he advised them to keep their seat belts fastened at all times. He told them how long the flight would take, and then let them inside to claim their seats. He noticed Jesse was able to climb into the aircraft by himself, despite carrying an aluminum cane.

Hootie climbed into the pilot seat and turned to look at the group over his shoulder.

"Someone can sit up here with me if you want," he offered.

Katie stood and made her way to the front as Hootie noticed the scowl on Jake's face. *Damn it; I should have left well enough alone*, he thought. Still, the plane flew better with that seat filled, but he decided not to mention anything about it.

Tom woke up early, and drove to the campus where he waited in the office of the bursar for the check. He knew he would need an assistant to travel with him to Mexico. A mental list of possibilities did not reveal anyone who fit his needs. He needed someone fast. Tom thought of Jesse and Jake first, because they helped discover Aquasaurus. He looked through his phone contacts until he found Jake Haw. He rang him up right away. There was no answer from either Jake or Jesse Perrine.

Scrolling down the list, Tom decided to call one of his student assistants, Mark Carter. Best of all, Mark answered on the first ring. Going down a list of requirements, Tom discovered that Mark had a passport and was willing to leave on short notice. He told Mark to be in his office in an hour; and then, he called the school travel office to book two air tickets to Mexico City for the next morning.

By the time Mark arrived, travel arrangements were final. Mark sat in the hallway outside Tom's office playing a game on his cell phone. Tom shook his head in wonder at how these mindless games could capture the young minds so completely. He called Mark into his office to bring him up to speed on what they would be doing.

"Mark, do you remember that huge crocodile from this spring?"

"You mean the one you and those guys found in that cave?" Mark did not even look up from his phone.

Tom wondered if Mark was going to be up to the task. *How many crocodiles did I find?* "Yeah, that one." Tom came around the desk, took the phone from Mark, and pitched it onto a table behind him.

"Hey!" Mark yelped.

"You'll get it back. I want you to pay attention – this is important."

"All right," the annoyed youth agreed. Mark gestured impatiently, waiting for Tom to continue. He wanted to get this over so he could get his phone back.

"We are leaving for Mexico in the morning. I want you to be ready; I'll send a cab at five-thirty to pick you up. Tell your folks we'll be gone for a month, maybe longer."

"What about school?" Mark asked.

"We'll be back in time for school. You'll get your regular pay, and you won't be out any money. I'll pay for everything: meals, lodging, and travel. All you have to do is help me."

"What do you want me to do?"

Tom pointed to the phone on his desk.

"Stay off of that thing for one. We are going to be doing serious work, and I need your full attention the entire time. If I catch you goofing off, I'll throw it in the ocean – understand?"

"You can't do that! That's my private property, man. It's illegal."

Tom looked at the youth. "It's either that, or I leave you here."

"Okay! Damn, can't I even use the phone to make calls? My folks might want to know where I'm at."

"Only that – and no games – and, only your folks! You get it?"

"I get it," Mark concurred reluctantly. "What are we going to do?"

"We're going to find that crocodile and take its picture."

"Oh, no way, man! That thing has been attacking things and killing ..."

"That," Tom interrupted, "is why I need your attention *all* the time. This trip is going to be dangerous. It's not a video game."

He watched Mark roll his eyes. Maybe this was not going to work out after all. Tom wondered which student assistant he could call next.

"We're just going to take a picture – that's all?" Mark asked, doubtfully.

"Maybe three or four, but yes, that is what we're going to do. We don't have to get too close to it; we can use a telephoto lens."

"Why do you need me?" Mark hesitantly inquired.

"To drive the boat and to keep it steady until I can get a good shot."

"Okay, I can do that. Why do we need to be gone so long?" Mark asked.

"Because we have to find it first," Tom explained. "I have no idea where it is."

The plane rolled to a stop at the HNH hangar in Galveston where Hootie would park it while they were away. HNH always housed Clint's aircraft. The van and a driver Darla arranged was waiting outside to take the team to the boat. Hootie stayed behind to bed down the plane as the others climbed into the van and headed for the docks.

After a short drive, the van pulled out onto the pier alongside *Miss Katie's* boat slip.

"How does it feel to have a boat with your name on it?" Rita teased Katie.

"We won't know whether we are talking about you or the boat," Jesse added.

"Don't be talking about me at all," Katie replied.

They laughed as Katie showed them around the boat, leaving Jesse in a deck chair near the bow. He would find his way around at a slower pace. When they reassembled on the deck, they told Jesse what they had seen. There was a dining room next to the kitchen, which Jake said was a galley. A wheelhouse stood above the main deck above a parlor-like room that held soft chairs and loungers. Jake called it a saloon, to the laughter of the others.

"I know we're in the wild west, but it's pronounced sa-lon, Jake." Jesse laughed.

Jake threw a flip-flop at him.

Katie assigned the cabins: "Rita and I will take the front two, and you guys can have the back two. Hootie will sleep in the cuddy cabin behind the helm. He'll steer all the time until he's comfortable with one of you two driving the boat."

"Wait!" Jake spoke up. "We're not sharing a cabin? I thought we'd be together. There's room enough in those cabins for the two of us."

"No," Katie asserted. "We're not sharing! What are you thinking, Jake? Under the circumstances, we should all stay in separate cabins – even Rita and Jesse."

"No problem here," Rita chimed in, as Jesse nodded in agreement.

"What circumstances?" asked Jake.

"Well," Katie hesitated, "You know … Hootie. What would he think? I wouldn't feel comfortable with him here and us staying together." Katie looked helplessly at Jake who was staring intently at the deck.

"Come on, Jake," Rita tried to smooth things over. "You guys are not a couple anyway, really – you know that. Sure, we have some good times; but you two hardly ever see each other anyway, except during the school year. It'll be for the best. If it were just the four of us, it might be different, but it's not. We don't want to make anyone uncomfortable. If it's okay with Jesse and me, it should be okay with you too."

"That's fine," Jake conceded as he walked to the rail. He watched a taxi pull up and saw Hootie climb out. *Some trip this is going to be*, Jake thought.

91

CHAPTER 14

Hootie cupped his hands around a warm cup of coffee and looked out upon the royal blue waters of the Gulf of Mexico. He read a faxed weather report and was relieved to see no significant storms were brewing. The only weather they could expect was localized summer showers that rarely lasted more than an hour. The winds might kick up a little choppy water; but if you spotted the storms soon enough, you could easily steer around them.

He wanted to stay close to the coast and remain in protected waters, but to do so, he would have to share the space on the Intracoastal Waterway with hundreds of commercial vessels. The big tankers and cargo ships were bad enough, but the small fishing boats were sometimes impossible to see. The tugs and barges stayed to their side of the channel, but the pleasure boats often crossed where they should not. If he were sailing directly to Mexico, he would have cut across the Gulf, but since he wanted to establish the trip as a fishing expedition, Hootie planned to hang out on the border for at least a few hours and fish.

A day and a half out of Galveston, Hootie needed to cross in front of Corpus Christi. He notified the Coast Guard and checked his GPS once more to make sure he was on the right route. Had he known far enough ahead of time, he would have positioned the boat in Corpus Christi and saved some distance. Who knew the hearings would end so abruptly? He laughed as he thought of how a simple hamburger and a phone call could clear a man's name. He was relieved that even if Clint did drop Pawson's, it was likely that he did not create the earthquake.

After clearing the shipping channels at Corpus Christi, it would only be one more day before they would pull up short of the international border. Not much had happened on the cruise so far, and he was beginning to feel a little bored. He put the autopilot on and went below to share lunch with the group. After a couple of days allowing them to get their sea legs, it was time to see if he could train someone to steer to give him some relief.

He entered the salon and found where Katie had laid out a sandwich tray. He built a ham and cheese sandwich, popped the lid from a bottle of tea, and wondered what they were talking about before he came in.

"Who's driving the boat?" Jesse looked up from his book and asked.

"It's on autopilot," Hootie advised. "We've cleared the shipping lanes out of Corpus Christi, so we are in the clear right now. Not much up ahead until we get to Brownsville."

"How long until we get there?" Jesse asked.

"Another day, if things go well. We are going to pull up there for a few hours before we cross over into Mexican waters. Since we are supposed to be a fishing charter, we probably should have a few fish in the freezer. So, once we get to the border, we'll do some fishing."

That announcement seemed to cheer the group up a little. It was clear that slowly sailing the coast was not nearly as exciting as climbing mountains or hurtling over a cliff on two wheels. Hootie was only about ten years older than this group, but it might as well have been thirty. They lived in entirely different worlds.

"Anyone want to learn how to pilot a boat?" Hootie offered. He was surprised no one rose to accept the offer. Jake's phone had his total attention, while Katie and Rita were engaged in a game of cards. Only Jesse sat looking out the windows at the expanse of sea, his book folded on his chest. He did not seem interested in moving from that comfortable position.

Hootie finished his sandwich and turned toward the door. "See you guys later," he stated as he walked to the door. He heard Katie's voice behind him.

"I'll do it – if you want to teach me," she decided, as the game ended. She dropped her cards on the table, "It's my boat; I guess I better learn how it works."

"Can I watch?" Rita asked as she stacked the cards and laid them aside.

"Sure," Hootie said eagerly. "Come on up when you're ready. It's a pretty good view up there. Meanwhile, I've got to get back up there now – just in case."

After fifteen minutes, Hootie could hear the women coming up the stairs.

"Man!" Hootie thought to himself "This world sure has changed. The two guys sit around playing video games while the two women take on the responsibility of working the boat. What are we coming to?" Still, he was happy for the company and the extra hands. They were sailing without a crew, so *they* were the crew. He had hoped Jake would show an interest. Maybe they could have eased some of the tension between them, but Jake seemed like he could not care less.

After showing the girls around the helm, he let one, and then the other take the wheel for a spell. He pointed out all the instruments. Rita wanted to sound the horn. No other traffic was in sight, so he let her give one short blast on the air horn.

Katie was scanning the shoreline with the binoculars, and she was surprised to learn she was looking at the beaches of Padre Island. They were so far offshore she could not make anything out. Tired of watching that side, she searched the port side and the horizon. She picked out some oil derricks and a few cargo ships heading into Corpus.

Hootie spent the next half hour showing the girls how to read the charts and pointed out the reefs and locations of buoy markers along the coast.

"The farther south we go," Hootie told them, "the more remote things get. By the time we get past Brownsville, we may not even have cell phone service in most places."

"What if we have trouble?" Rita wanted to know.

Hootie patted the instrument panel, "We always have the marine radio. We are in touch with the Coast Guard all the time. After we cross the border to Mexico though, they won't be able to help us much. We'll be pretty much on our own."

"That doesn't sound very comforting," Katie contended from her observation post.

"We'll need to be cautious," Hootie agreed. "We'll post a guard every night and make sure we are ready to run for it if it comes to that."

"What would we be running from?" Katie asked, worried.

"Probably drug runners, but we should be okay if we are careful," Hootie calmly responded.

Katie looked at Rita.

"You stay here," Rita told Katie, "I'll be right back."

Five minutes later, she reappeared with Jesse and Jake in tow. "Okay, Captain Hootie, show these guys how to run this boat."

Southwest Airlines Flight 581 landed in Mexico City late in the afternoon. After clearing customs and securing a rental car, Professor Tom Morrison and Mark Carter drove seven hours through the night to the main marina at Tampico, Mexico.

They parked in the marina parking lot and waited for the marina store to open. After explaining they wanted a charter, the merchant directed them down the long line of covered boats to Slip 14 to see a man named José Baca.

José listened to their story and slowly shook his head.

"I don't know, man," he hedged in English. "I do fishing charters. You guys want to go fishing? I know where to go. I can take you to where the big fish are running."

95

"No," Tom explained. "We don't want to fish. We want your boat."

"Without me?" José asked.

"Yes, without you. We want your boat for at least a month. I'll pay in advance."

"I don't know, dude, a month? I usually do three-four charters a week, man. I'll miss out on at least a dozen fishing trips, maybe more. Besides, I don't let my boat go out without me, man. What do you guys want with it?"

"We're going to…" Mark piped up, but Tom reached back and put his hand against Mark's chest to make him stop talking.

"We are photographers, and we want to take some pictures."

"For a month? You are going out there to take pictures for a month?"

"At least," Tom nodded.

"Without me?" José repeated.

"Yes, unless you don't mind being away that long. If you want to come, you'll drive the boat, but no extra pay."

"Man, my old lady will kill me if I'm gone that long."

Tom thought he would try a little humor.

"I thought you guys were in charge of your house, man. I thought you guys told your old ladies what was going to happen."

"What guys?"

"You guys – you know – you Mexicans."

José bent over double laughing.

"Man! I'm not a Mexican! I'm from California," he chuckled when he came up for air. "My old lady will kick both our butts if I go home and tell her I'm laying off for a month."

Tom thought he saw an opening. "Well, your name is José. Where in California?"

"I'm from Santa Barbara," José revealed. "I was born and raised there – so was she."

"Okay, here's the deal," Tom got down to business. "This will solve both our problems. Take a month off. I'll pay you for twelve charters, so you are not out any money. Plus, I'll buy you two round-trip tickets to Santa Barbara. Take a vacation back home and take the wife with you. By the time you get back, you can have your boat back."

José waivered, but still appeared worried. "I don't know, man. What if you wreck my boat? What will I do then? I'll be out of a living."

"Then sell us the boat; and when you get back, we'll sell it back to you."

"Naw, man," José hedged. "Too much paperwork and taxes and stuff. Do you know how much trouble it is to transfer a boat title in Mexico?"

Tom was not ready to give up yet.

"All right," he proposed, "this is the best I can do. I'll give you a check for $2,000 as a deposit. You hold that against damages to the boat. If you get back and we have not damaged your boat, you can give the check back. If not, you cash the check to pay for the damages," Tom argued.

José stalled, "Boat's worth more than that." He rubbed his chin as if he was thinking about it, but it was only a stall to get Tom to sweeten the deal.

Tom was desperate, and José knew it.

"$5,000 – that is it, man!" Tom shook his head. "If you can't do that I'll have to go find another boat."

"Cash," José insisted.

Tom thought for a moment. "Is there an ATM at the marina?" Tom asked.

"Sure," José assured him. "I'll go with you. You can buy breakfast – huevos rancheros," José specified with a toothy grin.

José and Mark ordered breakfast as Tom ran his card through the ATM. The card would not take because the machine had a limit. While Mark and José ate, Tom drove into Tampico to go to the bank. He brought back $5,000 American in a bank envelope.

After counting out the money into José's waiting hand, Tom thought he had a deal. He soon discovered the deal was not yet final.

"What about the twelve charters?" José asked.

Tom took out his wallet and fished out another $1,500, which he handed over. José handed the boat keys to Tom. He watched as the two Americans walked down the dock to his boat and loaded their gear inside. After they untied and were out of sight, José slowly walked over to the bulletin board, pulled the handwritten note out from under the yellow thumbtack, and tore it in two before dropping it into the wastebasket.

"Used Boat For Sale: $3,000 OBO. Contact José, Slip 14."

"I got a better offer," José laughed to himself.

CHAPTER 15

Satisfied that he had adequately trained his young crew, Hootie let them return temporarily to their video games. He placed the boat on autopilot once again and went into the Captain's cuddy behind the helm. He knelt, opened one of the drawers beneath the bunk, and pulled out a shiny aluminum briefcase.

Returning to the helm, he placed the case on the table in front of the wheel and scanned the horizon. He shook his head slowly as he eyed the metal container. They would get one shot – one shot only, and it had better work because he had nothing else with which to fight a giant crocodile. Aquasaurus would somehow have to swallow the canister inside that briefcase, but Hootie had no idea how to make that happen.

Hootie took the fire extinguisher from its hook on the wall and took it out on the foredeck. He pulled the pin, and held the lever down, throwing a billowing white cloud of fire retardant out to sea. The whoosh of escaping fire retardant was so loud it caught the attention of everyone else, and they rushed out on deck to see what was happening.

"What are you doing?" Jake asked above the sound of the escaping foam.

"I'm emptying this fire extinguisher," Hootie answered, trying to sound as casual as possible.

By now, the extinguisher was almost empty, and the discharge had slowed to a dribble. Hootie had a few seconds to come up with a reason as to why he emptied the fire extinguisher, which he knew would be the next question. The fire extinguisher was so cold that a rime of frost iced the upper part of the extinguisher.

"Because," he hesitated, "… it's defective. I got a fax from the manufacturer saying there was a recall. They directed us not to use it, so I emptied it to be safe."

The lie seemed to satisfy them as they turned back toward the salon to continue their evening activities.

"Dinner is ready," announced Katie, "if you're hungry."

"Thank you. Set a plate aside for me – I'll be down to eat in about an hour. I've got some things to do out here first."

Before they all went inside, he called out to Jake.

"Jake! Jake, do me a big favor. Will you go down in the engine room and grab a few items for me? You'll find a tube of adhesive in a drawer on the worktable. In the toolbox is a crescent wrench – and grab a can of red spray paint from the paint locker. Would you mind getting those things and bringing them to me in the wheelhouse?

"Sure," Jake agreed, as he moved toward the rear of the boat where the engines were.

When Jake returned with the supplies, Hootie thanked him for his help.

"Anything else I can do to help?" Jake volunteered.

"Sure," Hootie agreed. Maybe he was coming around a little. Having Jake feel more included would sure be a plus.

"Here, see if you can use this wrench to take the valve out of that fire extinguisher. Be careful. It might still have some residue left inside. You don't want to get that stuff on you."

"Why do we need to do that?" Jake asked. "You already emptied it."

"We have to make sure no one can refill it by mistake. It's a safety measure – you know how the Feds are. They have some stupid rules," he said with a grin.

While Jake fumbled with the wrench trying to get the valve off, Hootie moved the map chart over the top of the briefcase and pretended he was steering the boat. He did not want any questions about that case.

After a few minutes, Jake had removed the valve out of the fire extinguisher.

"Thanks," Hootie smiled, placing the valve on the table, "Good job! Now if you will go to the rail and carefully dump anything left inside the extinguisher body. Don't drop the canister into the ocean. That will help a lot."

"What if we need a fire extinguisher?" Jake asked when he returned.

"Oh," Hootie assured him, "we have other fire extinguishers. There is an extra one in the engine room. You'll find it in a locker marked spares. Why don't you go bring that one up? While you are there, you'll find a small plastic tarp. I'll need that too."

After Jake left, Hootie pulled his knife out of his pocket and cut the rubber hose and nozzle from the fire extinguisher. He placed the rubber and plastic parts in a drawer behind him. By the time Jake returned, Hootie had removed the nozzle holder by knocking the rivet loose. Hootie placed the loose pieces in a drawer just as Jake returned with the new fire extinguisher and the tarp.

"Thanks, Jake. You've been a big help. I really appreciate it. Tell Katie I'll be down for dinner in a little while. I've just got a few more things to do here before I quit for the night."

Hootie saw Jake flinch and reminded himself once more not to use Katie's name when talking to Jake – it was too upsetting for him.

After Jake was gone, Hootie brought the briefcase out on the deck. He spread the tarp outside the wheelhouse and taped the corners to the deck to keep it from blowing away. He looked to make sure no one was watching and flung the hull of the empty fire extinguisher as far into the sea as he could. Then he opened the case. He remembered the combination was the last four digits of Clint's cell phone number. Gingerly, he lifted the canister out and sat it upright on its base. Slowly and carefully, he began to paint the canister fire engine red.

The old wooden fishing boat was weak but appeared to be seaworthy. It was an old lobster boat that someone had converted in years past to a fishing and party boat. There was a fiberglass awning covering part of the amidships just outside a small cabin that housed the helm. Wooden benches, securely bolted to the deck, lined the outside walls. An open area beneath the awning covered the aft. It looked like the old wooden boat was equipped to carry a couple of dozen passengers. A long string of clear Christmas bulbs lined the inside edge of the fiberglass awning. A small counter stood in one corner of the open area, which appeared to function mostly as a bar. Deep-well ice chests lined the wall behind the bar, and empty wooden shelves were beneath. It was a day boat designed for fishing the bay, as it did not have cabins or berths – just benches. It was not exactly what Tom needed, but it would do so long as he didn't get into the open ocean.

After supplying their small boat with enough supplies to last a week, Tom and Mark set off in their party boat. Tom checked to ensure he had enough camera batteries to last, while Mark steered out of the Tampico harbor.

"Stay close to shore and head north," Tom instructed. "We'll stick to the back bays and estuaries. Just follow the shoreline for now, and watch the depth. We don't want to run aground."

"Where are we going to stay?" Mark asked.

"On the boat mostly – we might get out and sleep on the ground if we find a dry place – but mostly on the boat. Keep an eye out for anything that looks unusual."

Mark grumbled; but seeing that Tom was not paying attention, he focused on piloting the boat along the shoreline. By the time it was dark, they had gone several miles up the coast. Tom pointed out a little cove that looked inviting.

They entered an inlet that edged up against a small village. Tom searched for it on the map but did not find it. He thought he knew where they were. Tom had Mark get out the fishing gear and make a few casts while he took the wheel. It was dusk and quickly growing dark.

"There's no fish here," Mark grumbled. "Can we move to another spot?"

Tom shook his head no, "You aren't fishing to be fishing."

Mark threw down his fishing rod. "Then what am I doing fishing?" he barked.

"It's called a diversion," Tom replied patiently. "If someone sees us, we want them to think we are fishing. Now pick up that rod and make a few more casts!"

Mark snatched up the rod and resumed fishing, grumbling under his breath, "Fishing but not fishing in a place that's got no fish! I'm out here fishing in the dark with a lunatic!"

"I'm right here. I can hear you, Mark."

Tom was watching the lights in the villas that surrounded the bay. It was full dark now with no moon. Waves were slapping against the side of the boat, but the only other sounds were the high-pitched whirr as Mark cast once again and the click-click-click as he reeled the line back.

"Okay, you can stop fishing now," Tom declared, as he fired up the engine. A sharp *wheee* sounded just before the motor caught.

"Wait, I have a bite! Fish on!" Mark shouted.

"Shut up and cut it loose!"

"No! Let it go? I worked an hour catching this fish, and I'm bringing it in."

"Then bring it in, but we're moving."

"Don't go too fast; I've almost got it in the boat."

Mark did not have to worry about Tom going too fast. Tom did not head for the village as Mark expected he would; but instead, he slowly and carefully motored toward the closest shore. Mark's fish was safely in the boat by the time they turned toward the faint lights of the village. Tom kept about twenty yards away from the houses along the rocky beach until he came to a wooden dock behind a large villa. Tom pulled up to the pier and told Mark to tie them off.

The pier was rickety and moved with each wave swirling beneath. It was almost as though the sea and the dock were dancing a surreal mambo – each matching the sensual movements of the other. Even the thick posts wobbled back and forth with the waves. It was old and unpainted but still seemed secure enough to hold the boat. Tom killed the engine and cut all the lights.

"What are we doing here? Do you know this place?" Mark asked as he proudly hoisted his redfish for Tom to see.

"Welcome to the No Tell Motel," Tom laughed.

"We can't just pull up to someone's house and land our boat," Mark argued as he struggled to get the hook out of the fish's mouth. "What if they come down here and chase us away?"

Tom pointed toward the mouth of the channel as lightning lit the sky in the distance. With a storm coming, most homeowners were very liberal with boaters seeking shelter from a storm. They did not intend to get out of the boat, so it should be okay with the owners.

"Sometimes," Tom pointed out, as he scanned the shoreline, "it is better to beg for forgiveness than to ask permission. Besides, no lights came on in the house when it got dark. There is no one home. We'll be ok."

"What if someone comes to rob us? What then?" Mark asked, as he nervously looked toward the roadway leading toward the village.

"Not to worry," Tom grinned, pulling an AK-47 from beneath a blanket. "I got supplies in town."

At Port Isabel, Hootie motored beneath the bridge across from the lighthouse, through the cut at the end of South Padre Island, and into the South Bay. He anchored off Boca Chica State Park and cut the engines. South Bay was the last protected bay before reaching Mexican waters. It was dark on the water; so following the navigational buoys, Hootie found a safe anchorage near the shore. He left on his lights so other boats in the area could see them and then went below for dinner.

As he scrubbed the red overspray from his hands at the sink, he decided it was probably time to discuss precautions after they crossed into Mexico. Hootie went over all of the forms they would need and told them what to expect from the Mexican authorities once they came aboard. They should act naturally and answer the questions without offering any other information. He casually advised them that if they had anything they were not supposed to have, now would be a good time to get rid of it. He was pleased when they acted offended at his suggestion.

While he ate, he told them they were going fishing early next morning; and this might be their last chance to take warm showers, at the park camp, if any of them wanted to run ashore in the skiff to the boat landing. They all seemed game for hot showers; so after he finished explaining the plan for the next two days, the four of them gathered towels and soap and went ashore.

Alone in the boat, Hootie went topside to keep watch. He felt safe inside the park boundaries, but he worried about what they would find once they crossed the border. He looked at his map; and predicted that once Mexican authorities discovered them on their side, agents would direct them to go immediately to the port at Tampico to clear customs. It was a shame since Clint's villa was half the distance of Tampico – but laws were laws. After they passed inspection, they would have to double back and come north.

Hootie knew they were entering an area frequented by drug runners, corrupt police, and human traffickers. Mexican gun laws prohibited him from having any weapon to defend his boat or his passengers. He did not like going into that situation unarmed, but he had no choice. He had thought about it for a long time. There was no place on the boat he could safely hide a firearm. Therefore, they were unprotected – but there was no other option. The best he could hope for was that Katie would not want to remain in Mexico very long and they could quickly return to the relative safety of U.S. waters.

He stood at the rail and watched, as the laughing youths docked their boat and went up the trail toward the camp showers.

Tom pushed the button on the side of his phone and checked the time. He decided to try to reach Jake again. He dialed the number and listened to the digital tones of the phone ringing.

"Hello," Jake answered.

"Jake! Jake this is Professor Tom Morrison – remember me?"

"How could I forget? Hi, Professor, I heard you on the radio the other day!"

"Listen, Jake; I've got a job for you if you want it. I'm down in Mexico, and I need your assistance for about a month."

"Wish I could, Tom," Jake admitted. "But I'm down in Mexico, too – or at least I will be in a day or so! I won't be back in time to help you out, sorry."

"Mexico? What are you doing in Mexico?"

"You're not going to believe this, professor, but we're on a boat trying to find that huge crocodile – Aquasaurus."

Sudden sounds of approaching boat engines broke the silence of the night as Tom dropped the phone onto his duffle bag. Tom grabbed Mark's arm, to keep him from standing, as a jet boat roared by within yards of them.

"Stay down!" he ordered Mark, as a second boat passed in hot pursuit of the first.

"Don't we need to let them know we are here so that they won't make waves?" Mark yelled over the sound of the roaring motors.

"Not unless you want to die!" Tom warned as the boats made another pass, spraying waves of water over them. Tom pulled the charging level back on his AK-47 but kept the gun out of sight beneath the gunwales.

They crouched, unseen, and watched the two boats circle inside the bay. Tom was glad he had cut all the lights. In the darkness beneath the pier, Tom knew they were nearly invisible – unless one of the powerful searchlights picked them up.

Tom realized as soon as the lead boat stopped circling, things were not going to go well. As long as the lead boat circled and weaved, it made a poor target. He watched as the lead boat increased its advantage over the chase boat until, finally, it made a beeline toward the open Gulf. If it could make it out of the bay, it had a chance of escaping.

As soon as the lead boat straightened out, someone in the chase boat began firing an automatic rifle at it. Bright flashes of light and long streams of flame spurted from the barrel as the lead boat hit the surf and cut hard right out of sight. Gunfire still rattled the night even after Tom could no longer see either vessel. Tom remembered his phone call to Jake and retrieved his phone from the bottom of his bag, but the connection was lost.

Mark's eyes were wide.

"Who was that?" he asked. "What did they want?"

"Probably drug runners," Tom shrugged, as he redialed Jake's number. "The second boat was probably police or military. Who knows?"

"Are they gone?"

Tom hunched his shoulders in answer to Mark's question as he scanned the houses along the shore of the bay. He redialed and waited for

Jake to answer his phone. Tom noted that not a single home had turned on their lights. These dudes did not want any witnesses, and the residents were well aware that they should appear not to notice.

"Professor, what was that? Are you okay?" Jake's voice crackled across the connection.

"Yeah, Jake, we're okay. It was just a local dispute – that was all. They are gone now. Where did you say you were?"

"Boca Chica, I think. We're moving south tomorrow. We have to go to Tampico to clear customs."

"Tampico? Okay," Tom echoed loudly, as though he needed to yell for Jake to hear. "I'll see you there!"

CHAPTER 16

Satisfied they had caught enough fish, Hootie signaled it was time to stow the fishing gear. They had spent the morning playing and fishing in South Bay and had hauled in an impressive number of redfish and snapper. The guys cleaned and wrapped the fish while the young women took out one of the sea craft and rode double. Rita had tied her dark hair up on top of her head, but Katie let her blonde hair flow behind her in a yellow stream.

As they passed the boat again, Hootie could not help but be awed by sight of these beautiful women speeding by. He noticed how the sunlight bounced off Katie's hair as the jet ski bobbed and weaved along the starboard side. Memories swept Hootie unconsciously back to a time when he had watched another young woman ride by his boat, her long blonde hair trailing in the wind.

Hootie was a young Second Lieutenant in the Air Force celebrating his graduation from flight school on a fishing trip with some of his butter-bar buddies. His chest was still sore where they had "tacked" his flight wings to his chest. It was an old ritual for new pilots – something men did for some unknown reason. There had to be some pain with every achievement, so the first training wings were broken in half, and the presenter ceremonially punched the new pilot wings into the new pilot's chest. It was an attempt to ensure, ritually, that the emblem would remain on the pilot's chest forever.

Hootie had stood that day at the rail of the fishing boat rubbing his sore chest as a pleasure boat full of young women cruised by. On the rear seat was the most beautiful woman he had ever seen, her blonde hair trailing back in bouncing waves. Hootie knew that once women entered into the equation, fishing was over for the day. Their fishing boat fell in behind the women as they followed along. Hootie knew where they were going, and he knew alcohol would be the next element entered into the equation. As they neared the docks at the Officer's Club, Hootie moved to the front of the boat to keep the blonde girl in sight. He calculated in his head that there were six in his fishing group including himself, and eight women – so his odds were good if he could get to her first.

Hootie made sure he got to her first. Alice was as wonderful as she was beautiful. She was a student in a college nearby, and she was not looking for anything serious. However, love has a way of changing things; and by the end of the evening, Hootie was in love. They corresponded for a few weeks, with Hootie commuting a hundred miles up the coast on weekends. When Hootie received orders for California, Alice transferred to CSU - Sacramento. They were married a month later. She was everything Hootie ever dreamed.

"Hey, dude -- where you at?" Jake laughed. "We've been calling you."

Hootie snapped back to the present and realized he had been daydreaming.

"Miles away, in another place and time," he softly sighed.

Sunlight bounced off the water onto the bottom of the rickety dock and reflected across Tom's face. He yawned and sat up. Mark, who was supposed to be on watch, was sound asleep. It irritated Tom a little, but he decided to let the kid sleep. The gunfighter hoodlums had not returned, and they felt relatively safe back in the shadows of the old pier.

Tom calculated he was about fifty miles out of Tampico. Without navigational charts, Tom had to stay within sight of the shoreline as it wound and twisted along the Mexican coast. Besides, if they were going to encounter Aquasaurus, they would be safer closer to shore and not out in deep water.

Tom thought about his conversation with Jake. If Jake and his group were after Aquasaurus, then it might be a good plan to follow them until they located the crocodile. His little fishing boat had no radar or navigation systems, so he had no real idea where he was at any given time.

Tom decided to go to Tampico to see if he could make a deal with them to work together. It could be a win-win; each group would at least have some help if trouble arose.

He had not asked Jake why they were looking for the giant crocodile. He made a mental note to try to find out the next time they talked. What a stroke of luck! With another boat to help herd the crocodile into a shallow bay, they could quickly build a perimeter fence to contain the animal for study. While in Tampico, Tom planned to get a construction company under contract to deliver or build a containment pen once they isolated the crocodile. He did not know how many people were in Mexico with Jake, but Tom was willing to hire them all to help with Aquasaurus.

Having Aquasaurus contained would greatly help them study the creature, not to mention keeping it safely away from the public. It would also prevent accidental crossbreeding with any crocodiles that might be present in the area. One thing was sure; Tom did not want this thing to kill any more people, and he certainly did not want it to mate. It was hard enough to deal with one prehistoric crocodile. Controlling a dozen or more would be almost impossible.

Tom woke Mark and handed him a can of Vienna sausages and a sleeve of crackers.

"Breakfast," he proclaimed as he cut off a hunk of cheese and tossed it to the youth who sat rubbing his eyes.

"No breakfast tacos?" Mark yawned as he pulled at the pop-top on his can of sausages.

"Nope, but you'll be happy to know we're going back to Tampico today. You can have all the tacos you want when we get there."

"Great! Giving up, huh?" Mark guessed enthusiastically.

"What?" Tom asked, confused.

"Giving up – you know, that gunfight last night – we're going back and forgetting all this stuff about finding a giant crocodile…"

"We're not giving up anything," Tom told him firmly.

"Then why we're going back?" Mark asked as he stuffed a little sausage into his mouth.

Tom moved to the front of the boat and grasped the rope that tied them to the dock.

"We're going back," he grunted as he pulled the rope, "to make a new plan -- and to get reinforcements," he yelled as the motor came to life. "Untie us back there!"

Tom piloted the fishing boat out of the protected bay into the surf and turned south along the coast toward Tampico.

Jesse and Jake sat on the rear top deck as the boat sailed out of South Bay and turned south toward the Mexican border. It was a peaceful day, and the breeze blew softly beneath the protected overhang that covered the party deck.

"Hey, Jesse!" Jake suddenly remembered. "Last night, while you were in the shower, I got a call from old Professor Morrison."

"You did?" Jesse asked. "I wonder why he didn't call me?"

"He said he tried, but you didn't answer."

"Maybe it was when we were flying, or I was in a dead zone somewhere. What did the professor want?"

"Tom offered me a job, dude," Jake bragged.

"Doing what?"

"I don't know, field research, I guess. We got cut off before I found out. Anyway, he'll meet us in Tampico. We'll find out then, I guess. We probably can't do it anyway since we're on this trip; but it's pretty cool, huh?"

"Tom's in Mexico? What's he doing down here?"

"He didn't say, man," Jake continued excitedly. "And, there was gunfire too, dude! It sounded like the whole Mexican Army was after them. It sounded like a machine gun. Then the connection broke off, and I couldn't hear any more."

"They were being attacked?" Jesse asked, astonished.

"Nah, he called back in a few minutes. He said it was some local dispute kind of thing. Then he said he would meet us in Tampico and hung up. That was all."

"How did he know we are going to Tampico?" Jesse asked.

"Last night – at dinner – remember? Hootie said we'd have to go to Tampico to clear customs? Anyway, I guess the Professor will hang around the customs house until we get there."

Before Jesse could ask any more questions, a boat with flashing blue lights fell in behind them. A Mexican police boat pulled alongside them as Hootie cut the engines down to idle.

"We must be in Mexico," Jesse remarked.

Hootie came out of the wheelhouse and walked to the table under the awning where Jesse and Jake sat talking.

"Alright, guys. We are in Mexican waters now, they are going to board our boat, and there is nothing we can do about it. Be calm. Go below and tell Katie and Rita to get their passports out and not to worry – this is routine. They will check us out and tell us to go to Tampico to clear customs. It's nothing to be nervous about."

Hootie followed Jesse and Jake down the ladder to the main deck. Hootie unlocked the boarding gate as the Mexican officers indicated they wanted to board his vessel. Three uniformed officers came aboard *Miss Katie*. Without a word of permission, one of the three officers immediately went below to search the cabins along the companionway. The other two officers escorted Hootie up to the helm to check his papers.

"How many on board?" the officer with Major's oak leaves on his collar asked.

"Five," Hootie answered. "I have the travel papers and everything here in my desk, and they each carry their passports."

"We'll get to that," the Major said without looking up from the papers Hootie had given him. The other officer, who wore Captain's bars, looked around the helm, opened the door to Hootie's cuddy, and went inside. Hootie could hear him rummaging around back there, opening doors and pulling out drawers.

The Major handed the papers back to Hootie.

"That's all in order – give me your captain's log."

As the Major flipped through the log, the Captain exited Hootie's room leaving the door ajar. Hootie reached behind the Captain to pull the door closed, mostly out of habit. Hootie gave a little shrug of his shoulders as he and the Captain stood looking at each other while the Major studied the log.

"What's your purpose of being in Mexico?" the Captain asked.

"Pleasure – fishing mostly – I'm chartered out to the group below, and one of them has property at La Pesca. We plan to fish and hang out around that area mostly."

The Major looked up from the log, closed it, and tossed it onto the chart table.

"You are going to have to go to Tampico, you know? That is the closest port where you can clear customs."

"We're headed there now," Hootie nodded, "unless we can clear customs with you."

"That is not possible," the Major replied. "Are there any weapons on board?" he asked as he began opening doors and drawers in the console.

"No weapons here," Hootie assured him.

"You know this is a dangerous area, Señor Capitán Hootie. The border is crawling with pirates, drug traffickers – even human traffickers. You have no way to protect yourself?" the Major pressed.

"Unfortunately, your Mexican laws do not take the personal security of your tourists into account. We have no protection."

"Then, why you come to take such risks?"

"I only pilot the boat, Major. The lady downstairs tells me where."

While Hootie and the Major were talking, the Captain was nosing around the helm. From the corner of his eye, Hootie could see him bend forward and look closely at something.

"Hey! Señor Capitán Hootie! There is something wrong with your fire extinguisher!"

Hootie froze as a shiver ran down his spine. He turned to look at the officer tapping the gauge on the extinguisher!

"You got no pressure," he tapped harder. "Your fire extinguisher is empty!"

CHAPTER 17

Tom and Mark traveled along the mixed water estuaries of northeastern Mexico where fish and wildlife abounded. From the water, the tropical countryside seemed lush and beautiful. Tom knew from experience that on land, the barrier islands were hot, swampy, mosquito-laden hellholes. Often, in the larger waterways, bottlenose dolphins would play alongside their boat almost within reach. Wildlife depended upon the coastal wetlands for sustenance and survival. Tom used the time as a chance to show Mark the ecological benefit of wetlands. The freshwater influx at the end of upland streams and rivers acts as a natural filter, cleaning the water of impurities. The silt and runoff deliver a rich nutrient base for plants, which in turn adds to the food base for wildlife. As the water moves closer to the sea, it gradually turns brackish and attracts species that favor such habitat.

An endless series of sand spits stud the long lagoons between land and ocean. A confusing mass of small creeks and swamps, many of them unmapped, form a long string down the Mexican coast. Some lagoons were dead ends, and some had openings back to the ocean surf. The direction of flow often changed, depending upon tidal flows and sometimes on wind direction. Barrier islands and fingers of earth, mud, and sand protect the lagoons from the rough exposure to the relentless ocean surf.

The backwaters teamed with fish, fowl, and game animals, all of which depended upon the estuary for survival. These wetlands, especially in tropical climates, are ideal habitat for alligators and crocodiles. Alligators stay mostly in the freshwater outlets of rivers and streams, but crocodiles seem to prefer the more brackish backwaters. The two species do not mate, but in some places, they do cohabitate.

If you are looking for a crocodile, you want to stay in the more brackish areas and search among the reeds and water plants that provide cover. They are not usually hard to find if you know where to look. In the heat of the day, they lie on the muddy banks of the lagoons, warming themselves in the sun to the point where they become lethargic and motionless. You can almost mistake them for large, dead logs jutting half out of the water. It could be a fatal mistake. There are more crocodile attacks each year than shark attacks – and more than half of them result in death.

At night, a beam of light is all you need to find as many crocs and gators as you want. As the light reflects from their eyes, you see a red glowing dot, almost like a hot coal from a campfire. You will not know if the reflection is a crocodile or an alligator, but you will realize something is swimming in the water nearby. If you see two glowing eyes, you can be sure they can see you.

Tom happily lectured from memory and was pleased that Mark sometimes asked questions about one thing or another. Finally, to break the boredom of circling dead-end lagoons, Mark asked if he could fish while they traveled along. He would troll the mixed shallow water and try to catch some of the fish that trailed along, seemingly unafraid of the boat. Stripers, bass, and various other fish seemed to be attracted to their progress through the dark tea-colored water.

It was slow going. When Tom guessed wrong and reached the end of a lagoon without an outlet, they would have to double back – often a mile or more. If Tom went too far out to sea, he would have to deal with rip currents that could sweep the boat far out into the surf. Some rip currents were strong enough to upset small craft, so staying inside the barrier spits of land was the best practice.

At one point along the way, Tom ran the boat aground in the mud beneath the reeds and weedy plants along the bank. He reversed the engine and pulled back as hard as he could, but could not pull away from the muddy sand trap.

"You'll have to get out and push us off," Tom urged. "We're stuck fast."

"Why do I have to get out?" Mark argued. "You got us stuck."

"Because I'm the boss, and I said so," Tom snapped.

"Okay, okay, okay! I'll get out," Mark grumbled as he took off his boots. "You want to pull the boss card…"

"Well, hurry it up," Tom barked, exasperated at the delay.

Mark gave him a look as he swung his legs over the side, dropping into the water thrashing around noisily.

"I've got mud almost to my knees," he complained.

Mark slowly made his way toward the reed-covered shoreline, visibly laboring to pull each leg from the gummy mud with each step. Every time he pulled his leg out, the ooze made a sucking sound as his foot came free.

"Hear that sound?" Mark asked. "That's what this is like – it sucks!"

Mark nervously eyed the floating pads and weaving reeds as he moved toward the front of the boat in the dark, unknown water.

"What kind of snakes have they got down here, Prof?" he asked as he nervously spread the water with the palms of his hands.

"Just about every kind you can think of," Tom advised. "I'd keep my eyes open if I were you."

"What about that Aquasaurus thing? What about him?"

"No, I don't think it has worked its way down this far yet. Keep your eyes open anyway – lots of stuff in those weeds to worry about though. Hurry up and push us free so you can get back in the boat."

"I'm almost there! I'm almost there – be patient a minute!"

Suddenly, Mark came to a dead stop. He looked at Tom with panic in his eyes.

"Prof! Hey, Professor! I'm standing on something that's moving – I can feel it moving! What is it?" Mark was in full terror mode. "It's moving under my feet! Can you see it?"

"No! I don't see anything," Tom peered into the water.

"Well, something is down there – something big! I'm coming back to the boat; throw me a rope!"

"Mark, if you are standing on it, and it hasn't bitten you yet; it's probably a fish or a turtle."

"I don't care! I'm getting out of this water!"

"Push us off the sandbar first!" Tom yelled.

Suddenly, the reeds parted twenty yards in front of Mark as something large moved swiftly through the wildly weaving rushes. A flock of waterfowl took flight in noisy haste as hundreds of wings flapped along the muddy shore of the lagoon.

"What is that?" Mark screamed. "What the hell is that?"

Rested and fed, the crocodile renewed its search for more protective cover. It longed for the entrance to a dark cave where it could feel secure and hidden. Other needs press with an urgency that spurs the animal forward – searching for others of its kind. It does not know – cannot know – that it has been thousands of years since his kind has crawled the earth. Yet, the instinct for survival persists, pushing the crocodile onward – to keep searching.

The crocodile feels nervous and exposed. It searches the banks looking for an overhang or a cavity that might provide cover. Not finding refuge, Aquasaurus swims southward along the coast. With no sense of direction or purpose, the animal swims mainly at night, seeking food and shelter.

The crocodile prefers the night and the cool shadows of the late evening. Harsh daylight makes it almost impossible to see; but at night, the light is nearly perfect. The beast prefers to lie half-suspended in the salty water during the daytime, only eyes and snout above the surface of the warm water. The crocodile can sink or rise in the water, depending upon whether it is hot or cold outside. The glaring sun is hard to tolerate. The creature's unprotected back, unaccustomed to the sun by a lifetime spent in a cave, is sensitive and tender. Half blinded, it lies in the shallows to wait for darkness. Lying among the reeds along the shore, it becomes practically invisible.

Not finding any shade or covering vegetation, the crocodile rests on the bottom to regulate its temperature. Motionless, it sleeps beneath the water – its heart beating only two or three times a minute to conserve oxygen. It makes no outward sign of movement. After half an hour, the urge to breathe causes the animal to rise to the surface. Once on the surface, the crocodile opens its bulla and clears its throat and nostrils with a sharp snort.

While submerged, the crocodile keeps its mouth open and a valve within its throat tightly closed. The jaws snap shut with fantastic speed and strength when a fish or turtle is careless enough to swim or crawl inside the gaping mouth. If stepped upon, the crocodile immediately twists with astonishing speed, grips the prey in powerful jaws, and begins to turn and spin in a death spiral until the interloper drowns. Then, the awful gnawing and tearing of flesh as bones crunched between powerful teeth crack and the water froths with red sticky foam.

Hootie stepped quickly to the fake fire extinguisher before the agent could inspect it closer. Bending between the captain and the gauge, he blocked the captain's view as he tapped the gauge with his finger just as the agent had done.

"I have a spare," Hootie remarked, as he lifted the extinguisher from its hanger on the wall. He carefully placed the empty extinguisher on its side in a locker and pulled out a new one. After Hootie mounted the new extinguisher on the hanger, the captain peered at the new gauge, nodded his head in satisfaction, and began examining the other items inside the cabinet.

"You want to get rid of it? We'll take it," the captain offered offhandedly.

"Take what?"

"Your bad fire extinguisher – we can take it away for you, if you want, Señor."

"No," Hootie answers. "That's okay. I'll return it to Walmart for replacement."

Both agents exploded into laughter at the comment.

"He buys fire extinguishers at Walmart!" the captain snorted.

"No! I thought he bought it on Amazon!" the major hooted as he slapped the tabletop with his hands.

Hootie was relieved that the fake extinguisher didn't attract any further attention. His relief did not last long, as he looked on in horror as the Major picked up the little plastic box with the key fob inside. The major quickly flipped open the plastic lid and took the fob out of its protective case.

"My key fob – for my car back in Galveston," Hootie offered.

"Oh," the major nods. "Señor Captán Hootie. I am so sorry. I just opened the doors on your car!" Both agents convulsed in laughter and the major punched the unlock button several times.

"Do not worry, Señor, I will lock it back," the major chuckled as he fingered the lock button.

Hootie felt the paralyzing grip of fear. *Please don't push the red button!* Hot sweat rolled between Hootie's shoulder blades as he reached for the key fob. He struggled to keep his voice calm.

"Give me that, please. It is of no interest to you – it is only my car key. Please hand it to me."

"Señor Capitán Hootie," the major chuckled, "surely, you know we cannot open your doors from 300 miles away." Both agents found Hootie's discomfort extremely funny as they continue to guffaw. Hootie forced himself to laugh along with them.

"May I have it back, please?" Hootie asked as calmly as possible. "¿Por favor?"

The major smiled and flipped the fob in the air for Hootie to catch. Hootie quickly placed it back into its protective plastic box and stuffed it into the pocket of his jeans.

"You Americans – so jealous of your cars," the major shook his head. "What kind of car is it, Señor Capitán Hootie?"

Hootie wiped the sweat from his brow before he answered.

"Corvette ZR-1."

"Ay-ay-ay! That's one hot car, Señor."

"Hot?" Hootie nodded his head as sweat soaked through the back of his shirt. "You don't know the half of it!"

CHAPTER 18

In his panic, Mark lunged toward the bow of the boat as Tom revved the motor, trying to pull away from the sandbar. As the propellers caught water churning the surface behind them, the sudden jolt of Mark's body slamming into the front of the boat was enough to free it from the sludge. Tom quickly backed away into the middle of the lagoon with Mark clinging desperately to the front of the gunwale. His muddy legs swung wildly, leaving thick, filthy streaks against the side of the boat, as Mark tried to climb back into the vessel. Finally, with much effort, he rolled over the side and sprawled onto the bottom of the deck among the nets, reach-poles, and assorted fishing gear.

"What was that?" he screamed at Tom as he untangled himself from a throw net. "Did you see that?" he asked as he threw the orange net aside.

"I don't know, but we're going to find out!"

Tom throttled down and put the engine into a slow forward gear. The craft rocked and drifted slowly ahead in a graceful sweep back toward the small sand island. The flight of birds that flushed earlier came in for a water landing beyond the small cay. Nothing moved among the undulating reeds and floating pads as the gentle waves rocked the boat. The surface was calm as though nothing had disturbed the surface just minutes earlier.

"I'll tell you one thing; I'm not getting out of this boat again," Mark promised.

Distracted and half-listening to Mark, Tom surveyed the calm, dark water ahead.

"You'll do what I tell you to do," Tom absently reminded Mark, as he studied the opaque water in front of them. "Grab that long pole over there and start poking it into the water ahead of us." At a slow pace, barely above idle, Tom inched the boat through the shadowy sea soup. Whatever was in the water must still be there somewhere, and Tom was determined to make it rise again.

Mark selected a reach-pole with a curved hook in the end that boaters usually use to snag ropes when docking the boat. He stood holding it upright as he continued to complain.

"I'm not kidding, Tom – I'm not getting out of this boat again. If we get stuck again, *you* get out and push it off! You hired me to drive the boat, and that's what I'm going to do. You're not paying me to get eaten by some monster alligator!"

Tom continued to maneuver the boat toward the dense weeds and lily pads that masked the bottom of the lagoon. There was no sign on the surface of the water that anything was amiss, yet something had certainly rushed Mark and sent him into full-panic flight mode.

"Whatever," Tom absently responded. "Besides, it's a crocodile," he reminded Mark.

"I don't care what it is, damn it!" Mark swore. "I'm not getting back into that water!"

"Yeah, yeah – steer the boat then." Tom rose and took the pole from Mark and went forward to the bow. "Whatever you do, don't get us stuck again."

"I didn't get us stuck the first time," Mark snapped. "You did!"

Tom took his camera out of his bag and hung it around his neck. He turned it on so it would be ready to shoot immediately if needed. He cautiously poked in the weeds and delicately swept the pole beneath the surface as he kept up a steady stream of instructions.

"Slow ahead! Go left! Stop – hold what you've got. Move ahead! Slowly!"

As Mark pulled ahead, Tom spread the reeds and scraped the hooked end of the pole across the muddy bottom. He snagged something a time or two but pulled up only muddy stalks and gobs of seaweed. The rotten, decaying vegetation stank of spoiled fish and dead things mired in the thick gray mud. The more he stirred the water, the murkier and cloudier it became.

"I don't see anything," he yelled back at Mark over the clatter of the motor. The wind swept in from the ocean, bringing wisps of fog on the air as the tide began to rise. Rain clouds dotted the sky as the late afternoon sun began its long descent toward the tree-lined jungles on the shore.

A light, misty rain began to fall, but both men ignored it as they scanned the watery tangled mess ahead. A sudden motion in the reeds caught Tom's attention as he directed the boat forward and extended the pole as far ahead as he could reach. A wave of water built among the water plants. It swept through the reeds, toward the boat, and grew larger as it closed in on them.

"Here it comes," Mark yelled, as he pointed to the swaying reeds just off the starboard side of the boat.

The growing wave advanced rapidly toward the boat. A hard thump jolted against the hull in a loud thud. Whatever was in the water had found them and was now banging violently against the wooden sides of the boat. Tom dropped the pole into the bottom and raised his camera to his eyes.

"I see it! Holy cow!"

With the key fob safely in his pocket, Hootie could breathe a little easier. He was still shaking over how close the major's fingers were to the red button. One light touch on that red switch would have been catastrophic, and sure death for all of them would have followed.

Satisfied that there was nothing more to inspect, the agents prepared to leave the boat. The major blew a loud whistle and waved the police boat alongside so they could board. After warning the passengers once again about the dangers from pirates, drug runners, and slave traders, the three Mexican agents, including the third one who had searched below, climbed across to their boat. The major sternly admonished them to go directly to Tampico to clear customs. Once more, he covered the list of infractions they would be guilty of if they did not comply. Hootie assured him that he understood. The major saluted as Hootie pulled away from the agents. Hootie returned the salute as he set a course directly for Tampico. It would take a full day to get there, but they had no choice.

The police boat followed them for a few miles but eventually darted away into some coastal village along the shore. Hootie tried to visualize what would have happened if the major had pushed the red button. He tried to remember what Clint told him about the canister.

"It won't blow up," Clint had said. *"It will get hot – hotter than anything you've ever seen – ten times hotter than a blowtorch."*

Hootie remembered Clint warning him that it would burn through the steel floorboard of his truck and then make glass out of the sand beneath. *"It is a fire that can't be put out,"* Clint had warned.

Hootie shuddered as he imagined the canister igniting in the cabinet of the wheelhouse. The cartridge would start to heat up until it was glowing hot. Aerosol cans in the cupboard would begin to explode and catch fire as the canister burned through the shelf and into the bottom of the cabinet.

"Don't get it near the water," Clint had said.

With what he knew of physics, Hootie could picture what would happen next. After it burned through the bottom of the steel cabinet, it would burn through the deck of the boat down to the next level. It would continue to burn through layers until it dropped out of the bottom of the boat into the sea. Immediately upon hitting the water, the extreme heat would instantly vaporize tons of water into deadly steam. If they were still alive on the burning boat, lethal steam would be sucked into their lungs, killing them instantly. A huge cloud of vapor would hang over the sea, marking the place where the boat once floated. Everything not burned would sink to the bottom of the ocean.

"Hold it steady," Tom yelled as he focused the camera on the undulating waves. The swells rocked the boat as Tom struggled to focus the camera. "I see it! Damn, it's big!"

Tom peered through the viewfinder, as he twisted the lens on the front of the camera, trying to get the focus right.

"What is it? Is it that croc?" Mark yelled while he tried to keep the boat steady in the surging waves, as whatever was in the water kept thumping against the side of the boat. It was heavy and powerful; and, as it rolled against the side of the boat, it was even more difficult to hold the craft steady. Mark wanted to shift into reverse and pull away from the horror of what was going on unseen beneath the surface. He envisioned a gigantic crocodile rising above the boat, teeth gleaming white in a gaping mouth as it swamped the boat and threw them both into the filthy, stinking water. Scenes from the movie "Jaws" flashed through his mind, as he pictured Quint hung halfway out of the shark's mouth, crunched in two. Mark reckoned it would be the same result in a crocodile's mouth.

The sound of Tom yelling interrupted Mark's fantasy as Tom reversed gear. Mark backed away, happy to escape the threat beneath the water. Back in the middle of the lagoon, Mark wearily eyed the water, hoping that the advancing wave would not follow them into deeper water.

"What was that?" he asked, with his hands shaking on the throttle.

Tom's face was pale as he slowly handed the camera to Mark.

"It was the biggest one I ever saw. I didn't know they could get that big," Tom reflected in awesome wonder.

Mark scratched at his crotch as he looked on the camera screen at the rippled, blotched yellow skin in the picture. He could not see the head, but he immediately knew it was a huge snake.

"Anaconda," Tom reported, "a really big one!"

Mark sat, scratching his legs and backside as he swiped right, looking at the three frames Tom had snapped. He looked up at Tom as he handed the camera back.

"Something is eating me up," Mark grumbled as his entire body began to itch and burn.

CHAPTER 19

Tightly sealed in white and black plastic garbage bags, fifteen square bundles bobbed and floated on the sea a half-day out of Tampico. Black package tape tightly wrapped both ends of the bales making them watertight. Jesse, on watch in the afternoon, eased off the throttle and peered over the railing. He scanned the horizon with the binoculars, but no other boats were in sight. Training the binoculars on the bundles, he could see no markings or identifying information.

Jesse put the boat in idle and called down for Jake to come out to investigate his find.

"Grab that reach-pole, hook one of them, and bring it in. Let's see what it is," Tom yelled.

Jake reached as far as he could with the eight-foot pole but could not snag any of them. If he could hook one, he would draw it alongside the boat. The sound of the engine throttling down and the noise they were making trying to retrieve a package awakened Hootie who was taking a nap in his cabin. He stuffed his feet into his boots and went into the helm to see what the disturbance was.

"What's going on here?" he called.

"We found some stuff floating in the gulf," Jesse replied. "Jake's trying to hook one now…"

Hootie brushed past Jesse to look over the railing.

"Jake! Don't do that! Bring the pole back inboard."

Jake gave Hootie an annoyed look. "I've almost got one, just a few more inches. On the next wave, I can hook it," Jake grunted.

"Don't! Let it go! You don't want that. Do *not* bring it aboard this boat!"

"What's up with that?" Jesse asked. "It might be something valuable. It probably fell off a cargo ship."

"It is valuable," Hootie agreed. "Looks like about a million bucks worth to me."

"A million dollars?" Jesse's face lit with excitement. "Why can't we claim it? It's floating on the ocean, and no one else is around. We found it – why can't we keep it?"

"Oh, you can," Hootie nodded, "if you want the twenty years in a Mexican prison that comes along with it."

"Twenty years?" Jesse questioned. "For salvaging something that fell from someone's boat?"

"Jesse," Hootie explained patiently, "there are over a dozen packages there. Do you think those bales fell off someone's boat, and they did not notice?"

"I thought so. Otherwise, wouldn't someone be here trying to fish them out of the water?"

"Think about it," Hootie suggested, slowly nodding his head up and down. "Why wouldn't someone stick around to pick up cargo as valuable as this? Think about where you are," Hootie urged.

"Because," Jesse began. "Because … ooh." The awareness of what was inside the bundles began to dawn on Jesse. "It's contraband."

"Marijuana, probably," Hootie told him.

By this time, Jake had climbed up to the pilot deck where Hootie and Jesse were standing.

"Man, that's a lot of pot," Jake smiled.

"You knew?" Jesse asked.

"Sure, I knew," Jake punched him in the arm. "Why do you think I was trying so hard to snag one?"

"It's a good thing you didn't," Hootie laughed.

"What are they doing floating out here on the water with no one around?"
 Jesse wondered.

"Lots of reasons." Hootie took the wheel and pushed the throttle forward. "Sometimes these smuggler boats get chased by the police, and they throw stuff overboard so they won't get caught with it. Other times, they try to lighten their load so they can run faster, giving them a better chance to escape. It's odd not to have another boat around, though – guarding the bales. There might be one close by watching every move we make."

Jesse nervously eyed the shoreline looking for boats. "Do you think it was a trap?"

"No," Hootie decided, as he looked closely at the map chart. "Most likely, they left the bundles on purpose, letting them float until the pick-up boat arrived. If you had been caught harvesting their load, it could have been big trouble for us. Or, if the police were staking it out, they may have thought *we* were the pick-up boat."

"Do you think they're watching us?" Jesse asked.

"No, but I do think someone is going to come back and pick this stuff up – we better not be here when they do. Police or bad guys, either one would light us up if they catch us around here with this stuff."

"We could find ourselves between the police and the bad guys," Jesse realized.

"Sometimes," Hootie noted, as he pushed into high gear, "you can't tell the difference between the two."

"Sea lice?" Mark yelled. "What the hell are sea lice?"

Tom carefully inspected Mark's itchy skin. "Take your clothes off."

"What?" Mark asked. "Take my clothes off?"

"Yes, it's the only way to get rid of them. You are in for a few uncomfortable nights, my friend. Skin down and I'll see if I can help you."

"Leave my underwear on?" Mark questioned.

"No, take it all off – every last stitch."

Once Mark was down to his underwear, he stood with his hands protecting his private parts from Tom's view.

"Chill out," Tom smiled, "I've seen it all. By the time we are through here, being naked in front of me will be the least of your concerns. It's sea lice."

"What are sea lice?" Mark asked again.

Tom searched through his bag as he explained sea lice to Mark.

"Sea lice are, as you are about to discover young man, a hazard in tropical waters. They occur in the water from Florida to southern Mexico. They get between your swim trunks or t-shirt, and get trapped."

"I've got lice?" Mark wailed.

"They are the small larva of the thimble jellyfish. Not lice at all – you should be so lucky to have lice. *That* would be painless." Tim pulled out his credit card and showed it to Mark. "We can get rid of them with this."

"A credit card?"

"Yep." Tom moved to Mark's side and examined his body closely. "You've got them everywhere," he reported, as he examined the red, pimply bumps on Mark's back, legs, and backside.

Tom pulled out a pair of scissors and snipped away Mark's underwear.

"What are you doing? Those are my shorts you just cut off!" Mark yelled.

"I told you to get naked. Now you are." Tom laughed at him. "Sea lice are little jellyfish, about the size of a pepper flake that float around in the water just waiting for a host to latch onto – thousands – millions of them in every wave. Somehow, you got in a bunch of them; and they latched on to you. I told you – they get trapped beneath your clothes, and the spines hook in your skin."

"What are you going to do," Mark trembled.

"I've got to get the little spines out of you. It will burn and itch like crazy until they come out. See these little pimple-looking bumps?"

Mark nodded.

"I'm going to rub the edge of this credit card across your skin to pop the spines out – just as you do with a bee sting or cactus spines. If I don't press too hard most of them will pop free. Don't scratch them anymore – you'll just drive them deeper into your skin."

The red spots on Mark were beginning to welt up and form heads full of pus. Tom pulled a bucket of warm seawater into the boat and after ensuring there were no sea lice in it, poured the soothing water slowly over Mark's infected body.

"Ahhh," Mark sighed, "that feels better."

Tom began to run the edge of his credit card across Mark's shoulders, which immediately drew a complaint from Mark. Ignoring him, Tom continued to rub the card down Mark's back and across his buttocks.

"Prof! Have I got them there too?"

"You have them everywhere. Later, I'll let you take care of the other parts. Just remember not to scratch them – if they get embedded and infected you'll really have trouble."

Mark began to voice a low throaty moan as Tom worked over his body. The volume gradually began to rise until Tom could stand it no longer.

"Hush, Mark. Stop whining. I've got to do this, or you'll get an infection, fever, and you might even go into anaphylactic shock. It can be serious."

"Is there any other way?" Mark whined. "Is there any way to stop the pain?"

"Yes," Tom chuckled, struggling but failing to keep the laughter out of his voice. "I can pee on you. It will take the sting away."

"What? Are you some kind of pervert? You ain't pissing on me, Morrison. No way."

"Whatever you say, Mark," Tom laughed aloud.

After another fifteen minutes of moaning and writhing on the floor of the boat, Mark turned to look into Tom's face. Both men were red from sunburn, except around their eyes, which were protected by sunglasses.

"Prof? Have you still got to pee?" Mark pleaded with tears in his eyes.

Late that afternoon, *Miss Katie* pulled up to the dock at the main marina in Tampico. The dock master told them the customs office had closed for the day, and they would have to stay on the boat until the office opened the next morning. Hootie was disappointed. He was hoping they could clear customs and move up to La Pesca without any delay. Now they were going to have to hang out on the boat and wait for morning. At least it was not Saturday, so they would only have to wait one night. They would be under the watchful eye of a guard, assuring that no one left the boat until they cleared customs.

One of the local TV stations had English language movies, so most of the group settled in to watch after a light dinner of canned tuna. Hootie was not interested, so he went up to the wheelhouse to listen to the radio. At night, the radio signals were stronger and he could tune-in some of the news stations coming out of the states. There seemed to be nothing but a steady stream of talk-radio shows with an endless stream of know-nothing eggheads spouting off about one thing or another until Hootie flipped the radio off in disgust. He heard a sound behind him and turned to see Katie standing in the door.

"Not watching the movie?" he asked.

"No. I've seen it before," she shook her blonde head. "I decided to come up here and see the stars. Then, I saw you here."

"Let's take a look at what's out there tonight," Hootie offered, dragging his chair out onto the open deck. "Grab a chair, and I'll join you."

The two sat side-by-side in the pleasant evening searching skyward for something recognizable.

"They seem so bright," Katie noticed, "much brighter than back home."

"That's because we don't have as many city lights here washing them out. It's pretty dark down here; and you can see more of them, especially on a night like this with no moon."

"What's that little blurry blob of stars over there," Katie pointed.

"That," Hootie nodded, "is Andromeda. It is a galaxy actually – made up of thousands of stars, some are planets. It is the most distant object you can see with your naked eyes. Bring me those binoculars, and you can see it better. You'll see it looks like a tiny solar system."

Katie took the binoculars from their hook in the helm and focused on the star formation.

"Why do they call it Andromeda? What does that mean?" Katie asked.

"Well, they had to name it something. The ancient skywatchers named it for a princess. Didn't you take science or mythology in school?"

"Sure, but I don't remember the names of stars. Who was Andromeda?"

Hootie smiled. "That is a pretty good story – a love story actually."

"Tell me," Katie urged.

Hootie went inside the wheelhouse and returned with a laser pointer.

"See that "w" shaped constellation there?" he pointed. "That is Cassiopeia. She is another story, but look just below her 'W.' Now, see this one here – the one with the two legs?" Hootie traced the constellation with the pointer. "That one is Perseus. Just off his left leg is a triangle of stars. See them? Now look right above that triangle, and there is the Andromeda constellation." Hootie outlined it for her with his laser.

"Okay," Katie nodded, "but you were going to tell me about Andromeda."

"They are all part of the story. *So*, there was this mighty warrior – sort of like a superhero. His name was Perseus, and he was invincible. He killed the Gorgon Medusa – a fearsome female monster with snakes for her hair."

"I've heard of her," Katie laughed.

"Well, Perseus killed her by cutting off her head, snakes and all. On his way back home, he came across a beautiful young woman. It was Andromeda, chained to a rock near the sea."

"Who chained her there?"

"Her father did – King Cepheus. He was married to Queen Cassiopeia," Hootie pointed back to the "w" constellation.

"Why would they do that to their daughter? Didn't they love her?"

"Sure they did – very much," Hootie replied. "Maybe they loved her a little too much. The King and Queen constantly bragged about how beautiful Andromeda was. As punishment for their pride, the god Poseidon sent a terrible sea monster to destroy the kingdom. The only way to save the kingdom was to sacrifice their beautiful daughter to the sea monster, so they bound her to the rock. And that is where Perseus found her, helplessly chained, sadly waiting for her doom."

"Why didn't he save her?" Katie asked.

"Oh, he did. He killed the sea monster and set the princess free, but in doing so, he fell madly in love with Andromeda. He wanted to marry her, but her father had promised her to someone else – Phineus, her uncle."

"Her uncle? Didn't she have a choice in the matter?" Katie asked.

"No," Hootie shook his head. "So, the two foes, Perseus and Phineus, duked it out for the right to marry Andromeda."

"Who won?" Katie, amused, wanted to know.

"Who do you think won?" Hootie asked.

"Probably Perseus, I think. Wasn't he like a super-hero warrior? Phineus would not stand a chance against him."

"Well, you guessed right. Perseus won the fight by turning Phineus into stone using the head of Medusa he had killed earlier. So now Andromeda and Perseus circle the heavens in an endless dance for all eternity."

"Well, you know what would have been better?"

"What?" Hootie asked, curious.

"To let the lady choose, of course," Katie laughed.

"Then," Hootie chuckled, "there would have been no legend."

Tom steered the fishing boat into a slip at the marina. The dock master caught the rope Tom swung to him and tied them up to a pier.

"What are you doing with José Baca's boat?" the dock master asked in Spanish.

"I rented it for the month," Tom answered. "I've got to get this man to the doctor right away. Can you help me?"

"You rented it, Señor?"

"Yes! I rented it – can you help me get him to the doctor?"

"Sí, Señor. What is the matter with him?"

"Sea lice," Tom winced, as he draped a loose poncho over Mark's body despite his moans and curses.

"Aiee," the dock master nodded seeing the red bumps and welts. "Agua mala," he nodded as he assisted Mark from the boat and helped Tom support him as they walked down the dock toward the village.

CHAPTER 20

Jake stood in the shade of the awning outside the customs office in Tampico, Mexico. Jesse and Rita sat on a concrete block on the sidewalk as Jake watched Katie and Hootie walk toward them. Jake could not help but feel that Hootie was coming between him and Katie. He could sense a distance in her now. Jake was confused and did not know if she had moved on or if her new life simply required more of her attention than he did. Katie was spending more and more time with Hootie, and Jake felt the resentment building. *What was he after?* Jake wondered. *Was it the money?*

Jake put aside his thoughts as a short, bald man with a massive mustache and an equally impressive collection of keys came to unlock the door. A yellow, self-rolled, nicotine-stained, smoldering cigarette dangled from his lips. Jake wondered how he kept from setting his mustache on fire. The constable who had been keeping an eye on the small group until they cleared customs waved at the agent and went back toward the marina.

The customs office was bare, and the tile floor appeared not to have been swept since time began. A line of straight-backed chairs stood alongside one wall, while a chest-high wooden counter ran across the center of the room. A metal cage, like those bank tellers use, was in the center of the bar. The agent let himself in through a small door at the end of the service desk and rummaged around in the back room for a few minutes. When he finally came to the cage, he removed the "next window please" sign and looked out at the group assembling in the waiting room. Jake could not help but laugh because it was funny; there was no 'next window' – just the one.

The agent coughed a phlegmy hack, cleared his throat, and croaked, "Pass-a-portas, *por favor.*" It was a curious mix of mangled English and Tex-Mex.

Jake was the first of the group to step to the window with his papers. After the usual identifying questions about location and date of birth, the agent moved on to more pointed questions.

"Why are you come to Mexico – business or pleasure?"

"Pleasure – sport-fishing," Jake responded.

The clerk was confused. "Esporta, or fishing, señor?"

"Both," Jake affirmed.

"Where will you be staying while in Mexico?"

"On a boat," Jake responded, amused. "*Miss Katie* docked down at the marina." Jake pointed over his shoulder at Katie, "That's also Miss Katie," he laughed. "It's her boat."

"All of you will stay on the boat?" the agent asked the group.

Receiving only nods from the five, the agent turned his attention back to Jake.

"You must fill out this form. Are you bringing any of these items into Mexico?"

Jake looked at the list which included seeds and plants, cigarettes and alcohol, and firearms, and medications. He shook his head.

"Go over there and fill out the form and bring it back, por favor."

Jake signed his form declaring that he was not bringing anything illegal into the country and returned to the window. Jake waited beside the window until the last of his party had received their forms, and then handed his completed declaration through the window. The agent opened Jake's passport and picked up an ink-stained rubber stamp from his desk. He slammed the seal against Jake's paperwork. The agent placed the paperwork in a file basket and handed Jake's passport back to him.

"Have a nice day, Señor. Welcome to Mexico." The agent smiled, showing large yellow teeth behind what was left of the fuming cigarette butt still gripped in the corner of his mouth.

Jake stuffed the passport into his pocket and glanced at Katie. She was talking to Hootie in hushed tones and not paying any attention to Jake at all. Jake decided to go back to the boat rather than wait for the others. The stench of smoldering tobacco was too much to stand for much longer.

As he walked past the marina, he heard a voice calling him from a sidewalk café set beneath a shady awning on the waterfront. "Jake! Hey, Jake!"

Jake recognized Professor Morrison, but could not identify the young man sitting beside him. He looked about Jake's age and seemed in a very foul mood. The young one had some sort of pale pinkish, crusty, lotion stuff smeared across his face, arms, and legs. It looked like dried Calamine Lotion, only thicker. Jake had not seen Tom since the day they had come out of Honey Creek Cave, but he had heard Tom being interviewed on the radio several times. The media credited Tom with the discovery of the giant crocodile, but Jake did not care. After all, it was Tom who had identified Aquasaurus.

"Professor Tom! After talking to you on the phone the other day, I figured you would be around here somewhere. How are ya' doin'?" Jake looked again at Tom's companion. He seemed familiar, but Jake could not quite place him.

"Doin' great, Jake. You are looking fine! Aren't you going to say "hi" to Mark?"

"Hey slacker," Mark grunted. Mark peered at Jake through heavily coated circles around both of his eyes. It reminded Jake of those women who place slices of cucumber over their eyes and then smear their faces with skin moisturizer. He saw them around Barton Springs all the time. It was hilarious; when they finally stood, and the cucumbers fell off, they looked exactly like Mark looked now.

"Mark? Mark Carter?" he iterated dubiously. Jake looked back at Tom, "What did you do to him? He looks like a cracker with that canned cheese stuff on it that got left in the sun too long!" Jake hooted.

Mark extended his arm with his other hand across the inside on his elbow, making the classic 'stuff it' gesture, and then winced from the pain.

"Sea lice," Tom related. "He got a bad case of sea lice."

Jake got closer as he leaned forward so he could closely examine Mark's arms. This was too rich! Beneath the crusty lotion, Jake could see small red bumps that looked like pimply blisters.

"Sea lice?" Jake repeated. "What? You been sleepin' with slutty mermaids, dude?"

Mark spat on the ground and gave Jake a dirty look. "Yeah? Well just wait until you get 'em. Then, I'll be laughing at you, man!"

"It's a long story," Tom interrupted the string of insults. "Just be careful where you swim."

"What was that on the phone the other night? It sounded like gunfire. Were they shooting at you?"

"No," Tom assured him. "Some local druggers were shooting it out with each other, I guess. One boat was chasing the other and firing at them."

"The hell they weren't," Mark announced. "Some of those bullets were so close I could hear them cut through the air. They hit the pier that our boat was tied to – so close the woodchips fell on me. I thought we were dead!"

"They didn't even know we were there," Tom assured Mark. "We were in the dark without lights, so I'm sure they didn't see us. It was nothing." He turned back to face Jake.

"What were you saying about you guys searching for Aquasaurus?"

Jake looked around at the crowd and put his finger to his lips. "Ssssh, no one is supposed to know. We told the man we were on a fishing trip. Hootie told us not to say anything about the crocodile."

"Who's Hootie?" Tom asked.

"I don't know – all I know is he's some guy that worked for Katie's dad. He knows how to pilot the boat, but he thinks he's in charge of this whole damn thing."

"So let me get this straight. You, Jesse, Katie, *and* Rita are here with this guy Hootie trying to find Aquasaurus – right?"

"Yep, that's the fact, but don't tell them I told you." Jake looked up at the waiter who stopped by the table, "Bring me a Coke – no ice."

"Interesting – so are we. What do you plan to do when you find it?" Tom probed.

"Why do you order your Coke with no ice?" Mark wanted to know.

"I don't know. Katie said we'd report its location to the Mexican Army. The cowboy said he'd deal with it when we found it."

"How come you order your Coke with no ice?" Mark persisted in a louder voice.

Jake looked from Tom to Mark. "Mark, what is ice made of?"

"Water," Mark decided after consideration. When he smiled, dry ointment cracked in jagged lines around his mouth.

"Didn't they tell you not to drink the water down here?" Jake asked.

Mark's smile disappeared. He emptied his glass into the bay. The cracks in the orange ointment around his mouth came back together seamlessly.

"So, what's the plan?" Tom asked Jake again.

"Well, this Hootie guy – he thinks he knows how to kill it. But I don't know. We don't have any guns or weapons on the boat that I know of. I don't think he knows how big this damn thing is – how is he going to kill something that big without …"

143

Tom's face turned pale, "Kill it?" His voice rose several decibels.

"Yeah, that's what he said; but I don't give it much …"

"Why?" Tom asked as he looked around at the crowd and lowered his voice to an almost whisper. "Why does he want to kill it?"

"I don't know," Jake replied. "He's a cowboy – an oilfield roughneck. That's what they do – kill stuff."

"Jake, you can't let him do that," Tom pleaded.

"As I said, he don't have nothin' to kill it with – don't worry about it. He's just trying to impress Katie; that's all. What are you guys doing down here?"

"We've got a grant from the University to try to capture the crocodile – for research."

"Capture it? Are you crazy? That thing is dangerous – it's been killing people," Jake cried out, incredulously.

"That's exactly what I said," Mark croaked.

"Shut up, Mark!" Tom impatiently slapped the table. He looked back to Jake and explained, "The University has put up enough money to isolate this crocodile from the rest of the population. I've set up a construction crew to assist us. As soon as we can find it or drive it into one of those back bays, we can put concrete barriers in place to hold it there. Once we have it secured, it can be studied and protected from harm."

The waiter popped the cap from Jake's bottle of soda and sat a glass, straw, and napkin in front of him. Jake waited until the waiter left before he spoke again.

"Well, that sounds like a more reasonable plan to me than to try to kill it with our bare hands. I'll keep you guys posted. Maybe we can work together. We've got a big boat, and we're going to La Pesca this afternoon – Katie has a place there."

"No," Tom shook his head. "No, don't tell the others. They shouldn't know what we are doing. If they know about us, they might interfere with the plan – especially if they want to kill it. What Mark and I will do is follow along until you find it; then at least we'll know where it is."

"Okay, Professor – if you say so. We'll probably be leaving out of here this morning – to La Pesca," Jake reported.

"All right," Tom nodded. "We'll stay out of sight and wait until you spot the croc. We'll keep in touch as long as we can get the damned phone service to work. I can't get a signal half the time down here – no bars!"

Jake agreed that was a problem for him also.

"Where are the others?" Tom asked.

"At customs," Jake pointed toward the village. "They should be coming by pretty soon – back to the boat."

Tom rose from the table and tapped Mark on the shoulder. Mark winced at the contact. "Come on! We've got to go. I'll be around, Jake. Keep your eyes open; and if you see it, get in touch with me as soon as you can. And don't let them kill it!" Tom insisted.

"Whatever you say, professor."

Jake watched as Tom and Mark climbed into a small fishing boat tied to a pier near the marina store. He laughed as he watched Mark gingerly work his way onboard, complaining all the way. Jake swigged his drink from the bottle and watched Tom untie the boat and steer around the corner of the marina house out of sight of the dock cafe. The exhaust was black and sooty and hung in the air after they were out of sight. Jake took another sip of coke and laughed again.

"Sea lice," he chuckled to himself. "Whoever heard of flippin' sea lice?"

By the time the others arrived, Jake had finished his drink.

By mid-morning, *Miss Katie* left the port of Tampico and turned north along the coast. Hootie monitored the radio, hoping to hear news of Aquasaurus; but the giant crocodile had been silent for days. It was lurking somewhere among the marshes and bays along the Mexican coast. Hootie did not think the crocodile had come as far south as La Pesca yet, but it was time for another group meeting.

"Here's the plan," he told the gathered friends. "I don't think Aquasaurus has traveled far down the coast yet – at least not as far as La Pesca. Unless Katie objects, I say we go there and lay up a day or two, hoping to hear news of the crocodile's next sighting. We can pull into the dock at Katie's place and stay until we can get more reports. While we re-provision *Miss Katie* and get some fuel, you four can take the smaller craft out and explore around the bay searching for signs. If we had some way to find the exact location, we would have a better chance of finding Aquasaurus, but for now, this is all we have – sightings and radio reports. Agreed?"

No one objected, so Hootie went back to the helm to plot a course for La Pesca. If they were lucky, they would reach Katie's hacienda by early morning. Jake began mulling an idea around in his mind.

"Katie," he wondered, "whatever happened to your phone?"

"I lost it," Katie replied, "in the cave, I guess."

"Didn't it have like a solar recharging panel on it and a tracking device?" Jake recalled.

'It did," Katie admitted. "That was one fine phone – it was top of the line."

"When is the last time you remember having it?"

"When I was beating that huge, monster crocodile in the face with it," she laughed.

A mile to *Miss Katie*'s stern, a small fishing boat bounced upon the choppy seas, struggling to keep up with the bigger ship. At least Tom knew the lead ship was bound for La Pesca even though he did not know the exact location of Katie's house. Tom wanted to stay as close as possible, but he realized if he fell too far behind, or lost visual contact with the larger boat, it might be hard to find *Miss Katie* in the small Mexican vacation port. If he could keep them in sight, he would not have to search all the bays, harbors, and houses along the shore.

Mark lay in his bunk inside the open cabin. Each time the boat bounced across the waves, Mark moaned and loudly complained. Tom could do nothing else but remind him to take the pain pill the doctor had given him. Mark would doze back to sleep despite his pain, but eventually, a larger-than-normal wave would cross beneath the boat throwing Mark into the bulkhead, and waking him again. It was going to be a long, bumpy trip.

CHAPTER 21

The seas grew rough on the way up the Mexican coast. Hootie moved farther out into the Gulf, but the wind kept pushing up choppy whitecaps on the surface. Hootie checked the radar for weather but saw nothing important. He flipped the switch to see a larger range, but no storms were brewing. It was the beginning of hurricane season in the Gulf, so it was wise to be aware of building storms. The whitecaps were due to the southeast wind pushing past the coast.

Katie's hacienda was located nearly a mile southeast across the Rio Soto la Marina. The house sat on a narrow cove protected from the wind on all sides. The house had its own dock and a small beach; also, the location offered a great vantage point for entry and egress out of the bay. The town of La Pesca was reachable by smaller craft, which could dock at the marina or at the restaurant piers that stretched across the waterfront.

With only a couple of hours of daylight left, Hootie dropped off the four friends and went across to the main marina to buy fuel. By the time he returned, darkness had covered the little bay, and he had only the marker lights to guide him to the right dock.

Hootie tied up at the pier and walked down the wooden walkway that led to the house. The builder had oriented the hacienda so that most of the windows looked out on the water. The yellowish lights within lighted the yard around the house and made the dwelling seem warm and inviting.

Hootie knocked on the glass door and entered through the combined kitchen-dining room. Most of the group was in the living room. Katie took Hootie on a quick tour of the house, offering him one of the larger bedrooms.

"You know, I appreciate your offer, but I really think I should stay with the boat. You never know who is going to come meddling around in the dark. I'll be fine out there."

"Okay," Katie pouted, "but, I was hoping you would stay here with us."

"I'm not that far away. Besides, I think you guys need some time alone together. Go have fun, party a little, and don't worry about me. I'll be okay. I'll monitor the radio and the news; when it's time to leave, I'll give you all plenty of warning."

"Okay. You know you are welcome to join us any time – like … for dinner? Luna and her husband, Miguel, live here; and Miguel is preparing a special dinner tonight. You won't want to miss it – he is such a great cook."

"Sure, thanks. Let me ask you something."

"Okay – anything. What?" Katie winked. Her smile was so enchanting Hootie almost forgot his question.

"Did your dad have a bedroom here that no one else used?"

"Yes, he did. As a matter of fact, it was the room I was going to put you in."

"Do you know if your dad kept any guns here?"

"No, he never mentioned any."

"Do you mind if I check out the room? If there is a gun around, it sure would be helpful if we had it on the boat."

"Come on, I'll show you his room. You might want to change your mind and stay there after all."

Katie did not have a key for her father's locked bedroom, so she called for Miguel to unlock the door.

"I should have remembered he kept it locked. No one ever goes in there," Katie said. "I haven't had the heart yet," she mumbled.

Miguel arrived, and Katie introduced him to Hootie. After he opened the door and returned to his cooking, Katie stood by the door as Hootie looked around the room.

"Pretty nice, huh?" she asked. "Are you sure you don't want to stay in here? It's okay."

Hootie looked at her. "I might, it is very nice. I'm going to look around a bit to see if there is a gun here or something we can use. Do you mind?"

"No," Katie agreed. "Make yourself at home; stay as long as you like.

After a few minutes, Katie left Hootie alone in the room and went back to her friends. In a far corner of the closet, behind Clint's clothes, Hootie found the safe – locked of course. Hootie looked under the bed and saw a gun case; but when he pulled it from beneath the bed and opened it, there was no gun inside. Disappointed at not finding a gun, Hootie thought his only option was to ask Katie to open the safe. He was not sure how she would feel about doing that, so he decided to look around the room a little closer. Maybe he would find something.

Hootie went into the bathroom and ran his hands around the inside of the cabinets beneath the sink. Nothing hung there. He pulled out all the drawers in the bathroom and the chest in the bedroom – no false bottoms. He checked all the pockets of the clothes hanging in the closet but found them empty. He looked behind the window curtains and the furniture. He searched beneath the cushions of the chair and the loveseat that sat in the corner. After checking all the air vents, Hootie was ready to give up. The safe was all that remained.

He sat at Clint's desk, trying to think of all of the places someone might hide a gun. Toilet tank? No, too damp. Ceiling? No, there were no ceiling tiles. There was only a single stucco ceiling.

A small short-wave radio sat on the desk, and Hootie absently pushed the power button – maybe he could pick up some news. Nothing happened – the dial wouldn't light – no static – no music – nothing. Hootie looked under the desk to see if the radio was plugged in, but discovered there was no power cord coming out of the back of the radio.

He placed his fingers under the small ridge on the back of the lid and pulled up. With a little force, it opened. There were no guts in the radio, but sitting inside the case was a 1911 Colt .45 semi-automatic handgun and two full clips. Delighted, Hootie stuffed the two clips into his pocket and stuck the .45 in his belt. *"Thank you, Clint,"* Hootie thought as he closed the door behind him. *"I knew you wouldn't bring your daughter here unless you had some protection somewhere."* As a last thought, Hootie went back into Clint's room and took the short-wave box back to the boat.

Tom had not realized how many little coves and inlets surrounded La Pesca. There seemed to be miles of shoreline to cover, and he began to doubt that he would ever be able to find the right house.

Mark seemed to feel better as his skin began to heal. He was still sore, but after scraping away some of the ointment, he no longer looked like one of the living dead. He still refused to go overboard to swim in the ocean. He was trying to wash from a bucket of seawater he had pulled onto the boat.

"There are no sea lice here," Tom assured him. "Look in your bucket. They look like little flakes of pepper. See? Nothing."

"Well, I don't care. I'm not going in that water," Mark declared.

"You should. The salt water will do wonders for your skin. Rubbing that ointment off with sea water will make it heal a lot quicker."

"It will?" Mark asked dubiously.

"Of course it will. Salt water cures everything. Look, take off your clothes and jump in. It's dark, and no one is going to see you. We'll sit here for a while and then start searching for the boat again when you're done."

Tom cut the engine on the boat and threw out the anchor. It was quickly growing dark out on the water. Maybe he would have a better chance when the lights in the houses along the beaches came on. At least he would know which houses were occupied. Tom decided to let the boy take a swim while he decided what to do.

"There, see? We're standing still. Heave ho, old boy!"

Light shorts and a t-shirt were all Mark could stand to have against his skin, so it did not take much for him to disrobe. He splashed into the water and bobbed up quickly.

"Oh, man! This feels great," he sighed as he rubbed the caked medication from his arms and legs. "It even feels good to rub the scabs off," he laughed.

"When you get out, we'll put some more of that salve on you. You'll be okay in a few days."

As Mark eased his aches and pains in the warm water of the Rio Soto la Marina off La Pesca, Tom searched the shoreline for the sight of *Miss Katie*. His back was toward the opposite shore in the growing darkness when he heard the unmistakable sound of a boat approaching.

"Mark!" Tom yelled, "Boat passing! Stay away from the hull, a swell is coming."

Tom stood on deck and watched *Miss Katie* pass by a hundred yards off his starboard side.

"Come on, Mark – show time!" he jubilantly shouted.

After Mark safely climbed aboard, Tom again fell in behind *Miss Katie*. He watched from a distance, as it pulled in to a pier in the small, protected cove outside La Pesca. Now that he knew where they were staying, it would be easy to keep tabs on the group. He did not expect they would be leaving, at least not until morning. He and Mark would be ready to tail them all day if necessary.

"Hey, Mark? How would you like to spend the night in a real hotel?" Tom inquired.

"Are you kidding? Heck, yeah!"

"There is a hotel right over there called the El Fortin. What d'ya say we get a good meal and a clean bed for tonight?"

"Okay," Mark eagerly agreed as he groaned and rubbed his lower belly.

Tom pointed across the water at *Miss Katie* as he watched Hootie stroll up the walkway toward the house. "See that boat?"

"Yeah, that's the boat we've been following," Mark acknowledged, as sweat began to form on his forehead.

"Exactly right. Remember it well. That boat is going to lead us to our crocodile!"

Mark began to feel a rumble from deep inside his stomach just as a sharp pain began to grow in his gut.

"I think you'd better hurry and get us to that hotel, Professor. Soon!"

CHAPTER 22

On the half-mile trip across the bay, Tom paused the boat three times for an agonized Mark to roll himself into the Rio Soto la Marina to clean himself. Even after Mark entered the water, Tom could still smell the stench left behind. As Mark bathed, Tom sluiced the deck with seawater.

"It was that damn ice I drank at the café back in Tampico," Mark moaned, as he crawled back into the boat for the third time. "It gave me the revenge!" Mark wailed.

"Could be," Tom agreed, "but, most likely it's nausea from the sea lice. You probably have a fever along with it, too. I had a friend once who had it so bad he lost fifteen pounds in a week."

"Great!" a sardonic Mark yelled. "I feel like I just lost fifteen pounds of something."

"I don't mean to laugh," Tom said, trying to hide his amusement, "and I don't want to scare you, but I also had a friend who got into sea lice and came out with a bad infection in his urethra."

Mark rolled his eyes and sat on the deck as Tom steered toward the hotel dock, trying to hide his grin. By the time they came ashore, Tom was beginning to realize that Mark might be seriously ill. Mark was almost too weak to walk. Tom enlisted the help of a hotel employee to help drag him to a cabana on the beach.

Esteban, the hotel porter, looked closely at Mark while Tom explained about the sea lice.

"Si, señor, he has got it bad. And, something else too, I think," Esteban scrunched up his nose. He sadly shook his head and made a 'tsk-tsk' sound with his mouth.

"You do not worry, señor – I know what must be done – it is an old family *remedio*. *Por favor*, take this card to the desk and tell them to give you this cabaña – *número vientiuno*. When you return, your son will be much better – you will see."

As Tom turned to leave, he could not help notice Esteban's puzzled look and the expression of helpless terror on Mark's face, as he struggled with the stranger who was trying to remove his shorts.

Hootie sat on the deck and enjoyed the summer breeze that drifted along the river. He would call this water a bayou in Louisiana or Florida, he thought. He considered tossing out a line with a lure or two but decided it was too much work for such a lazy night. He popped open a cold beer and leaned back on the comfortable chair to enjoy watching the twinkling lights along the shore. From somewhere inside the house, he heard Katie's laugh carried lightly on the wind; his mind immediately flashed back to Alice.

He did not know why he was thinking so much about Alice lately. Maybe it was because he had more time on his hands these days. The oilfield did not leave much time for thinking, which was what Hootie thought he needed at the time – no time to think. Maybe, if he did not think about it, he would forget somehow. Through the years of hard work, fistfights, booze, and other women, he believed he had finally forced Alice way back into the recesses of his mind. Then he met Katie, who was so much like her, and he realized he had not forgotten any of it at all. The memories came flooding back. And, just like the day it happened, he could feel Alice with him again – watching over him from somewhere.

He could almost sense the smell of her – not her perfume or shampoo – the fragrance of *her*. It was unlike anyone else. Maybe it was pheromones – Hootie did not know – but it was on her skin. Maybe no one else seemed to notice it, but Hootie did, and it got into his system. He became addicted to the nearness of her in a way that was incomprehensible to him – and the withdrawal was numbing.

155

He wondered if anyone ever really knew when they were going to die. His grandmother knew – he was sure of that. She told Hootie so just hours before she drew her last breath, but then she had been eighty-eight years old. Hootie thought a person might have a clue at that age – but at twenty-two? What in hell does anyone know about life or death at twenty-two? Hootie certainly had not. At that age, everyone thinks it will last forever. Alice probably had thought the same.

Hootie closed his eyes and slipped into a dream world where the two of them – he and Alice – danced among bluebonnets. Hand-in-hand, they mowed a trail among the weedy flowers in a circular path, as they orbited each other until they were dizzy. Falling on their backs, they made bluebonnet angels that joined at the top. As Hootie slipped deeper and deeper into the dream, he could actually see them lying there in the flowers, as if through a magic motion picture camera that continued to revolve and rise into the starry heavens above them, leaving them far below.

Had his fingers not relaxed, allowing the beer to fall to the deck and roll to the edge of the bulkhead, Hootie might have stayed asleep on the deck all night. He opened his eyes, looked around for Alice and bluebonnets, and realized he had been dreaming. He slowly rose, mopped up the mess, and went inside to bed – hoping to dream again.

By the time Tom returned to the cabana, Mark was resting comfortably. The porter had left a small glass of liquid with instructions that Mark was to drink it straight down upon awakening. Tom picked up the glass of weak milky-looking liquid and sniffed. It did not have much of a smell he thought, as he put the glass back down near the note Esteban had written.

Tom took a long, hot shower that steamed the sweat and stale seawater brine from his body. Hot, fresh, clean water never felt so good. He rinsed the soap, dried off, and changed into fresh boxers and a T-shirt. He was going to sleep well tonight.

He slid the patio door open and went out onto the veranda. He thought he could make out the lights of *Miss Katie* across the Rio. Just as he planned, any movement of the boat would bring her past his hotel – unless she went upstream – but there was no reason to go in that direction – not if they were searching for a crocodile. To find a crocodile, you would want to stay in the marshy, brackish waters of the back bays and low-lying flats.

Tom sat in a chair near the railing, unwrapped the fresh cigar Esteban had left beside the note, and fired the tip. The gray smoke curled up with a satisfying aroma, as Tom watched the far lights flicker on the water.

He went back inside to check on Mark again. He felt his forehead as he pulled the covers up over the boy's shoulders. He resolved to try to take better care of the kid despite his quarrelsome attitude. Then he set the alarm for six a.m., turned off the light, and went to bed.

After the evening activities died down, each of the friends retired to their separate bedrooms for the night. Jake still did not understand why Katie was giving him the standoff. Any other time, they would be making out. Even Jesse and Rita were sleeping in separate bedrooms, so it rather spoiled the romantic idea of being together.

He tried to call the professor but was unable to get through. Service down here was terrible. Too bad the professor did not have one of those neat satellite phones like Katie's. 'Had' was the operative word – she did not have it anymore. She believed she lost it in Honey Creek Cave, but Jake was not so sure.

Powerless to change the way things were, Jake tried to read himself to sleep but did not have much luck. He put down his book and stood by the window for a moment. He pushed the curtains aside and looked out on the amazing view of lights of La Pesca wiggling across the water.

He kept going over in his mind about Katie's lost cell phone. He remembered it was a super-nice satellite phone with a solar charger built into the waterproof case. Maybe he could do her a big favor and help her find the lost phone. She thought she lost it in the cave while fighting Aquasaurus – but what if she didn't? Maybe she had dropped it in the Parks and Wildlife truck they used that night, and it was under the seat of her car or something. On the other hand, maybe it was somewhere in her apartment, and it got pushed under something in the excitement of the cave rescue. Maybe it was still there.

Wouldn't there be a way to get a fix on it and track it down, he wondered? He pulled a chair up to the computer on the desk in the little room, signed on to his account, and began researching ways to find a lost phone.

He found what he was looking for – he read the step-by-step instructions about how to "ping" a lost phone and get coordinates from its location. If Katie lost the phone in the cave, where she thought she lost it, then it would be a dead signal by now. However, if it was anywhere but in the cave – anywhere the light could reach it – Jake believed he could locate it. It wouldn't hurt to try. What else did he have to do?

All he needed was her phone number and various other registration numbers to attempt to get a fix on its location. Earlier in the year, Jake and Katie had cloud-stored all of the data for their phones – just in case one of them was lost. Jake showed her how to do it. He pulled up the information he had stored in the cloud and entered Katie's phone number into a search engine. Satisfied that he now had enough information to ping Katie's phone, he decided to wait for morning and surprise her. He printed out the last of the instructions, turned off the computer, and went to sleep almost as soon as his head hit the pillow.

CHAPTER 23

The entire situation was frustrating Hootie. No news had surfaced about Aquasaurus for at least a week. It was as though the great crocodile had vanished. Hootie found nothing printed in the newspapers, nor was anything broadcast on the radio or posted on the internet feed. The last known sighting was sixty miles north up the coast of Mexico.

Nothing needed doing for the next several days, so Hootie decided it was time to scout the back bays and coves farther up the coast. If the crocodile came south toward them, the search would give them some advance knowledge of the area. They would find places that were preferred by the species. That would give them valuable clues of where it might hole up for a while, and they might even find a place where they could stage an encounter. If they knew the area better than the crocodile, it would give them a slight advantage.

Hootie rounded up the group and laid out a plan so that everyone was on the same page.

"We don't know where the crocodile is – yet. But there are some things we can do until it turns up. We can go look for it. I'd like us to pull out of here in an hour, so get ready. We are going to head north and search along the coast to see what we can find. I don't expect to run into Aquasaurus, but we can at least familiarize ourselves with the coastal waters. This morning, I'll move the boat about twenty miles north and anchor as close to shore as we can.

When we get there, you can take the small craft out in pairs to explore the marshes and islands along the shore. Memorize everything about our location. See if you can spot anything that might help us locate the crocodile, or predict where it might be. Look for a dead-end on a slough or creek outlet. It likes briny water. Test the depth and scout the passages where we can get in and out rapidly, if necessary. Any questions?"

"How long will we be gone?" Katie wanted to know.

"Not long this first trip. If all goes well, we'll be back late tonight. We might move farther north in a few days, and if so, we may have to stay out a couple of days – but not this trip. The information we uncover will come in handy when we find out where the crocodile is hiding. We can never have too much information about these waters. We may have only one chance. If we find the crocodile, we can't let it slip away."

It did not take them long to gather their gear and board the boat. By noon, Hootie was dropping anchor near a group of islands east of *Isla Panaleros*. The area was the landward side of a long barrier island called *La Yegua* that protected the inner bays. There were no cuts or openings to the Gulf of Mexico until you got to *San José de Los Leones*, some fifty miles north. At *La Pesca,* Hootie had to decide to stay inland of the *La Yegua*, or outside on the Gulf side. Hootie chose to search on the inside, protected loch. If the crocodile came south from its last known location at *Laguna Madre y Delta del Rio Bravo*, it would keep inside the barrier islands. Hootie counted on the crocodile favoring the slower, less turbulent waters of the lagoon. As the map depicted, there was no place to cross over to the ocean below *Los Leones*.

Jake and Katie launched one jet ski, and Jesse and Rita took the other one. Hootie killed the engine on *Miss Katie*, set the anchor, and pushed off in the light skiff. The water was calm behind the protective island, and the breeze was low, keeping the water surface smooth. Hootie looked out on a blue paradise of sea and sky. The only sign of human life was a fishing boat nearly a mile to the south. He cranked the motor on the runabout to life and steered in the direction the Jake had taken.

Tom was sitting on the veranda when he noticed *Miss Katie* preparing to leave. Mark was feeling much better after a restful night and was now eating a breakfast taco stuffed with egg and bacon. The redness in his welts was starting to heal, and his skin tone began to return to normal. His diarrhea was also finally gone.

"Okay, Mark. Game on! We've got to go!"

"I'm not finished with my breakfast yet," Mark complained.

"Take it with you – we've got to shove off; *Miss Katie* is on the move!" Tom ordered.

It surprised Tom that Mark did not continue to argue. He stuffed his breakfast taco back in the wrapper, pulled on his shorts, and followed Tom to the dock. Tom fired the engine while Mark untied the boat from the pier, as *Miss Katie* was passing the hotel dock. Tom waited until the larger boat was a half-mile ahead before he pulled into the Rio. At the end of the lagoon, they would either cross into the Gulf, go south toward Tampico, or turn up the inside passage.

After turning north, Tom soon lost sight of *Miss Katie*, but it did not matter much. The group had no place else to go for the next fifty miles, without turning back. If they came back, Tom would be sure to see them. If they pulled over to anchor off the barrier island, Tom might not see them in time to get out of sight. So he maintained a northward course until he caught sight of them again. *Miss Katie* lay anchored close to one of the endless mazes of sandbars dotting the inside lagoon. Tom would stay as far away as possible to remain beyond recognition of anyone who might be watching.

If they found the crocodile, Tom would be able to tell. He planned to rush in with his little boat and disrupt any attempt to destroy the animal. Likely, they had no more idea of where the crocodile was than he did. Still, to be safe, he would keep the group in sight until he figured out what to do. Tom anchored across the narrow waterway, taking precautions to point his bow toward *Miss Katie*.

It was time to go fishing – or at least appear to be fishing.

Tom allowed Mark to stay beneath the fiberglass awning as he arranged the empty bait buckets and placed a fishing pole at each position. Mark sat in the shade and watched Tom position each fishing pole in a precise arrangement. The sun was beginning to bake the boat deck so that walking without shoes was out of the question. After a few minutes in that sun, everything exposed would be searing hot.

Mark wiped sweat away from his face, as he watched Tom fiddle with the fishing rods. After Tom made the rounds on both sides of the boat to check that the rods were secure, he sat on the bench next to Mark. He took off his hat and used it to dry his head.

"That's it, then?" Mark asked.

"It, what?"

"You aren't going to catch many fish that way. You didn't even throw out the lines or put bait on the hooks," Mark said, exasperated.

"You just don't get it, do you, Mark?"

"Yes! I get it. Fish like to eat. Put bait on hook. Throw out line. Fish eat bait. Catch fish on hook. Pull in fish. We eat fish, and repeat."

Tom felt his ears grow hot. He looked at Mark and felt the urge rise within him to haul off and slap the kid. However, Mark had been through so much the last day and a half. Tom decided to cut him some slack.

"See that boat way out there?" Tom asked instead, trying to stay as patient as possible.

"Where?" Mark looked 180 degrees north and south.

"There," Tom pointed.

Mark scrunched up his eyes and peered into the distance in the direction of the finger.

"I don't see nothin'."

"Go get the glasses by the wheel and come back," Tom urged the boy.

Mark went into the wheelhouse. Tom could hear him rummaging around inside the little cabin. While waiting, Tom flipped through an old copy of a magazine someone had left behind.

"Come on back out here, Mark," Tom called, after a few minutes.

"I can't find them," Mark yelled from inside the wheelhouse.

Frustrated, Tom rose from his bench and threw the magazine in disgust. He walked to the door of the wheelhouse and pointed next to the wheel – the binoculars sat in plain sight.

"What are these?" Tom nodded toward the binoculars sitting beside the wheel.

Mark slanted his head along the focus of Tom's stare. "Binoculars?" Mark said as if he were not sure.

"Isn't that what I sent you after?" Tom asked.

"No, I was looking for your *glasses*," he shook his head, not understanding.

Tom slapped his own forehead and pulled his hand down across his face.

"Bring those *binoculars* and come back on deck," he ordered. Returning to his seat on the bench, he wondered how the boy had enough sense to survive.

When Mark sat down, he said, "I thought you meant your reading glasses; like all you old dudes use to read."

A shiver ran down Tom's spine. The urge to slap Mark arose again but, instead, he pointed out the boat ahead.

"It's there – against that little green island. See it?"

"Oh, yeah! There is a boat out there," he exclaimed.

"That, my young friend, is *Miss Katie*."

163

"How do you know? It's so far away."

"From the shape and the color of her," Tom told him. "Memorize her because we are going to be following that boat for a few days – probably as long as we are out here. Before you ask, we don't get closer because we don't want them to know we are following them. Yes, if we can see them, they can see us. That is why we pointed our boat directly at them. We only want it to look like we are fishing," Tom explained, attempting to stay as calm as possible. "If their boat moves, we will also move, trying to stay as far away as possible while keeping them in sight."

Mark nodded at each point as if he understood.

"Your job, Mark, is to keep an eye on that boat; and if it moves, to tell me right away."

After Tom assured him that surveillance of *Miss Katie* was his only task, Mark wised off with a sharp, "Aye-aye, sir!"

Tom went back into the wheelhouse, shaking his head as he popped the top from a lukewarm Dos Equis.

"I'm going to need a lot of these," he mumbled to himself.

After moving the *Miss Katie* several times that afternoon, the day was ending. The setting sun was turning the sky the color of plum marmalade. All hands were aboard, preparing to return to La Pesca. It was Jesse's watch. Just before Hootie gave Jesse the order to go, he noticed something out of place.

"Jesse, can you see that boat over there?"

"That fishing boat? Sure," Jesse nodded toward the boat in the distance.

"Have you noticed that it's been around all day?"

"Yeah," Jesse agreed, "I remember seeing it this morning. I think it is just a fishing charter."

"Have you noticed that every time we move – they move?" Hootie asked.

"Come to think of it, you're right. Maybe they think we know where the fish are."

"Maybe," Hootie agreed. "I wonder why they never get very close. Let's wait for it to get fully dark before we head back to La Pesca. It will only be about thirty minutes now. I want to try to get close enough to see who they are."

The rosy sky turned violet-purple as the sun sank and the stars began to pop out of the deep heavenly blue. In the distance, Hootie could see the navigational lights of the suspicious boat shining red and green on the horizon. "Go ahead below and get something to eat," Hootie told Jesse. "I'll take her now."

Once Jesse was gone, Hootie raised the anchor and started the engines. Turning north, he crawled ahead until he was sure the boat in the distance was following. Hootie was positive now that the fishing boat was tailing them. But, why? Were they a lookout for the drug runners or the pirates planning to hijack them at the first opportunity? Were they Mexican police watching them for illegal activity?

Hootie took a sharp turn to starboard and ran a short distance. Ensuring that nothing stood between him and the island, Hootie switched off his running lights. It was a violation of navigation law, but Hootie was desperate. From a distance, it would look like he had gone behind a small island. Hootie took another sharp turn to starboard and struck a direct course toward the navigational lights of the small fishing boat. If they were the Mexican police, Hootie would be in big trouble. If they were anyone else, Hootie planned to sneak past and return to La Pesca.

Hootie opened the fake radio box and stuck the .45 into his waistband.

"Let's see what you are up to, mister."

CHAPTER 24

In that time of day between the setting sun and falling darkness, sounds amplify in the dewy-laden air. Things ignored in the light of day become magnified and ominous on the breeze. Insects rub their legs in raspy tenor chirps, frogs sing bass, and the leaves and stalks of various plants rustle in rhythm with the wind. It is three-part harmony in an orchestra of organic originality.

Like wispy curls of gray smoke softer than feathers, evening fog swirled on the surface of the opaque water. As the minutes passed, the fog thickened and grew in intensity, lifting from the water like spirits rising from the grave.

The sound of the surf on the other side of the barrier island rolled in as the incoming tide broke and hissed on the shore like cymbals adding to the symphony of the night.

"I think he's moving," Mark shouted as he peered through the growing gloom.

Tom emerged from the wheelhouse, glasses in hand, and focused on the distant boat.

"Yeah," he agreed. "*Miss Katie* is on the move."

Tom laid down the binoculars and went back inside to start the engine.

"He's probably ready to head back in," he speculated aloud. "We'll need to move aside and stay out of sight. Once he passes, we'll go back to La Pesca keeping a safe distance behind him."

Mark squinted into the dimness as he stood on tiptoes trying to get a better look.

"Professor! He's not moving toward us – he's moving off to the side," Mark called.

"What?" Tom yelled. "What do you mean?"

"He's moving to the right!"

"Our right – or his right?" Tom called.

Mark looked at both of his hands.

"Our right," he hollered.

Tom stuck his head out of the window and shouted, "It's an illusion, Mark. Light, playing on the water and the fog, is messing with your perception."

"I don't think so, Professor. He's moving across us – not at us. You better come take a look!"

Irritated at the interruption while busy hauling in the anchor, Tom stomped out onto the foredeck and picked up the glasses.

The fog was increasing rapidly, but Tom could tell instantly that the kid was right. *Miss Katie* was moving toward the east.

"What are they doing?" Tom asked himself, not realizing he was speaking aloud. "She can't get out that way – the cut is at least twenty miles north of here."

Tom could not believe his eyes. There was no good reason for the boat to move in that direction. Home was due south – directly past them – not east across a spit of sand.

"Keep an eye on her," Tom said. "I'm going to try to get in closer to see what they are up to."

Before he could put the boat in motion, Mark was calling for him again.

"Professor! She's disappeared!"

"That can't be," Tom screamed back at him. He stuck his head and shoulders out the window and peered ahead. He scanned the water for the distant boat's red and green navigational lights only to see nothing but darkness. The fog was beginning to shroud the night, but those navigational lights should still be visible at this distance.

"Maybe they went behind an island," Mark suggested.

"No. There is no island between us." Tom scratched his head and tried to think.

"They went through a cut, then," Mark offered.

"There's no cut there!" Tom assured him once again.

"Well, he's making one, then – because he is gone!"

Tom searched his mind, trying to find an explanation that made sense. What could be the cause of such peculiar behavior?

"He hasn't disappeared," Tom decided. "We just can't see him. He's cut his lights off."

"He can't do that," Mark objected. "It's against the law – even I know that! Why would he do that?"

"He spotted us, and he doesn't know who we are. He will either sneak up on us to find out who we are or try to slip past us in the fog. He's probably fixed his course on our position so he can run in the dark, and he's headed directly at us."

Tom realized his cover as a fishing charter was blown. He knew he had not been acting like a fishing charter or a party boat – neither of which would have been way out here in this foggy night. *Miss Katie* probably thought he was a pirate or a drug runner – neither of which they would want to come upon in the night.

"He's got a bead on us," Tom called to Mark. "He's headed right for us, trying to see what he's up against."

Tom pulled the AK-47 out from beneath the seat and pulled back the handle, charging the weapon. He did not think *Miss Katie* was armed, but he was not going to be flat-footed.

Even if *Miss Katie* had all her lights on, she would have been difficult to see in the enveloping fog. Tom could barely see the shoreline five hundred yards away. The visibility was getting worse by the minute.

He is definitely headed right toward us, Tom thought. He is trying to get a visual on us before wheeling off a few degrees to pass. Well, two can play that game. Tom thumbed the toggle switch on the dashboard and shut off his navigational lights. He has a fix on our location. We had better not be sitting here when he comes whistling by. Tom turned east to move closer toward the shallows along the shore to clear the way for the unseen, approaching vessel.

"What are you doing, Professor?" Mark called.

"Getting out of her way," Tom shouted, as he pushed the throttle up and steered toward the edge of the invisible barrier island he knew was there.

"So you want to play a little cat and mouse?" he asked the distant boat. "I'll be the cat," he chuckled to himself.

An impenetrable wall of fog was rolling in from the Gulf of Mexico. Hootie turned on his wipers, but all that accomplished was to smear his windshield even more. He throttled-down and went outside with some glass cleaner and a sponge. It took several minutes to clean the glass in front of the cockpit, but soon the smudges were gone. He should be able to see a little better now.

He looked out into the misty night as the fog curled like smoke across the inky black water. The fog was so thick that wisps of it could obscure the lights of a distant fishing boat. Hootie suddenly remembered he was running without lights, so he returned to the cockpit and took control of the wheel.

By now, the weather was disintegrating so quickly Hootie could not even see the distant boat's navigational lights. This fog was going to be a thick one, he decided. He reckoned that he must still be two thousand feet away from the smaller boat in the distance. He had not changed course, so she must be dead ahead.

In this dense fog, it was going to be almost impossible to identify who had been following him all day. Hootie decided not to risk getting too close. If the smaller boat drifted even a few feet, he could be on a collision course. Hootie did not want to run into that boat. If he were to become disabled, he would not be able to get away from whomever it might be – good guys or bad guys.

The fog was good for one thing though; it gave ample cover to slip past silently in the fog bank. Hootie dropped the throttle another two notches so that they were barely making any headway at all. At that slower speed, Hootie knew his boat would be much quieter. He figured the other crew would hear them; but with Hootie's lights out, it would be difficult to determine precisely where he was. They might turn on their big floodlights if they had them, but Hootie knew that in this fog, the floodlights were more likely to bounce back toward them than to reveal his precise position.

With this in mind, Hootie altered course five degrees to port. At two thousand yards and with his present speed, Hootie calculated that would take him some five hundred feet to the east of them. She had been standing about a thousand yards off the barrier island, so he should end up about halfway between the mysterious boat and the shoreline. There should be plenty of water to sneak past and return to La Pesca.

Hootie turned on his GPS and navigated by the dark blue and green light. He could tell from the small screen that he would have plenty of room to pass. At the rate he was going, he would be able to stop and back up if he encountered unexpected shallow water. Hootie remembered he had hugged that same barrier island this morning at a distance of fifty feet and still had water. With the tide rolling in, Hootie did not expect to drag bottom.

Hootie decided he had at least five minutes before he sailed between the mystery boat and the island, so he flicked on autopilot and went below.

Immediately, Jake asked, "What's going on? Why are we going so slow?"

Hootie got everyone's attention and calmly made his announcement.

"Someone – I don't know who – has been spying on us today. It could be the Mexican police, or it could be bad people. I can't tell. It's so thick out there that I'm sure they can't see us either. What we are going to do is try to slip past them and get back to La Pesca as quick as we can. I need your help."

"What do you want us to do?" Katie asked.

Hootie raised his hand above his head and leaned against the bulkhead by the doorway, not realizing the butt of the .45 was showing above his waistband.

"Douse all the lights – everything. We'll quietly sit until we get past, and things will be okay. I'm going as slow as we can to cut the engine noise; but once we get past them, we'll open her up and get out of here."

"Expecting trouble?" Jake asked, pointing at the weapon.

Hootie looked down and pulled his t-shirt over the gun.

"Sorry," he said. "No – let's hope not. I just thought it would be safer if we had some way to defend ourselves. I've got to get back up to the wheel. Meanwhile, you guys put out all the lights you can and stay as quiet as possible. Once you hear me rev up the engines, you'll know the danger is past."

He pointed a finger directly at Jake.

"Jake, if we come to a dead stop, then there is going to be plenty of trouble. Put the girls in one of the cabins and try to hide them both as well as you can. You guys may have to fight them off if it's the bad guys."

"What if it's the good guys?" Jake asked.

"Then we are probably going to jail," Hootie answered, "but at least they won't murder us – I hope…"

Back at the wheel, Hootie calculated he was only five hundred yards from where he needed to be to pass the unseen boat. He peered deeply into the darkness and gloom. *Why can't I see them?* He wondered to himself. The GPS had not updated his last position so he could not tell for sure where he lay. The fog did not seem that thick – but it was hard to judge. Somewhere out there to his right, the little fishing boat stood at anchor – that is, unless they moved. If they moved, Hootie would have no idea where they were.

Hootie thought if he were driving that mysterious boat, he would head back to the nearest port or maybe go to one of the hidden coves nearby. He would not leave his boat sticking out in the passageway at night with no lights. That was probably why he could not see them – they had tucked themselves in a small cove for the night. There were not many places to dock, so Hootie guessed they would head due south back to La Pesca. If they were police, they were more than likely out of the port at La Pesca. If they were bandits, they would go to whatever hideout they had around the lagoon.

Hootie peered through the swirling fog, afraid to shine a light for fear of revealing his position. He placed his hand upon the vibrating dashboard and strained to see. Behind him, heat lightning illuminated the sky over the Gulf but did nothing to help light the way before him. Hootie could see nothing but fog and a light mist in the vapor.

Without warning, a dark shape appeared directly ahead in the darkness. *What was that?* Was it a shadow or a cloud? Hootie strained to see. Suddenly, Hootie broke out in a cold sweat as his heart thumped in his chest.

They moved!

The fishing boat had cut its lights off and now sat only thirty yards directly ahead of his bow! Hootie spun the wheel as hard as he could to turn right to avoid a collision. Hootie's larger boat loomed over the smaller craft, which was now slipping beneath his bow. *Miss Katie* blocked

Hootie's vision. Hootie turned full right, but the smaller vessel remained beneath *Miss Katie's* bow. Hootie did not even have time to tell his passengers to get a grip.

Hootie pulled the rope on his air horn, hoping the smaller craft might be underway and could avoid an impact. Hootie grabbed a rail and held his breath. Nothing more could be done. *Why were their lights off?*

Slowly, at a crawl, *Miss Katie* began to respond to the turn. Hootie could see only the top of the fishing boat now. A low toned scraping sound, like fingernails on a chalkboard, began just to the port side of his bow, and the yacht trembled as a grinding, crunching sound filled the air as they scraped down the hull of the small fishing boat.

CHAPTER 25

Tom pulled as close to the shoreline as he dared; he did not want to become stuck in the muck again. He turned back toward the north in hopes of getting a glimpse of *Miss Katie* as she passed, if possible. He could hear the faint hum of the engine in the distance. It was difficult to determine the direction of noises in the dark fog bank. He knew sound carried better across the water than on land. From the hum of her, he guessed she was still a few hundred yards away.

Miss Katie would pass off his port side – there was no way she could get around his right without running aground. Tom toyed with the idea of lighting his vessel again but decided to stay in the dark and wait it out. If he did not have to reveal his location, *Miss Katie* might pass without seeing them. It would make getting back to La Pesca unobserved that much easier. Even so, Tom knew that a boat the size of *Miss Katie* would likely have radar and know precisely where he was lying. Even if not, Tom did not think they would come so close to the shallows around an island.

A boat that large, running without lights at night, was a considerable risk. With nothing to guide her, except what her pilot could see, the ship was dangerous. Only a fool or a desperate man would even attempt to run at night without lights. Tom did not know Hootie, but the man was not a fool. He wanted to avoid contact with *Miss Katie*, but not at the price of being run over by the larger vessel. Tom expected her to pass between his current location and his previous position – somewhere about 500 yards to the west of where he lay. The noise of the engine grew louder with each passing minute and spread across the water in the misty darkness beneath a cloaking fog. Lightning lit the eastern sky out in the Gulf. The sound of the invisible boat grew louder and closer.

The distant storm crept around to the north. The wind shifted, now coming across the barrier island from the open gulf. Lightning, diffused by the low-lying fog, put on an incredible show. The sky ignited through the clouds in a fantastic display of silver light and dark patches. During one long sheet of lightning, Tom noticed that the fog bank seemed to break off in a curved, smooth line like the outline of an enormous boat. Tom stared ahead, as a cloud of fog swirled and opened a hole in the wet wall. From out of the swirling mist, the bow of *Miss Katie* appeared monstrous above him.

The only thing Tom had time to do was scream for Mark to grab hold of something. The more massive ship loomed from the fog right on top of them! Tom grabbed a nearby post and hung on for dear life as a horrible screech of clashing boats pierced the shrouded night.

When the horrible scraping stopped, Hootie jammed the throttle up as far as it would go and sped away into the night. He threw on every light to help guide the way. He mentally kicked himself for running at night without lights and markers.

Hootie had no idea who he had rammed. Under normal conditions, he would have stopped and rendered aid. Mexican police would have flagged him down and arrested everyone on board by now. He was also sure they were not a fishing-party boat. If the mystery boat was not the police, then that left two ominous alternatives – both deadly. They were either pirates or drug runners – neither of which he wanted to deal with on the water in the middle of the night. Luckily, they had not opened fire, and they did not seem in pursuit. He checked his gauges and saw nothing to concern him about the condition of his boat. He decided to get back to La Pesca as soon as possible.

Motion from the corner of his eye grabbed his attention, and he jerked the .45 from his waistband. Seeing it was Jake, Hootie placed the gun on the table in front of him as he steered the boat.

"What was that?" Jake asked wide-eyed.

"We almost collided with that boat," Hootie admitted. "She didn't have any lights on, and she changed her position from the last time we saw her."

"We didn't have lights on either," Jake reminded him.

Hootie did not bother arguing with the obvious.

"Jake, I need you to go below and check to see if we are taking on water on the port side. We need to get back to the house at La Pesca as soon as we can; but if we are taking on water, we may not make it. Please go now. We can talk about this later."

"I'm on it," Jake agreed, aware of the seriousness of the situation.

Once Jake had left the cockpit, Hootie wiped sweat from his face. He prayed that everyone on the other boat was safe. He checked his rear-view mirror and saw no lights coming from behind. It was a good sign. He knew swift boats that could outrun any police boat, often ran interference for drug runners. If they had one of those, Hootie was sure they would be attacking them by now, intent on killing them all. He stuffed the .45 back into his waistband and increased his speed as he guided the boat toward La Pesca and safety.

The fishing boat rocked in the wake left behind by *Miss Katie*. She had already disappeared behind the curtain of fog. Tom fought to regain his balance on the pitching, slippery deck.

He called out to Mark: "You okay?" There was no response. "**Mark!** Are you okay?"

"Yeah," came the surly answer. "Man, you almost got us killed!"

Tom ignored the complaint and began checking the seaworthiness of their fishing boat. They did not seem to be taking on water. Tom was thankful he had not set the anchor. Unmoored, the wooden vessel was able to bounce away from the impact, reducing the damage. However, the fishing boat was so close to shore it could not move away far enough to avoid being damaged. Tom marveled at how close they came to being crushed like a beer can. Mark was right. It was a foolish thing to do —

sitting in the dark without lights or warning devices. A few more inches and the larger boat would have crushed them to death.

Tom switched on the entire bank of lights. The refracted light bounced and rippled on the face of the choppy dark water. An unseen hand smoothed the water as the wake dissipated and the surface calmed. There was no longer any sight or sound of the larger craft.

A deep gouge ran down the entire port side rail where *Miss Katie* has sideswiped them. The joints were still holding, and the seams appeared intact. Tom could see no damage below the protruding rail that ran all the way around the boat. The impact had splintered the railing in places but had not pierced the hull. The sides from the bulkhead to the waterline seemed secure. Tom checked the bilge and was satisfied they were not taking on water. It was a narrow escape.

"Well, we're not going to sink," he told Mark, who was busy stuffing loose gear into the cupboards and cabinets.

"Glad to hear that," Mark called over a pile of life jackets in his arms. "Guess we won't need these." He threw a caustic "yet" onto the end of his comment.

Tom ignored the jab and swung the wheel as far left as he could and then spun it back to the right. The tiller moved without obstruction. Satisfied that the boat was steerable, he hit the switch and fired the motor. She caught on the first try. The glowing gauges and dials showed the mechanical parts of the boat were working well.

Tom shifted the boat into gear and made a sweeping turn to take them back toward La Pesca. The damage was not too severe, he calculated. A sanding down, some wood filler and a little bit of paint and the boat would be as good as new. Well, not as good as new; but better than it was when they rented it. He doubted that José Baca would care once he replaced the rail and had it painted. Of course, he would want more money.

On the long trip back to their hotel, Tom thought about his plan to get a photograph of the giant crocodile. He had no idea where the animal was. Tom knew he was in over his head. His vessel was too small, he did not have the equipment he needed, and he had an untrained assistant – not to mention his own incompetence as a sailor. Tom realized he had almost gotten them both killed. What would happen when they met a giant crocodile? They had survived sea lice, knee-deep mud, massive anacondas, and now, a near-miss boat wreck.

In addition to that, he still had no idea where Aquasaurus was. His only plan, to trail *Miss Katie* until they found the crocodile, had almost ended in tragedy. Who knows what would happen next?

Tom decided that if things did not improve in the next few days, he would return José Baca's boat and go home with Mark. He needed a lucky break. He was sure Mark would have no objection to going back. Without a photograph, *Discovery Magazine* would have to wait for the DNA results. If those DNA results would just come in early, none of this would turn out to be necessary.

Because of the weather and poor visibility, Tom relied on the GPS as he steered the boat all the way up the lagoon to La Pesca. They floated in a sea of mist stretching from horizon to horizon. There were no visual clues of their whereabouts, nor sign of any other living soul nearby. As Tom guided the little boat back to the hotel, Mark slept on a wooden bench with an orange life vest for a pillow. Asleep, without the wiseacre comments, Mark looked calm and vulnerable. Tom knew he had almost killed the lad. He pulled a blanket from the wheelhouse and spread it across the sleeping youth.

CHAPTER 26

In the light of day, Hootie could see *Miss Katie* was not as damaged as he had feared. A long, deep scratch ran down the port side about three feet above the water line. The accident had not punctured the hull, so she only needed some fill, a good sanding, and a little paint. He found an electric sander in the boathouse, along with paint in a rusty can that was the same color as the boat.

Thankful the scratch ran down the port side, Hootie realized he could work from the dock. He tied on extra bumpers to keep the floating boat from pinching his hands against the pier as he inspected the entire length of the abrasion. He decided he would go up to the house for a cup of coffee so he could tell Katie what he was going to do to her boat.

Inside the house, the group was quiet and subdued. Hootie sat at the table, as Katie brought him a plate from the kitchen – scrambled eggs, bacon, toast, and coffee. She sat in a chair next to him.

"Is it bad?" she asked.

"No, not really – it sounded a lot worse than it was. I should have it fixed by this afternoon. I apologize, Katie; the accident was my fault – I screwed up."

"What about the other boat?"

Hootie took a sip of coffee and admitted with a shake of his head, "Don't know. I'm sure we didn't sink them. They may have suffered a little damage, like us, but we were going very slowly. If they didn't set their anchor, they likely bounced off, limiting the damage."

"Do you think anyone got hurt?" she wondered.

"I don't know that either, Katie. I don't think so. We didn't know who they were. If we had stopped, they might have attacked and killed us all. I don't know what they were doing, but I am positive they weren't a fishing party – or the police. They were either pirates or drug runners. I'm hoping for pirates," he said, trying to smile.

"Why pirates?"

"Because drug runners get even," Hootie told her.

"Listen," she confided in a quiet voice, "we got a lot more than we bargained for here. It was a dumb idea to come down here, I guess. Maybe we should go home before someone gets seriously hurt."

"We can do that," Hootie agreed. "If that's what you want, I'll fix the boat, and we can head for home tomorrow."

"Thanks, Hootie. Don't you agree that would be for the best?" She squinted into the light reflecting from the patio window. The morning sun shining through her blonde hair carried Hootie back to a memory of Alice. Hootie stuffed the memory back in his mind, as he always did.

"The boat wreck took the fun out of it," Katie continued. "We can only dodge pirates and drug runners for so long. What happens when they catch us?"

"It could be pretty bad," Hootie admitted. "We had a hard enough time with the customs people on the boat." He decided not to elaborate further. "I'll fix the boat today, and we can sail home tomorrow or the next day."

While Katie announced the new plan the other three, Hootie went back to his boat repairs. He plugged the sander into a long extension cord and reeled the line out down the length of the dock. He switched on the sander and was satisfied that it worked.

Before long, he had smoothed the surface of the hull more than halfway down the scrape. He heard the group coming down the path toward the docks.

"How's it going?" Katie asked.

"Good," Hootie nodded. He showed her the length of the scratch while the others launched the wave runners. "I'll be ready to paint in an hour or so. When I finish, you'll never know it was scratched."

Katie smiled, "We're going out on the jet skis to explore the back bays around here. We'll be back before dark. Are you going to need any help?"

"No, I'll be fine. Y'all go have some fun, and I'll see you back here around dark-thirty."

Hootie watched as they roared off into the sunny bay. Within the hour, he had finished sanding the boat. Returning to the boathouse, he picked up the paint can. It seemed heavy enough; about half a gallon should do. Prying the lid from the rusty can, he found the paint dried and solidified in the bottom. There was nothing left to do but fire up the boat and go across the bay to buy a new can.

At mid-morning, Mark was still sound asleep in his bed at the hotel. Tom woke early but did see a need to disturb the boy. Let him sleep. Tom left a note and took the fishing boat over to one of the many mom-and-pop boat repair facilities along the stretch of the Rio. Tom decided on one and pulled into the shipwright's dock. He needed to have the boat inspected and repaired right away. There was no telling when *Miss Katie* and her team would decide to go back out. Tom still planned to tail them and to disrupt their plans to destroy Aquasaurus if he could.

He tied off at what seemed the largest repair facility near the hotel. Luckily, the boat master spoke English and Tom was able to communicate with him about what he needed. The carpenter could see that the collision split the upper rail and almost ripped it off in several places. There was no damage to the hull. The boatman did a quick inspection and quoted Tom a price.

"When can you have it finished?" Tom asked.

"Oh, …" the boat master stalled, "Mebbe, three weeks, I think."

"No, no, no, no," Tom stressed. "I need it fixed quicker than that!"

"How much quicker, señor?"

"Today! Tomorrow at the latest."

"*Imposible*, señor," the boatman shook his head. He spread his arms wide to encompass the entire boatyard. "I have all these others before you."

"Do you have the materials to do the job on hand, or do you have to order?"

"Si, señor. I have the wood for the new railing, but I must cut and use the papel de lija. Then there is the laca. It will take two days, at least, to dry."

"What if I lacquered it myself? Could you have it cut and installed by tomorrow morning?"

"But, señor, as I said, the others are waiting."

"Could I pay extra for express service?"

"Espress?"

"Yes, you know. Pay extra to go ahead of the others."

"Oh, ràpido! Si! Si! I understand now. You will pay more money to go ahead of los demás." The boat master sucked in his cheeks as he looked around the boatyard. "How much more do you pay?"

Tom looked at the boat master. He had been down this road before. The first one that names a price is the loser. "How much more will it cost?"

"Mucho, señor. Maybe as much again as I said before."

"Okay. Deal! You can have it finished by morning – early?"

"Si, señor. Mebbe, I can have it by this afternoon."

Tom knew then he was out-negotiated again, but he did not care. He needed that boat back as soon as possible. Tom looked up as another ship sailed into the receiving dock of the boatyard. He froze as he realized it was *Miss Katie*!

Tom finished his business, shook hands, and hurried toward the main gate out by the highway. He wanted to avoid whoever was on *Miss Katie*. If he could reach the cyclone fence and get through the gate on the road, he could call for a taxi – if there was one. It was not going to be that easy.

"Hey! You!" Tom heard from behind him. "Wait up! I need to talk to you!"

Tom pretended not to hear. About halfway to the gate, the stranger caught up on the run.

"Hey! Didn't you hear me?" Hootie pulled at Tom's elbow. "I need to talk to you."

Tom decided to go on the aggressive as he spun around. He knew it was Hootie, but Tom decided to play dumb for a little while.

"Who are you?" Tom barked. "What do you want?" Tom looked beyond the tall stranger to see if anyone else was with him. Any of the others would know Tom at a glance. He was glad that Hootie was alone.

Hootie sized him up, "Are you the guy that's been followin' me in that fishin' boat over there?"

Tom faced him. "Why? Are you the guy who almost ran me down last night – the idiot who almost sunk my boat? Was that you who almost killed us all?" Tom tried to make his voice as angry and as loud as possible.

Hootie was at a disadvantage. He knew he had violated all the rules of boating and felt guilty about causing the crash. "Yeah, that was us. Look, I'm sorry." Hootie held up his hand palms out. "You were lyin' there with no lights on – there was no way I could see you in that fog!"

"You might have if you had **your** lights on," Tom admonished. "You could have used your search light to clear the path ahead, but you didn't. You could have come back for us to see if we were okay, but you didn't. You could have done lots of things, but you didn't. You endangered the lives of our passengers and the safety of our boat. I should call the police now and report you!"

"Are you hurt? Was anyone aboard injured?" Hootie asked, filled with genuine concern and regret.

"No. We're fine, thank you," Tom said, with ice in his voice. "Why on God's green earth were you running without lights at night with the fog like that?"

"I'm sorry," Hootie repeated. He made his voice sincere and contrite. "I'll pay for your repairs. It was my fault. But, why have you been followin' us every time we go out?"

Tom decided to stay on the offensive, "Why were you running without lights?"

"Look," Hootie reasoned, "I didn't know who you were. You weren't acting like a fishing charter, that's for sure."

"I'm not a fishing charter."

"I was afraid you were either smugglers, pirates, or drug runners. You were blockin' our way back to La Pesca. I was trying to sneak past you in the fog. I've got young women on-board. You can understand that. Can't you?"

"You are lucky I wasn't the police," Tom huffed.

"No kidding! Like I said, I'll pay for your damages and your inconvenience. I admit it was my fault; we don't need the police. We can settle this between ourselves – don't you think?" Hootie stuck out his hand, "I'm Hootie Johnson."

"Tom Morrison," Tom mumbled and took the offered hand. "I guess I can see why you needed to avoid the bad guys. What are you doing down here anyway?"

"I've got some college kids down here for fishin' and water sports. They are doin' a lot of drinking, partying, and whooping it up," Hootie lied. "You know the deal. What about you, and why have you been following us?"

Tom realized Hootie did not know. Jake had kept his word and kept quiet.

"Following you? Why do you think we were following you? I'm a professional photographer out with my assistant on a rented boat. We're trying to get some nature shots for a travel magazine, that's all. We don't have time to be following you. That said, having a distant boat in the photograph is not bad, you know. It kind of shows perspective – at least, that's what my publisher says."

"Photographs," Hootie repeated. "Then why go to all the trouble of putting out fake fishing lines?"

"We wanted to use the boat in a sort of surface shot yesterday for a tourist ad. So we laid out some lines and paddled about a hundred yards away and shot it like that."

The story sounded believable enough, even if a bit odd. Hootie realized his own story might not stand scrutiny either.

"Yeah, well those kids I'm with have some strange ideas about havin' fun! Look. Now I know who you are, we won't be thinkin' you are the bad guys. Maybe we can watch out for each other."

"You know," Tom agreed, "it may be a good idea to stay fairly close together in case one of us needs help out there. Besides, there's some giant crocodile or something on the loose down here – a big one I heard."

"Yeah," Hootie agreed, "I keep hearing stories about that monster. They say he is huge! It might be good to stick close together; so long as we don't spoil your photography."

Tom nodded, "Mind if I shoot your boat in the distance if I need to?"

"I don't see why not."

"Sounds good," Tom admitted. "We'll see you out there then." Tom nodded, as he watched Hootie turn to walk back to the boatyard.

"I'll take care of that bill," Hootie shouted over his shoulder.

"Yeah, you do that, buddy," Tom mumbled to himself. A beat-up yellow taxi stopped across the dusty road from the gate and honked. "Watersports," Tom thought. "He probably doesn't believe my story any more than I believe his." Tom pulled the taxi door closed and sat back in the seat.

At the dock, Hootie turned back toward the road and watched as the taxi pulled away.

"Photographer, my eye," he thought. "I don't know who that guy is, but he is no photographer!"

Out on a back bay fifteen miles out of Rio Soto la Marina, Katie and Jake were making rooster tails. Rita and Jesse were taking things slower in the small runabout along the shore. Jesse was trying to convince Rita that he did not need the cane any longer. His leg was healing fine. Jesse was sure his leg would support his weight. He contemplated cutting off the lightweight cast himself.

Rita urged him to wait. "We're going back home tomorrow. You'll be able to see your doctor on Friday; why don't you wait and see what he says?"

"Yeah, I guess you're right," he admitted. Jake and Katie made another pass on the wave runner causing a wake that rocked the boat side to side. Jake passed so close he sprayed them with about fifty gallons of cold water.

"Show offs!" Katie yelled as they skied away.

The pair laughed as they dried each other with a towel. Jesse moved close to Rita and held her hand, as they watched Jake and Katie make circles and rooster tails in the distance.

"Wanna get married?" Jesse asked without warning.

Rita could not hide her surprise. Her mind raced as she tried to regain her composure. Sure, she figured she and Jesse would marry one day, but there was a lot to do. They had another year of college to go. Then, who knew what the job situation would be like then? His asking thrilled her, but she needed time to answer. It was so unexpected, and certainly not like Jesse!

She decided to stall. "That's hardly a proposal, Mr. Perrine!" she teased.

"That's hardly an answer, Miss Martin," Jesse responded, teasing back.

Rita jumped to her feet, "Oh, my God!" she screamed.

"That's more like it," Jesse grinned.

"Look! Katie fell off the wave runner!" Rita pointed. "Come on! We have to get over there!"

Jesse cranked the motor and put the boat in motion. They crossed the bay in a rush, gliding to a stop where they last saw the rooster tail. They began calling for Katie. Jake was already circling the small island coming back around. Somewhere in a mass of floating plants, Katie was struggling to stay afloat.

"Over here," came a faint call.

"Katie, are you okay?" Rita called.

Katie emerged from a thick maze of water plants and reeds, as she slogged in water up to her waist toward the runabout. "Damn you, Jake!" she yelled in disgust.

"I'll come around and pick you up," Jake hailed across the water.

187

"Don't bother," Katie shouted, as she battled her way through mud and thick vegetation. "The boat is closer! I'll ride back with Rita."

"Are you hurt?" Jake called as he came to a stop nearby.

"No! I'm okay – just mad!"

"I'm sorry!" Jake called.

"Don't even…" Katie threw up her hands, as she fell backward into thick muddy slime.

Gathering her feet beneath her, she stood in the muddy, murky mess. Her hair was a matted wad of mud and filthy water. With tentative steps, she waded toward the edge of the weeds where Rita and Jesse waited in the boat. It was clear that Katie was not injured. She was more mad than hurt. Jake was going to be in the doghouse tonight for sure.

As Katie neared the pick-up boat, she appeared to be pushing against something in the water. It seemed to be moving in the up and down motion of the water.

"There is something here," she shouted to Katie. "It feels like a heavy log or something. It stinks to high heaven! I can't push it out of the way, and I can't get around it!" They watched as Katie tugged and wrestled with the stubborn, slimy mass.

"I can't move it out of the way," she finally yelled. "It's stuck in this sea junk! I'm either going to have to climb over it or go under it!"

"Don't go under," Rita warned. "You don't know what's under there!"

"This thing stinks so bad I think I'm going to throw up!"

She and Jesse watched as Katie threw one leg over and hoisted her body up onto the floating mass. As Katie straddled the barrier, she began to wave her hands as the log rolled beneath her. She looked like a rodeo rider on a wild bronco. Something heavy rammed the mass next to Katie's leg and jolted the mass from the binding weeds. Katie waved her hands wildly and squealed as the log rolled over with her on it. Coming back to the surface, and standing waist deep in the putrid, nasty water, Katie slung her mud-soaked hair back out of her eyes and screamed in rage and frustration. Then, she looked down in horror and screamed even louder.

Two lifeless, unseeing eyes of a dead man stared up at the clear blue sky.

189

After several months in the open sunlight, it was becoming easier for Aquasaurus to see during the day. The brightness still stunned him at times. Sometimes, the bright sun was blinding. The discomfort was irritating. When it was too bad, the massive croc would lie on the silty bottom or climb halfway out of the water onto the muddy banks. There, half shaded and partially in the sun, the animal would lie soaking up the heat.

The crocodile stayed as close to shore as possible. It was most comfortable near the stream outlets and estuaries. The salt content was lower there than in the bay. Shrouded from view, it would linger in the sand for hours. Aquasaurus missed the cave in the aquifer and often searched for an opening to crawl inside. The cave had been a perfectly protected habitation. Because parts of the aquifer had been briny, the salty waters of the estuary were not a problem. The croc missed the cave but enjoyed having more space in which to roam. Instead of a dark and confining passageway, the expansive lagoons offered ample space, new experiences, and abundant food.

Traveling greater distances was more tiring, but a short rest brought new strength and vigor. After the cold and damp of the cave, the outside felt bright and warm. The crocodile adapted well. Here, the warmer waters invigorated and excited the creature. Stronger and healthier each day, Aquasaurus searched for others of its kind.

Food was abundant. There was a great quantity of fish; and along the shore, birds, turtles, and other creatures provided a steady source. There was no hunger now. It did not matter whether the catch was alive or dead, but the crocodile preferred live meat. The act of survival thrilled. The struggle for life as his massive jaws closed upon prey was exhilarating. The giant croc loved to roll and tumble in the water while subduing and drowning whatever wandered past the deadly jaws. The streamlined body and narrow head were perfect for building speed. A massive tail, whipped back and forth in the water, propelling the croc to incredible speeds – such speed as was only a dream in the cave where there was no room to maneuver.

Tucking huge webbed feet close to its sides permitted the croc to gain even higher speed. Speed was not necessary inside a cave. In open water, though, the rapid movement with as little noise as possible was a significant advantage. Then, coasting to a slow glide, letting momentum carry him forward among the weeds and rushes at the water's edge, with only snout and eyes above the water line, the massive animal would beach in the cool sand at the water's edge.

On land, the behemoth could run fast enough to catch most land mammals. Surprise and ambush were the tools that bagged larger prey like deer and hogs. The creature would kill even when not hungry. It would stash the kill in little holes dug along the bank, in a low-lying tree, or beside a decaying log lying at the water's edge. On land or in shallow water, huge webbed claws would dig deep into the mud and sand. In this way, it could launch great leaps unexpectedly. If rested, it would lift its entire body on short legs and walk along the shore for a short distance. This activity was tiring, and shade-speckled sunny spots beckoned as places to soak up the warmth and doze along the bank, its head resting in the shade. The water was calming as it lapped against the huge dappled body.

It was quiet and peaceful, with few noises to disturb the peace. Boats would pass, whipping up waves that often surged over the patterned, leather back. The rush of water only cooled the skin allowing it to bask longer and absorb more warmth. The cooling effect of the waves was temporary. It would lie with its mouth open in mid-day to release heat through the salt glands on its tongue. As an apex predator, no other creatures were a threat to its life or safety. Often, the crocodile would fall asleep in the sun, unaware of how much heat it had absorbed. Awakening and salivating with his sides heaving and struggling to catch its breath, the croc quickly submerged to cool down. Unable to extend its tongue, it was necessary to go back into the cooling water to regulate its body temperature.

Frequently, it would hear the sound of boats long before they came into sight. The noise the boats made was irritating, driving the croc to the bottom until all was quiet again. The increasing *putt-putt-putt* sound they made and the high-pitched buzzing grated and angered the beast. The croc became nervous and jittery. The sounds provided ample time to move into deeper water and submerge before the machines arrived. Shutting nostrils and the flap in its throat the croc could stay on the bottom for an hour or more, if necessary, while boats passed overhead on the surface. Once the noises faded away, Aquasaurus would resurface to continue the southward journey.

The crocodile preferred capturing larger mammals as opposed to the smaller aquatic fish and wildlife. They fight harder, which increased the thrill of the killing. A nocturnal hunter, the crocodile had great ability to see in low light, providing it a distinct advantage. The odor of rotting or decaying flesh spread for long distances in the water. Submerged, with the nostrils closed, few odors were detectable. However, on the surface, navigation toward the target with absolute precision was possible. It could track decaying carrion for great distances.

Aquasaurus had not encountered any species of its type. There were stray and often single caiman and small alligators along the way. However, no crocodilian seemed to exist in this part of the world. The steady movement southward was a result of both the environment and instinct to find others. As the geography of the area funneled toward the south, it would be useless to circle back. If there were others, they would be ahead, not behind.

The need to hunt was stronger than the need to eat. Months could go by without eating, if necessary. Often the kill, safely cached in easily accessible hiding places, would act as a lure for larger prey. The crocodile would often go days or weeks without hunting. Hunger was no longer a motivator. Other times, Aquasaurus would hunt and eat daily, rarely returning to cached meat because of the bounteous supply of fresh kill available. Some unconscious but irresistible instinct compelled the beast to keep baiting its caches with dead, rotting flesh. The massive crocodile did not think or plan but only reacted by instinct.

The tropical bay spread out and became broader and shallower. Small spits of sand, like islands, studded the sparkling bay. Vast slabs of dense sea plants that wound in thick wads covered most of those sand spits. The bay was a matrix of islands and sandbars. The crocodile glided, silent and undetectable, attracted by the scent of rotting flesh that filled its senses. Only eyes and snout protruded above the water. It lay for long moments, trying to locate the source of the decaying meat.

Smaller prey swam nearby, but the crocodile was not interested. It knew from the strength of the stench that a much larger prize was close. Being dead, whatever it was, would take less energy to capture.

The crocodile was an ambush killer. It preferred to lay in wait for unsuspecting animals to cross its path. Often it would lie on the muddy bottom of the water, mouth agape. Fish, turtles, and frogs would swim between jagged-toothed open jaws unmolested. Tiring of this waiting game, it would often turn away. Sometimes it would close its massive jaws and crawl aside to avoid taking the small prey.

Today, in this open waterway, the stench of a rotting corpse was luring the crocodile forward. Although the crocodile was not hungry, the odor of carrion drew it like a magnet. The beast had other uses for a rotting corpse. Steaming through the water using only its tail, the animal followed the scent. If it found the source, the crocodile would try to secure the meat in a safe place secure from other predators. Rolling it in weeds and mud, Aquasaurus would use the horrible corpse as an enticement to lure fresher prey. The cache would be bound securely to ensure that other predators would not carry it away.

Aquasaurus soon found the floating body of a dead human in the shallow waters. The croc swam in circles around the motionless, stinking body. Nearby was a small island of floating vegetation. Nosing the carcass forward, the crocodile jammed the corpse into the mass of weeds and plants and flipped it several times among the water plants. The long tangled ropes of water plants bound the body into a tight bundle. The crocodile jammed the grisly package even deeper into the mud and silt of the shallow basin.

193

Keeping an eye on the prize, the crocodile moved away a few feet and sank below the surface. Swimming along the floor of the lagoon, Aquasaurus wove in and out of long stems of floating plants. It surfaced on the other side of the island of weeds and waited, trusting the power of the luring, rotting meat. Before much longer, something of a larger size would come to investigate. When that happened, the crocodile would have fresh meat as well as the dead bait.

The horrible, irritating buzzing sound came again. Unsettled by the noise, the crocodile surfaced and searched for the offending intruder. Only eyes and nostrils showed above the water as it waited for the noises to abate. However, instead of fading away as before, the buzzes grew louder and closer. Now the crocodile could feel the vibrations in the water. The droning interfered with its ability to locate objects nearby, confusing and confounding the crocodile.

The behemoth sank again to the bottom and waited. Several times, the horrifying whine passed right above the croc. Before the crocodile could rise to the surface and attack, the buzzing moved on. Instead of fading away, the racket would resume, making circles around and around, repeatedly. The crocodile had learned the pattern now. It crouched, preparing to leap and rise from the water in a snapping, toothy attack intended to end the nuisance.

Without warning, a large splash disturbed the water behind the agitated crocodile. Something substantial and alive began to move in the water. The prey had arrived. Aquasaurus turned toward the swimming creature. It peered through blurry eyes into the dark and murky water. Something was swimming and hopping among the weeds near the corpse bait. Whatever it was, the intruder walked on two pale, thin legs, bounding and leaping as it fought to pass through the tangling mass of reeds.

The crocodile watched the sallow creature move toward the fleshy, morbid lure. The intruder was taking the bait. The crocodile slipped underwater, snapping at the vines and weeds blocking the target. The mat of vegetation that separated it from the creature was thick and unyielding. Before the crocodile could seize the intruder, the legs drew back up and disappeared.

The intruder was taking the bait!!! One pale leg was dangling in the water. Aquasaurus lunged as the leg rose out of sight above the water line. His snout stuck the entangled mass with a thump, breaking it loose from the confining weeds. The angry crocodile moved backward from the stinking mass of entangling weeds. Ready to snatch anything that tried to escape, it circled back around the other side of the matt of plants.

There! A high-pitched screaming replaced the *putt-putt-putt* sound and the buzzing. Then, he could see the legs again vaulting through the water on the other side of the carcass. Now was the time to strike! With a mighty sweep of its tail, the crocodile lunged forward to grasp the churning legs. Without warning, the legs once again pulled up and disappeared above the water surface. Circling back, the crocodile ensured that the corpse was still there and sank beneath the weeds waiting for another opportunity.

The loud buzzing noises began again, this time moving away. Sinking to the bottom, the massive crocodile closed its eyes as the noisy buzzing faded into the distance. At last, now all was silent; and the crocodile slept.

CHAPTER 28

Hootie stepped back to inspect his handiwork. He knew he would never be a painter, but the job was not bad. The long, deep scratch was almost undetectable. He was putting the final touches on *Miss Katie* as the jet skis roared back to the dock. Hootie noticed that Katie was in the boat now instead of on the jet ski behind Jake. As soon as they reached the docks, she ran headlong up the walkway to the house. The others mobbed Hootie all at once.

"We found a dead body!" Rita squealed. "It was horrible and nasty."

"It was in the water – stuck in the weeds on a small island," Jesse added.

"Did you call the police?" Hootie questioned.

"No. We hurried back here to tell you," Jesse croaked.

"Okay. You two," Hootie pointed to Jesse and Rita, "hoist the jet skis back onto the boat. Jake, you check on Katie and phone the police. Have them meet us here at the house. Then you can lead us back to where you found the body. How far away is it?"

"About fifteen miles north of here," Jesse volunteered.

"I'll get the boat ready." Hootie climbed onboard and began to stow equipment in preparation to launch.

By the time they were ready, they could hear the sirens of the police boat echo across the Rio. The police boat tied up alongside their dock, and three police officers climbed out.

After scribbling some quick notes, the officer in charge, a Sergeant, asked questions. "Where is this body, Señor?"

Hootie nodded for Jesse to reply. "It's about fifteen miles north of here, near a little sand island almost covered with seaweeds and vines."

"You will take me there, of course. Who discovered the body?"

"Our friend, Katie," Jesse pointed up the path. "Here she comes now."

Katie, freshly showered but looking pale and sick to her stomach approached with Jake at her side. Jake reached to take her hand, but she snatched it away giving him a dirty look.

"*Señorita*," the police officer began, "you are the one that found the body? Are you sure it was dead?"

"Yes, I am absolutely sure." Katie shuddered at the memory. "Nothing could smell that gross and still be alive. It was rotting in the water."

"Si – si. You will show us now?" he asked, indicating the boats.

Hootie steered *Miss Katie* out into the wide bay with the police boat close behind. There was no time to waste. It was getting late in the day. There would not be much light when they arrived.

Jake pointed the way up the coast as the boats bobbed and sheered in the waves. The wind was picking up little whitecaps on the water. Hootie cruised to the spot Jake indicated and cut his engines. The police boat came alongside and bumped into their side annoying Hootie. *"Right!"* he thought, *"smear up that new paint job."*

"Dónde, Señor? Where is the body?"

"Over there," Jake pointed.

The Sergeant nodded, and two of the officers stripped down to swimsuits, jumped into the water, and swam to where Jake pointed.

"Follow your nose," Jake called. "Man! How could they not smell that?"

The officers poked at the weed-covered cadaver that floated like a tethered cocoon of some sort. They yelled back and forth in Spanish to their Sergeant, who had now lashed the police boat to *Miss Katie*. The Sergeant tossed them a coiled rope which unreeled across the water. The officers wrapped several loops around the corpse. The officers jerked and pushed the body to free it from the entrapping weeds. Once untangled, the Sergeant slowly pulled the body back to the police cruiser.

The crocodile awoke to more annoying sounds – the noises were louder this time, and there were more of them. Intruders were stirring the water. They were attacking the cache! Strange legs churned in the water and roiled the surface. Something was trying to steal the bait!

Aquasaurus snapped at the nearest set of churning legs and missed, as the encroacher moved out of reach. With a mighty thrust of its tail, the great beast lunged forward and stubbed its tender snout into something solid and hard. The pain raced through the animal's jaws, as blood oozed where teeth were broken and missing.

The croc regrouped and returned to check on the bait. It was missing! The absence of the body enraged and excited the massive crocodile. Aquasaurus could tell by the diminished scent that the body was no longer there. Instinct and anger took over. Propelled by a powerful flip of his tail, the animal wheeled and swam circles around the small sandbar. Something large and hard had taken the prize. Rage coursed through the crocodile's body – what manner of creature was this that could stand against such a charge? The buzzing faded into the distance, taking the rotting meat with it.

As time passed, the awareness of the permanency of the loss became apparent. Whatever had intruded earlier had stolen the lure. The trap needed fresh meat. When the invaders returned, the crocodile would be ready and would spew anger and vengeance out on the next unfortunate creature that crossed its path. The crocodile lay half-submerged in the dank water as waves slopped across its rippled back. Silently, the croc crouched in the mud and waited.

The men opened a large plastic bag and drew it over the lifeless body. As the Sergeant maneuvered the police boat nearby, the officers zipped it closed and hastily lifted the body bag aboard. The two wet officers climbed into the boat and leaned the body bag against the gunwale. Together they raised the body and turned it upside down over the rail. Seawater that had been scooped up inside the bag drained from the opening. A disgusting, stringy, brown liquid dripped grotesquely from the plastic. Afterward, the officers placed a stretcher under the bagged corpse, strapped it down, and rolled it to the rear of the boat where they set the brakes and tied the gurney to a cleat.

Once they secured the body, the Sergeant once again moved the police boat alongside *Miss Katie*. Hootie once again felt a heavy thud as the police boat drew alongside. He thought they had rammed him intentionally!

"Watch out," Hootie yelled, "I just finished painting this boat!"

"Sorry, Señor, but your boat moved and struck ours unexpectedly; my apologies."

The Sergeant motioned that he wanted to come aboard. Hootie could feel the police cruiser was rubbing against his hull right where he had painted. The action and the sound grated on Hootie, fraying his patience.

The Sergeant asked everyone to take a seat in the salon as he continued his investigation.

"Did you know this man?" the Sergeant began. "Have you seen him before?"

"No," they answered at the same time.

"None of you have seen this man in the past?" he pressed.

Negative headshakes and verbal denials circled the room.

"How is it that you found the body?"

Katie explained that she was riding on the jet ski and was thrown off. Jake could not help noticing her expression as she answered the question. She spoke to the Sergeant, but she looked right at Jake as she explained how she flew from the jet ski. Turning her attention back to the Sergeant, Katie finished her story. She described how she found herself trapped in a mass of floating weeds and debris. Not being able to force her way through and not wanting to go under, Katie decided to climb over the tangled mass. Looking down at the floating mass, she discovered she was sitting atop a dead body. Katie still shivered in disgust as she related her part in the discovery.

"Have you seen any other boats or noticed any other activities on these waters in the past few days?"

Hootie answered that he had not. He did not feel the need to mention the photographer. He was sure they had no connection to the body. The others followed Hootie's lead and shook their heads.

"Do you have a gun aboard this vessel, Señor?"

"How did he die?" Jake interjected, glancing at Hootie.

"Was he attacked by an animal – like that huge crocodile I've heard about?" Hootie asked, hoping to change the subject.

"Señor, we would search your boat now, if you please."

"Search our boat? Why? We only *found* a body; we didn't put it there."

"We must see if you have drugs or weapons. It is a formality we must follow."

"But, Sergeant, we had nothing to do with this," Hootie protested.

"Señor, the man was killed by a gunshot to the back of his head with his hands tied behind his back. I must determine that you had no contact with this man before I can release you."

The Sergeant remained in the salon with the group, as the other officers searched the boat. After a short while, they returned and spoke to the Sergeant in rapid Spanish.

The Sergeant spoke to Hootie, "Señor, would you be so kind as to accompany me to your wheelhouse?"

All Hootie could think was they had found the gun. He had taken the precaution of placing it back inside the empty radio casing. His heart stopped at the realization that they could have detected it as quickly as he had discovered it that first time in Clint's room.

Entering the wheelhouse, Hootie stood with his hands at his side as more rapid Spanish exploded from one of the officers. The Sergeant listened intently, as the officer picked up the radio case and waved it at the Sergeant. The Sergeant nodded. Hootie's pulse raced.

"Señor, your radio is inoperable," the Sergeant advised. "Were you aware it has no power cable?"

"Si – yes! Of course, I know. It is a backup radio I am trying to repair." Hootie reached up and snapped on the overhead radio, which lit and came alive with static. "This is the main radio. That one …," Hootie reached out to take it from the officer, "that one is only a broken spare." He was thankful that the foam rubber packing did not allow the gun to rattle around inside the radio case.

To Hootie's great relief, the young officer released the radio to Hootie's hands. Hootie realized that they had not found the .45 inside after all.

Another policeman arrived with a spool of rope. The Sergeant examined the cord closely and determined it was not the same type that was used to bind the body.

The first policeman pointed to the fire extinguisher hanging on the wall as he told the Sergeant something in Spanish.

"Are you also aware," the Sergeant asked Hootie, "that your fire extinguisher has no pressure?"

"Oh," Hootie stalled. "Uh, yes … you know kids," he shrugged at the Sergeant. "I caught them playing with it the other day." Hootie opened a cupboard door and pulled out a new fire extinguisher. "Here," he gestured, "here is a new one – I just haven't hung it up yet."

All of the police officers nodded, understanding. *They bought it,* Hootie thought. The search turned up nothing that could tie the group to the dead man. The .45 remained concealed in the shell of the radio. The Sergeant thanked Hootie and left with a warning to stay in the area until the investigation was over. It may take a day or two, but the Sergeant assured them it would not take long.

"We have these things happen often. It is usually between warring drug gangs. They compete with each other for the right to transport and deliver contraband. I am sorry, but we must ensure that you were not involved. We will present the facts to the authority in La Pesca, and I am sure he will release you from the investigation soon. Do not worry my friends," he smiled a toothy grin. "It is only procedure."

The cantina was alive with jukebox music, dancing, and loud conversation. The din was so loud that Tom and Mark moved to a table on the patio near the outdoor bar. After ordering cervezas, they sat back to enjoy the evening. Cooling breezes blew in across the Rio.

"No more Coke and ice, huh?" Tom joked and laughed at the string of expletives spat by his younger companion.

"You eat with that mouth?" Tom added.

"Not lately! I'm starving! But, I'm not drinking anything that's not in a bottle! I'm not going through that again."

The night was early, but several couples were already dancing to the jukebox. A small guitar band arranged microphones and instruments on a tiny outdoor stage. Other couples gathered around umbrella-covered tables and chatted in low tones. Lovers sat off by themselves in the darker areas of the outdoor patio. At the bar behind Mark, single men sat in a long row and nursed their beers.

As they waited for their food, Mark wondered, "When are we going home, Prof? Have you had enough yet? We've been down here three weeks now, and nothing! There hasn't been a single sighting of that crocodile since we've been here."

"Yeah," Tom began. "I've been thinking about that. It has been a rough trip. Look, Mark, if I've seemed like a jerk to you, I want you to know it's not because of you. I've just been so bent on finding this big croc that I couldn't think of anything else but that."

"You have been pretty rude sometimes – but I figured it was just your way."

"Come on, Mark, glasses versus binoculars?" Tom laughed as he reminded Mark of his confusion on the boat. "You have to admit that it's funny."

"You didn't seem to think so at the time," he smiled.

"Not in the moment," Tom admitted. "I'll bet there are a lot of little things that have happened on this trip that we'll be laughing about for years to come."

"Like what?"

Tom pointed to the healing scabs on Mark's legs below his shorts, "Like sea lice… maybe?"

"Oh, man!" Mark rubbed his legs. "Don't remind me! That was the pits!"

"Well, I think you are right," Tom admitted.

"Of course, I'm right! Those little things itch like fire!"

"No, I mean about going home. Maybe it's time we think about going home."

Mark perked up. "Really? Great! Tonight?"

Tom held up his hands, "Whoa, buddy – not tonight, but soon. We've got some loose ends to finish up first; but, I think we'll be out of here in the next few days."

"What loose ends?"

"Well, we've got the boat repaired; I picked it up this afternoon. We have to go back to Tampico and return it to José Baca. No telling how much extra he is going to charge for the damage. After that, we can go to Mexico City to catch the plane home. I'll make the flight arrangements tomorrow morning, and then we can head out."

"Let's do it! I'm ready to get out of this place!"

He wasn't such a bad kid, Tom decided. "You did good, Mark. In spite of my complaining, you did real good. I'm glad I brought you."

Mark smiled, "Thanks, Professor. It means a lot to hear you say that. But, right now, I've gotta go to the can, man."

Tom took a sip of warm beer as Mark made his way to the baño the bartender pointed out. Two police officers pushed by him and climbed on bar stools behind Tom. As they sat at the bar talking and sipping beer, Tom could not help but overhear their conversation. He was paying scant attention until he heard one of them say the words, "gringos."

"Americans – are they talking about us? Tom wondered. He listened in. Although he did not understand everything they said, he knew enough Spanish to get the main idea.

The police had found a body. No, some Americans had reported a body floating in the sea somewhere nearby. Thoughts swirled in Tom's mind as he listened and tried to interpret at the same time. *Were they talking about Hootie and Miss Katie?* The Americanos had taken the police to the site, several miles up the coast. Tom heard them mention,

"Miss Katie." Yes! It was them. Did they find a body? He searched his mind for the meaning of *atado – atado – tied, like tied up?*

Yes, he understood, they had found a corpse, bound with rope – hands behind its back. The police seemed to agree it was due to drug runners or gangs – or both. *The victim had been murdered – shot in the head!* But, there was something else – something he could not quite make out in his limited Spanish. They seemed quite animated and puzzled about whatever they were discussing. After a few moments, they finished their beers and left the bar.

Tom turned around and motioned the bartender. "Excuse me, but what were those policemen talking about just now?"

The bartender looked at the departing officers, "Those guys?" he pointed.

"Yes. What did those men say? I made out most if, it but I got lost at the end."

"They were police officers, my friend. They were talking about a dead guy that was found out on a sandbar north of here. They don't think he drowned. Someone tied his hands behind his back and shot him in the head. *Asesinado* – executed," the bartender put his finger against his temple.

"Yeah – yeah. I got that part. What was the last part? I'm trying to learn Spanish. Help me out here."

"I was not paying attention, but they were getting off duty soon. They spoke of going over to a sister's *casa* to get something to eat."

"No, before that. They seemed confused about something."

"Oh! Yes. They were saying it was strange how they found the body."

"Didn't someone take them to it?"

"Oh, si! Si! Yes, the Americans found it and showed them where it was."

"But, what was the confusion?"

"Ah, yes, *that*," the bartender nodded. "Yes. The condition of the body was very odd. Someone wrapped it in the seaweeds and vines. It was like it had been rolled into a blanket, with weeds and mud wrapped around it, over and over. It must have been the waves, but they did not think the waves could have done that. Moreover, it was jammed into a bed of seaweed, as though it was put there to stay for a long time."

The bartender wiped his glasses as he continued, "They didn't believe the gangs would have taken the time to anchor it so well to prevent it from floating away. They usually don't care. These drug guys usually throw bodies overboard and just sail off. This time they made sure that the body would stay put for some reason. It was like they intended for it to stay where they left it."

Tom thanked the bartender and returned to his table. He was deep in thought as he had the waiter bring a "to go" bag. When Mark returned, Tom barked, "Come on! Let's go! We gotta get out of here. Now!"

Mark shook his head, "Now? I haven't eaten yet!"

Tom tossed him the plastic bag. "Take it to go – we're leaving!"

Mark stuffed his food into the bag, hurrying to stay up with Tom. "What happened? What's the hurry? What got into you? Where are we going?"

Tom stopped on his way to the door looking back at Mark, his eyes wide with excitement.

"We've found it! I know where it is," he whispered

"Found what?" Mark shook his head in confusion.

"Aquasaurus – the giant crocodile! I know where it is!"

CHAPTER 29

Katie avoided Jake all the way back to the hacienda. When Jake tried to apologize, she raised her hand and showed him her palm. Katie was not ready to forgive Jake yet, but he kept trying. Tiring of his repeated attempts, she left the salon and went to the wheelhouse to sit with Hootie.

"What's up, Buttercup?" Hootie asked as she hopped into the co-pilot's chair.

"Nothing," she mumbled. "Boy trouble."

"Yeah. I know," Hootie nodded. "Jake messed up and threw you off the jet ski – and you ended up finding a dead body. You're still in shock."

"I guess so. But it seems more than that."

"Such as?" Hootie sensed that she needed to talk.

"He's such a jerk sometimes. He thought it was funny. He laughed."

Hootie knew better than to laugh or make light of the situation. She was so much like Alice; he knew she would get mad and leave. He was happy for the company and did not want her to go away.

"I did that once," he admitted, pretending to be concentrating on the water out front.

"Did what?" she asked.

"I was married once. Did I tell you that? It was so long ago it seems like another life. My wife had a little thing like that happen, and I laughed. I didn't mean to, and it didn't mean I didn't love her, but it seemed funny at the time. She felt the way you do about it. She didn't speak to me for a week. I guess I was insensitive; I thought I lost her at the time. Jake must be feeling the same way."

"What's her name, Hootie?"

They talked all the way back to the hacienda. Even after they docked and the rest of the group went inside, Katie stayed in the wheelhouse with Hootie. Katie wanted to know about Alice, so Hootie told her. He remembered things he thought were buried long ago – things Hootie believed he had forgotten. It all came back now in vivid detail. Hootie relayed stories he had never shared with anyone. He told her everything – except for the ending.

He even told Katie how much she reminded him of Alice. She seemed interested in that and wanted to know how they were alike. Hootie tried to explain, but the more he tried, the less alike the two women seemed. It was more than appearance – it was the attitude. It was their shared love of life and her joy of being young and free. Katie wore the same fragrance as Alice. Her hair was the same shade and style. Both women felt compassion for others and often put themselves last. They were so much alike they could have been sisters and so different at the same time. It confused Hootie, so he stopped trying.

Hootie managed to shut up before admitting his attraction to Katie, but he felt closer to Katie now than ever. Somehow, he felt closer to Alice at the same time, and that was confusing. Maybe it was talking about Alice that was bringing all these emotions out. He wanted to stop thinking about Alice but knew he was talking about her too much for that to happen. And, he sure didn't want to start drinking again. He sat without speaking for a long time, looking out the window of the boat while Katie sat beside him. It was too surreal – he could almost reach out and touch her. Hootie did not want to talk anymore, but he did not want Katie to leave either.

She tried to change the subject once, "I see Andromeda," she pointed, but Hootie did not look. He sat lost in his thoughts somewhere with Alice.

"I know how she felt," Katie said under her breath.

Hootie snapped out of his reverie, "Who? Alice?"

"No," Katie giggled pointing up, "Andromeda."

Jake came out of the house once and walked halfway down the path toward the dock.

"You guys comin' in?" he called to the couple on the boat.

"We'll be there in a minute," Katie shouted back. "We're talking about things. Go on in; I'll be there soon."

Jake turned and walked back to the hacienda, feeling rejected and alone. Katie was not mad at Jake anymore, but she was not ready to let him off the hook yet. She felt like Hootie was trying to tell her something – something important. If he was, he was saying it in silence. She struggled to understand what he could not verbalize. She did not want to miss what he might say.

She got out of the chair and stood next to Hootie in the dark. She could not see his face, but she could tell he was fighting to say something – wrestling with the words. She reached out and touched Hootie's arm. He flinched but did not pull away.

"What is it, Hootie? What happened to you and Alice?"

Maybe it was the closeness of Katie or the nearness of Alice, but Hootie could not stop the tears. Emotion gripped him, and for the first time, he found he could not put her memory into the dark hole of the past. He did not sob or cry out, but he could feel the tears streaming down his cheeks. He did not want to say it. He had never said it to anyone – not even himself. Katie's voice was so soft and understanding – like Alice's. He could not stop himself. When he answered her, it was as if he was speaking to Alice.

Katie held him close, as it all came pouring out. He cried for the first time since the day Alice died in the tragic car crash all alone. Hootie had not even had a chance to say goodbye. Alice was just suddenly, irretrievably, gone, leaving behind her fragrance and her things. When she died, she took all the life, joy, and happiness Hootie had ever known with her.

Mark tried to eat his taco, as he followed Tom back to the hotel. It was not easy. More of his meal was dropping on the ground than was reaching his mouth. Tom was in an awful hurry.

"Where are we going?" Mark asked as he struggled to keep up.

"Back to the room – we can't get decent cell phone service down here half the time. See?" He held his phone up to Mark. "No bars! Just the other day I had five and no problems at all. Now, I've got nothing! I have to get to the phone!"

Tom pushed through the door to their room and grabbed the telephone by the bed. He ordered Mark to pack up and prepare to push off as soon as possible. He punched the numbers on the phone and waited for someone to answer.

"Hello, Tom Morrison here. Give me Gilberto – right away."

While waiting for Gilberto to come to the phone, Tom barked out instructions. Mark began carrying their gear down to the boat.

"Gilberto? Tom Morrison here! Yeah, yeah, yeah, listen. I'm at a place called La Pesca. Do you know it?"

Tom listened to the answer.

"Great! Now listen – those concrete highway barriers I ordered – have you got 'em? Great. I want you to put them on a barge tonight and float them down here to La Pesca. Try to get here by daylight if you can."

Tom waited for the reply, twisting the telephone cord into knots.

"Yes, daylight tomorrow! Do it! Get them up here as soon as possible, and bring a crane to drop them in place! We're located about fifteen miles north of the town on the inside waterway. You'll find us; there won't be anyone out there but us. I'm going to need those barricades placed precisely where I show you."

While he listened, Tom pointed things out in the room he did not want Mark to leave behind. Mark took two more armloads to the boat while Tom continued yelling instructions to Gilberto.

"Don't worry about what I'm using them for. I don't care what it takes! Get them here pronto." Tom paused and asked, "What?

Tom untangled the kinks in the phone cord as he listened. He finally answered, "You'll be placing them in the water of an estuary. It's a float job, but the water is shallow. We may need to stack them two deep, but no more than that. I need to get them in place as soon as possible."

There was a short pause. "Yes, I have the permits," Tom lied. "It doesn't matter why. I want you to load up and come now – tonight! I'll be waiting!" Tom snapped.

When Mark returned, he looked around the room. "That's everything, Professor," he panted.

"Great! Let's go!"

"What was that all about?" Mark asked.

"I'll tell you on the way," Tom answered, as he hurried Mark down the dock.

The two shoved off from the hotel pier and motored into the inlet. Tom hugged the left bank, not wanting anyone from the hacienda to see him leave. He saw dim lights on *Miss Katie*, but there were no lights inside the main building. They would not expect Tom to be motoring away in the middle of the night.

Once on the inside waterway, Tom called for Mark to come forward to the wheelhouse.

"Okay," he confided, "here's the deal. We've found Aquasaurus."

"That's great! How?"

"Remember when we were in the bar tonight, and you went to the bathroom? Well, two Mexican police officers came in. I don't speak much

211

Spanish, but I could tell something happened that excited them. They seemed to be arguing about something. When I heard them say the word *"Americanos,"* I reasoned they had to be talking about our friends across the bay. There are no other Americans down here right now that I'm aware of. If they were talking about us, they would have been talking *to* me."

Tom continued, "I thought they had heard about the boat crash and were trying to figure out who was involved. Then I heard one of the cops say *"Miss Katie."* That cinched it! I thought we were in deep trouble. I expected that any minute, they would notice me and start asking questions about the boat crash. They babbled on for a few minutes, and I picked up a few more Spanish words, like *cadáver.*"

"That sounds like a dead body," Mark said.

"Exactly – these Americans had found a corpse in the water about fifteen miles north of town. They found the body trussed up and stuffed in the seaweeds. The police said it was an execution – he'd been shot."

"Wow! That's not far from where we had the boat accident," Mark said. "What does that have to do with a giant crocodile? Drug runners kill people down here all the time and dump bodies overboard. If they assassinated some guy, how would that help us?"

Tom nodded. "Yes, that's what I thought, too. Some poor sod got offed by the cartels. But there was something else about the story that didn't make sense."

"What was it?"

"I couldn't tell – my Spanish was too weak, but when the police left, I asked the bartender."

"Yeah?" Mark waited for the reply.

"He said they were confused by the way the body was left. Something or someone had wrapped the carcass in the weeds and mud and bound it into a tight bundle, rolling it over and over – like they didn't want it to float away."

212

"Why would the drug people care if it floated away?" Mark asked. "They dump bodies all the time; sometimes on people's docks in the daylight. The waves could have rolled it around, and it got wrapped up tight."

"I know, that's what the police thought too. But I know that is not what happened." Tom assured him.

"How would you know?" Mark questioned, doubting Tom's assessment.

"Mark, long before I met you, I lived and worked in South Florida."

"So?"

"Do you know what they have in Florida? The Everglades," he said, not waiting for an answer. "And, do you know what is in the Everglades?" Again, Tom did not wait for an answer. "Gators and crocs – thousands of them. In fact, that is the only place in the US where both species share the same habitat. I grew up down there, and I worked at a tourist trap in Alligator Creek. Do you know what I did?"

This time, Tom waited for Mark to answer.

"I don't know – took tickets, maybe?"

"Took tickets?" Tom laughed. "No. I was the lead alligator wrangler for the park. I trained the other wrestlers to handle the gators. We *never* fight crocodiles. Do you want to know why?"

"Sure," Mark said, with a new respect for Tom in his eyes.

"Crocodiles will kill you – that's why. Alligators are dangerous, but crocs are deadly. Do you know how they kill their prey?"

"Chomp?" Mark asked.

"Not at first. First, a croc will latch on to you; and then start a slow death roll out into deeper water where they drown you before they start pulling you apart – limb by limb."

"That explains the rolling," Mark said, "but you said this guy didn't drown – someone shot him! As far as I know, crocodiles aren't packing!"

"That's what had the police so confused. They thought the cartels stashed the body. I know better. No, crocodiles don't carry guns – you goof! They are ambush killers. That means they will bait a trap with dead animals and wait for it to rot. They bundle it up, stick it in a secure place, and wait for something to come get it. That's when they strike. They rise up without warning in an explosion of water. The prey is too stunned to resist as the croc drags it away into deeper water. It's awesome – I've seen it many times."

"You think a crocodile put that rotting body there as a lure to attract something else it could kill?"

"Exactly!"

"Wow! So you think it was this Aquasaurus?"

"I do. The ocean waves may have rolled the body and wrapped it up, but waves could not have secured the cadaver that way. The drug runners would not have taken the time. It was the giant crocodile – I'm sure of it!"

"What was that phone call about?"

"I called a man named Gilberto in Tampico. While you were with the boat and José Baca, I went into town for more cash. Remember?"

"Yeah," Mark admitted.

"I met Gilberto in town. He owns a construction business out of Tampico. I passed his yard and saw huge stacks of those concrete barricades. You know? The ones you see alongside highways under construction. They are massive – about four feet high and weigh tons."

"Yeah, I know the ones you mean."

"I realized if we had a way to move them to where we spotted the crocodile, they would make a perfect enclosure. I arranged with Gilberto to bring them to me if and when I ever needed them. Now, I need them. In the morning, Gilberto's crew will arrive with 200 concrete barriers and a crane. We're going to make an enclosure. If we can trap Aquasaurus inside, I can get my picture. But, better than that, we can study it and so can others. Do you realize what this means?"

"Yes. We've found the crocodile."

"More than that; this thing – this giant crocodile – this is not a *normal* crocodile."

"What is it?"

"I believe it is a descendant of a species of crocodile long thought to be extinct! It is so huge; it has to be the one?"

"The one, what?"

"*Carnufex Carolinensis!*" Tom stated, with excited assurance. "The Carolina Butcher!"

CHAPTER 30

Jake sat on the side of the bed, forlorn and lost. He should have been on the happiest vacation of his life. Instead, there Katie was – out on the boat with Hootie, and here he was – alone in his room. Jake could have kicked himself for being reckless and throwing Katie from the jet ski. He had never seen Katie as someone weak. She had always seemed strong with an independent streak. He had seen her climb mountains most girls would not even attempt. He thought they were having fun until she lost her balance. Now, she was blaming him, and with good cause. He felt responsible.

He had noticed the attraction between Hootie and Katie since the beginning of the trip. No one could miss it. She was acting differently when she wasn't acting indifferently. It was as if she did not want Hootie to know she and Jake were a couple. In the old days, there would have been no question about them being together, but that is not the case now. With Hootie around, she changed from a girlfriend to a sister. Now, she was an angry sister.

Did Katie have a thing for Hootie? It sure seemed that way. But, Hootie was an old man – at least fifteen years older than they were. Jake felt a little intimidated despite the apparent differences between them. Though Hootie seemed old to him, Jake knew Hootie must seem worldly and adventurous to Katie. Despite the extreme sports, Jake felt immature and inadequate for the first time in his life. Was it all bravado – a put on? Nothing Jake had done seemed important now – essential. Jake had lived his life for adventure, fun, and the thrills of taking chances. Jake realized, he had been trying to compete with Hootie. He had been taking unnecessary risks like making breakneck turns on the jet ski to show off. It had backfired big time this time.

He was grateful that Katie was not injured. Looking down and seeing that stiff must have been the shock of her life – especially since she had been riding it like a dirt bike! He wanted to comfort Katie, but she kept pushing him off. She rode back to the boat on the skiff with Rita and stayed in the wheelhouse with Hootie all the way back to the hacienda. She was there with him still – talking about who knows what.

Jake picked up his cell phone and saw he had almost two bars. Finally! Now he had a chance to do something he had wanted to do for a week. He searched his backpack for the scrap of paper he needed to ping Katie's phone.

He opened the LOC application on the phone and carefully tapped in the numbers he had copied. He watched the wheel go round and round until a map appeared on his screen. Jake scrutinized the small map on his screen. Nah! The ping brought back a false return. He must be pinging himself because the location came back close to the hacienda. He scrubbed the identifying information from LOC and reset the input fields to null. He retyped the information into LOC again digit by digit, making sure there was no mistake. Same result.

He examined the refreshed map on his screen. Something did not add up. Katie's SAT phone was pinging in the same location it had minutes earlier. He enlarged the map by spreading his fingers across the screen. The ping site was not the hacienda after all. Her phone was pinging about fifteen miles north of their location. What would Katie's phone be doing out there?

A sudden thought occurred. That location was very close to where they found the dead body! At first, he did not understand how that could be. Katie said she had lost the phone while they were in Honey Creek Cave or soon after they came out. She had not seen it since. It was not in her gear, her car, or anywhere in her apartment. She had looked everywhere. How could her phone be alive and pinging down in Mexico? It seemed impossible. If she had lost it in the cave, it would have been dead by now, and no ping would have been possible.

The only answer that seemed plausible was she had not lost it at all, and it was somewhere loose in her gear. Did she leave anything out at the crime scene where they found the body? Jake did not think so. Was it on the jet ski? No. She would have had to put it there. In that case, she

217

would have known she hadn't lost it. It was not in her clothing since they were only wearing shorts and tank tops on the jet ski.

What about when they went back with the police? No. Katie had not left the boat. And, if the SAT phone were on Katie's person, it would be pinging right here, not fifteen miles north.

Jake's original thought was someone might have stolen her phone after the Honey Creek rescue. It was too much of a coincidence to imagine that the thief would have followed them all the way to Mexico. It could not have been with Rita or Jesse unless it was in their gear and they didn't realize it. Even so, it wouldn't be pinging now out there where they found that dead body.

Jake scratched his head as he tried to solve the mystery. Nothing he thought of fit, except this far-fetched idea that would get him laughed out of Mexico. The last time Katie had remembered having her phone was in Honey Creek Cave. She was beating a giant crocodile on the snout with it. Was the phone in the croc? That was impossible! The phone would have shorted out in seawater, or the battery would have died.

Then he heard Katie and Hootie in the kitchen.

Hootie felt drained. He had never confided in someone the way he had with Katie. He felt embarrassed and vulnerable.

"I'm sorry," he mumbled, wiping his face. "I don't know what came over me."

"It's okay, Hootie. I know you must have loved her very much."

Hootie wiped his eyes and laughed, "Don't get me started again. Come on. Let's go up to the house. I could use a cup of coffee. You know, I will stay in your dad's room tonight. I could use a hot shower and a soft bed."

"It's yours," Katie said as she climbed down the ladder onto the dock. She waited for Hootie to put the lights out and secure the boat. Katie walked down the pier toward the rear of *Miss Katie* watching the sky. She sighed as she spotted Andromeda again. Kaite did not know many constellations, but she could recognize Andromeda now. She felt the emotions of Hootie's story sweep over her once more. She felt like she knew how Andromeda must have felt. Her father chained her to a rock to appease the monster. Wasn't that the same way her father, Clint, had chained her to an oil company she did not want. She had no idea how to manage an oil company. Thank goodness, Hootie did. The thought of Hootie always being close made her feel warm and protected. As long as he was around, things would be okay. Katie would let Hootie have free reign in that area. Since the fire and earthquake, Rio Frio had been inactive anyway. She figured she would sell it to Hootie one day – or to someone else who wanted it.

At the end of the dock, Katie turned back toward the ladder. Hootie climbed part way down and dropped to the dock. Katie noticed something didn't look right. There was a dent in the side of the boat near the waterline. Looking closer, she called Hootie.

"What?"

"Hootie, come and look at this. Bring some light. Something hit our boat."

Hootie switched on a high beam LED flashlight and lit the damage. "Wow! Something hit us hard," he agreed. "It was probably that police boat." Then he remembered the police boat had tied up forward amidships.

"Katie, remember? As the officers were coming on board our boat, their boat thumped us so hard that I had to shout at them to be careful. Remember that?"

'No, I guess I was still thinking about that putrid body."

"Well, they hit us pretty hard. The only thing is, the police were up near the front not back here on the rear. Here, hold this light a minute while I check out the damage."

"Do you think it was from the crash the other night?"

"No, this dent wasn't here this morning."

Katie held the light on the place while Hootie leaned far over the edge of the dock. He ran his hand across the damaged hull. She heard him say, "What is this?"

"What is what, Hootie?"

Hootie stood and held his hand out under the beam of the flashlight. "This," he said looking into her eyes, "is a tooth – a big tooth! Look at the size of this thing! Do you know what this is?"

"No. Did a shark attack our boat?" she guessed.

"Maybe, but this doesn't look like a shark tooth. Come on! Let's get the others. I want to talk to everyone before we decide what to do!"

Tom steered the fishing boat through the dark waters of the Mexican night, using his fish finder to navigate.

"How do you know where to go?" Mark asked.

"I don't, but I know it is near a group of sand spits about fifteen miles north of the Rio. We should see some signs of a police recovery operation out there. They may have put buoys out or some yellow tape. Or, we should see some signs of a disturbance – marks on the sand or in the vegetation. Look for anything that looks moved or out of place. Why don't you man the spotlight when we get there?"

"Right," Mark agreed. "Even if we find the spot, how are we going to find the crocodile?"

"Their eyes glow in the light at night. Look for one or two flashes on the water that look like red-hot coals. That will be the croc," Tom instructed.

Mark opened the window and took the handle of the spotlight in his grip. He moved it around to get a feel for its operation.

"Don't turn it on yet! The light will spoil our night vision."

They drove on through the moonless night. It often seemed they were floating on an endless sea of water with no land in sight. The GPS showed only small islands and sand spits sprinkling the inside passage. A long barrier island on their right protected them from the Gulf of Mexico. You could not see it unless it was daylight. At the fourteen-mile point, Tom slowed and guided the boat to a string of small islands. He navigated with his green display screen.

The boat was at a crawl as Tom wound in and out and around the small cays. They were creeping ahead by inches when Mark turned on the searchlight. Moving it around the edge of the water, he kept a sharp lookout for red eyes. After a few minutes, finding nothing, Tom would change gears and move on to the next group of sand islands.

After two hours of searching, Mark was ready to give up, but Tom was not satisfied.

"It has to be around here close by. Keep watching and moving that light around."

Even Tom was about to give up and catch a nap when Mark noticed something near the edge of a weedy waterline.

"Professor," he pointed, "there's something over there that looks like it is moving away from us. I don't see red eyes, but it is definitely moving."

"Spot it," Tom ordered.

Mark turned the searchlight in the direction of where it might be, but could not find it.

"It's gone now. Let's get a little closer."

Mark placed the spot in the area where he last saw the movement, as Tom moved the boat toward the location.

"Stop here," Mark said. "This is where I saw it."

"Was it glowing red? What do you think it was?"

"I thought I saw something like a red reflector from a bicycle. I'm not sure. It could have been a piece of broken glass or something. I didn't see what you described, but it was big, and it was moving fast."

Tom took over the light and ran it around the edge of the water. He did not see anything out of place. There were no signs that the police had recovered a body there, but that did not mean it did not happen. The GPS showed only this small string of islands in the vicinity.

"This must be the place," Tom nodded. "I'm going to move over to the back side. Here, take the light and keep a lookout."

Tom ran the boat around the left side of the island mass as Mark lit the edges.

"Professor!" Mark shouted.

"What?"

"Look!" Mark pointed. "Tiny coals, you say? Those things are as big as cannonballs! They must be three feet apart!" Mark could feel his stomach twist in terror.

"Grab hold of something," Tom yelled, as fear froze his eyes on the unbelievable sight. The crocodile was larger than he had imagined – bigger than any animal he had ever seen.

"Why?"

"Because that monster is coming right toward us!" Tom shouted.

CHAPTER 31

"What's up, guys?" Jake asked as he entered the kitchen. "Guess what I found."

Katie crossed the room and hugged Jake before she led him toward the table, "Jake! We found something." Her eyes were wide with excitement.

"I found your phone!" Jake blurted out, not hearing Katie's news.

"My phone? You found my phone? How? Where?"

"Katie, this is crazy. I don't really understand it, but it's not lost at all. It's here in Mexico with us. The phone is still working, so it must be getting some sun. If we search, we'll find it hidden in our things somewhere."

"How do you know that?" Hootie asked.

"I finally got some bars on my cell phone, so I pinged Katie's old SAT phone for the fun of it. I thought I might be able to locate it for her or something. Guess what? The ping came back from here!"

"Here? You mean here in the house?" Katie asked.

"Well … not exactly. It actually looks like it is about fifteen miles north of here. It could be a calculation error, or it fell off the jet ski when we were out there this afternoon."

"It's pinging from out there? Where we found that dead body?" Katie asked, her eyes wide with excitement.

"That's what it looks like. But how could that be? Really?" Jake looked from Katie to Hootie.

"Jake, we found something, too," Hootie replied.

"Found something? What?"

Hootie reached into his shirt pocket and handed Jake the tooth. "It's a tooth of some sort. Whatever hit our boat, got its tooth stuck in the side of the hull."

Jake peered at the giant, blunt tooth trying to figure out what it might be.

"Want some coffee?" Katie asked Jake.

"Sure," Jake said. He was grateful that she asked – that was a good sign.

"What is this thing?" Jake asked Hootie.

"I'm not sure. It's a tooth, of course; but I know it's not a shark tooth," Hootie declared. "I remembered something rammed us while we were out recovering the body. Whatever it was, it almost knocked a hole in the side of our boat. My imagination is running wild, but I wanted you all to see it first before I jumped to conclusions. What do you think?"

Katie handed Jake his coffee and said, "I know it sounds crazy," she said, "but that looks like a tooth from that giant crocodile from the cave! Do you think it could be?"

Jake shook his head. "Katie, the last time you saw your phone you were beating that crocodile on the snout with it, weren't you?"

"Yes," she agreed.

"Hootie, is it possible that the phone could be inside that crocodile and still stay charged?"

Hootie took the tooth back, "I don't know. But let's wake up the others and see what they think. If this is what we think it is, we've found our crocodile."

A canopy, held up by bolted aluminum posts, shaded the deck of the boat. Mark let go of the light and grabbed the nearest pole. He held on as tightly as he could while he waited for what would happen next. Unattended, the beam of light dropped and streaked across the deck. Mark could no longer see the monstrous burning eyes coming toward them in the dark. He saw Tom jump back into the wheelhouse and spin the wheel, trying to move out of the way of the charging animal. Mark prayed it would turn off or dive under them.

A sudden loud crash erupted amidships almost directly below Mark. It sounded and felt like a car crash, as the boat splintered and cracked. Mark could hear the engine rev up as Tom attempted to move away from the attacking crocodile.

"Are we taking on water?" Tom screamed from the wheel.

"I don't know. I'll go below and check," Mark yelled back.

Mark lifted the wooden hatch in the center of the deck and peered inside. It was too dark to see, but the clear sound of rushing water was unmistakable.

"Yes!" Mark shouted back to Tom. "We've got water coming in fast!"

"It's breached our hull. If we don't stop that water, we're going to sink!" Tom warned.

The boat was getting underway, but already the weight of the water was slowing their escape. Mark went to the bulkhead, grabbed an emergency flashlight from its mount on the wall, and went back to the hatch. His heart leaped in his chest as he shined the light into the darkness, realizing he was going to have to go down into that dark bilge.

Water was gushing into the boat at an incredible rate. Cracked and jagged boards from the side of the ship jutted inward into the small hold.

Mark believed, if he could push those boards back into position, he could slow the leak.

Mark eased himself down inside the small compartment. Water was already up to his waist. The hold was so small Mark could not stand erect, so he crawled to the bulkhead where the damage was. He sat on the bottom of the boat as he placed his feet against the cracked wood and pushed as hard as he could. Gradually, the broken planks moved back into position; but as soon as Mark released the pressure, they gave way again. The water gushed through the opening and covered Mark's face so that he had to move to the side. Mark realized that in minutes the entire compartment would be full of water. He hoped he would be able to find the hatch again to climb back out.

He looked around for something to prop in front of the rupture, but he found nothing he could use as a brace. Mark thought he might try to hold out as long as he could with his feet propped against the broken boards. The leak had slowed, but the water was already up to his neck — he only had a few minutes before he would have to evacuate.

Topside, Tom was trying to steer the boat away from danger. The added weight of the water was slowing their progress. Where was Mark? He pushed the throttle as high as it would go, hoping the added horsepower would move them forward. The crocodile had hit them on the starboard side. Tom turned the wheel to the left, hoping to take the pressure off the breached hull. If the kid knew what he was doing, he was down there trying to block off the water.

The boat shuddered and shook, as greasy black smoke huffed from the exhaust. The fishing boat won't take much more of this, Tom thought, as he kept the engine whining as high as possible.

Tom realized he had turned the wrong way, as a sudden concussion as hard as the first, pounded aft of the first blow. The crocodile hit them again! I must have turned right into it! What happened to Mark?

The impact knocked Mark across the bottom of the boat, and as he slid beneath the water, Mark's head slammed into the opposite bulkhead. He saw stars but did not black out. He came up for air, spitting and coughing up seawater. He could tell from the increased flow of water across his chest that the boat was sinking fast. The level was rising so quickly; Mark barely made it to the hatch in time to climb back on deck. They were going down, and there was nothing to do about it. He needed a life jacket. They were going to be taking a swim.

As he climbed through the hatch, he went to the locker to grab two life jackets. Before he could open the door, he saw a sight that almost stopped his heart.

The giant crocodile rose from the water and stood on its hind legs, lunging at the boat. It loomed almost twice as high as the boat itself; the fat throat and horrific gape of the crocodile towered some twenty feet in the air. It hung there, then in slow motion crashed down onto the boat like a giant oak tree. The entire bulkhead gave way, as the ship split in half.

The collision hurled Mark through the air as the boat gave way. Tumbling head over heels, he landed in the water, confused and disoriented. Wiping salt water from his burning eyes, he looked for the boat. The two pieces of the craft were floating away from each other. In the stern half, the engine smoked, coughed, and died as it upended and quickly sank out of sight. The front end bobbed and swung around as it floated with its bow pointed toward the dark sky. It twisted and turned as it drifted like a big fishing cork with a catfish on the line. Tom was nowhere in sight.

Where was the crocodile? Mark turned three-sixty, as he scanned the surface of the water. He expected the crocodile to attack at any moment. In the darkness, Mark made out what hopefully was a small island about fifty yards to his left. Disturbing the water as little as possible, he tiptoed on the bottom, moving his body toward the sandy shore.

A blood-curdling scream filled the air. Mark's blood turned to ice. He bobbed in the water on tiptoes and shuddered – the professor was alive! Mark tried to locate the direction of the screams, but it was too dark to see very much.

Off to his left, Mark saw motion and heard wild splashing in the water. The screaming had stopped. Through the smoke and gloom, Mark made out a horrifying scene. The giant crocodile rolled over and over and over again. That must be the death roll Mark thought. He remembered the professor telling him that crocodiles did that. They would drown their prey by rolling before tearing the victim limb from limb. Did the monster have the professor in his jaws?

Despite the danger to himself, Mark knew he had to help if he could. He started moving toward the gruesome scene. Getting closer, he could see the crocodile rolling in the water. As it came up each time, Mark could see Tom clutching the crocodile's back.

"Don't let go," Mark prayed. He knew if Tom came off the crocodile's back, he would end up in its mouth. Each time Tom surfaced, he had slipped a little farther down the crocodile's back toward the deadly tail.

The croc stopped rolling as Tom tried to regain his grip on the leathery hide. Mark watched amazed as Tom jumped to his feet on the back of the giant animal like a surfboarder and dove headlong into the sea.

"No!" Mark screamed in terror. "No! You don't have a chance in the water!"

Tom was out of sight in the darkness as the crocodile turned and pursued the swimmer. Mark knew that once Aquasaurus killed Tom, it would turn its attention to him. Mark began to swim wildly, not knowing where he was heading but putting distance between him and the beast. Mark sensed movement behind him in the water. He stopped swimming and turned into the face of the crocodile.

Mark lowered his arms into the water and tried to make himself as tiny as possible. The crocodile floated with deadly eyes locked onto Mark's terrified eyes.

Looking toward the shore, Mark decided he had no better chance on the sand than he did in the water. Crocodiles could run thirty miles per hour. There was no place to run on the small island even if Mark could keep ahead of it – which he could not. But maybe, if he could stay still enough, the monster might go away. Sinking as low in the water as possible, Mark left only his nose and eyes on the surface. Sea lice crossed his mind, and he wished with all his heart that sea lice were his only problem right now. The crocodile advanced, inching closer with each passing second.

The croc seemed to have calmed now. Its attack had slowed, as its anger dissipated. Moving to within a few feet of Mark, the giant animal floated motionlessly. Transparent eyelids, like cataracts, slid up from grey-green flecked eyes. Frothy bubbles began to leak from beneath the eyelids as they formed in droplets and ran down the animal's face. In his senseless terror, Mark almost laughed as he thought of what a beautiful pair of boots that leather would make. Mark realized he had only seconds to live. He waited for the inevitable teeth to grab him and roll him under the water. In his imagination, Mark could hear his bones crunch beneath the ivory tusk-like teeth.

With a deafening roar, the crocodile bellowed directly in Mark's face but did not grab him. Mark sensed that the crocodile was trying to make him swim away so it could catch him from the unprotected rear. The animal was smart. A small splash sounded to the left of the crocodile, as Tom surfaced and got his bearings.

In a calm, soft voice, Tom spoke to Mark. "Mark, listen to me. I'm going to draw attention away from you. Don't splash or make any sudden moves. Slowly sink, and swim underwater as far as you can go! Don't come up until you can't stand it anymore. Now, go!"

Tom slapped the water with cupped hands, making a loud noise. The sudden movement on his flank alerted the giant crocodile. It threw back its head and roared so loud it almost broke Mark's eardrums. Mark, frozen with fear, forgot to sink and swim away. The croc twisted toward Tom, and with one mighty swipe of its tail, catapulted Tom bodily from the water. Tom tumbled through the air, cleared a small island by yards, and splashed into the lagoon on the other side.

The crock turned back to eye Mark. It glared as it undulated its powerful tail from side to side. Mark dipped fully beneath the surface and swam as far underwater as he could. He felt his lungs about to burst as he surfaced and looked around. He crawled from the water and knelt on the sand. Looking out to sea, Mark could not see the crocodile. Across the island, in the water on the other side, he saw something bobbing on the surface. It was Tom!

Mark did not know where the crocodile was, but he could not let Tom drown. He got to his feet, ran to the rim of the sea, and plunged into the dark water. A few vigorous strokes brought him alongside Tom, who was floating face down in the royal blue ink. Turning Tom face up, Mark grabbed Tom's hair and towed him to shore. At the water's edge, Mark stood and dragged the heavier man farther up on the sand.

Tom was struggling to breathe. Mark tilted Tom's head to the side to keep him from swallowing the seawater that came gurgling from his mouth. The unconscious man began to moan. At least he was alive – for now.

Mark sat on the sand, stripped off his wet shirt, and covered the unconscious professor. He shivered as he cradled Tom's head in his lap and waited for sunrise. He watched as starlight reflected on the wriggling water like a million slithering snakes. Every motion and every wavelet that rushed ashore at his feet brought fresh new terror.

He waited for death – or for dawn; whichever came first.

CHAPTER 32

In the pale blush of dawn, Hootie boarded *Miss Katie* beneath an orange-streaked sky. As he waited for the group to gather, he topped off the jet skis with gas and checked the straps that held them to the boat. Back in the wheelhouse, he placed the fake fire extinguisher on the dashboard. He rummaged around in his bag for the key fob that would activate Pawson's Bitter Pill.

He wondered what was inside the tank that made such a powerful reaction. He wished Clint had told him more about the device. He tried to remember the instructions Clint had him memorize.

"Don't push the red button," he had admonished back in the pump house at Dilley Chalk #1.

> *"That wooden box should never be found again," Clint said pointedly. "Don't burn it, and don't throw it in any water. Get rid of it and don't tell me where. Best way would be to bury it deep; somewhere out in the brush." Hootie nodded. "And that locking aluminum case," Clint continued, "I want you to hide it too – somewhere closer. Somewhere you can put your hands on it really fast if I need it. Wrap it in a garbage bag and hide it in a different location than where you got rid of the box. Make sure no one will ever find it and dig it up. Remember where you buried it. If I need it, I'll ask you to get it for me. So hide it somewhere you won't forget. DO NOT keep it in your truck – bury it! Understand?"*

> *Hootie nodded, "What's in there?"*

> *"Damn it, Hootie! Sometimes you ask too many questions. All right ... what's in there? You want to know? Follow me." Clint turned and led Hootie back into the shed. Clint shined his flashlight on a smooth,*

aluminum cylinder lying on a shelf. "What's in the briefcase is another one, just like this one," Clint said. "That and a key fob like you use to unlock your truck. The combination on the case is the same as the last four numbers of my cell phone. Whatever you do; whatever happens; do not push the red button within a hundred yards of that cylinder. You understand?"

"It'll blow up, huh?"

"No," Clint slowly shook his head. "It won't blow up. It'll get real hot, though – hotter than anything you've ever seen. Ten times hotter than a blowtorch or a welding rod. It will burn right through the steel floorboard of your truck, and then make glass out of the sand underneath. It'll keep burning until the gas tank blows. If you are too close when it goes off, it'll incinerate your clothes, boil the flesh right off your body, and set your bones on fire. Do not push the red button."

Hootie patted the round cylinder he had disguised to look like a fire extinguisher. "What did old Clint put inside you, buddy?" he asked aloud.

"Probably CO^2," Jake said, as he entered the wheelhouse behind Hootie.

The cylinder slipped from Hootie's hands. He fumbled it a few times, finally catching it before it hit the deck.

"Yeah, that's what it is," Hootie agreed. There was no need for Jake to know what was inside the fake fire extinguisher …yet. Hootie knew, sooner or later he would have to reveal its secrets.

The black night sky lightened to blue and orange as that magical time before dawn spread across the water in front of Mark. Tom was still unconscious. He was in obvious pain, as he had not ceased moaning the entire time. With growing light, Mark could, at least see that he was not bleeding. One of Tom's legs bent at an odd angle. Broken, Mark thought. There was nothing on this sandy beach to use for a splint.

Mark piled sand into a heap and eased Tom's head from his lap onto the makeshift pillow. Tom groaned and sucked in his breath, but did not regain consciousness. Mark inspected the rest of Tom's body but found no open wounds – only some scratches and bruises. One large purple-green bruise ran from under Tom's left arm to his hipbone. He hoped the hard landing had not broken Tom's ribs. A broken rib could puncture Tom's lung, and he might die. Mark decided to move Tom as little as possible, but he had to get them some protection from what was going to be a relentless sun.

Rose-colored air hung above the water, matching the sky above until it was impossible to tell sky from sea. The sun was a red ball peeking over the horizon. Mark knew once it was high they would be baking on the little sand island. He stood and scouted along the water's edge until he found a jagged board that had washed ashore. Chances are it came from their wrecked boat.

Returning to Tom's side, he began to dig a trench in the soft sand using the board. He planned to build a shelter from the sun then use the board to splint Tom's leg if he could. By the time the sun changed from a red ball into a blazing yellow orb, he had dug a large hole in the damp, cool sand. The hole was about 8-feet wide, and 5-feet deep. It spooked Mark to think how much it resembled a grave. He hoped it would not become one. Satisfied the pit was large enough, he sat the board aside. He roamed the edge of the island looking for anything he could use to cover the shelter.

He peered out on the water scanning for the giant crocodile. Not seeing any sign of danger, Mark waded into the water and began pulling seaweed and other plants up by the roots. They were easy to remove, but they smelled of rotten mud from the bottom of the lagoon. He gathered an armful and carried them back to the trench.

Starting at one corner, he laid the plants across the opening. He did the same with the other edge, and then put more plants across those. He continued that zigzag thatch pattern until he had the entire hole covered except at one end. He had made a sand ramp at the narrow end of the trench leading to the bottom. He would drag Tom inside to lie in the cooling sand, shielded from the blazing sun. Despite the rising temperature, the sand at the bottom of the hole had not dried out and remained moist and refreshing. It wasn't much, but it was a shelter.

He grabbed Tom beneath the arms and began to pull him toward the opening. He saw movement on the lagoon and breathed a sigh of relief as *Miss Katie* appeared in the distance. She was moving slowly but in their direction. He stripped his white t-shirt off, tied it to the end of the board, and began to wave it in the air. After a while, *Miss Katie* seemed to come to a halt. Why did they stop? Didn't they see us?

"Please see us," Mark prayed. "Don't let them turn around," he pleaded.

"Help!" he yelled, knowing *Miss Katie* was too far away to hear him.

"It's only an old piece of driftwood," Jake said, as he pulled the board from the water.

"Let me see it," Hootie requested.

After examining the wood, Hootie asked Jake to bring everyone up on the main deck. Holding the broken wooden board up for all to see, Hootie explained, "This is fresh broken; see how the ends are sharp and jagged? If it were driftwood, it would have smooth edges worn away by the water. It smells like fresh wood, too. I want everyone to keep a lookout on all sides of the boat, please."

"What are we looking for?" Katie asked.

"Look for anything that is out of place or doesn't look right. I think there has been a boat accident out here – somewhere close by. Keep your eyes open."

In fewer than five minutes, Jake called from the starboard bow, "Hootie, turn this way!"

Hootie swung the wheel in the direction Jake pointed. "What have you got?" he called through the window.

"I don't know, but something is lying in the water ahead."

Hootie pulled the throttle down to slow the boat. "Let me know when we get close," he instructed.

"Okay! Stop," Jake called. Hootie idled the engine and came out of the wheelhouse to look at the object Jake had found. Everyone came forward to see.

Fifteen feet below in the crystal water lay the stern of a fishing boat. The stern was pointing towards the surface as if it were resting on its bow, which they could not see.

"The front of the boat must be stuck deep in the mud and sand," Jesse offered.

Hootie shook his head. "No. It would not have happened that way; the rear of the boat is the heaviest part because of the engine. If anything, it would be sitting on its stern – even that would be unusual."

"Then, what?" everyone asked in unison.

"That," Hootie pointed, "is only half a boat. Something ripped off the front half of it!"

Jake found that hard to believe. "What could break a boat in two?"

Hootie did not know, but he wanted a closer look. "Jake, take the wheel. I'm going down there to check it out. Keep watch, and if you see anything, throw that ring into the water." He pointed to the round lifebuoy ring hanging on the bulkhead. "Smack it on the surface real loud. I'll be able to hear it down there."

Hootie stripped down to his swim trunks, donned a snorkel mask, and slipped over the side of the boat. The group watched as he swam to the wreck. The water was so clear that if not for the ripples Hootie made, it would have looked like Hootie was floating in space.

Everyone watched as Hootie swam around the wreck and pulled at certain sections of the hull. At one point, he peeled something from the side of the hulk and stuck it under his arm. Everyone was glad when he finally rose to the surface. Spitting water and out of breath, he threw his mask onto the deck and climbed aboard.

"That boat didn't sink," he panted, once he had wiped his face. "She was sunk by someone – or something."

"Pirates?" Katie wanted to know.

"I don't know. That boat looks like it's been in a war. It looks like a torpedo hit them. There is a huge crack where the boat split in two and another one aft of that – smaller than the first." He laid the piece of the wreck he had found on the deck. "And, I found this."

"What is it?" Rita asked.

"What is that? Someone's leather wallet?" Jesse asked. "Hey! Let me see that."

Hootie handed it over. "It looks like that hide we found in the cave. Jake! Come and take a look at this," Jesse called.

"Hootie!" Jake yelled from the front of the boat. "Hootie!"

"What is it?"

"Someone is waving a white flag up ahead," he pointed. "Someone is in trouble!"

CHAPTER 33

"He doesn't look to be in very good shape," Hootie said beneath the binoculars. "The photographer looks like he might be dead – he's not moving. His helper is building some kind of shelter for them. It looks like we got here before something worse happened!"

"Photographer?" Jake repeated. "You know them?"

"Yeah, I didn't get a chance to tell you guys. That boat on the bottom back there is the boat we rammed a few nights ago."

"The very same boat?" Katie asked.

"Yeah," Hootie admitted. "I met him while we were getting the boats repaired."

Jake looked at Jesse and mouthed the word "photographer." Jesse shrugged and made a quizzical expression.

Hootie throttled down and stopped *Miss Katie* as close to the small island as he dared get. If they mired in the mud flats, they would not be able to help anyone. Both groups would need rescuing.

"Jesse, do you feel strong enough to help Jake?" Hootie asked.

"You bet! I haven't used the cane in a few days. I'm okay. What do you need me to do?"

"Help Jake launch the skiff, go get them, and bring them aboard. We'll take them back to the hospital in La Pesca."

"Be careful, Jesse," Rita urged. "Let Jake do most of the work. You run the boat."

Jesse blew her a kiss as he went to the stern with Jake to launch the shallow watercraft. Katie tried to comfort her.

"Jesse will be okay," she assured her friend. "He's not even limping much anymore. You know how those guys are – if there's macho in it, you can't stop them."

"Katie!" Rita snapped. "There's a giant crocodile out there, for crying out loud! For all we know, that Aquasaurus is what sank their boat! Think what it could do to that tiny runabout!"

Katie hadn't thought about that, and now she looked worried too. She watched Jake steer the small boat toward the sandy bit of island. They could not take their eyes from the smooth glassy water – imagining a giant crocodile coming to the surface at any moment.

"Wake up, Professor!" Mark tried to shake Tom awake by roughly pushing on his shoulder. Tom's eyes fluttered as he groaned at the pain Mark was causing by rousing him. Worried that Tom may have more than cracked ribs, Mark stood and went toward the small boat as it came ashore.

"I can't wake him up," Mark explained. "He's alive. He's still breathing, but I'm afraid he has cracked ribs. I'm afraid to move him very much. I don't see any wounds on his head, but he may have a back injury. I'm no medic! I don't know!"

Jake knelt next to the unconscious man. "Professor! Professor, can you hear me?"

Tom did not respond. "What happened?" Jesse asked Mark.

"We got attacked by the biggest crocodile you ever saw in your life!" Marks eyes grew wide as he related the story. "You know that body they found out here the other day?"

"Yeah," Jake chimed in, "that was us! We found it, or rather Katie did."

"Yeah, we know," Mark admitted. "The professor figured it was a crocodile that put it there, so we came out here last night to check it out. The damned thing attacked us. It almost killed us. It ate our boat!"

"I know. We found what was left of your boat over there," Jesse motioned with his head. "It looks snapped in two."

"It is!" Mark agreed. "That thing was so big it broke us in two like a pretzel. Then it went after us in the water. The professor tried to save me, but the monster smashed him with his huge tail. He flew through the air across this island and into the water on the other side."

"Wow! That has to be fifty yards. No wonder he's out," Jesse marveled.

"Well, we can't stay here in the open. That crocodile could come back any minute – we can't protect ourselves here. We've got to get the Professor aboard *Miss Katie* so we can take him to the hospital," Jake said, putting their situation back in focus. "Jesse, go get a tarp out of the flatboat and bring it here."

They folded the tarp into a triangle since they only had three people to carry. "Tie a knot in your corner," Jake told Mark and Jesse. "That is going to be your handle as we try to carry the Professor to the boat."

They formed the tarp stretcher into the shape of a giant diaper. Being as gentle as possible, Jake took Tom beneath the arms. With Jesse and Mark on each leg, they laid Tom on the tarp, shoulders at the wide end. Tom moaned in agony but did not regain consciousness. That was probably a good thing.

Once they positioned Tom on the tarp, each gripped and lifted their assigned corner. As they carried and half-dragged Tom to the runabout, his feet made two furrows in the sand.

They laid Tom in the bottom of the runabout, still on the tarp, covered him with a blanket, and pushed off from the sand island. Everyone helped bring Tom on board *Miss Katie*. Rita recognized Tom immediately. Tom was the professor who had helped rescue them in Honey Creek Cave.

"It's Professor Morrison!" she exclaimed. "What is he doing down here in Mexico?"

"He's a professor?" Hootie asked. "He told me he was a photographer. I met him in town the other day as he was fixing the boat we damaged. He told me he was taking vacation shots for a travel magazine."

"Travel magazine," Jake snorted. "Discovery is no travel magazine – he was trying to get a picture of that giant crocodile."

"How do you know that?" Hootie wanted to know.

"He told me," Jake admitted. "I saw them in Tampico while you guys were clearing customs. He said he wanted to get a picture of Aquasaurus for that magazine."

"It's true," Mark admitted.

"Why didn't you tell us, Jake?" Hootie demanded.

"I didn't think it was important," Jake responded. "We all know him – he's Jesse's Earth Science professor at Texas State."

"How come you all know him?" Hootie wanted to know.

"Professor Morrison was with Jesse and Jake in Honey Creek Cave when the earthquake hit," Rita told him. "Katie and I decided to try to rescue them. We didn't know that huge crocodile was in there with them. It attacked us, and that is how Jesse got hurt. Professor Morrison helped us escape."

"Who else knew this professor was down here and didn't tell me?" Hootie demanded.

Jesse raised his arm and looked at the deck.

"Jesse!" Rita exclaimed. "You didn't even tell me. Why didn't you let us know?"

"I didn't think it mattered," Jesse explained. "Jake told me, but I didn't think any more about it. It didn't have anything to do with us. I didn't know it was them we hit the other night."

"I didn't know that either," Jake said as he shook his head.

Hootie stared at the group for a moment, then said, "Okay, first things first. We'll deal with this later, for now, we have to get your professor to a doctor. You guys make him as comfortable as you can, and I'll get us there as soon as possible."

Hootie shook his head as he turned to go into the wheelhouse. In moments, *Miss Katie* was speeding toward the safety of the Río Soto la Marina.

Swimming in the murky depths amongst the reeds and seaweeds, the crocodile searched. The two large swimming bodies had disappeared. Aquasaurus tried to find them. Where were they? They were not bobbing on the surface nor were they floating beneath the water. Those noisy, buzzing raiders had stolen another prize.

Anger coursed throughout the creature's limited mental awareness. The instinct to protect its territory was natural. Twice these interlopers had cheated by stealing his prey. The survival impulse demanded a fight until the threat was gone. There was room for only one master of these waters. Those hard-shelled floating platforms that made the awful buzzing sounds must leave. Aquasaurus would destroy them just like the last one that entered the realm. The crocodile had bashed and battered the foe by ramming them. They were vulnerable. With a few well-placed blows, they sank to the bottom never to rise again. Once attacked, the tender edibles floundered in the water – helpless and alone.

Not many targets escaped those massive jaws. Aquasaurus remembered eyeing a helpless creature swimming in the water the night before. The animal lowered lenses over soapy eyes when another large swimmer surfaced behind. Fearing an attack on the left flank, the crocodile flipped its tail in an ominous sweep. The new threat sailed out of sight. During the delay, the giant beast found the first swimmer had also disappeared. That did not happen often, and the giant crocodile could not determine how the swimmer had escaped.

The crocodile swam among the islands and sandbars searching for the missing prey. Where had it fallen? Where had the other one gone? They had to be here in the water somewhere. The crocodile hunted all night until the morning light.

The giant crocodile was a mile away when the buzzing began again. Using every ounce of strength, the crocodile swam toward the sounds it hated. Too late, the buzzing had moved away again.

Here was their gathering point. Aquasaurus sensed that the invaders would return soon. This time would be different. Lying in wait for their return, the crocodile dreamed of satisfaction and revenge.

Crawling from the water onto the small sand island, the crocodile slid ashore. It left great divots in the sand as sharp claws pulled its huge body forward. The scent of prey was everywhere. Nosing the pit, the giant animal found the hole too small to enter. Using its feet and snout, it moved enough sand to allow partial entry. Turning around inside the pit was impossible. The crocodile swung its massive head to clear an opening at the other end of the trench and lay facing the open water. The crocodile was uncomfortable in the narrow hole, pressed in on either side. There were other uses for sand. It dug smaller pits, exposing cool, dark sand beneath the dry, grainy surface. The sun and the afternoon heat of Mexico bore down upon the makeshift roof above the giant reptile. Stretching full length on the sugary sand, the crocodile slept.

CHAPTER 34

The hospital at La Pesca was rural and far less modern than any you would find in Austin, but at least there was a doctor on duty. The small group sat in the waiting room as the doctor examined Tom and Mark. When the doctors were finished with Mark, he sat with the group and waited for word about Tom.

"How is he?" Hootie asked as Mark sat in the hard, steel chair. Mark rubbed at a rough bandage covering his arm and turned his swollen face toward Hootie. Mark looked like he had lost a boxing match.

"He's conscious now, but not making any sense," Mark reported. "They gave him a shot, and he's kind of babbling. The doctor said it was a good sign, but he looks in pretty bad shape to me."

"Tell us what happened," Hootie inquired.

Mark repeated what he had told Jesse and Jake on the island.

"That thing came out of nowhere," he related. "It was on us without warning – like it was waiting for us. It was the biggest alligator I've ever seen."

"It's a crocodile," Hootie reminded him.

"Alligator – crocodile – whatever! That thing is a killer! You can't imagine how big it is!

"I can," Katie said as Jesse, Jake, and Rita nodded.

"We've met it before," Rita told Mark.

"No kidding! Where?" Mark asked.

"That same crocodile trapped us in Honey Creek Cave last spring. It attacked Rita and me on a lake deep inside the cave," Katie told Mark. "When Jake and Jesse jumped in to save us, it flipped Jesse clean out of the water. That's how Jesse's got injured. Professor Morrison took over, drove the monster away, and got us to a safe place. Did you know Professor Morrison used to wrestle alligators in Florida?"

Mark shook his head, "Yeah. No wonder he knows so much about 'em. Anyway, this was no ordinary alligator!"

"What are you two doing down here in Mexico?" Hootie asked Mark.

"We came to get a picture of that monster crocodile! Professor Morrison needed it for a magazine."

"So that much is true," Hootie said. "Morrison left out the part of him being a professor and tracking the same crocodile. What did he intend to do if he found it?"

Mark looked at the floor and admitted, "He wanted to catch it and study it for scientific purposes. What are you guys going to do if you find it?"

Hootie looked at Katie, then back to Mark. "I'll let her tell you," he answered.

Katie brushed her hair back from her forehead and looked at Mark with a deadpan expression, "We're going to kill it!"

Tom opened his eyes and looked around at the sterile, white-sheeted room. Where was he? A hot, bright light was shining in his face. He shut his eyes and turned his face away from the glare, and tried to sit up. Instant pain erupted in his lower back, and his entire left side throbbed. White streaks flashed beneath his closed eyelids. He felt the pressure of a hand on his chest and heard a soft female voice.

"Easy, Señor, do not try to get up. You have been in an accident."

"Where am I?" Tom wanted to know.

"You are in a hospital in La Pesca. The doctor is next door reading your X-rays. He will return soon. Try to stay calm and still. We have given you medication for the pain; but if you are not calm, it will not help much."

Despite the warning and the sharp pain, Tom raised his head enough to check out both arms and legs. Relieved that they were still attached to his body, and dropped his head back to the pillow.

A Mexican doctor in a white lab coat entered the room and greeted Tom. "I see you are awake now. How do you feel?"

"Like a truck ran over me," Tom groaned. "There was a kid with me – his name was Mark. Where is he?"

"He is fine, Señor. He saved you from drowning. Your friends from the other boat brought you here to the hospital."

"He's okay?" Tom asked.

"Yes, he is fine. He has only minor injuries. I understand that a giant crocodile attacked you – one that has been in the news lately."

"Yeah," Tom admitted, "*that* … Aquasaurus."

"You are fortunate, Señor. Others have not survived its attack. Is it truly as large as they claim?"

"They didn't do it justice," Tom assured him.

The doctor made a sizzling sound and shook his fingers of his right hand. He wrote a note in Tom's chart and then looked up. "I have examined you and looked at your X-rays; and I can tell you that you are fortunate, indeed. There are no bite marks. You have three broken ribs and a wound below the left knee. I see swelling in your knee, but it is merely sprained – not broken. However, you have a break above the ankle. I'm going to tape your ribs to restrict movement, and after that, I'm going to immobilize your knee and leg. Once you return to the States, you should see your doctor." The doctor nodded at the nurse who injected another dose of painkiller into Tom's IV.

"Return to the States?" Tom mumbled, already feeling groggy again.

"Si, Señor. I'm afraid your crocodile fighting days are over for now."

Tom laid back his head as fatigue and drowsiness began to overcome him.

"This will hurt some, Senor; but it will be over soon. Relax please."

Tom drifted into a merciful anesthesia-induced fog as the doctor set his broken leg. He did not remember the doctor taping his ribs.

Mark had escaped the attack with only minor bumps and bruises. Once Tom was able to travel, he planned for them to return to Texas. There, Tom could get better medical attention and would be able to recover at home under the care of his doctor.

Mark and Tom were safe, and Hootie and the group had done all they could do. They said goodbye to Mark and returned to *Miss Katie*. Once back on board the boat, Jesse, Rita, and Jake went to the salon to lie down and rest. Katie stayed with Hootie in the wheelhouse as he steered the back onto the bay.

"What now?" Katie asked.

Hootie looked forward as he spoke, measuring his words. "Well," he started, "at least we know where the crocodile is now. Do you still want to get rid of it?" he asked.

"Yes," Katie admitted. "I think we have to if we can," she added. "What if that thing kills someone else? How are we going to feel? I know how I'm going to feel – horrible."

Hootie nodded.

"Hootie," Katie asked, "are you sure you can kill it?"

"Oh, yeah," Hootie nodded, "no doubt about that. We can kill it if we can get close enough to it."

"You never told me how," Katie reminded him.

Hootie did not want to go into too much detail in case anyone ever questioned her. "It's a little trick I learned from your daddy," he admitted. "It's probably best you don't know too much about it, but remember – no matter what – it is *not* an explosive," he emphasized. " If we get caught, it is important that you keep saying that to anyone who will listen. Bringing explosives into Mexico is illegal. Understand? We *did not* do that. When this thing goes off, it may look like a bomb, but it is a far different reaction – not an explosion. Got it?"

"What do I tell them?"

"Tell them you don't know anything. Tell them to ask me. Describe what you saw, but do not ever say the word explosives. Got it?"

"I got it," she assured him, "I got it. Won't they find out anyway? They have tests, you know – and dogs that can pick up the scent of a bomb."

"Don't worry," Hootie assured her. "You won't be lying. I told you – it's not a bomb. The dogs won't pick up the scent, and there won't be any residue for them to test. But it will make the biggest waterspout you ever saw or will ever see."

The sun was setting on the Rio as Hootie turned *Miss Katie* northward. The red-cloaked sky to the west looked like the clouds were floating over a sea of Big Red soda.

An hour out of La Pesca, Hootie slowed *Miss Katie* to a crawl. He swung the big searchlight in a long arc from bow to stern, then down the other side. Other than waving grasses on a few sandy islands, nothing moved in the darkness.

Katie was still in the wheelhouse. From the sound of it, everyone else on board had gone to bed. Nothing was moving.

"I can't believe Jake didn't tell us," Katie said almost to herself.

"It wouldn't have changed anything," Hootie answered. Katie had not realized she had spoken aloud.

"I wonder why he didn't," Katie said, almost as a question.

"Who knows? He said it didn't occur to him. He didn't think it was important."

"Would it have been important?" Katie asked.

"No, not really," Hootie admitted, "except, we may have had two boats instead of one."

"And four more pairs of eyes. Maybe it wouldn't have attacked two boats."

"No way of knowing," Hootie admitted, as he continued swinging the beam of light out on the water. "Give Jake a break – I have. He's telling the truth."

"I'll give him a break alright!"

"Easy, girl," Hootie laughed. "I'm sure he's punishing himself enough already."

Hootie scanned the surface of the water as he moved the light from side to side. "The croc has to be close by," he muttered. "It's lying on the bottom."

"It's the deception, you know," Katie moaned. "We trusted him, and he didn't tell us. I don't know if I can trust him anymore."

"I guess you'll have to give him the benefit of the doubt," Hootie said. "He screwed up."

"No," Katie said. "I don't have to give him anything. He almost got the Professor and Mark killed – you said so yourself – it may not have attacked two boats."

"I didn't say that; you did," Hootie reminded her.

"You didn't disagree," Katie countered.

"Well, you're tired," Hootie said in a gentle voice. "Why don't you go below and get some rest? Nothing's going to happen out here tonight. We'll be up by daylight and start searching again."

"What about you?" Katie asked.

"I'll keep watch until morning. I'll catch a little shuteye during breakfast. By then, I figure it will be on the surface."

"I'll stay with you a little longer if you don't mind."

In less than ten minutes, she was sound asleep in her chair. Hootie draped a blanket over her sleeping form and touched her hair. He felt like he imagined a father feels. He realized that more than anything else, he wanted to protect her. Katie slept in the wheelhouse as Hootie steered the boat into the bay. He cut the light and laid his head back against the pilot's seat.

The day broke clear and fresh, as the sun was a bright yellow ball in the eastern sky. Hootie realized he had dropped off to sleep sometime during the night. He woke Katie and suggested she go below for some coffee. She promised to bring some up for him.

Hootie scanned the surrounding water through the glasses. Nothing was moving, not even waves. The surface was glassy smooth. Small shadows traced each little sandy island like eyeliner while above, each cloud had a silver lining. Any bumps or mounds he could see on the beaches were all natural and were not moving. Somewhere among those shadows the giant beast lay – waiting.

Hootie realized it was time to reveal the plan. He called everyone topside for some instructions. When they were together, Hootie stood before them and got their attention. He placed his coffee aside and lifted a red fire extinguisher. He looked from one to the other as he spoke.

"We are sitting right where we were yesterday. The wreck of the sunken boat is right over there. Dead ahead is the island where we picked up Mark and the Professor. I am convinced that the crocodile is nearby – it may be right beneath us right now."

"What are you going to do," Jake joked, "beat it to death with a fire extinguisher?" No one laughed.

"Shut up, Jake! This is serious," Katie warned giving Jake a hateful glare.

"Actually," Hootie admitted, "I am." He cradled the fire extinguisher in his arms. "As a matter of fact, this is not a fire extinguisher," Hootie admitted. "I painted it to look like one." Hootie pulled the hose away from the canister body and pitched it across the deck behind him.

"Why did you paint it up like a fire extinguisher?" Jesse asked.

"Because. I didn't want the police to find it if they boarded us. I needed everyone to think it *was* an empty fire extinguisher. It worked," Hootie said.

"So I wasn't the only one holding back information," Jake said in a half whisper.

Hootie continued, "I want everyone to listen and remember this. There won't be time to remind you of these things later. You have to understand it right from the start. Pay attention," he said in a firm voice.

"I know what you are thinking," Hootie said. "This is *not* a bomb. Get that out of your head right now. It is not an explosive – it *won't* blow up. I already explained this to Katie. It is important that you all understand this one important thing. If the police think we used a bomb, we will go to a Mexican prison for the rest of our lives. You have to remember – this is not a bomb. If they arrest us, never confess to using a bomb. You won't be lying – this is **not** a bomb!" Hootie emphasized again.

"It may look like a bomb, it may look like a bomb when it goes off, but it is critical to your freedom to remember that one fact. When it does go off, it's going to shoot a geyser of water about two hundred feet in the air. There will be a loud noise like water boiling, but no boom. There will be no explosion – because why?" Hootie asked.

"Because it's not a bomb?" Jake offered.

"Exactly! Good job, Jake."

Hootie pulled a key fob from his shirt pocket. He held it up for all to see. "This is a normal key fob like you use to unlock your car. Katie, come here, please."

Katie stood and joined Hootie in front of the group. "Katie, see this little plastic square glued on top of the key fob?"

"Yes, sir."

"Beneath the little plastic square is a red button. Whatever happens, do not move that square or press that red button until I tell you. Okay?"

"You want me to do that?" Katie asked.

"Yes. Once we find Aquasaurus, I'll motion you like this." Hootie crossed both of his arms over his head in an "x" shape. "When you see me do that you pull that little tab off, and press the red button."

"Okay. Where will you be?" Katie asked.

Hootie pointed out over the water. "Out there. Jake and I will be on the jet skis. Jesse, you steer the boat, and Rita I need you to take out the small boat and be ready to come to pick us up if we get in trouble. Katie, you'll be here on the deck with this key fob ready to push the button when I give the signal."

"What are you going to do?" Katie asked.

"Jake is going to get the crocodile to open its mouth somehow, and I'm going to toss this canister down its throat. Then I'll give the signal, and you'll press the red button."

"Then, what?" Jesse asked.

"Crocodile goes poof!" Hootie exploded his hands outward.

CHAPTER 35

The airliner rose over Mexico and swung outwards over the deep blue Gulf. The cabin tilted left as the pilot set a course northward toward Houston. Mark leaned back into his seat, hoping to catch a few winks before landing.

Throughout the boarding and takeoff briefing, Tom sat silent and deep in thought. As the plane rose over the coast, he looked out the window at the landscape gliding by far below. La Pesca and the long, narrow inter-waterway were recognizable below. Tom could almost make out the exact spot where the giant crocodile attacked them. Somewhere along that slender inland sea, Hootie and the rest of them were going to track down Aquasaurus and kill it. Tom wished he had some way to stop them, but that chance had slipped through his fingers. Tom felt defeated and sore as he readjusted his aching leg. Still looking out the window, he spoke to Mark in the next seat.

"I never said thank you."

Mark grinned and poked Tom with his elbow.

"You didn't have to. You'd have done the same for me – *you did*! You told me how to get away from that croc," he joked. Tom smiled.

"You did well," Tom admitted. He poked Mark back with his good arm, "There's a job for you down in south Florida if you ever want to work as an alligator handler."

"No. Thanks!" Mark laughed. "I'll be happy if I *never* see an alligator or crocodile again."

"Right now, I tend to agree with you," Tom admitted, as he lay his tired head back against the seat. In five minutes, both had dropped off to sleep. Neither one of them knew what waited ahead at Houston's airport.

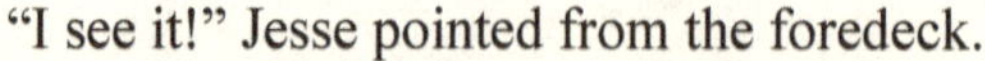

"I see it!" Jesse pointed from the foredeck.

Hootie jerked the glasses to his eyes and scanned the sea in the direction Jesse indicated. He passed it over a couple of times before he realized what he was seeing. It was big! It was so much bigger than he expected. There, stretched out on the sandy bank, lay the largest crocodile he had ever seen. It was monstrous – it seemed as long as a twenty-nine passenger school bus, but not as tall! The island was a sandy hook with an enclosed section of water behind it. If they could get the crocodile to slide off the other side, they might be able to trap it in the shallow backwater.

Hootie, realizing the opportunity at hand, called a quick strategy meeting.

"Okay," he informed them. "The crocodile is beached on that island right ahead of us. We need to get it back into the water. I don't think it has spotted us yet, so we have the element of surprise. Here is what we need to do." Everyone paid close attention to Hootie as he repeated the plan.

"Jesse, take the wheel of this boat. Rush that island at the highest speed you can reach. Pull up as soon as you see the crocodile move. If you surprise it, it will scramble across that small beach and go off the other side. That is what we want. When it gets back into the water, move the boat around to the right to block the channel that goes back into the lagoon."

"What if it doesn't move?" Jesse asked.

"Push it as close as you dare. Be careful you don't run aground. If the crocodile won't move, or it comes at you, back off and outrun it if you can. Whatever you do, don't let it get broadside to you."

He handed Katie the black plastic key fob.

"Katie, as soon as I cross my arms over my head, like this," Hootie demonstrated, "peel away this plastic chip and press the red button beneath. Do not press it before then," he stressed. "Understand?"

"Yes," she nodded and asked, "What about you?" Hootie did not answer.

"Rita, you and Jake come with me," he turned and walked to the rear of the boat. Rita and Jake followed.

Hootie untied the runabout and both jet skis. After they buckled their life jackets, Hootie spoke to Rita.

"Rita, stay as far back as you can. If one of us gets in trouble, we will need you to come to pick us up – if you can do it without putting yourself in danger. Don't take any chances. You won't have a chance on the water in that little johnboat. We will need you to pick us up – if you can get to us without crossing its path. Got it?"

"Yes, sir, I've got it."

"Jake, I'll have the canister with me. Your job, if you can do it, is to get close enough to its snout to make it open its mouth wide. Watch out for that tail – it's quick. Don't get alongside it – try to stay across the front of its snout. If you get close enough, it will open up wide, and I'll be there to throw this thing down its throat."

"Got it, boss," Jake grinned. "Open wide, baby!"

"Once I get the canister inside it, we all high tail it back to the boat. Don't waste any time getting back on the boat even if you have to leave the jet skis loose in the water. We don't want to be anywhere near when this thing goes off. Rita, once you see us head back to the boat, you do the same."

"Yes, sir," Rita acknowledged.

Hootie lowered his goggles and shouted, "Let's go!"

Jake and Hootie moved off side-by-side and waved to Jesse to start the charge. Rita moved around to the other side of the boat and raised her glasses to watch the action. Once Jesse moved *Miss Katie*, she planned to move closer to the end of the island, just in case they needed her.

Jesse eased the throttle forward and moved ahead, slowly increasing speed. *Miss Katie* kicked up a wave of foamy water as it roared ahead, picking up speed as it went. The bow of the boat rose, and the propeller cut into the frothy water. Jesse watched as the giant crocodile turned its head and glared at the approaching ship. Jesse yelled as loud as he could and pulled the air horn chain. The horn drowned out his voice as it pierced the air.

He smiled as the crocodile turned and scrambled for the opposite side of the island. Once Aquasaurus had entered the water, Jesse pulled the throttle back. *Miss Katie* slowed to a crawl a hundred yards offshore. Jesse turned to the right and moved into position to block the entry into the open lagoon.

With hurrahs and high fives, Hootie and Jake moved into the still backwater hunting the crocodile. Each took opposite ways around the lake, waiting for the animal to surface. Rita saw Aquasaurus enter the water and moved her boat into position near the entry into the back lagoon. Behind the island, the two jet skis circled – searching. Somewhere beneath the dark, glassy water, the giant crocodile lurked and waited.

A crowd had gathered at the airport in Houston. Almost every local TV station and news service had a van parked at the arrivals entrance. Police with loud whistles and rude gestures were standing in the road moving traffic along as well as they could. Heavy, rubber-coated wires snaked across the sidewalk in front of the doors. Police officers lost the battle for order. The best they could do was string yellow "crime scene" tape around both sides of the media mob.

"There he is!" one reporter shouted, as Mark pushed Tom's wheelchair through the automatic doors. What in the heck was going on?

The crowd surged forward, shoving and elbowing each other, jostling for position. Photographers held cameras high in the air and filmed over the heads of those ahead of them. Dozens of electronic flashes burst at almost the same time.

"Professor Morrison, can we have a word?" Bewildered, and unsure of what to do, Mark struggled to push Tom's wheelchair over heavy communications wires and came to a stop in front of the reporters who did not yield or open a way for them to pass. The swarm of news reporters tightened and pressed them in on every side.

"Professor Morrison, do you have a comment for our listeners?" the nearest one asked.

"What's this all about?" Tom asked.

"You haven't heard?" A murmur moved through the crowd.

"Heard what?"

"The DNA results came out this morning. You discovered a living specimen of a crocodile long thought to be extinct!"

Tom looked from one reporter to the other. "Aquasaurus," he muttered.

A rapid stream of questions erupted from the crowd as they all spoke at once. "Have you found it?" "Are there any others?" "Your school said you were going to Mexico to get pictures." "Do you have any photos?" "Can you give us a statement?"

Tom blinked at the crowd of reporters. They could not have heard him if he had answered. The questions were coming so loud and too fast too loud for Tom to think. He raised his hands to the crowd as if pushing them off. Like adoring fans before a rock star, they quieted. Cameras and audio recorders rolled as they waited for his words.

"I've been in Mexico," he told them. "I haven't heard the results yet. What did they say it was?"

"Why," one reporter checked his notes, "they called it *Carnufex carolinensis*, Professor."

"I knew it!" Tom shouted. "Mark, that proves it," he called over his shoulder. He turned back to the media crowd using his best dramatic voice, "It was the Carolina Butcher!"

"Professor, why are you in a wheelchair? How were you injured?"

Despite his pain and the fog of his painkillers, Tom realized the position he now owned.

"We tracked the crocodile down, and it attacked us. It sank our boat! We're lucky to be alive."

The crowd pressed even closer. Tom, realizing the power he had over the media, announced; "Ladies and gentlemen, I am on my way to see my doctor. I plan to hold a news conference at 10 o'clock tomorrow morning at the St. Regis Hotel. There will be no further comments until then. Thank you for your concern and cooperation."

The crowd parted as an ambulance with red and blue flashing lights, squawked and braked to a stop at the curb. Two uniformed paramedics rushed forward and pushed Tom toward the waiting ambulance.

The crocodile was startled by the sudden roar of the motor and the blast of the air horn. Instinctively, it rose and lumbered with astonishing speed across the sandy beach toward water and safety. It slid into the quiet pool on the other side without a splash.

Below the murky still water, the giant crocodile knew it was in control. It was larger and superior to creatures now buzzing on the surface. The small backwater hampered its movements as it kicked waves up onto the barren beach. The irritating buzzing closed in and confused it for a moment. It must find a way to stop the annoying buzzing. Crawling along the muddy sea bottom, Aquasaurus followed the edge of the sandy island. It inched its way toward open water it knew was close. Reaching the laguna and sensing it was free, the crocodile swam for deeper water. After five hundred yards, it stopped and surfaced.

It swam in a broad arc back in the direction from which it came while surveying the surface from beneath. The crocodile floated, only its eyes above the water. It spotted the buzzing nuisances nearby. They circled the back lagoon like giant water flies. In a rage, the crocodile rose to its full length from the bottom. Aquasaurus towered high and bellowed a terrifying roar that vibrated across the water. Birds nesting in the shallows flapped, squawked, and took panicked flight. Setting its sights on the nearest annoyance, the monstrous crocodile lunged forward. In a mindless rage, it rushed toward a wide-eyed Rita in the small boat.

Jake could not hear Hootie shouting over the wind and engine noise. He saw Hootie point and followed his lead. Aquasaurus had eluded them below the surface and had entered the open lagoon. Gunning their jet skis even faster, Jake and Hootie shot tall rooster tails into the air as they raced toward Rita.

Almost as planned, Hootie went around the left side as Jake steered to the right of Rita's small boat. Jake remembered that Hootie wanted them to crisscross in front of the monster crocodile. They hoped to distract it away from helpless Rita. Their plan worked. The monster crocodile watched them speed past and snapped at them with its giant jaws: close, but no cigar. The giant crocodile turned away from Rita and focused on the even smaller watercraft. Jake slowed and turned back to make another run as Hootie circled his arm above his head like a rodeo rider. Jake understood that this was the pass that had to count. His job would be to make sure the crocodile opened his giant mouth this time.

Jake threw open the throttle of his jet ski and barreled forward, aiming to get as close to Aquasaurus as he dared. Meanwhile, Hootie would angle to be in the right place to throw the cylinder down the crocodile's throat. Jake ducked his head against the spray of seawater and coaxed as much power as he could get from the jet ski. He did not see the submerged sand ramp just beneath the waves. Jake slid up a hidden sand ramp and went airborne. Jake and the jet ski hurdled skyward as the crocodile rose again, vulgar fat jaws opened wide.

259

The world shifted into slow motion for Jake. Aloft on an unsteady jet ski, Jake no longer had any control over his direction or his trajectory. The momentum was carrying him and the jet ski on a direct course toward the crocodile's open mouth. Jake saw the red canister tumble through the air below him and disappear down the crocodile's throat. Success!

Jake sailed between the animal's huge teeth as the massive jaws snapped closed. He felt enormous teeth clank against the metal of his ride. The jet ski stopped, but Jake's forward force carried him tumbling into the sea. Jake plunged past the handlebars and went head over heels into the sea. With a mouth full of twisted metal and plastic, the crocodile fell upon Jake with the full force of its entire body weight.

Hootie, traveling in the opposite direction did not know Jake had crashed. He stopped in the water and raised his crossed arms above his head.

"Push the button, Katie! Push it now!" he screamed, knowing she could not hear. Katie peeled the small plastic square away from the dreaded red button. Nervous, shaking hands fumbled the key fob in her grasp. The fob slipped between her fingers, and she snatched at it twice before it fell too far for her to reach. She watched horrified as the fob splashed into the sea below and sank.

Katie had swung one leg over the rail, prepared to dive in to retrieve the fob. She took one glance toward Hootie and Jake and froze when she realized that she could no longer see Jake. The giant crocodile was churning the water in a slow death roll at the exact location where Jake had last been.

The key fob swayed and swerved as it sank into the salty depths. It swung and played like a falling leaf in a sea-green forest. It dipped and spun in the currents as it dropped out of sight beyond reach.

CHAPTER 36

Hootie raced toward *Miss Katie* thrilled with the success of their plan. He looked back and saw Rita speeding in the same direction as fast as her little boat would carry her. Hootie saw no sign of Jake, but Hootie was not worried. Jake knew the plan, and Hootie knew he would be joining them as soon as he could. He saw the roiling water beyond Rita's boat and wondered if the reaction in the canister could be taking effect already. He did not know how long it would take to work. He thought it would happen very quickly since Clint had warned him not to be anywhere close to the thing when it went off.

Sliding sideways into the rear of the boat, Hootie jumped from the jet ski. He tied the lead rope to a cleat and waited for Rita and Jake to arrive. Within seconds, Rita motored up, and Hootie helped her secure her boat and climb on board *Miss Katie*. There was no sign or sound of Jake.

"Come on, Jake!" Hootie shouted to no one in particular. "Where are you?" He scanned the surface of the water but did not see Jake approaching. For the first time, he became worried. Where was Jake?

Rita had already climbed onto the deck. "Rita! Did you see where Jake went?"

"Yes! I don't know how he did it, Hootie. He Jake flew right through that crocodile's mouth – in the air!"

"What?"

"Yes! I don't know how he did it, but his jet ski took off and flew through the air. Jake went between the crocodile's jaws. I lost sight of him; then you signaled us to come back to the boat. I didn't look back. I thought he was right behind you."

"Rita, go up front and tell Jesse to move the boat back to where we started. I'm going after Jake!"

Hootie jumped back onto the jet ski and untied the rope. He fired up the motor and swung back toward where he could see the crocodile rolling over and over in the water. "No!" he screamed into the wind and salty spray.

Hootie made circled wide around the animal as he searched the water beyond the thrashing crocodile. He did not see Jake anywhere in the lagoon or even behind the small island. He moved as close to the flailing crocodile as he dared and caught the flash of metal in the sun. When the crocodile rolled upright, Hootie could see the twisted remains of Jake's jet ski in its mouth. Parts of the jet ski protruded from the animal's jagged teeth as it yawned wide trying to dislodge the machine. Where was Jake? Did the crocodile have him in its grasp? Was that why monster rolled and lurched around so wildly?

Hootie knew that the canister would ignite any second now – if it hadn't already triggered. He had signaled for Katie had pressed the red button. Surely she did. He wished he knew how much time he had. He wanted to keep searching for Jake, but he remembered Clint's warnings. Clint said when it touched water there would be a violent reaction. Hootie did not want to give up, but he had to think of the others.

Jesse was moving *Miss Katie* farther away as instructed. Hootie knew he had to leave but still could not force himself to abandon Jake. Circling once more around the angry crocodile, Hootie searched for any sign of Jake. There were none. Hootie roared past the crocodile as he dared, hoping it would open its mouth again. Maybe he could catch sight of Jake – or what was left of him. The crocodile was writhing, trying to disgorge the remains of the jet ski and paid no attention to Hootie. Hootie peered intently at the flames deep inside the crocodile's throat. The reaction was beginning. He blew the air horn several times as he went around the sandy islands, hoping Jake would hear and come out if he was hiding. The sandy beaches and shallows flew by in a dizzying blur. There was no sign of Jake.

At last, Hootie swung his craft back toward the boat. Speeding toward *Miss Katie*, Hootie imagined the worst –Aquasaurus had taken Jake. Even if Jake were alive, the heat reaction when the canister contacted water would kill him. Hootie knew there was nothing he could do. Katie had pressed the red button. There was no taking that back. Clint's words echoed in his mind as he realized he had to get the group as far away as possible.

A thousand yards short of *Miss Katie*, an evil-sounding hiss sounded behind Hootie. It grew so loud Hootie could hear it over the roar of his motor. It was so loud Hootie's ears ached. He looked back as the sea roiled and rippled, like a boiling pot. He realized what he was seeing was more than a crocodile in a death roll. It was the kind of reaction he expected – all hell was about to break loose!

On board *Miss Katie*, a worried Katie began to quiz Rita.

"Where did he go?" Katie pressed.

"He said he was going after Jake. Jake didn't come back – Hootie went after him!"

"What happened?" Katie's lips trembled as her eyes grew large with fright.

"I don't know, Katie. Jake hit something in the water, and he flew through the air right toward the crocodile. It reared up with its mouth wide open, and Jake flew all the way through its jaws! It was unbelievable! Then, Hootie made the sign, and I turned the boat to head back. It all happened behind me."

"Did Jake make it out the other side?"

"I don't know, Katie," Rita cried. "It all happened so fast. When Hootie gave the sign to come back, I just thought Jake was behind us. When he didn't show up, Hootie went back out after him. I don't know if there is time before that thing goes off."

"I didn't push the button," Katie admitted. "It slipped out of my hands, and it sank in the ocean," she wailed. "We've got time to help Jake!"

"What? You didn't push it?"

"I tried! Never mind – we've got to go get Jake!"

They rushed to the back of the boat and climbed down to the boat launch ramp. Rita remembered how desperate she had been to save Jesse from the cave and did not hesitate. She knew how Katie felt.

"The only thing we have is the skiff," Rita shouted. "Get in, and I'll untie it!"

As Katie scrambled aboard, Rita struggled with the knotted rope. Her hands shook so hard that she could not make her fingers work. Before the runabout floated free, Hootie came roaring up in a spray of seawater.

"What are you doing?" he shouted. "Get back on the boat! We've got to move further back. That thing is about to go off!"

Hootie tied off the jet ski as Katie stood in the boat. "Hootie, I didn't push the button!" she shouted. "I dropped it, and it fell into the water. I didn't push it! Where is Jake?"

Hootie grabbed at her wrist and pulled her out of the boat. "Get on deck! We've got to get away from here."

"Why? I didn't push it! Didn't you hear me?" Katie shouted.

"Well, something sure did," said Hootie pointing over the water. "Can't you hear that? *That* is not normal!"

The noise sounded like an old-time coffee pot beginning to percolate. Only this noise was a thousand times louder. They scrambled onto the deck and watched as the water roiled and boiled in the distance. The water bubbled higher by the second, stirring up large white-capped waves. Something about those waves looked odd to Hootie. It took a second for him to realize that the waves were moving toward the bubbling, not away from it. Something was pulling a massive amount of water into the center of what looked like a giant vortex. The surface where the crocodile had been was now a giant whirlpool as a gigantic swirling hole opened on the surface of the lagoon.

Without warning, a geyser of water erupted from the vortex and shot skyward. An upside-down funnel-shaped fountain formed and grew taller and thicker with each passing second. The increase in water thickened the shaft of the spinning funnel until it looked like a waterspout. Spray ballooned out at the top. Hootie thought it looked like an oil well gusher or an atomic bomb cloud – only with water.

The geyser doubled in size as the noise grew as loud as a jet engine. Water continued to swirl down the throat of the whirlpool and shot out of the mouth of the maelstrom. New water rushed in to replace the water that boiled off, and clouds of white steam rose two hundred feet into the sky, blotting out the sun.

A spray like light rain fell on them as they watched from the deck of the boat.

"It's hot!" Jesse reported.

Hootie reached out his hand to catch some droplets. "Wow! It feels like hot tub water! It must be boiling that crocodile alive!"

Katie began to cry. "And Jake with it!" she sobbed.

The hot geyser erupted for a full fifteen minutes growing larger all the time. After a while, the waterspout grew smaller and sagged back toward the surface, yet a rolling mountain of steam remained in the air. It looked like a thick fog covering the sky that grew and spread in all directions.

Jesse stood with Hootie at the rail, watching the incredible eruption. Behind them, Rita comforted a distraught Katie beneath a tarp.

"That was awesome!" Jesse marveled. "I've never seen anything like it before. Have you?"

Hootie could not turn away from the sight. "No," Hootie shook his head. "I haven't."

"You haven't? It was your thing that did it – that canister thing."

"I didn't know what it would do exactly," Hootie admitted. "I knew it would be bad – I didn't know how bad."

"Where did you get that thing?"

Hootie looked toward Katie, sobbing in Rita's arms. He took Jesse's arm and moved him further up the deck so the women could not hear them talk.

"I got it from Katie's dad – Clint. One like it may have been what killed him."

"There were more of them?" Jesse asked alarmed.

"That was the last one – there were only two. If Clint put the first one down the well, and it reacted like this one did..." his voice trailed off.

Jesse whistled. "Man! That thing must have boiled off a million gallons of water!"

"It atomized the water – it was so hot and quick, it vaporized that water in the blink of an eye. Anything nearby would have boiled like a shrimp."

"What about Jake?"

Hootie looked out on the sea. The water was calming, and the misty fog still clung to the water as far as they could see.

"Jesse, I saw the twisted wreckage of Jake's jet ski in the crocodile's mouth," Hootie admitted. "I don't think Jake made it through. The crocodile got him."

"What are we going to do?" Jesse asked.

"Come on," Hootie moved toward the rear of the boat. "We've gotta go back out there and try to find his body," Hootie said. "Hopefully he drowned before he got scalded to death."

Before they could launch the small boat, squawking sirens and horns filled the air. A Mexican Coast Guard boat and two police cruisers surrounded *Miss Katie*. Uniformed soldiers with automatic weapons lined the rails of the police boats.

CHAPTER 37

The Coast Guard officer scowled as the passengers lined up aboard his vessel. He ordered them to be silent as he walked back and forth along the line of handcuffed prisoners. Rows of campaign ribbons perfectly aligned above his left pocket. His sunglasses were so mirror-like Hootie could see his face in them. The officer moved up and down the line surveying each of them – measuring them. He held his hands behind his back at parade rest in military fashion. After several passes, he stopped in front of Hootie. Hootie did not blink or take his eyes off the officer's sunglasses. The officer rocked back and forth, as he looked Hootie up and down. His calm silence was more intimidating than if he had cursed or yelled at them. Something about his calmness disturbed Hootie; he knew the type, and he had heard the stories.

He had the bearing of a veteran military police officer. The sunglasses sat beneath heavy black eyebrows that neither twitched nor narrowed. Hootie sensed that beneath those glasses were dead dark eyes that revealed no clue as to what he was thinking. He may as well have been looking at a fish he was about to eat for dinner. Hootie knew it was no act; this man would be willing to use any force necessary to get the information he wanted. In an instant, Hootie flashed back to a desert in Afghanistan.

"¿Cuál es su nombre, señor?"

Without thinking, Hootie reverted to his military training. He gave his name and nothing more.

"¿Puredo ver su pasaporte, señor?" While he waited for an answer, the officer stretched his neck and rubbed his left temple with his right hand. He is tense and trying not to show it, Hootie thought. Hootie switched his attention to the back of the officer's hand. If he was going to get punched, Hootie wanted to see it coming.

Nodding toward *Miss Katie*, Hootie answered, "It's on the boat in my cabin. All of our passports are onboard the boat. Sir, now that we're allowed to speak, we have a passenger missing."

"In due time, Señor. Primero – first, we must determine who *you* are."

"But he is out there somewhere – drowning!" Hootie nodded toward the small island in the lagoon, "He's out there. A crocodile – a huge crocodile, attacked him as he was riding on a jet ski! We don't know what happened to him."

"Un cocodrilo gigante? – A giant crocodile?" The officer removed his glasses. Hootie was right about the eyes. "But what was the explosion?"

"We don't know, officer. We were fishing and riding jet skis when we saw the crocodile attack our friend. Sir, this crocodile was huge – bigger than any crocodile I ever heard of! Then, it – it evaporated or something!"

"Si! ¿Quién inició la explosión? Who is responsible? Who set off the bomb or hand grenade – or whatever you used."

"Sir, I will tell you all I know, but please help our friend. He's out there somewhere," Hootie motioned with his head. "He's hurt ..." Hootie looked at Katie and stopped short of saying 'dead.'

The officer replaced his glasses and turned to his sailors. In Spanish, he ordered them to begin searching for a missing person on the water. They immediately began to prepare a smaller craft to search for Jake.

"Señor, we will do all we can, but you must cooperate with us. Who are these people?" the officer indicated the others.

"This is Jesse Perrine, a student at Texas State University. Next to him is his companion Rita Martin, also a college student. The woman crying is Katie Marshall, also a student. Our passports are on our boat."

"Why is she crying?"

"Our missing member, Jake Haw, is her boyfriend – her fiancé I suppose."

"This crocodile you mention, ¿Qué tan grande es? How big was it? Was it the monster crocodile we have heard so much about?"

"With all due respect, who am I speaking to, Sir? How must I address you?"

The officer snapped to attention and proudly announced, "Señor, I am Capitán de Corbeta Rodrigo de Guzmán. You may address me as Capitán or Captain if you wish."

"Thank you, Captain. Why are you detaining us? We are victims of a crocodile attack and an accident at sea. We are survivors of a terrible attack – we're not criminals!"

"You are not under arrest, Señor. As the senior officer on the scene, I must determine if you have committed a crime or if you are a threat to security. If so, I will turn you over to the Chief of Police for arrest and prosecution. I have many, many questions about what occurred here."

"Can you at least take our handcuffs off? As you can see the young lady is quite upset, and this is not helping."

The officer thought for a moment and then ordered a sailor to remove their handcuffs. Hootie rubbed his wrist and thanked Captain Guzmán. The Captain's eyes had softened somewhat in the past few minutes, but Hootie knew the Captain had managed to contain his rage for now. It was still there inside, just waiting to leap out without warning.

"Capitan, why would you think we committed a crime? We are innocent tourists. A wild animal attacked us!"

A shout from *Miss Katie* aroused Guzmán's attention. Hootie looked and saw a sailor holding the fake radio box! The seaman was asking why the radio did not have a cord. Hootie was glad he had snapped the radio case back together.

The Captain looked at Hootie with a questioning expression. "Señor, why would you have a radio transmitter with no electric cord?"

"Captain, the radio does not work. The cord had a short in it, and to keep from getting shocked, I removed it. I haven't had a chance to replace the cord yet."

Guzman yelled to the sailor to put the radio back where he found it.

"My men are searching your boat for contraband. Do you have weapons, drugs, or explosives on your boat?"

"No, Captain! None of that." Hootie was emphatic.

"Señor, crocodiles do not blow up by themselves. What caused the explosion?"

"I do not know, Captain. I did not hear an explosion, but I heard a loud boiling noise. It sounded like a boiling caldron. All I know is a giant funnel of water formed as we were searching for our friend. It looked like a large waterspout. The water around us grew hot, and a large cloud of steam formed above us. Then, after a while, the column collapsed, and a boiling hot mist soaked us!"

"Si! I saw it myself. I also did not hear an explosion, yet something occurred. You must agree that it was not the weather that caused such a reaction."

"I told you all I can," Hootie said. "I know nothing about an explosion. It was more like an eruption."

Captain Guzmán motioned his sailors to return to the Coast Guard boat. Shortly after that, the smaller craft returned with the twisted wreckage of Jake's jet ski. After a short conversation with his men, the Captain returned and pulled Hootie aside for a private conversation.

"Your yacht has no evidence of contraband that we can find. It will remain here at anchor while we transport you to La Pesca until we complete our investigation. I am sorry; we could not find your friend, but we have recovered his wrecked jet ski. My condolences – he is lost."

Despite the Captain's discretion, Katie realized they had not found Jake, and succumbed to her grief with whimpers and cries of mourning.

Capitán Guzmán turned them over to the police chief. A police boat pulled alongside the Coast Guard vessel, and officers herded the group onto the new ship. The Chief identified himself and apologized as he ordered his men to reattach their handcuffs. Another police officer read them their rights in Spanish, while someone made a comical attempt at translation. It would have been funny, had the situation not been so serious. Hootie did not know that Mexico used Miranda warnings. Now, Hootie realized, they were now officially under arrest.

Once Capitan Guzmán left with his sailors, the Chief of Police assumed command. His attitude, calm and sympathetic, changed as soon as the military boat departed. His manner became colder and less friendly. He was not cordial, and he did not identify himself. He asked them to call him Jefe.

The officers searched each of them, and dumped everything in their pockets into a black plastic garbage bag, along with the items Jefe had received from Captain Guzmán. What worried Hootie the most was Jefe placed their passports in a pocket of his cargo pants. The officers made no inventory or any attempt to identify who owned which articles. In mixed Spanish and English, Jefe listed off a variety of charges. The only one Hootie recognized was setting off a bomb. Hootie spoke for the group that they did not wish to answer questions until they could have a lawyer present.

Jefe nodded his head in thought and then had his men take Katie and Rita to a different compartment of the boat. Hootie objected! Hootie insisted that they be kept together. The women were still handcuffed and had no female escort. The Chief ignored Hootie's objections.

The Chief was not waiting for the boat to arrive ashore. He intended to interrogate Hootie immediately. Hootie realized their circumstances had changed. Instead of a Coast Guard Capitan who would follow official protocol, they were now in the hands of a local Chief of

Police whose career, and possible promotion depended on solving the case and getting a confession.

Jesse watched as a police officer pulled Hootie to a table and shackled Hootie's legs to a chair. They cuffed his hands to metal rings embedded in the sides of a metal table. Despite Hootie's repeated request for an attorney, the interrogation continued.

"As per the rights you have read me, I will not answer questions in the absence of my attorney. I am requesting an attorney for me and my companions!" Hootie repeated.

The Chief ignored Hootie's complaints as he continued to try to get information. Hootie realized that the Chief would not attack him so long as Jesse was present. All the Chief could do was curse, bluff, and bluster. Hootie worried that Jesse might be next, so he decided to give a little information. He wondered what might be happening to Rita and Katie. It was time to dangle some bait.

Hoping to keep the attention on him, Hootie pleaded, "Don't hit me, señor. I don't know anything about a bomb. We are innocent tourists. We came here for sports and fishing. We are staying at a casa in La Pesca," he repeated for the tenth time.

The ploy worked. After getting some useless information from Hootie, the Chief calmed down. Hootie realized it was all about pride and saving face with his fellow officers. After an hour, the boat pulled into the harbor at La Pesca. Hootie indicated the house where they were staying.

"You are staying in Señor Marshall's house?" The Chief asked with wide eyes.

"Yes! Yes," Hootie admitted, "Clint Marshall. You have his daughter handcuffed somewhere on this boat."

The Chief's attitude immediately changed. He ordered his police officers to remove the handcuffs. Hootie hoped they would remove Katie's and Rita's as well.

"Señor, my apologies. I know Señor Cleent Marshall. He is long time a friend. How is he?"

The Chief had not heard of Clint's death. Hootie filled him in, grateful that Katie was not in the room. It was bad enough to lose Jake. A reminder of losing her father might be too much for her to handle all at once. The Chief's face showed sympathy. His former stern attitude had melted away. Jefe was all smiles and friendly gestures now.

"I have removed your handcuffs, but you must see the Judge. The charges against you are serious. You must not leave Mexico until we have investigated these charges."

The boat made its way through the harbor to the police dock. The occupants climbed onto an old school bus for the short ride to the police station. Rita assured Hootie they were fine.

When the van stopped, they marched in a single file line into an official-looking government building. A small courtroom was in a room off the front lobby. It was small, and hard wooden benches were in rows in front of a high Judge's bench. Two wooden tables with straight chairs stood in front.

A bailiff appeared and asked why the Chief had not handcuffed the defendants. The Chief whispered into his ear and pointed toward Katie. The bailiff disappeared through a door behind the Judge's bench. He reappeared a few minutes later to whisper into the Chief's ear.

The handcuffs came out again. However, Jeffe was apologetic. "I am sure you understand, my friends. It is court rules – that is all." He spoke to Katie, "Señorita, we are friends. Unfortunately, your charges are federal and not local. We know your father – he is a great friend of the town of La Pesca. We mourn his loss, as I know you do. We will be quick to release you as soon as possible."

Katie nodded her understanding, and stood with her head down, trying to stifle her tears. The Chief motioned for them to sit on one of the benches.

Soon, a Judge in black robes entered as the bailiff instructed them all to rise. The Judge looked out onto the courtroom and motioned Katie forward. His face gave no clue to his mood, but he knew who Katie was and greeted her by name.

"Miss Katie," he said in a soft voice, "how very good to see you once again. We are so sorry to hear about your dear father – he was such a friend to us."

"Yes," Katie admitted, "I miss him very much."

After a few minutes of quiet talk that Hootie could not hear, the Judge motioned them all to come forward.

"Mr. Hootie Johnson," the Judge referred to his notes. "Are you in charge of this group?"

"Yes, Your Honor, I am the eldest. I work for Katie. The others in our party are her guests. So, as far as responsibility for the boat, I'm in charge."

The Judge nodded. "I understand. You all face serious charges. You do not need to enter a plea this moment. Your arraignment will be tomorrow when the federal prosecutors arrive. What we are deciding now is whether you will remain in jail or not. Do you understand?"

"Yes, sir."

"I want you all to know that if this were a local case, I would have more authority. The authorities have charged you with a federal case, and the *Federales* are in control. It is complicated. Tonight, we will house you in our jail. If there is no objection from the prosecutors, we may be able to release you to your casa under guard tomorrow. Do you have an attorney?"

"Not one in Mexico," Hootie responded.

"The court will appoint one then, as per our laws. He will consult with you this evening at the jail. His name is Mr. Morales. He is a fine attorney. He will represent you well. If you wish, you may have your own personal attorney appear in your defense."

"What are we charged with, Your Honor?" Hootie asked.

The Judge consulted a sheaf of papers and flipped from one to the other as he read.

"They charge you with possessing explosive materials and other contraband. There are several bio-environmental charges of pollution and damaging the environment. They claim you caused an illegal detonation and other serious crimes. Your attorney will explain them all to you later, I am sure."

"But, Your Honor …" Hootie started.

The Judge raised his hands. "No! Please do not speak now – it is not the time. We will hear your defense soon in the presence of your attorney. These are serious charges, and you may not address the court without representation. I am doing this for your protection – believe me."

The Judge called the bailiff forward and instructed him to take the prisoners to jail. As they turned to leave the courtroom, the Judge halted them.

"One more charge, I see here, Señor Johnson."

"Yes, sir?" Hootie turned to face the Judge.

"Señor, you are also charged with espionage."

"Espionage? We are not spies – we are tourists! These are only college kids."

The Judge shook his head, "Not them, Señor. Only you."

CHAPTER 38

The cellblock consisted of rows of steel-barred cages on each side of a long cement hallway. One cell ran across the far end of the corridor, so there was only one way in and one way out. Rita and Katie occupied the last corner cell, with Jake and Hootie in the center cell, with just a steel-barred wall between them.

Concrete benches two feet high, intended for beds, lined three of the four walls. Thin, lumpy mattresses lay rolled at the head of each hard shelf. Katie stepped onto the cement bed and sat on top of her mattress. Hootie took the same position on the opposite side of the barred wall. Jesse unrolled his mattress and carefully inspected it before he lay down, while Rita roamed the cell like a caged animal. She finally settled where she could see down the long hallway.

A small window, also barred, sat centered high on the concrete wall above each cell. The window was unscreened, but it was not large enough to pass through anyway. The rays of sunlight coming through the window shimmered as evening approached and soon, only the dim incandescent bulbs that lined the hallway provided the faint light they had.

No one spoke for a long time. "Do you think he is dead?" Katie finally asked Hootie in a sad voice.

Hootie did not want to think of that much less reveal his true thoughts. He hedged, "I don't know, Katie. There is a chance he survived. We can always hope."

"He's dead," she said. "It feels that way. I wish I had never brought us here."

"Katie, don't blame yourself. We all came here freely; you didn't force anyone to come."

Katie sat silent for minutes as her eyes circled the room. She raised her eyes toward the window and sighed. She did not want to voice it, but she knew Jake had no choice. There was no way Jake was going to let her leave alone with Hootie. She wouldn't have wanted to leave him behind. She looked at the darkening sky beyond the small window.

"There it is," she pointed.

"There *what* is, Katie?"

She pointed a thin finger toward the window. "Andromeda. I can see her outside the window in the sky – still chained to her rock. Just like me."

Hootie was confused. "I don't understand. What do you mean chained to a rock? We won't be here long. They don't have enough to hold us for long. Don't despair. We'll be out of here soon and on our way back home."

"Oh, Hootie, don't you see? My life is exactly like Andromeda's. My father chained me to this rock – this oil business that I don't want and don't know anything about. Aquasaurus is the giant sea monster, and *you* - you are my Perseus. My hero – and I love you for it."

Hootie ducked his head as he mumbled, "Sometimes, heroes fail, Katie."

"Never on purpose," she reached between the bars to touch his face.

"The mythology turns into a prophecy. My betrothed – my Phineas -- Jake, is dead. Can't you see the similarities?"

"Yeah, I guess you could look at it that way. I wish I had never told you that story."

Katie brought her hand back to her side of the wall. "How else can I look at it, Hootie? I've lost Jake, and I'm trapped by Rio Frio Oil Company trying to drill through solid rock. That's your world, Hootie – not mine. I don't have any business owning an oil company. I don't know anything about it – and I don't care. It doesn't interest me. I'll give it to you!"

"Katie, I know it doesn't have much value right now, but it can provide an income to you for the rest of your life. There will be other wells. You can't just give it away."

"All right. Then you run it. Take what you want and send me the rest – I really don't care," Katie said sadly, her voice cracking.

"You're upset right now. I'll be there to help you. I'll take care of you. It'll be okay."

Katie shook her head, "I'm not Alice, Hootie. And you aren't Jake. I love you, but I was *in love* with Jake. But, I don't want you to leave me; I need you to run Rio Frio."

Hootie knew she was right. Hootie realized he was still in love with Alice. At that moment, he understood how Katie felt. "I'm not going anywhere, Katie. I'll be with you as long as you need me."

"I'll have Mr. Charles at Bruner, Bartholomew and Zackery draw up the papers putting you in full charge of Rio Frio. He'll transfer half of my shares to you. As soon as they let us make a phone call, I'll see if he will send someone down to get us out of this place."

"I hope we'll be out before he has to come. Mr. Morales will meet with us tonight, and we'll see what he has to say."

The muffled sound of clanging metal doors announced someone was coming. The door at the end of the hall opened, and a uniformed guard carrying a four-legged stool entered. Behind him, a short, stout man in a grey suit followed him down the hallway. It appeared their attorney had arrived. At the cell door, the jailer introduced Eduardo Morales and assured them he was the finest attorney in La Pesca.

Mr. Morales balanced on the stool and requested the jailer to leave. The jailer moved back up the hallway and through the jail door. He reappeared after a minute with another seat and sat facing them. It was clear that this was as much privacy as they were going to get. The jailer could hear everything they said.

"I must ask you, señores and señoritas, a very critical question. To defend you, I must know the truth. I do not care if you are innocent or

279

guilty, but I must know the truth to prepare your best defense. Did you bring explosives into Mexico and use them to destroy the feared Aquasaurus?"

"Mr. Morales," Hootie responded, "these are college students. They came here because Ms. Marshall owns a home here on the Rio. They came to celebrate summer break and to fish and ride their jet skis. They have no access to explosives."

Mr. Morales' eyes narrowed, "And you, Señor?"

"I work for Miss Marshall, piloting the boat and providing other services on the trip. Has there been any word on our missing friend – Jake Haw? Is there any news at all?"

"No, señor – nothing. Now, allow me to ask you. I understand Mr. Marshall was in the oil business in Texas. It is also my understanding that you worked for Mr. Marshall in the oil fields. Is that correct?"

"Yes, I worked for Clint Marshall for a long time – until his death this past spring."

"My condolences," Morales nodded to Katie. "In the oil business, is it true that you use explosives often?"

Hootie could see where this was going. "No – very infrequently, I would say. I don't think I ever used explosives during the entire time I worked there," Hootie added. "Explosives and flammable liquids do not go well together, Mr. Morales."

Morales nodded in understanding. "That is true. Nevertheless, there was a claim recently that Mr. Marshall used an explosive in Texas. It was reported that he might have caused the same earthquake that freed the giant crocodile."

"That was never proven, señor. In fact, testimony at a recent hearing shows that Mr. Marshall was alive after the earthquake began. There were no explosives involved."

Mr. Morales began to tap his foot on the concrete floor. As he considered the facts in his mind, his eyes searched from one prisoner to the other.

"Your boat will be moved to the police dock tonight," Mr. Morales reported.

"Your defense depends upon the Judge and the Federal prosecutor believing your story. They will search your boat with scientific equipment for evidence of explosives. Can you tell me they will find nothing?"

Hootie thought of the gun in the radio case. They did not find the pistol, but the instruments or dogs might detect gunpowder. Hootie took a gamble, "They will not find anything explosive in that boat, Señor."

"For your sakes, I hope that is true," Morales said pointedly.

"Señor, for many months, I stored a gun in the wheelhouse for protection at sea and in port. When we determined that we would be traveling to Mexico, I had it removed and stored in Galveston. If you ask Miss Darla Dunn at HNH Oil Company, she can verify that I gave her a rifle to store until we returned."

Mr. Morales pulled a small notepad from his suit pocket and wrote down notes. "I will verify that, Mr. Johnson. Thank you."

"If she is unavailable, you may check with Mr. J.R. Howlett, one of the owners. He will tell you that we had no explosives with us and that we did not use explosives on any of our wells in Texas."

After scribbling Howlett's name, Mr. Morales looked up from his notes. "I can defend you if what you say is true. But, I will need help – you need someone familiar with the oil business on your defense team. The government will only pay me a small stipend as a public defender; however, it could cost many thousands of dollars for an adequate defense." Mr. Morales' mustache twitched. "Do you have access to cash?"

"Not with us, Señor." Hootie could not help but get a dig in, "Your laws limit how much money we can bring to Mexico."

"I do," Katie spoke up. "When I can call my attorney, Mr. Charles Bruner of Houston, he will bring what we need – if I can get a telephone call."

Hootie cringed.

Missing the signal, Katie continued, "As soon as they let us use a phone. He will bring the money. How much do you need?"

Hootie tried to signal her to stop talking, but she did not see.

"At least $20,000, Señorita Marshall. Can he bring that?"

"Yes, I will tell him. He will arrive with a cashier's check for that amount."

Hootie hung his head and placed his hands on the top of his head. *Here it comes*, he thought.

Mr. Morales shook his head and looked at the floor, "Señorita, I hope you understand." Morales looked at Katie. "The money must be in cash. I will see you get your phone call soon."

I'll bet you will, Hootie thought. *I bet you will.*

After Morales departed, Hootie stomped around the cell in anger.

"That damned crook!" he shouted. "He's trying to rip us off! Granted, Mexico doesn't pay him much to defend us, but he's trying to take advantage of us!"

"I know you're right," Katie agreed. "But, what choice do we have? I'll tell Mr. Bruner, and we'll see what he says."

"Isn't it illegal to bring that much cash into Mexico?" Jesse wondered.

"Yeah, unless it is going to the Mexican government anyway," Hootie replied. "Katie, we have to get word to T.J. in Houston. When you talk to your attorney, will you ask him to call HNH? They may be able to help us. And one more thing – ask him to call that guy," Hootie tried to remember. "What was his name – that congressman in Austin? Pudgy? No, Tubby! No … ." The memory suddenly returned, "Pokey! That's it! Pokey Marin. Have him call Representative Pokey Marin in Austin. He was Clint's state representative – and yours too so far as that goes. That is why he was at the hearing about the Dilley Chalk fire. Your company is in his district."

"Well, sure," Katie agreed. "Mr. Bruner will notify all of your folks too," indicating Rita and Jesse. He'll let them know you are safe – except for poor Jake. I – I don't know what to do about Jake," Katie began to weep again.

Rita sat beside her and took Katie in her arms, stroking her hair until she cried herself to sleep. After saying goodnight to Rita, Jesse lay down on the thin mattress and slapped at "no-see-ems" until he dropped off to sleep. Hootie continued to pace the cell in deep thought. Somewhere in the night, an idea occurred to him. It was an idea so good Hootie was unable to sleep at all.

The Judge called them back to court the next morning. The Federal prosecutor had arrived. The bailiff swore them in and showed them where to sit. "Remain silent," Mr. Morales advised. The Judge motioned the prosecutor and Mr. Morales to his bench. Most of the talking was in Spanish and very quiet. Hootie could hear the words 'explosion', 'espionaje,' and 'Crocodrilo' repeated several times. No one made an effort to translate the conversation into English.

Mr. Morales returned to their table to consult with his clients. "The Magistrate," he pointed to the robed man behind the bench, "is listening very hard to the prosecutor. The prosecutor is arguing you caused an explosion that killed your friend, and the charges should include homicide."

"Homicide? Mr. Morales, how could we have set off an explosion without leaving evidence? There is no evidence at the scene, and our boat has no traces of explosives."

"Except in the wheelhouse," Mr. Morales pointed out.

"That was from the gun," Hootie reminded him. "There was nothing there to make an explosion that large. It would take tons of dynamite to do what we saw. Have you thought that this was a natural event?"

"Natural? How could that be?"

"Beneath the sea, there are high temperatures that often rise close to the surface. Has anyone suggested that this may have been a volcanic vent that opened up right beneath us?"

"Volcán?" Mr. Morales's eyes revealed he had not considered this possibility.

"Yes," Hootie empathized. "There are plenty of them just a few miles south of here near the coast. What else could cause the sea to boil? It is far more likely than us smuggling explosives into Mexico without leaving a trace."

Mr. Morales nodded and returned to the conversation before the Judge. This time, the prosecutor became animated and angry. Both attorneys shouted at each other in loud voices until the Judge hit the table with his gavel several times. Now the Spanish word for volcano gained frequency of use. Hootie wished he had thought of it earlier.

After a heated discussion, Mr. Morales returned to the defense table. "The prosecutor, of course, is in disagreement. He does not believe it was a volcano vent – but!" Morales raised his finger, "There is hope – he is not positive. We will continue to argue that possibility. Meanwhile, I am afraid that the prosecutor will not allow you to go to your home tonight. You will have to go back to your cells."

"Phone calls?" Katie reminded him.

"Solo un momento," Morales said and returned to the Judge's bench. He returned shortly with a smile. "The Judge says that you may have one phone call between you. You must choose who will make the call, and it may last only three minutes. The charges against you are very grave," Morales reminded them. "You should call your attorney about the money," Morales reminded Katie. "That way, I can get a second attorney – the prosecutor is very powerful here."

After her call to Mr. Bruner, Katie hung up the phone and followed a police officer to the waiting bus for the trip back to the local jail. The others wanted to know what Mr. Bruner told her. The group huddled in the back of the bus. Hootie pointed out the wire mesh that someone had welded over the emergency exit.

"Hope we don't crash," he half-joked. "What did your attorney say?"

"He's coming – he's coming himself," Katie reported in a low voice.

"Is he bringing the money," Jesse asked.

"No, I don't think so," Katie said. "He said he would bring whatever was necessary to get us out of jail."

"What about our defense? Mr. Morales wants $20,000." Rita reminded her.

Katie looked to each one before she spoke. "No. Mr. Bruner is not bringing hostage money. They would confiscate it from him and take it for themselves. Mr. Bruner is coming for one reason only."

"What's that?" Hootie asked.

"He's going to represent us personally. As soon as he arrives, he is going to dismiss Mr. Morales!"

The bus moved through the ornate reinforced gate that surrounded the federal courthouse. Hootie gazed at the concertina wire that topped the fence. He wondered if the prison used the razor wire to keep people in or to keep people out. The bus rolled out onto the public street, lined with yelling locals. They hoisted signs and cheered the coach as it passed. "What is this all about?" Hootie yelled to the driver.

"Don't you know?" the driver yelled back. "These are your fans!"

"Fans? What do you mean fans?" Hootie asked.

"Can't you read the signs?" the driver laughed. "See? *Free the Americanos!* They are happy you destroyed the vicious animal that has killed so many. You are heroes!"

One sign worried Hootie. The sign read, "Viva la explosión!

CHAPTER 39

Morning brought subtle changes that Hootie could not determine were good or bad. Before sunup, a rosy pink hue filled the sky as new jailers came to lead them from their cold, sterile cells. This time, the jailers addressed them with broad smiles and great courtesy. They guided rather than pushed them through the sally port. Each guard along the way went out of his way to be polite and accommodating – despite the handcuffs. One significant improvement was that the jailers fastened the cuffs in front and not the back. These were all good signs, but Hootie remained hesitant and suspicious.

Outside the walls, they climbed into a late-model van for the drive to the Justice Center. It was not a worn out school bus this time. This van featured plush seats with armrests and air conditioning. They drove along streets full of busy workers hurrying back and forth to their jobs. Other groups cheered and waved from the street corners with hand-painted signs supporting the Americanos. At the Justice Center, friendly guards led them into a well-stocked dining room. The guards removed their handcuffs, and uniformed girls served them a hot breakfast. It was clear that some change had taken place somewhere.

Jesse cupped his hands around a warm coffee cup and looked at Hootie. "Nice, huh? What do you think is up?"

"I don't know," Hootie said, "but this is much better."

"I think it is a good sign," Jesse said, as he shoveled a fork full of scrambled eggs into his mouth.

"No, that's not it," Rita spoke up. "They think because we are Americans the media will cover this, and they want to show how well they are taking care of us."

"Either way, it's better than the slop they gave us last night at the jail. What was that stuff?"

"Whatever it was, it was inedible," Jesse said, as he buttered a tortilla and folded it into a pie-shaped taco.

After breakfast, they sat on comfortable leather couches facing a large picture window. The window looked out on a well-maintained tropical garden in a flowery courtyard. The room had the feel of a posh hotel lobby.

"I don't think this is where they hold the regular prisoners," Jesse said. "Katie, do you think your lawyer arrived? What's his name?"

"Mr. Bruner. Charles Bruner. When I was able to talk to him yesterday, he said he would be on his way immediately. I'm sure Mr. Bruner arranged this for us."

Tall stone walls and the sides of buildings formed a perimeter around the garden outside their window. The place did not have the appearance of being a prison at all. It had wide walkways that ran from the court building to their structure. In the center of the garden was a paved circle with an ornamental fountain. Water splashed across the basin into a pool below. Sidewalks ran from each building, around the cascade, and out to the guarded gates that breached the rock wall. Palms and flowering plants lined the sidewalks. Comfortable benches stood beneath the swaying palms. It looked much like a courtyard in a five-star hotel.

"That's got to be it," Jesse agreed. "Otherwise, we'd still be in handcuffs and sitting on those hard wooden benches in the courtroom."

A civilian waitress offered them hot coffee or hot chocolate. Hootie sipped his coffee and muttered aloud, "I wonder what happens next?"

"If we are lucky, we get out of here," Jesse said. He stood and wandered over to the steam table where a young girl was cleaning the serving area. Rita saw him talking to her in hushed tones. *What was he up to?* Rita was not amused. *What could he be talking to her about?*

It did not take long to find out. Jesse returned and informed the group he had gathered some news. They huddled around Jesse as he spoke in hushed tones.

"She said our attorneys have arrived – plural. There are two attorneys."

"So, Mr. Morales has brought his second attorney. When do you think we'll see him?" Rita asked.

The girl overheard them talking and whispered to the group, "No, Señorita. They are saying your attorneys from Estados Unidos have arrived. I am not supposed to say nothing, but you must not worry. I cannot say more." She returned to her cleaning. "Would you like more coffee?" she asked in a loud voice as another court official entered the room.

Hootie was ecstatic, "Katie, your attorney is here! What is his name – Mr. Bruner? He'll get us out soon," he promised. "I'm sure of it! That's why they're taking such good care of us. I'll bet he's over there with the Judge right now!" Hootie pointed across the courtyard.

Katie had sat all morning quietly lost in her thoughts. She had not touched her breakfast. At this news, Katie perked up. "Mr. Bruner is here?" She brightened as her hopes rose. She called out to the bailiff, "Sir – Señor! I understand our attorney is here. When may we see him?"

The bailiff cast a stern frown at the nervous waitress. She ducked her head and carried a large tray of dishes and silverware out of the dining room. The irritated bailiff turned back to Katie and managed a polite smile.

Hootie could not help but think of the old military adage, *"The beatings will not cease until morale improves!"*

"Señorita, I may only tell you that it is true that your attorneys have arrived. They are with the Judge in his chambers even now, as we speak. I am sure you will see them shortly."

He pointed down the sidewalk leading from the large building on the other side of the courtyard. The full sun was rising behind the roofline, and long shadows stretched across the garden and pathways. Someone opened the large wooden door in the far building. Señor Morales and an elderly white-haired man stepped out into the garden.

"That's Mr. Bruner," Katie identified him. "He's here!"

The two men paused at the fountain circle and talked. After a few minutes, the two shook hands and embraced. Señor Morales walked toward the gated wall and left the compound. Mr. Bruner continued toward them as the sun slipped over the rim of the far roof.

Charles Bruner entered the room with a confident expression. "There you are, my dear! Do not be worried. I'm here to take care of you, as promised. Have you been well treated?"

He took Katie into his welcoming arms and hugged her as long as she wanted. When she pulled away, she asked, "Did you pay Mr. Morales?"

"My dear, you must leave such things to me. No, I did not pay Señor Morales. Señor Morales is an appointee of the court. It would not be proper for Señor Morales to receive money; besides, Senor Morales is no longer on the case. The judge dismissed him once we arrived."

Katie introduced Mr. Bruner to her companions as he went around the room to each of them. "My friends, I am here to represent you as well. Do not worry. The court will release you today."

"All of us?" Hootie asked.

"Each of you," Mr. Bruner assured him.

Smiles and cheers rose from the worried group, and the girls hugged while Hootie pounded Jesse on the back.

Mr. Bruner continued, "The Mexican government is dropping all charges against you. There is no evidence that you committed any crime."

Katie smiled and hugged him again, "Thank you, Mr. Charles," in the Southern tradition of adding 'mister' when using the first name of elders. "How did you do that?"

"Oh, not me," Bruner laughed. "It was your other attorney who pulled that part off. He flew down here with me from Texas."

"The attorney Señor Morales hired?" Hootie asked.

"Oh, no," Mr. Bruner laughed. "It was your other attorney who came with *me* that arranged your release." Mr. Bruner nodded down the sidewalk to where the door in the other building was opening again. "Him," Mr. Bruner pointed.

The full sun was over the top of the building now. It looked like a red ball resting on the ridge of the roof. The rays of sunlight flooding the garden cast a glare on the large window glass making it difficult to see. A tall man walked toward them, but in the harsh light, they could not see him for the glare on the glass. All they could see was white cowboy boots and long thin legs sheathed in a bright, white western suit. The tailored suit fit his body, and a black string tie hung down almost to the shiny silver belt buckle. He had a wide-brimmed cowboy hat pulled down low over his face concealing his identity. Blonde curls, shining like gold in the morning sun, surrounded his head. He looked exactly like a country singer minus the guitar. Jesse said what they were all thinking.

"You got Alan Jackson for our attorney?"

"Even better," Charles Bruner's belly jiggled as he laughed. "You'll see," he promised.

The mystery attorney passed out of sight of the window as he climbed the short steps to the door. Mr. Bruner smiled as he watched them stare at the door, waiting for it to open. What was he doing out there? Why didn't he open the door and come in? They stared, mesmerized, as the door handle turned in slow motion. When the cowboy entered and removed his huge hat, a shock ran across the room.

"Hey, guys!" Cody Hughes smiled. "¿Còmo **estás**?"

The group swamped Cody immediately. Everyone wanted to hug him. Laughter filled the room as each of Cody's friends tried to get to him first.

"What are you doing here?" Jesse pounded him on the back. "You're an attorney? How did you know we were here?

Finally, Mr. Bruner asked them all to take a seat, as he explained what had occurred over the past few hours.

"When Katie called last night," Bruner explained, "she gave some instructions. I was to contact a representative named Pudgy or Pokey – she could not remember which. With a little research, I found Representative Pablo Marin – Pokey Marin. He directed me to Representative Sara Hughes, who represents the district where the Dilley Chalk well is. Then, as you requested, I reported your arrest to J.R. Howlett at HNH. J.R. arranged a private jet immediately. I'll let Cody finish the story, as he was responsible for everything that happened after that."

"What are you doing here?" Jesse asked. "The last time I saw you, you were still recovering from a head injury after being in the hospital in a coma."

"I got over that with no permanent brain damage. I still can't remember most of it, except the part where we went into Honey Creek Cave. I don't remember coming out. Y'all need to fill me in on that part."

"You are an attorney now?" Katie asked. "How did that happen?"

"After graduation, I went down and took the bar exam, and I passed! But, Texas won't let anyone practice law without a law school degree anymore. A Criminal Justice degree won't do it. So, I had to go to Wyoming, where the state allowed me to practice law. It's one of the few states left where you only need to pass the bar."

"How did you get here?" Rita wondered.

"When Mom got the call, she recognized that you were the friends who pulled me out of that cave when I was hurt. You guys saved my life. She got the Governor to write a letter to the Magistrate here in Mexico. It was a friend-of-the-court letter, you know, an *amicus curiae*. Do you know how rare that is? Then, she called me to tell me what had happened to Y'all, so I asked Mom to let me come down here to deliver the letter. She put me in touch with Mr. Bruner, and here we are," Cody smiled like the football hero who scored the winning touchdown. "Besides, I had to get you all out of jail so that you could come to my mother's wedding."

"She's getting married? How wonderful," Rita clapped. "Who is the lucky groom?"

"Dr. Bryan – the doctor who cared for me while I was in the coma. He's going to marry my mom, and you are all invited!"

After rounds of congratulations, Cody and Mr. Bruner shook hands. "You did well, Cody." Mr. Bruner advised the others, "There is nothing to hold you here; we are free to go."

"You mean we can just walk out of here?" Hootie asked.

"Just like this," Cody answered as he led the way outside toward the gated wall. "They've moved your boat to the city docks," he said. "We'll use that to sail over to your house, which I understand is across the water here."

Cody showed the release papers to a smiling guard who opened the gate for them to pass. He politely saluted as they went through the gate. It felt so good to be free. Rita, Katie, Cody, and Jesse held hands and made a circle. Hootie looked at the sky and thanked his lucky stars that he was free.

Jesse could not miss the irony that Cody kept his papers in a glossy crocodile valise. "Nice case," he joked.

The van dropped them off on the waterfront near *Miss Katie*. Officials reviewed their papers, as the group boarded the boat for the short trip across the Rio. It was like coming home. Everything on board was where they left it. Hootie went to the wheelhouse and immediately noticed that the broken radio was gone. He figured that one of the detectives had discovered its secret and kept it for himself. Hootie did not care. He didn't feel like he needed it anymore.

The dock crew threw off the ropes, and the boat pulled away from the police dock. Hootie steered toward Katie's house. It was so great to be free! Hootie could not wait to get out of Mexico, and he vowed he would never return. At least T.J. at HNH knew where he was now. He would call in as soon as he could get to a working telephone.

In the salon, Rita found all the beer, soda, and coffee gone. The only thing she could offer was ice water. She placed cubes from the freezer into glasses as she passed around the refreshment. "I'm sorry, but everything we had in stock is gone. Taken for evidence, I guess," she laughed.

Cody was still catching everyone up on his activities and his mother's wedding. Cody's mother had found happiness with Dr. Bryan, and he could not wait for them to marry.

"He's such a neat guy," Cody bragged. "He's good to my mom, so I'm happy for her. She needs to be happy. You are all invited. I mean, that's why I came down here to get you all out of jail! You owe me! You must attend the wedding of one Dr. Colton Bryan and Representative Sara Hughes," Cody laughed. "Otherwise," he continued, "it's back to a Mexican prison for you convicts! It'll be in Austin, next month. You gotta come! I'm giving the bride away!" Cody flashed that charming smile. How could they say no?

The conversation turned to what they had been doing in Mexico for the last two months. He knew about Aquasaurus, of course, but was unaware that the group had been searching for it all summer. They told him about Professor Morrison and Mark. They filled him in on the collision that almost sank the professor's boat. Then they related to Cody how the crocodile attacked and injured Tom. They described how the giant crocodile split Tom's fishing boat in half. They acted out how they dragged Tom off that sandbar and took him to the hospital.

When they got to the part where they encountered the crocodile, Cody told them, "It's been all over the papers how a group of American kids down in Mexico killed a dangerous crocodile. You guys are either heroes or villains, depending on who you talk to."

"We didn't kill it," Katie told him. "Our plan didn't work. It was all my fault. I dropped the key fob."

"Well, something sure happened. I won't ask how you managed to do it and avoid detection. It is clear something blew that crocodile into so many little pieces they could not find any! It's best if I don't know any more about that," he hinted.

Mr. Bruner agreed, "Let's change the subject," he suggested. "Attorney/client privilege only goes so far."

"Come on," Rita encouraged, "we are getting near Katie's house. Let's all go up on deck and celebrate."

Together, they stood on the deck and laughed. Katie's house grew slowly closer. Cody remarked how great it was for them to all be together again.

"Not all, Cody," Katie said as tears filled her eyes. "I'm sorry, I don't feel like celebrating," Katie said as she turned away.

Cody was confused. "What's up?" he asked Jesse.

"You know, we lost Jake?" Jesse answered.

"What?" Cody said, shocked.

"Yes, we lost Jake," Rita confirmed. "Cody, Jake tried to fight off that giant crocodile. It tried to attack me, and Jake tried to distract it. You should have seen him. He flew through the air right through the crocodile's huge open jaws. But he crashed – they arrested us before we could find his body," Rita felt the tears running down her cheek.

Cody's eyes grew wide with astonishment. "Jake is dead?"

"I'm afraid so, Cody," Jesse confirmed. "I'm sorry to tell you. We'll go out tomorrow and try to find his body."

"It shouldn't be hard to find," Cody could not help laughing. "It's sitting over there on the end of the dock fishing!"

CHAPTER 40

Katie was in Jake's arms almost before the boat touched the dock. She flew down the pier in shouts and squeals of relief and happiness. They did not release their tight embrace as the others gathered around.

"I'll never let you go again," Katie wept through tears of joy.

"Man," Jesse got a word in edgewise. "We thought you were dead!"

"Your jet ski looks like a mangled mess," Rita added.

"I'll tell you all about it later," Jake promised. "We'll see you all at the house in a little while. Okay?"

Jake and Katie walked arm and arm toward the house. The others smiled and rejoiced that their friend was safe and well. It seemed like a miracle he could survive a crocodile attack, but here he was.

"They need a little time, you guys," Hootie grinned. "Why don't we go across to one of those hotels and do a little celebrating?"

"I'm buying," Mr. Bruner offered.

"Might as well," Jesse joked. "I'll bet we won't see those two again for a couple of days."

Rita punched him in the arm as they climbed back on *Miss Katie* for the short ride back across the Rio.

It was late afternoon when they tied up back at Katie's house. Rita carried the white take-out boxes intended for Jake and Katie, as they walked up the pathway.

"I wonder if they are ready for company yet," Jesse mused. "I can't wait to find out how he got away from that crocodile!"

"And how he avoided the Mexican Coast Guard," Hootie added.

Katie and Jake were sitting on the couch in the living room. Jake dove into the meal Rita offered him.

"Thanks, guys! I am *so* hungry," he said, as he filled his mouth with rice and beans.

"Out with it, man! The last time I saw you, you were flying through a crocodile's mouth on a jet ski! How'd you do that, man? It was awesome!"

Between bites, Jake told his story. "I don't know, man. It was unreal – like something out of a sci-fi movie! I didn't know a jet ski could get that much air!"

"It was awesome, dude! I couldn't believe it," Jesse raved.

"Shut up and let him tell it," Rita said.

"I was going full out – as fast as I could get that mo to go! I'll bet I was topping fifty! I didn't see the sand ramp, but it was down there barely under the water, and up I went. I could see Hootie, and I could see I was heading right for the croc's mouth! He was like a dog after a Frisbee, man. He saw me comin', no doubt!"

Jake took another bite and continued, "So I'm flyin', right? I don't have any steering. I swear that croc is timing my flight like he's waiting for me. I'm still gaining air when I see Hootie's red tube go down its throat. It was like everything was in slow motion, man. I could not believe it! Before I know it, I'm sailing right between its teeth. Maybe it felt the canister, I don't know, but it started to slam its mouth shut!"

"I'm thinkin'; I'm going to make it through after all. I can see open water through these huge white teeth. But then I felt its teeth chunk against the back of the jet ski. The ski came to a dead stop, and I tumbled over the handlebars and out the other side. It must have happened in a split second, but it felt like forever. I hit the water hard, and it knocked the breath out

297

of me. When I caught my breath, I looked around and thought, okay, I'm out of danger."

Jake was wound up. "But I wasn't. The thing rolled over on me, trapping me underwater. It was laying heavy on me. I thought it was going to crush me. I was drowning, man, pure and simple. It was all over. I thought I was going to die under this giant crocodile when it started to roll over. I caught my breath and latched onto a big leg, and it pulled me out and over the top. I grabbed a lung full of air, and I could see the croc wasn't after me at all. It was snorting, and groaning, and trying to spit out that wrecked jet ski. The plastic and metal hung up in its big teeth. I let go, swam off a little way, and looked around for you guys, but I couldn't see you."

"We thought you were right behind us," Rita said. "We didn't know you crashed."

"Anyway, I moved a few feet away, and the croc was doin' gymnastics, tryin' to cough up that jet ski. It rolled back right side up, and I could see parts of the jet ski burning inside its mouth. I remembered what you told me would happen when you pushed the button. So I headed out toward the closest island. It was that same island where we rescued Mark and the Professor. I didn't make it. I got blindsided. It felt like a bus hit me, and I was flying again – this time without a jet ski."

"It must have clobbered you with its tail," Hootie said.

"I guess, but this time I hit the sand hard! I landed on the back of my neck, and it knocked me out. When I came to, I was lying half in and half out of the water. I'm lucky my head was the part that was out. I'm lookin' around, tryin' to figure out where I'm at when the water starts bubbling, man. I swear the water was popping. That water was so hot I saw steam comin' off of it. It was boiling, man! Boiling. With the croc doin' flip-flops, the water was sloshing around like in a washing machine in mid-cycle when you raise the lid to throw in your shorts. The water was foamin', dude!"

"I'm still thinkin' you guys are comin' to pick me up. The water started swirling around like a huge whirlpool. It looked like the eye of a hurricane. It looked like water going down a toilet. This giant vortex pulled in all the water around. It was like a black hole, man – nothin' could get out. The wet hole sucked down about a ton of water. I couldn't see the croc anymore because it was on the bottom with everything else!"

"Then without warning, it all swooshed out! It was like all the water in the ocean was shooting up in this huge big funnel cloud. It was as loud as a jet at the airport! I thought my ears would burst. At the top of the column, a huge cloud formed, and it started to rain down hot water. It was scalding hot, man. I saw that hole on the beach with the thatched roof that Mark built as a shelter, so I dove in it as quickly as I could. At least that kept me from boiling alive."

"When it finally stopped raining hot water, I crawled out to flag you guys down. That's when I saw three boats with red and blue flashing lights surrounding *Miss Katie*. I figured it was the police, so I went back into the hole again to hide and wait it out. I thought if they arrested you, I could help more on the outside than sitting in prison with you. Sure enough, they hauled y'all off, and left the boat behind. I figured that monster was crocodile soup now, so after they were all gone, I swam out to *Miss Katie*."

"Aquasaurus is dead?" Rita asked.

"Oh, yeah! There ain't no way it could survive that boiling pot! Now I know what it's like being in a crock pot," Jake joked. "No, that thing couldn't survive the kind of heat that threw up the steam cloud I saw. It almost boiled me alive too, and I was fifty feet away."

"Then what happened?" Jesse asked.

"When everyone was gone, I hid out on the boat and waited. I was afraid if I moved the boat, the police would figure out I escaped. So, I waited. I figured someone would come back for the boat, and sure enough next morning a couple of cops came in a boat and towed it in. I hid out on board. First, they docked it at your dock over here," Jake pointed. "So I got off in the middle of the night and came in the house. Next morning, they came and towed *Miss Katie* back across the Rio. They didn't even see me. I was sitting right here on the patio drinking coffee. If I had a phone, I would have called for help."

"I wonder what made it blow up? Katie dropped the fob, and it sank in the ocean." Jesse mused.

"She didn't push the red button," Jake asked, amazed.

"I dropped it," Katie explained.

"Well," Hootie said, "I saw fire deep inside the crocodile's throat. I think the jet ski caught fire, and that set off the reaction. If Katie didn't push the button, it had to be that," he assured them. "Anyway, it's dead, and we can all go home now."

"Oh! That reminds me," Charles Bruner stood up, "I've got to call the airport and have the plane ready to fly back to Houston. I assume you folks will be taking the boat back. Am I right?"

"You have a phone that works down here?" Hootie asked. "We haven't been able to get any signal most of the time we've been here."

Mr. Bruner looked shocked. "You mean you haven't talked to T.J.?"

"No. Why?"

Charles handed his phone to Hootie. "Then I suggest you call Darla Dunn right away. Her number is in my contacts list. You might want to go outside on the patio," Charles suggested.

"That doesn't sound good," Hootie joked as he made his way outside. "They're probably goin' to fire me," he grumbled.

Tom Morrison rolled his wheelchair toward his desk in his home office. He held the phone a moment before he punched in the numbers.

"Yeah," Mark answered.

"Did you hear the news?"

"Yeah, I heard. They killed it. Thanks for the money. I got the check yesterday."

"Well, I'm grateful to you, Mark. You saved my life, man."

"You'd have done the same for me," Mark repeated his standard reply whenever Tom brought up the subject. "What are you going to do now?" Mark asked.

"Mark, when do you graduate, and what is your degree in?"

"I'll graduate next year in public relations and advertising," Mark said.

"Perfect! I'll need someone like that – if you are interested," Tom dangled.

"Interested in what?" Mark said with suspicion in his voice. "I'm not going croc hunting with you again," he half-joked. "That last trip almost killed both of us!"

"I'm starting a new foundation," Tom replied, "I'm calling it 'The Aquasaurus Project.' Are you in?" Tom asked.

"In?" Mark laughed. "In what? The crocodile is dead. We didn't even get a picture! What is The Aquasaurus Project?"

Tom laughed, "Ye of little faith." He fingered a thick hide lying across his desk. "For your information, Mr. Vice President and spokesman, I've got DNA – lots of it!" Tom responded.

"So what?" Mark asked.

"Mark, did you ever see the movie 'Jurassic Park'?"

CHAPTER 41

Darla Dunn sat in her apartment in Houston waiting for the phone to ring. *Why doesn't he call? He promised to call right away.*

She changed channels a dozen times without even realizing what was on the screen. *What was going on down there? What if something has happened to Hootie? What if Mr. Bruner couldn't get them out of that jail? Then what?* Time dragged by as the numbers on the clock took forever to change. For the fourth time, she checked her phone to make sure the ringer was on.

Dozens of scenarios played out in her mind as she imagined the horrors of Mexican prisons. She had heard all the stories about brutal jail guards. *People have ended up missing or dead down there,* she fretted as she imagined five heads in a duffle bag. She stopped flipping channels when the news appeared. They were reporting on some college kids the Mexican police had arrested in Mexico. Darla's attention snapped to the present as she turned up the sound. She sighed in relief when she realized the report was not about Hootie's group. It occurred to her that she might care for Hootie more than she realized. She thought about that for a while and decided it was not something she wanted to analyze right then. She was too nervous and too excited to give Hootie the news.

Darla thought back over her relationship with Clint Marshall. He had been so charming that Darla could not help falling head over heels for him. That phase did not last long, because, over the years, Darla realized it was never going to work. Clint was older and had different interests. The physical attraction was strong, but it was not enough for either of them. Darla found herself firmly entrenched in the "friend zone." She did not know how to move past that stage of the relationship. Clint had raised his daughter on his own and gradually evolved into an old bachelor type. Darla understood Clint had enjoyed being single and was not likely to change his ways. When Clint perished in the oil well fire, Darla's hopes of an intimate relationship between her and Clint had been dead for years.

Hootie, though, interested her a lot. Hootie was closer to her age and had that fierce independent streak she had admired in Clint. He had that roughneck attitude that thrilled her, and he was even more of a cowboy than Clint was. There was a story behind Hootie that she could not quite put her finger on, but she was determined to find out what it was.

Now Darla waited for Hootie to return, just as she had waited for Clint dozens of times before. Great things were happening, and the company needed Hootie back right away. Darla looked forward to working with him.

The sudden ringing of her phone made Darla jump. She did not understand why she was feeling so nervous lately. She looked at the screen and read Mr. Bruner's name.

"Hello, Mr. Bruner," Darla could hear her voice echo back over the connection. It made her sound like she was speaking into a barrel. "Were you able to find Hootie? Is he okay?"

"Darla! It's me, Hootie. I'm using Mr. Bruner's phone to call you. He said you needed to talk to me," Hootie answered. "What's happened?"

"Hootie! Oh my God! I'm so glad to hear from you at last!" Darla could not contain her excitement. "Isn't it great? Imagine. Clint was right all along!"

"Darla, slow down. What are you talkin' about?"

"What am I talking about? Haven't you heard? Didn't Mr. Bruner tell you?"

"Heard what? They've had us locked up down here for a few days, and we only got out this morning."

"I know, but Mr. Bruner didn't tell you? Oh, gosh! He should have told you …"

"He didn't say anything other than that I needed to get in touch with T.J. right away."

Darla, calm and collected most of the time, sounded like she was using her couch for a trampoline. Hootie could not help thinking: *what the heck is going on in Houston?*

"Oh! My! Yes! T.J.! Hootie! You've got to get back here right away! We need you! T.J. is buying out HNH and reforming the company under Rio Frio. He wants you to take Clint's job with the new company! He's making you the head of all field drilling operations for Rio Frio!"

"How's he gonna do that? Rio Frio is flat broke and dead in the water."

Darla realized she had circling the couch in a fast walk. She was out of breath. She stopped, put a hand to her chest, and said, "Not anymore cowboy." Something about this situation struck her funny, and Darla began to laugh. She could not stop laughing out loud.

"What's happened?" Hootie was very confused at her hysterical response.

"What happened? Why -- why we hit the biggest oil strike in Texas history – that's all! Rio Frio is worth billions! Clint was right about that giant oil field under the granite dome. The earthquake must have cracked it open. As soon as the pipe passed the blockage, the well started blowing out like gangbusters! We have to punch four more wells over that field as soon as possible! T.J. wants you back as soon as you can get here!"

"Fantastic! Old Clint was right – I knew it! Did you say millions with an 'm'?"

"Hootie, it's billions with a 'b' and a whole lot of zeros! T.J's putting you in Clint's old job. He needs you up here right away!"

"Wow! That's just great! Tell T.J. I'll be back in three days! Meet us at the dock!"

"Three days? Hop a flight tonight! It's that important."

"I can't Darla; I've got some business to take care of here first."

"You didn't find some little señorita down there did you?" she half-joked, not believing she said it out loud.

"No!" Hootie laughed, "Nothing like that; I made a promise to Katie Marshall I have to finish first. I'll see you in three days."

Darla laughed, but she felt a surprising pang of jealousy. *Was he involved with Katie now?* It surprised Darla that she cared. *What was that all about?* She wondered.

Stunned, Hootie returned to the group. Mr. Bruner took his phone from Hootie's hand and asked, "Did she tell you?"

"Yes, sir," Hootie nodded. He pointed at Katie, "Did you tell **her**?"

"Tell me what?" Katie looked up. "Hootie, you look like you just saw a ghost! What's wrong?"

"I didn't tell her yet," Charles grinned. "I wanted to let you do that."

"What's going on?" Katie asked. "Someone tell me something. What's going on?"

Hootie went over and took her by the hand, "Katie, we have to talk. Do you mind, Jake? Let's go out on the patio."

"Jake can come too," Katie said as she rose from the couch. "Come on, Jake."

Outside, in the warm tropical evening, they sat in wicker chairs on a stone patio. The warm evening breeze washed ashore from the Rio, blowing Katie's blonde curls. It was that perfect time of day, before night, that Hootie always loved.

When he was with Alice, it was their favorite time of day. It was a time of light blue skies over dark shadows that made everything magical.

Watching Katie with Jake now, Hootie began to understand his feelings for her. It was not that romantic kind of love Katie felt for Jake or that he had once felt for Alice. The love that Hootie felt for Katie was the kind that made him want to protect her – like a father. Hootie was glad Jake was alive and that Katie was happy in love. He wished they could stay that way forever as he struggled for the words that would change Katie's life forever.

"What do you need to tell us, Hootie?" Katie interrupted Hootie's thoughts.

"Katie, your dad was right on the money. You know how I told you that Rio Frio owed more money than it was worth?"

"Yeah, I remember. Are we in trouble?"

"No," Hootie laughed. How do you tell a woman she is filthy rich?

"We're not in trouble," Hootie laughed. "Katie, there was an ocean of oil right under Dilley Chalk #1. Your dad was right. After the earthquake, the crew was able to drill through that granite dome. You own 25 percent of what must be worth billions of dollars. They say it is the biggest strike in Texas history! Congratulations."

After the celebration quieted down, Hootie continued. "You may want to think about changing our agreement about Rio Frio. After all, you could have me a whole lot cheaper than for half of your share. Besides, T.J. offered me your father's job. You wouldn't have to pay me anything at all, really."

"No way!" Katie responded without pause. "No! I'm not Andromeda! You're not going to chain me back to that rock!"

"What rock?" Jake asked.

"It's a metaphor, Jake. I'll tell you later," Katie laughed.

She turned back to Hootie, "I still need you to handle my affairs with Rio Frio. I'm glad we're making money, but we made a deal, and I'm sticking to it!"

"Katie, you don't have to – you didn't know about this oil strike when we agreed to be partners."

"Nothing's changed, Hootie. Nothing's changed for me. I still need you!" She reached out to take Jake's hand, "Jake and I need you. Jake and I don't know anything about the *oil* business. The agreement stands as far as I'm concerned. Besides, I already told Mr. Bruner to draw up the papers dividing my interest in Rio Frio with you."

"But, Katie. You are giving away millions of dollars. I can't ever pay you for that!"

"You already have," Katie smiled as she threw her arms around Jake. "No," she shook her blonde head as curls fell from her shoulders, "I've got what I want. Jake and I are going back to finish college. After that, whatever we do, we'll do it together – the three of us!"

"The three of us?" Hootie asked, confused.

"Hootie, you are the first to know! Jake and I are getting married, and we need you to run the oil company. Besides, you promised," she reminded him. "We're partners!"

When Hootie neared Galveston, he contacted the marina to prepare for their arrival. Earlier, a small storm had churned up the Gulf, and the chocolate-colored water was choppy. A pair of bottlenose dolphins escorted them through the back bay all the way to the dock. It felt so good to be home.

Hootie eased *Miss Katie* back into her slip at her home marina. He stopped the engine and made his final shutdown checks. Down below, Katie and her friends were packing bags and preparing to leave. Hootie could see Darla had arranged a luxury van to take them back to Austin. Classes would begin in a week. Hootie laughed aloud, as he imagined them answering the age-old question, *"What did you do on your summer vacation?"*

"Oh, we just blew up a monster crocodile and spent time in a Mexican prison – that's all."

Hootie locked all the compartments and looked around the wheelhouse. He made a mental note to replace the fire extinguisher. He picked up his duffel bag and climbed down to the main deck. The marina staff had already put the gangway in place, so he stepped onto the dock and waited for the others.

The crew lined up to greet Hootie as he stepped ashore. There were warm hugs and kind words all around. Rita even kissed him right on the lips. Jesse slapped him on the shoulder and thanked Hootie for everything. Jake gripped Hootie's hand, and without saying a word, motioned with his head back toward the boat.

"She wants to see you in the salon before we leave," Jake told him.

"Sure," Hootie agreed, "come on, let's go in."

Jake shook his head, "Not this time." Jake smiled at Hootie's confused look. "It's okay. Go ahead. She's waiting for you."

Katie was standing at the large window looking out at Galveston Bay. The sun on the water made her hair glow. She turned as Hootie entered the salon and was in his arms in an instant. They kissed warmly before she laid her head on his chest.

"Oh, Hootie, what would I do without you? I don't know what I'd do …" her voice trailed off.

"You don't have to worry. I'm right here, and I'm not going anywhere," Hootie assured her.

She pulled back and looked at him from arm's length. "I'm going to miss you," she started and faltered again.

Hootie shook his head. "Nah, you won't miss me that much. You're going to be so busy with school this fall, and then you and Jake will get married. Time will fly by. You'll see."

"Hootie, I want you to give me away at the wedding. I want you to walk me down the aisle. Will you do that?"

"You know I will. It'll be my honor," he smiled. He felt the need of something to keep from tearing up, but he could not think of anything to do. Instead, he sniffed, scrunched up his nose, and made a feeble attempt at a joke, "Sure thing, boss. Whatever you need, boss."

"That reminds me," Katie said as she broke their embrace and retrieved something from the countertop. "Don't ever call me *'boss'* again." She handed him the sheaf of papers.

"What's this?" Hootie squinted at the writing.

"I told you," Katie reminded him. "Mr. Bruner drew up the papers to transfer 12% of Rio Frio to you. These papers are your copy, of course. He took the real ones back to Houston to formalize and register."

"Katie…" Hootie began.

"Now, shut up," she hushed him. "We talked about this. Mr. Bruner thinks I'm nuts too, but I know what I'm doing. I'm crazy like a fox! I'm making you an owner! That way, you can't ever just walk away and leave me. Now, I'm chaining *you* to this Rio Frio rock," she laughed. "You're stuck with me forever!"

"Oh, yeah? You think you're so smart don't you?" Hootie joked. "I could just sell all my stock, and then where would you be?"

"Oh, Hootie," Katie pouted. "You forgot – I'm Clint Marshall's little girl," she said like an innocent child. "Those papers have a little old clause in them that says you can only sell them back to me," she laughed. "Daddy didn't raise no fool."

Hootie must have heard Clint say that line a hundred times. "He sure didn't," Hootie agreed.

Then she said the words he had heard Clint say even more often. "This ain't my first rodeo!" She pronounced it *ro-day-o*, just as Clint used to do.

"What the heck am I getting into?" Hootie wondered as he hugged Katie close.

After the van left with everyone on board, Hootie stayed behind to secure the boat. Everything handled, he pulled his cowboy hat low over his eyes and walked toward the parking lot at the end of the dock. He planned to hail a taxi to take him back to Houston. He would get a room somewhere until he could find a more permanent place. In the morning, he would be at HNH offices – or was it Rio Frio now?

"Hey! Cowboy! You want a ride?" At the end of the pier, a top-down Mercedes waited with Darla Dunn behind the wheel.

Hootie threw his things in the back seat and climbed in next to her. Darla leaned over and gave him a peck on the cheek. Three beautiful women had kissed him in the last five minutes.

"What is this," Hootie laughed, "Kiss Hootie Day?"

"Whatever you say," Darla laughed and planted a wet kiss right on his lips. "Welcome home."

Hootie felt his cheeks turn pink, "That was some welcome home."

"Want me to do it again?" she asked.

Hootie thought she was joking, so he cracked, "Well, … *yeah*!"

Darla held the next kiss a little longer, and Hootie felt himself kissing her back. "*This could get complicated*," he thought, as he looked into her eyes.

"Where are we goin'?" he asked, to change the subject.

"Oh!" Darla turned back to the wheel and started the engine. "Yesterday, we got a notice to transfer ownership of Clint's condo to you. That's where I'm taking you first – unless you want to go somewhere else. Clint's daughter sure must like you a lot."

"She sure does," Hootie agreed. He left her hanging in suspense on purpose.

They did not speak for several miles. Hootie let her stew a little while, knowing she would be thrilled when she heard the rest of the story. As they neared the Houston city limits, Darla pulled a manila envelope from between the seats. She passed it to him, "This is for you."

"What is it?" Hootie asked.

"It's T.J.'s job offer. "He's making you a Vice President in charge of drilling operations. He wants you to take over Clint's old job. It's quite a deal: six figures, with all the perks, profit sharing, and all that. You'll be pleased, I'm sure."

"Do you come with the deal?" Hootie asked as the pages flapped in the wind.

"Only if you want me," Darla gave him duck lips.

Hootie laughed and pulled out his cell phone. "I've got to get a picture of that face!"

"Don't you dare," Darla laughed and turned her face away.

A few more miles passed before she spoke again. "So?" she finally asked.

"So, what?" Hootie played with her. He knew full well what she was asking.

"So, do you want me?"

Hootie could not help himself, "I'll bet those words never came out of *your* mouth before," he joked.

"Well! Mr. Johnson! I'll take that as a compliment!"

"You should," Hootie agreed. He stuffed the papers back into the envelope and handed it back to her. "But the answer is, no."

Darla swerved into the nearest parking lot and came to a sliding stop. "No?" Her eyes were wide with astonishment.

Hootie looked at the distant Houston skyline and shook his head. "No," he repeated.

"No, what? You don't want me working for you?"

"Yes, I want you working for me – no, I don't want the job. I got a better deal."

Darla was even more dumbfounded. "A better deal? What deal? Who with? Whatever it is, we will match or beat it. What do you want? Name your price."

"You can't match it," Hootie teased. He knew Darla was a woman who was not surprised often, and he was enjoying this turn of events.

"You're turning down T.J.'s offer? Then, how am I going to work for you?"

"The same way you do now," Hootie said, eyes twinkling, "except you don't work for T.J. anymore; you work for me."

"Okay, cowboy, I'm completely lost. What have you been smoking down there in Mexico? I work for HNH – well, Rio Frio, now. If *you* don't work for T.J., how am *I* going to work for you?"

Hootie broke into a wide grin and decided to let her off the hook. Relishing the look on Darla's face, he extended his hand for her to shake.

"Meet Rio Frio's newest minority-share owner." Hootie could not help laughing. Darla looked attractive even with her mouth hanging open.

Two weeks later, Hootie and Darla walked the state Capitol lawn to attend a wedding. Hootie had to miss the rehearsal dinner at the state Capitol, but he and Darla were in their reserved seats early on the wedding day – front and center. Hundreds of bright, white, wooden chairs in rows lined the green grass. Well-connected people packed the Capitol grounds. The herd included the Governor, Senators, and dignitaries of all sorts. Hootie was glad he had dressed for the occasion, but he still felt a little out of place. He was happy Darla was there with him. She squeezed his hand.

The minister, the groom, and the best man moved to the center of the stage up front. Hootie waved at Jake and Jesse. He did not know the rest of the attendants. He wondered where Cody was. When everything was in place, the ceremony began. One-by-one the bridesmaids came walking down the center aisle. Rita Martin came first, followed by Katie who blew Hootie a kiss as they passed and stood in their places.

The wedding march sounded, and soon the bride appeared. She looked beautiful. Cody wore a white tuxedo, as he walked his mother down the aisle. Hootie wondered how they would handle the introduction at the end. Would she be Mrs. Colton Bryan, Mrs. Dr. Bryan, or Representative Mrs. Dr. Bryan? Hootie did not know the protocol for such things.

The answer came as the minister spoke for all to hear after the service.

"Ladies and Gentlemen, I present for the first time, Dr. and Mrs. Colton Bryan."

The reception was much less formal. Hootie felt less out of place, as he fished a couple of longnecks from a tub of ice. He twisted the tops, wrapped a napkin around one and handed it to Darla. Hootie felt a sharp poke in the middle of his back, and heard a soft voice say, "Stick 'em up!" He turned to see Katie smiling at him.

After they hugged, Hootie introduced Darla to Katie.

Katie could not help teasing Hootie, "So, this is the woman you picked up on the docks the day you dropped us off, huh?"

Hootie blushed, "No. I … She picked me up. Uh… I knew her before -- a long time before that." Everyone laughed at Hootie's discomfort, including Darla. What was it about this girl that could get his goat every time he saw her?

Hootie introduced Darla to Rita, Jesse, and Jake as they arrived at their table on the Capitol green. It was a beautiful fall day, and squirrels scampered beneath the giant oaks. Hootie wondered how many people had been married there before. He did not think there were many. You had to be a VIP he guessed.

Cody, in his white tux, stopped by for a chat. "Hey! They're getting ready for the bouquet toss. Katie? Rita? Y'all come on."

"I'm already engaged," Katie protested.

"Aw, come on," Cody encouraged. "It'll be fun. It's a Texas tradition." Katie realized that Cody would make a great politician one day – maybe even Governor.

Katie gave in as she, Rita, and even Darla joined the group. The single women lined up in preparation of the age-old ritual, as the bride turned her back to the group. There must have been a dozen of them Hootie mused. They were laughing and jostling each other under the cloudless Texas sky. Finally, the bride was ready, and her white and yellow spray soared skyward. There was some pushing and shoving, as the women reached for the bouquet. Hootie watched as Darla's hand brushed the falling bunch of flowers. It bounced off her hand and tumbled behind her. It surprised Hootie that he felt a little disappointed. Rita snatched the bouquet before it hit the ground. Everyone surrounded her and applauded the fated "next bride."

The small group returned to the table laughing and kidding each other. "No," Rita mused, "Katie, you'll be next. I haven't accepted yet."

When the laughing died down, Rita stood in front of Jesse. She smiled down at him, as he looked up at her, not knowing what to expect.

"Yes," she said smiling.

Jesse looked around the table, trying to get a clue about what was happening. He got no help at all.

"The answer is, yes," Rita repeated.

Jessie shook his head, confused. Rita helped him out. "Remember when we were in the boat when Katie rode that dead body like a bronc rider?"

"Oh, God!" Katie cried. "Don't remind me of that! Gross!"

"You had just asked me to marry you," Rita reminded him. "The answer is, 'yes'!"

CHAPTER 43

It had rained in the afternoon, raising the moisture content of the air. Now, the warm, humid night air wafted across the tropics, invigorating the night things. They rustled the leaves and vines that grew next to the sandy shore. The day feeders huddled in their dens and trembled with fear at what the night may bring. The white sand twinkled like a million tiny diamonds under the risen full moon. Emerald reflections glinted on the rippling water as it lapped at the edge of the shore. Night sounds overcame the day noise as the hours marched toward the birth of a new day. The calm waters of the bay surged and receded to a set rhythm as precise as the cosmos itself and nearly as old.

On the silky, sandy beach, fat plovers foraged at night searching for insects. Other night feeders swooped across the sparkling water seeking sustenance beneath the moonlight. They made no sound as they soared on silent wings. Other night birds skipped across the sand inspecting anything that washed ashore. A solitary sandpiper swooped low across the water, feeding. It flew toward a series of off-shore islands, many of them only small tufts of sand. It landed on one and immediately began to search for food. On spindly legs, it raced across the sand to a pit covered with dried seagrass. It performed a curious dance at finding hundreds of insects in the withered leaves of grass.

Beneath the thatched cover lay a shallow depression in the sand. Inside the pit, beams of the full moon danced and swung as the ceiling fluttered in the breeze. On the floor of the hole, the sand began to shake and pulsate. As the quivering continued, more sand fell away revealing a white oval egg case. Vibrations became tremors, which gradually progressed to a throbbing thud.

At last, a small crack began to appear on the eggshell. The embryonic fluid leaked and ran down the egg casing. It glistened in the light of the moon, as the break grew wider with each impact.

At last, a small opening began to form in the egg as a pointy beak emerged. The gap widened and spread until the entire top of the shell flipped away and slid down the grainy sand. The fresh-born crocodile crawled forth and greeted the night.

It scampered up the sandy slope toward the beach, smelling water, which it knew was close. It crawled on four legs toward the safety of the ocean it was born to inhabit. It caught the scent of its progenitor. By instinct, it followed a tail drag furrow that led toward safety. Pausing at the edge of the water, it turned its face toward the full moon. For the first time, it voiced its rapture at being alive. The voice emerged as a hissing screech that caused even the shore creatures to freeze. The rustling among the trees and the rattling beneath the leaves ceased as everything nearby huddled in fear. The sandpiper left the banquet on swift fluttering wings.

The infant crocodile closed powerful jaws with an audible, fearsome clap of teeth. Without a backward glance, it slithered into the warm tropical sea.

The end